THE ALTAR OF PERGAMON

JONATHAN CAHN

FRONT LINE

The Altar of Pergamon by Jonathan Cahn
Published by FrontLine, an imprint of Charisma Media
1150 Greenwood Blvd., Lake Mary, Florida 32746

To access the bibliography for this book, visit booksbyjonathancahn.com/pergamonbibliography.

For more resources like this, visit MyCharismaShop.com and the author's website at booksbyjonathancahn.com.

Cataloging-in-Publication Data is on file with the Library of Congress.
International Standard Book Number: 978-1-63641-615-1
Signed Copy ISBN: 978-1-63641-649-6
E-book ISBN: 978-1-63641-616-8

1 2026
Printed in the United States of America

CONTENTS

PART I
BEGINNINGS

PART II
KINGDOM

PART III
FURY

PART IV
DESTROYER

PART V
POSSESSION

PART VI
CATACLYSM

PART VII
SACRIFICE

PART VIII
CONTAGION

PART IX
REVOLUTION

What you're about to read
appears in the form of a story.
But the mystery it reveals
is not fiction.
It's real.

PART I

BEGINNINGS

Chapter 1
THAT WHICH IS TO BE REVEALED

I have come into a cataclysmic knowledge...

I COMMIT THESE WORDS to writing in trepidation and awe, not knowing what will happen when I finish.

I begin this in secret. There are those who, if they knew where I was and what I was doing, would do everything in their power to stop me from completing it, even if it meant taking my life. They have already tried.

I sit with pen and paper in the midst of a vast desert. By the time you read these words, I will be gone from this place and hopefully still alive. Whatever happens next, I have no choice. To see what I have seen and to know what has been revealed to me and to keep it to myself would be to commit an immoral act, a colossal sin of omission.

That which is to be revealed, that which you're about to read, is a mystery, an ancient and cryptic knowledge, hidden for ages in the dust of the Middle East, a mystery that holds the secret behind the most critical, pivotal, calamitous, and catastrophic events, the greatest evils ever to come upon this world—wars and revolutions, the rise and fall of kingdoms and superpowers, unfathomable darkness, and the prospect of global destruction.

I am the least likely of people to take up such an undertaking. I didn't choose the mystery. The mystery chose me. I have no choice but to reveal it.

I have decided that the best way to bring it forth is to disclose that which I saw with my own eyes. So I will tell a story. I will recount a journey—a journey that changed everything. But that which the story contains is a mystery on which the future of the world now hangs, the future of every life in the world, and the future of you who are now reading these words.

The story will span the world, from an unexpected encounter in New York City to a Turkish bazaar in Istanbul; from a dark gate in a German city to a strange man in Red Square, Moscow; from a desert of white mountains and white sand to an island in the Caribbean; from a city of seven hills to the city of God. I will tell you of my encounters with the "guides," the revealers of mysteries—an old man playing a solitary game of chess in the Balkans; a young Polish woman with a knapsack on her back; a thin, bearded man who appeared to be homeless but wasn't; a Native American stoking a desert fire; a woman with long, dark, wavy hair at the birthplace of a monster; and more than these.

I will also tell of those on the other side, of a very different nature and purpose, the keepers and guardians of an ancient secret. They had their own agenda—to stop the mystery from being revealed and the revelation from going forth. They were watching, they were everywhere, and they were deadly. They would seek to take my life and the life of another. It was only by a twist of events that I am alive to now reveal what they so zealously and violently tried to stop from being revealed.

The journey will also involve a book, or rather, the pages of a book. The book itself is unknown to the world and of a most cryptic nature. Those who wrote it never intended it to be read or seen by those outside their circle, much less by me. It was that book that began the journey. And it was that book that contained the clues and keys concerning what was hidden and then revealed.

As for the mystery, it centers on an ancient object, hidden from the world for ages. And then it was unearthed, and everything began to change, and the world was altered.

And the mystery involves even more than this, something that, before the journey, I would have mocked and derided—and did. But I can no longer do that. Though it exists outside the confines and realms of modern notions and speculation, I know now how real it is and how it has acted upon and transformed the modern world. It is ancient, dark, and dangerous. It is now for me to reveal it and how it has altered the existence of everyone on this planet.

It began on the other side of the world in a place as different from my present surroundings as two places could be—New York City. I was giving a lecture for an association of skeptics, cynics, and unbelievers, during which I mocked and deconstructed the idea of the supernatural. It would be the last time I would ever do so.

It was at the end of that lecture that I had an encounter that would change my life.

Chapter 2
THE VISITOR

My name is Ariel Herzog. I have made a reputation of being a skeptic. It was at first my disposition and then my profession. I became a debunker of hoaxes, frauds, delusions, and deceptions. I wrote and posted articles exposing them and those who promulgated them as frauds, charlatans, or simply deluded. And whenever I could, I debated them. I investigated everything from Bigfoot to the Loch Ness Monster, Area 51, UFO abductions, psychics, witches, mediums, ghosts, spirits, and the claims of the religious—divine healings, angelic encounters, and miracles. I challenged them and debunked them all.

I was also a public speaker, having given countless lectures around the country, mostly preaching to the choir of fellow nonbelievers and cynics. It was at one of those lectures—presented in a library in New York City to an audience of about thirty-five skeptics and scientific rationalists—that my life would be irrevocably altered. I had given that lecture more times than I could remember and always ended it with the same summation and finale:

> We are no longer children of superstition, no longer the heirs of fantasy and folklore. We are the disciples of science, rationality, and progress. The days of witches and fairy tales, goblins and boogeymen, monsters, fiery dragons, and knights in shining armor have passed. There are no creatures lurking in our enchanted forests, and there are no enchanted forests. We do not hope for winged men with halos to come flying down to our rescue or for the white-bearded man upstairs to save us. Nor do we fear the red-caped man with a pitchfork and horns. There is no one to save us but we ourselves, no monsters to frighten us, no angels to bear us on their wings except those born of our dreams, and no devils to haunt us but those forged by our nightmares. It is time for us to put away the illusions of our childhood

> and walk out of the dark forest of superstition into the light of scientific rationality. It is time for us to put away childish things and grow up.

For that I received a standing ovation. It was what they came for and expected me to say. But it would be the last time I would ever give that speech.

Several of those in the audience came up to me afterward to tell me how much they enjoyed my lecture and to thank me for my work. Some asked for my autograph. That went on for about half an hour. It was only as they began dispersing that I noticed him still sitting there in the middle row of now-empty folding chairs, just staring at me. He was middle-aged, with a weathered face, somewhat disheveled dark hair, and an old, worn trench coat. I had noticed him earlier as I was delivering my lecture—restless, intensely serious, troubled, continually scanning the room as if for signs of danger. He waited until the last person had left before he approached me.

"Mr. Herzog," he said with a foreign accent I couldn't place, "I have to talk with you."

It was not unusual for someone to want to speak with me in private after a lecture. It was almost always because they had some revelation, some insight or theory they had to give me, convinced it was of urgent and world-shaking importance, which, of course, it never was.

"I appreciate that," I replied, "but I'm on a tight schedule and really have to get going."

"I *have* to talk to you. It's something you *have* to hear. And I'm not leaving without telling you."

"All right," I said, relenting. "Tell me."

"It has to be in private."

That would have normally ended it right there, except that one of the librarians overheard the exchange and offered us one of the library's private rooms. We sat down on opposite sides of a meeting table in the center of the room.

"I don't know how much time I have," he said.

"How about five minutes?" I replied.

"I didn't mean that."

"Then what?"

"Before they come. I don't know how much time I have before they come."

"Before who comes?"

"Those who would not want me to give you what I'm about to give you."

"What are you talking about?"

"I was once one of them, but I'm not anymore. I broke away. That's why I'm here."

"I'm not understanding. Who are 'they'?"

"'They' are those whose mission is to ensure that his plans come to fruition in the world."

"Whose plans?"

"I believe you referred to him in your talk...the red-caped man with horns and a pitchfork...only he doesn't have horns, or a pitchfork, or a red cape. And he's not a man. He's the Dark One."

"The Devil?" I asked. He was silent. "You're talking to me about the Devil? You know who I am?"

"Very much so."

"You're not serious."

"I came to tell you of a mystery...of mass calamity, mass destruction, the future of this world...and that on which everything else is hanging. Yes, I would think I am most serious, Mr. Herzog."

"I have a different word for it," I replied. "How about *crazy*? How about you're seriously crazy?"

"We have no time for this," he said. "This is why I came."

At that, he scanned his surroundings, then reached into his trench coat and took out a large rolled-up piece of paper. It looked aged, brownish-golden. He laid it on the table and unrolled it. It looked to me like a medieval parchment, an illuminated manuscript. At its top was an illustration in a mix of colors—brown, crimson, blue, purple, and black. Around the image and below it was text, stylized and ornate, as if written by a calligrapher. I had no idea what it said. The words were not in English, and the letters were not of the Roman alphabet.

"It's an illuminated manuscript," I said.

"Yes."

"An original?"

"Yes."

A disheveled man in an old trench coat with what appeared to be an original illuminated manuscript...I couldn't imagine what he was doing with it or how it came into his possession.

"I hate to ask you, but is this stolen?"

"Taken…and given."

"From a museum?" I asked.

"No," he replied.

"Then from what?"

"From a book."

"What book?"

"A book of pages, loose manuscripts. The book of 'them.'"

"Of 'them'?" I said. "The people who don't want you to give it to me?"

"Yes."

"It's understandable that they might be upset, on account of it being stolen."

"Taken," he said, "but more than that, because of what it reveals."

"And what does it reveal?"

"The mystery…the chronicles of the Dark Angel…his purposes for the world. They have seen it as their mission to safeguard those purposes for ages. The book isn't supposed to be seen, Mr. Herzog, by you or anyone outside their circle. It's their book. They made it for their eyes only…as a testament to his workings."

"But somehow you managed to obtain it."

"I have one page. Others have the others."

"Others? Others, like you?"

"Others very much *not* like me," he said. "It was when I finally broke away, when I thought I was finished with them, that I encountered the others. They told me to go back, to get the book. They said it was of critical importance, and it was time. I believed them, and so I went back…and took it."

"And you gave it to them?"

"Yes."

"Why did you trust them?"

"The story is longer than the time we have. The others have the other pages. They gave me this one, the first page, the opening…the beginning of the mystery."

"Why?"

"So I could bring it to you. They told me it was time."

"They wanted you to show it to *me*?"

"No, they wanted me to *give* it to you."

"You're giving me a stolen illuminated manuscript…because…"

"Because you're the one."

"The one for what?"

"The one to open the mystery."

"I don't open mysteries," I replied. "I close them."

"Perhaps. But you're still the one."

"I have no idea what this is all about or why you would go through all the trouble of coming here with this elaborate story about what I'm sure will turn out to be nothing."

"You're a debunker, Mr. Herzog. Debunk it."

At that, he rose from his seat. "I have to be going," he said and with that began heading for the door.

"Wait," I said. "Take your manuscript."

"I told you I came here to give it to you. It's yours now. But that means you'll have to be more careful, much more careful than you've ever been. It tends to attract danger. Take care, Mr. Herzog."

Those were the last words I heard him say. I would never see him again.

I sat there in that room for at least ten minutes, alone with the manuscript, deliberating over what had just happened. I tried to come up with a rational explanation, but I couldn't. I placed the paper in my inner coat pocket and went home. If it weren't for the event that would soon transpire, I don't know that I would ever have pursued the mystery presented to me that night. But it happened.

Chapter 3

THE FALL

When I came home to my apartment, I put the manuscript inside the top drawer of my home office desk. Throughout the next few days, I returned to it, taking it out, staring at it, and trying to construct some rational explanation that would make sense of the man's visit and his cryptic story. It went on like that for about a week.

It was evening. I was watching the news on television when the anchor announced the story of a strange homicide that had taken place in the city in the late hours of the previous night. A man had plunged to his death from the forty-second floor of the hotel in which he had been staying in central Manhattan. The police suspected homicide, as there was evidence of a forced entry and a violent struggle.

They found a picture of the man among his papers. It appeared as part of the news story.

"No!" I said to myself. "No."

It was him, the man who had visited me and given me the page. I, of course, didn't believe his story. I came to the conclusion that it was either the elaborate construct of a conspiracy theorist or the fabrication of a lunatic. His speaking of "them" coming for him, his anxious scanning of the room for danger, I wrote off as paranoia. But, apparently, the danger he spoke of was real. So then, perhaps, was the existence of those he warned me of. He believed they were trying to stop him. Apparently, they were, and if not "them," then others. And they were also, as he had warned, dangerous—enough to throw a man to his death from a high-rise building in New York City.

How much more of his story was true? If there was an organized network of people committed to keeping the book or the page from being known, then for what reason? What was it about the book that was so critical that it would warrant a man's murder? What did it reveal? What mystery could be so important that it would involve a man thrown down over forty stories to his death?

I took the page out of the drawer and, again, just sat there staring at it. But now, in light of what had just happened, it seemed different, as if there was an aura, a gravitas about it that it didn't have before. And if they killed a man to stop him from giving me that page, what was there now to stop them from doing the same to me? I went to the door of my apartment to make sure it was locked. I slowly drew the curtains of my living room window and cautiously scanned the street for any sign of danger, of being watched. But I didn't see anything. The street was quiet.

At least my apartment wasn't anywhere near forty-two stories up. It was just above the ground floor. Still there was no shortage of ways to kill a man at ground level. My mind raced through the possibilities. Finally, I turned out the lights and went to bed. It would be hours before I was able to fall asleep.

As soon as I woke up, the thoughts of how I might meet my death again began racing through my mind. Those who killed the man were trying to stop him from giving me the page, but he gave it, and now I was its possessor. That alone would appear to place me in danger. On the other hand, as I told myself, they might not even know I existed. They may have known he was trying to give it to someone, but it didn't mean they knew it was me. No one actually saw him give it to me. And as long as there was no connection between him and me, I was safe, perhaps.

The following evening I noticed a text on my phone from a Detective Richter. He needed me to call him as soon as possible. So I did. Though it was after hours, he picked up right away.

"Mr. Ariel Herzog?"

"I am."

"Detective Adam Richter with the New York Police Department. I'm investigating a homicide. What do you know of a Max Yildirim?"

"Nothing. I've never heard of him."

"We don't believe it's his real name. It's the name he was using. We believe he was murdered, pushed out of a window in his hotel room. We found a paper in his pocket, and it had your name on it and the address of a library in the city."

"It had to be the library where I was giving a lecture."

"On what?"

"On the supernatural, rationality, and skepticism."

"From what we've been able to gather, Mr. Yildirim had worked for the security forces of the Turkish government. Why do you think he would come all the way to America with your name in his pocket and the address of where you were giving that lecture?"

"Maybe he thought I would say something interesting. I have no idea. Those who attend my lectures come from all over and from all backgrounds. I don't know them, and I certainly don't know their motives."

"Did he speak with you?"

I knew that if I said yes, I would be making my connection with the man official, and if that connection became known to the wrong people, it could mean my death. Further, it would lead to my being asked why he had come to see me—the giving of the manuscript. I paused.

"Nobody with that name spoke with me." What I said was technically true. The man never gave me his name. Thankfully, the detective didn't press me on my answer.

"One more question," he said. "The man was found with a note tied around his neck. I wanted to know if the words on the note meant anything to you."

"What were they?"

"*Thieves don't live long.*"

"I guess it sounds as if his murderers thought he had something that belonged to them and would stop at nothing to get it back."

"Do you have any idea what that was?"

"How could I possibly know that?"

There was a good answer to that question, but I didn't choose to volunteer it.

"If I need to talk with you again, Mr. Herzog, and I have a feeling I may, I'll use this number to reach you."

Those who pushed that man out of that window did so to stop a mystery from being revealed. Instead, they would set in motion a journey that would lead to the mystery's revelation—and to the changing of my life.

Chapter 4
LARA

A MAN WAS DEAD because of an illuminated manuscript, a page from a mysterious book hidden from the world. I had to find out why. The page was an elaborate creation of artistry and calligraphy. An entire book of such pages would have involved countless hours of painstaking work. Why would anyone, or any organization or sect, take the time and effort needed to produce it?

The one person I could think of who could possibly help me and with whom I was personally acquainted was the same person least likely to do so. I would think she viewed me as something of an enemy. Her name was Lara Winter. She was a woman of intelligence, passion, and strong convictions. Had we met under other circumstances, things might have been different. But we didn't. She was one of those on the other side, one whom I counted as an opponent. She was a Christian—not by name but by conviction—a true believer who took the Bible and her faith seriously.

She belonged to an organization that posted biblical apologetics—defenses of the faith—online. She was a frequent contributor to their site, writing articles on reasons to believe and citing testimonies of healings and answered prayers. I would send emails to her office inviting her or those of her organization to debate me. But they never accepted. I would post articles arguing against faith, specifically attacking the articles posted on that site and, more specifically, the articles she had authored. More often than not, my responses were contemptuous and derisive. But Lara never attacked in response, never responded at all, nor did she ever cite my name in any of her writings. I was a thorn in her side and in that of her colleagues. But it was what happened when we first saw each other in person that would seal her animus toward me.

Her organization had decided to host a seminar on the subject of angels, featuring testimonies of those who claimed to have encountered them. The event was open to the public. I decided to attend. It was while I was sitting in the audience, waiting for the presentation to begin, that I first saw her. She was on the panel. She was young and pretty with dark, wavy hair.

The format allowed several opportunities for those in the audience to ask questions. I used every one of them. I turned the seminar into a courtroom. I cross-examined each witness, looking for inconsistencies and contradictions in their testimonies, anything that would discredit their claim.

"Have you ever seen a fairy?" I asked one of them. "Do you believe in fairies? Have you ever had an encounter with a pixie or a boggart?"

"No," said one of the witnesses. "I don't even know what they are."

"Then how," I asked, "do you know that you've never encountered them? Is it possible that what you took to be an angel was actually a pixie?"

"Do you often see things?" I asked another. "Have you ever been on medication?"

Those hosting the event wanted to stop me but decided it was better to let me finish asking my questions than to try to silence me. When it was all over, I saw Lara from across the room, gazing at me with a troubled look on her face as if asking me, "Why?"

And now I needed her help. She worked in a museum. The museum's most prominent and celebrated exhibit was of illuminated manuscripts. She was the exhibit's curator. And so my dilemma: the person whose help I most needed was the one with the most reason not to give it. Despite that, I decided to take the risk. I took for granted that the exchange would be awkward and possibly hostile but believed there was a chance she would help me. I would be extremely friendly and would act as if the past had never happened. I phoned the museum. They put me through to her line.

"This is Lara Winter," she said.

"Lara!" I said enthusiastically. "I hope you're doing great! I don't know if you remember me, but this is Ariel Herzog. We've corresponded a number of times by email."

There was dead silence.

"Yes, well, I could use your expertise. You see, I came across an illuminated manuscript, but I have no idea what it means. So if you could help with this, it would be…"

"Yes, Mr. Herzog," she interrupted. "I certainly remember you. But my memories of you are not pleasant. Why are you calling me?"

"Because I need your help. Someone gave me an illuminated manuscript, an original illuminated manuscript, and I can't figure out what it's about."

"Someone gave you an original illuminated manuscript. Really? And where did they happen to get this manuscript? Walmart?"

"Well, I don't really know. I never saw the man before, and he…"

Again she interrupted. "So you just happened to be given an original illuminated manuscript, and I just happen to deal with original illuminated manuscripts. What a coincidence! And you were given this manuscript by some man you had never seen before. And how did he just happen to obtain this illuminated manuscript?"

"Actually, he said it was stolen."

"Stolen? So you just happened to be given an original illuminated manuscript that was stolen from somewhere, but you don't know where. It's amazing."

"I thought it was."

"And you called me because I happen to know about such things."

"And because it seemed to have something to do with spirituality and faith. The man who gave it to me spoke of the Devil. So I thought that you might…"

"Why are you doing this, Mr. Herzog?" she said. "Is it because this is what you do? You mock people of faith? I don't believe your story, and I'm sorry, but I don't trust you."

"How about we meet, and I'll show it to you?"

"How about we don't," she replied. "I don't know what you're doing or why you're doing it, but whatever it is, I'm not interested. I don't want any part. I'm sorry. I don't have time for this. Goodbye, Mr. Herzog."

And with that, she hung up. It didn't go as well as I had hoped. But I wasn't about to give up. If she could see the manuscript, I thought, if I could find a way to show it to her, she would know I wasn't making it up. I would bring it to her office. It was another risk, but it was the only way she would believe it. So I decided to show up at her place of work, the museum. I made my way over to the exhibit of illuminated manuscripts, where I saw one of the museum's staff.

"Do you know where Lara Winter is?" I asked. "I'm here to see her."

"And you are…?"

"An associate."

"Wait here."

Less than a minute later, Lara appeared on the exhibit floor looking for the associate who had come to see her. We were about thirty feet away when she spotted me and recoiled in horror.

"No, no, no!" she exclaimed. "He's not my associate!"

"I have it!" I exclaimed. "I have it to show you."

"No," she said again, then turned around and began walking away.

I began pursuing her. A security guard intercepted me. "Sir, I have to ask you to leave."

"I haven't done anything," I responded.

A second security guard now joined him. They began escorting me out. I took out the manuscript, unrolled it, and held it up as high as I could. "Lara!" I shouted. "Look!"

She turned around and saw it. She appeared somewhat stunned. She was silent, just staring at it.

"I told you it was real," I said. "Come. Look at it."

Slowly, she walked over, her eyes fixed on the manuscript. The guards backed away but stayed close by. She touched the paper and carefully began scanning the text. Finally, she looked up at me.

"Come," she said as she turned to walk back to her office.

"Should we accompany you?" asked one of the guards.

"No," she said. "It's all right."

She led me back to her office.

"I told you it was real," I said. "Listen, I know what the past has been, but please set it aside for now. I'm totally sincere. And I need your help."

She asked me to lay it down and unroll it on the table in her office. She must have stared at it for at least a minute without saying anything.

"What can you tell me about it?" I asked.

"For one thing," she said, "it's not like any illuminated manuscript I've ever seen."

"Can you tell where it's from?"

"I can't."

"How old is it?"

"By normal standards, old, but compared to most illuminated manuscripts, very new…too new. Most illuminated manuscripts date from around the fifth century to the sixteenth century. But I would guess that this was made somewhere around the nineteenth century. It doesn't make sense…And something else doesn't make sense. The overwhelming majority of illuminated manuscripts are written in Latin. There are some later ones written in other European languages. But this one isn't in Latin or in any language one would expect with such a late date."

"What language then?"

"Greek…Koine Greek."

"Which is…?"

"A form of *ancient* Greek. That's what's even stranger. Though there are some illuminated manuscripts in Greek after the Middle Ages, there are very few written in *Koine* Greek. So why would anyone write an illuminated manuscript using ancient Greek in the nineteenth century? It doesn't make any sense."

"What does it say?"

"I don't know. I don't read Koine Greek. I just know enough to recognize it. But now that you know, it shouldn't be hard for you to get it translated."

"I guess I just have to find someone who reads ancient Greek."

"Or an app. So you still won't tell me how you got it?"

"I told you, but you didn't believe me. It was given to me. And the one who gave it to me said it was stolen."

"If it actually was stolen, you could be in big trouble. I hope you know what you're doing."

"I *don't* know what I'm doing. That's why I came to you. So hopefully, you could help me."

"And hopefully, I have. I don't believe there's anything more I can tell you about it. And I still have no idea what this is all about. And I have to say, Mr. Herzog, this is not like you. You don't seem your normal cynical self. It's almost as if you're searching for something."

"To disprove it."

"No," she said, "I think it's more than that. You seem sincere. Are you sure you haven't come down with something?"

I smiled.

"I hope you find what you're looking for."

We said goodbye. The end of our reunion was more pleasant than its beginning. But it wasn't the end.

What happened next one might attribute to chance or coincidence, but it almost seemed as if events were turning in a set direction—the direction of the manuscript. Not that I believed it then, but it was as if there was some kind of purpose in it.

Less than twenty-four hours after I parted from Lara, the missing piece began to fall into place. It would happen through what seemed to be a chance meeting. But it would lead to the first unlocking of the manuscript's contents and to the opening of the first mystery.

Chapter 5

A THRONE ABOVE THE STARS

I WAS STILL SLEEPING when my phone rang. It was Lara.

"Well, this is a surprise," I said.

"For me too," she said. "OK, so this is what happened. The museum is opening an exhibit of newly obtained manuscripts. To mark the opening, it's presenting a series of lectures to be given by a special guest speaker, Lorens Marinus, a professor from the Netherlands. He's one of the world's foremost experts on illuminated manuscripts and ancient history. Last night the museum held a reception in his honor. During the reception, he approached me. We got into a long conversation. I happened to mention your manuscript and that I couldn't make any sense of it. I described it to him. He was intrigued. He asked me if I could show it to him. I told him I would contact you. So that's what I'm doing. If you want to figure out what it is you have, I wouldn't pass up the opportunity."

"How long is he here for?" I asked.

"A few days."

"I'll meet with him whenever he can."

Professor Marinus must have been anxious to see the manuscript, as he agreed to see me that same day. The meeting would take place in the museum at night. He wanted to do it after hours so there wouldn't be any distractions. I arrived just after nine o'clock, as I had been directed, at the museum's side door entrance. Lara met me there and led me upstairs to where the professor was waiting. It was a massive room, the place where they examined and treated old parchments and manuscripts. The professor was sitting at the end of a small table designed for the examination of scrolls, manuscripts, and parchments. As I entered the room, he stood up.

"Mr. Herzog," said Lara, "this is Professor Marinus. Professor Marinus, Ariel Herzog."

He was tall, thin, and of a distinguished bearing. He appeared to be in his seventies. His face was long and angular, marked by the deep lines of age but in a way that only enhanced the dignity of his appearance. His head was crowned with a wispy halo of white hair.

"It is an honor to meet you," he said with a Dutch accent.

"The honor is mine," I replied.

"Lara has told me so much about you," he said.

"All of it good, I'm sure," I said, knowing that all of it was definitely not good.

"You have the manuscript?"

"I do."

"Would you please place it on the table?"

So I did. He hit a switch, and a multitude of lights came on over the table, around its sides, and from its surface. He then strapped on what appeared to be a jeweler's glass over his eye and began examining the manuscript. Lara and I stood silently around the table, watching him perform his examination. Several minutes passed before anyone said anything.

"Is it real?" I asked.

"It depends on what you mean by real," he said. "It's a real object. The text is Koine Greek. And it was made in the nineteenth century."

"You're sure?" I asked.

"About when it was made? Without question. Lara, can you hand me the scanner?"

It was a compact, pistol-shaped object with a short, snub-nosed barrel and a small display screen—a spectrometer, used to analyze chemical composition. The professor held it over the manuscript and began scanning. Then he showed Lara and me the results as they appeared on its screen. They confirmed the professor's dating.

"So it begs the question," he said, "why a manuscript of Koine Greek from the nineteenth century? You say this was given to you by a man you had never seen before. And he told you he stole it...from whom?"

"He called them 'them.'"

"'Them'? And who are 'them'?"

"He said they've been around for ages."

"You didn't tell me any of this," said Lara.

"Well, it was kind of challenging to get it all out in between 'I don't trust you' and 'I don't want any part of this.'"

"And he told you *where* it was before it was stolen?" asked the professor.

"Not where, but that it was a page taken from a book."

"And did he tell you what book?"

"The book of 'them.'"

He was silent after that, staring not at the manuscript but into the distance as if in deep thought. Then he spoke.

"Do you want to know what it says?"

"Please," I replied.

"I'll read you my translation:

His Throne
Upon the Mountain
His Altar
In the Midst
For Ages Hidden
Unearthed
It Rises
He Ascends
Above the Stars
Of God."

"What does it mean?" I asked. "Who is it talking about?"

"The imagery and phrasing," said the professor, "come from Scripture, from the Bible, from the Book of Isaiah:

> I will ascend into heaven,
> I will exalt my throne above the stars of God."[1]

"Who will ascend to heaven," I asked, "and exalt his throne above the stars of God?"

"The answer," he said, "is found in the preceding verse of Isaiah's prophecy:

> How you are fallen from heaven
> O Lucifer, son of the morning!"[2]

"The red-caped man," I said.

"What?" said Lara.

"The one with the horns and the pitchfork—Satan."

"The word comes from the Hebrew *Sahtan*," said the professor. "It means the Adversary, the Opposer, the Enemy…Satan."

"It matches what I was told. The man who gave me the manuscript said that its previous owners saw it as their mission to fulfill the plans and purposes of the Dark One. So does this all have to do with some kind of sect or cult?"

"It would appear that way." The professor then turned to Lara. "You were wondering why an illuminated manuscript would be created after the time of such things. It's because of this. In the worship of the Devil, the things of God are inverted and employed for the purposes of the Evil One. Illuminated manuscripts were used overwhelmingly for sacred purposes, for the presenting of Scripture, in holy texts. So it would make sense that those on the other side would use the same things for the glory of their own god, Satan—an inversion."

"What about the throne?" asked Lara. "What is that about?"

"The Scripture in Isaiah," said the professor, "speaks of Satan's will to take the place of God, to ascend above the stars, to become like the Most High, to sit on the Throne of God."

"His Throne upon the Mountain," said Lara. "The Throne of God?"

"No," said the professor. "The Throne of Satan."

"But it's talking about something specific," I said, "something tangible, physical, something hidden on a mountain for ages and then unearthed."

"Yes," said the professor. "It's speaking of a physical throne of Satan...And such a thing does exist."

"An actual throne of Satan," I said, "in this world?"

"Yes. And would you like to know where it is?"

"Please," I replied.

The professor would now open the mystery of an ancient object that, up to that moment, I had no idea existed, and yet would alter the course of my life.

Chapter 6

PERGAMON

A THRONE IS THAT upon which a ruler sits," said the professor, "and from which his authority and power go forth. From the throne comes the kingdom. So the Throne of Satan is the seat of Satan's authority and that from which his power goes forth, from which his kingdom emanates."

"And it exists on earth."

"Yes," said the professor. "It is identified in the Scriptures. In the second chapter of the Book of Revelation, it is written:

> I know your works, and where you dwell, *where Satan's throne is.*"[1]

"And you know where that is?" I asked.

"The previous verse reveals it:

> And to the angel of the church in *Pergamon*...[2]

"The Throne of Satan was in Pergamon. Pergamon was an ancient Greek city in Asia Minor, not far from the Aegean Sea. In the second and third centuries BC, it was the capital city of the Kingdom of Pergamon. By the time the Book of Revelation was written, it had become part of the Roman Empire."

"And what language did they speak in Pergamon?" asked Lara.

"Koine Greek," said the professor.

"The language of the manuscript," she replied, "because it was the language of Pergamon."

"But what was it about Pergamon," I said, "that would cause it to be called the place 'where Satan's throne is'?"

"Look at the image on the manuscript," said the professor. "What do you see?"

"A mountain," I said, "and an object on top of it...It could be a throne."

"His Throne upon the Mountain," said Lara.

"Yes," said the professor. "Rising over a thousand feet above the city of Pergamon was what the ancients would have called a mountain or a high place. On top of it stood temples and monuments of the gods. But it was one specific structure that stood out among them in its uniqueness—an altar."

"His Altar in the Midst," said Lara.

"A gigantic altar," said the professor, "almost a hundred and twenty feet wide and over a hundred feet deep—the most colossal known to ever have been erected in the Greek world. It was built to the supreme king of the gods, Zeus, and was known as the Great Altar."

"And why," I asked, "would it be connected in the Bible to the Throne of Satan?"

"For one thing, it was a pagan object, and among the most immense pagan objects in the world. It was an altar, a vessel of sacrifice, the ultimate act of devotion in the worship of the gods.

"And then there was Zeus. According to the Scriptures, the worship of gods involves more than mythology."

"What would be more than mythology?" I asked.

"Spirits," he said. "It involves spirits. In the Hebrew Scriptures, they're called the *shedim*. In the Greek of the New Testament, the word is *daimónia*, from which you get the English word *demon*. In other words, in the view of Scripture, the gods were only facades, the masks of demonic spirits.

"And who would be ruler of those spirits?" he asked. "In the Greek, Satan is called the *archon* of demons. *Archon* means chief, head, ruler. So Satan is the chief, the head, and the ruler of demonic spirits. And Zeus was the chief, king, and ruler of the gods. And if behind the gods were spirits, then the ruler of the gods, Zeus, would correspond to the ruler of spirits, the archon of demons, Satan. The Scriptures even refer to Satan as 'the god of this world.'[3] And Zeus, or Jupiter, was the god of that world. Zeus would thus be a mask of Satan, and his Great Altar, a satanic vessel."

I couldn't believe I was now engaged in a conversation about Satan that seemed to almost imply his actual existence.

"And beyond all that," said the professor, "if Pergamon was the Throne of Satan, it was the Great Altar that would become the embodiment of Pergamon to the world and thus the embodiment of Satan's Throne."

"What I'm not getting," I said, "is what all this has to do with now. Everything you spoke of took place in ancient times. Why would the manuscript be created thousands of years after ancient times? And if what the man told me was true, it has to do with what's happening now…with mass calamity, mass destruction, and the future of the world...How could an ancient object be affecting anything in the modern world?"

That was followed by a long silence. The professor's answers had only opened up more questions, larger questions. And now he would answer my question with yet another.

"Why don't you find out?"

"What do you mean?"

"Why don't you find out what it means and what it has to do with now? You're an investigator, Mr. Herzog. Investigate it."

"This wasn't something I was planning to launch an investigation into. I just wanted to know what it was or wasn't."

"Sometimes you don't choose your endeavor," he said. "Sometimes it chooses you."

"How would I even know where to begin?"

"You might want to start in Turkey. You might want to begin in a place called Bergama."

"Why there?" I asked.

"Because Bergama is the modern name of the ancient city of Pergamon. That's where you'll find the high place and the ancient ruins."

"I'm supposed to travel across the world on a mission having to do with an ancient object that may or may not have something to do with a strange manuscript that may, in some way, be relevant, and maybe not. And it all has something to do with the Devil, who I don't believe exists."

"Strange," said the professor. "Lara told me you were in the business of debunking. I wouldn't think that unbelief would stop a debunker from debunking."

"Bon voyage, Mr. Herzog!" said Lara with a smile.

"Lara," said the professor, "your specialty is illuminated manuscripts. And you're the one who arranged for this meeting. It's not often that one gets the chance to uncover something new about them, to actually make a discovery. Something like this may never come your way again. I think you should consider going as well."

"Bon voyage, Lara Winter!" I said with a smile.

"I appreciate your words, Professor Marinus," she said, "but I don't think so. It's not for me. And I have too much going on in my life to even consider it. And even if by some miracle I were to consider undertaking such a mission, it would not be with him."

"The pursuit of truth," said the professor, "like politics, can sometimes make for strange bedfellows."

"Except in this case," said Lara, "there are no fellows—and no bed."

"What we have here," he said, "is a unique mystery and a once-in-a-lifetime opportunity. If I were younger, if I were you, I would jump at the chance." At that, he rose from his seat, as did Lara and I. "And now, I must thank you for a most memorable evening."

He walked toward the door but then paused and turned around. "Mr. Herzog, you *will* take good care of that manuscript. It could be of great value, and there *are* ethics concerning stolen artifacts. It really does belong in a museum."

Again he moved toward the doorway, and again he paused and turned around. "And you should take care of yourself as well, Mr. Herzog. If what the man told you was true, there are others who have a similar interest in your new possession."

And with that, he exited the room. Lara and I were left there standing by the table.

"You do realize," she said, "that the chances of me going on a journey with you to Turkey or anywhere else on this planet are less than zero. I just wanted to make sure you realized that."

"Stranger things have happened," I replied.

And stranger things would.

Chapter 7

THE DREAM

I COULDN'T GET THE professor's words out of my head. I just wanted to know the meaning of the scroll. And now I knew what it said—but had no idea what it meant. I knew how to investigate a story. I had done it countless times. But I had never traveled across the world to do it—and not for something that might mean nothing. It could end up being a wild-goose chase or, worse, a rabbit hole of clues that led nowhere.

Still I couldn't shake his words. Here was the expert telling us that, if he was able, he wouldn't pass up the opportunity. He would jump at the chance to embark on a journey to unlock the mystery of that manuscript. It was clear that he believed there was more to it, something potentially important. What if there was? And what if I missed the chance to find it?

It was about two weeks after that meeting that I came to a decision. I would go to Bergama, to the high place, to the ruins of the ancient Altar. And if I didn't find something significant, some clear or solid leading, and if I didn't find it soon, that would be it. I would finish my journey and bring my search to an end.

It was the day after I made that decision that I received a text. "Call me," it said. It was Lara. I couldn't imagine what she wanted to tell me.

"Did you decide?" she asked. "Are you going to go to Bergama?"

"I am."

"I was so hoping you would say you weren't."

"Why?"

"Not long after our meeting, I was called into the office by one of my directors at the museum. Apparently, Professor Marinus had approached the board to tell them that they needed to send me along with you on a fully funded research mission concerning a certain unique and enigmatic illustrated manuscript that he believed to be of historical significance."

"And..."

"Because it was Professor Marinus and because he was connected to many of the museum's most important funders, they didn't think it wise to offend him. So they said yes."

"And what did *you* say?"

"I said no. They gave me a week to reconsider. Now, I know this won't mean anything to you, but throughout my life I've had dreams that often come true."

"How?"

"I don't know how—a revelation from God? I have no idea, but it happens. And you were in it."

"So you dreamed of me."

"Not by choice. You were in a maze, an outdoor maze of hedged bushes. You were wandering through it aimlessly, ending up back where you started over and over again. I heard a voice telling me to help you. I went into the maze, found you, and led you out.

"We walked through a landscape of ornate domed buildings and then into another maze, this one of old stone streets covered with arched ceilings, some kind of Middle Eastern bazaar with vibrant colors, hand-woven rugs and fabrics, intricately crafted trinkets, ceramic plates and vases, golden lamps, the voices of merchants haggling with buyers, the aroma of spices and incense, and the sounds of Middle Eastern instruments echoing through the walls.

"We turned down street after street. Somehow, I knew where to go. Finally, we came to a wooden door where I stopped. The door was framed by two painted pillars of brown, yellow, black, and red. In the center of the door was a small carved image of an eagle. I turned to you and said, 'He's in here.' I opened the door…and the dream ended."

"And so…"

"And so after waking up from that dream, I prayed you would tell me you weren't going to Bergama."

"I guess prayers aren't always answered."

"Or," she said, "given answers we'd rather not have been given."

"Does that mean I'm the answer to your prayers?"

"Definitely not. But it means I have to go to Bergama…with you."

I was quiet as something just hit me.

"What?" asked Lara.

"I didn't tell you this before, but I have to tell you now…The man who visited me, who gave me the page—he's dead."

"Dead?"

"He was murdered—thrown out of a window."

"Who would…?"

"I would think those from whom he took the page. He told me that there would be dangers. If there are, and you go with me, you'll be facing those same dangers. So you may want to reconsider…"

She was silent for about half a minute. I said nothing, letting her contemplate what I told her. Finally, she spoke.

"I'll trust," she said.

"You'll trust me?" I asked.

"No," she said, "I'll trust God. You, I don't trust. Speaking of which, I haven't told you my two conditions…"

"What?"

"Number one, if we don't find something of significance—some clear, solid lead—and soon, we end the journey."

"All right," I said. "I'll agree to that. And the other…?"

"Separate rooms."

"Of course."

"I can't believe I'm doing this," she said.

"And you're the believer," I replied.

We would now embark on a journey that would take us across the world and to that which was far beyond anything either of us could have prepared for or imagined. And as the man had warned, it would place our lives in danger.

It would all begin with a journey to the Throne of Satan.

Chapter 8
THE UNEARTHED

WE BOARDED THE plane for Turkey. Lara was quiet on the flight as if in deep thought, undoubtedly wondering if the whole thing was a big mistake.

We landed in the city of Izmir and checked into our hotel—separate rooms, of course. Izmir is one of Turkey's port cities on the Aegean coast. In ancient times, it was called Smyrna. I would later come to find out that Smyrna was also mentioned in the Book of Revelation, along with Pergamon.

The next day, we rented a car and set out for Bergama, modern-day Pergamon. We arrived there in less than two hours. Bergama sits in the valley below the ancient ruins. We could see it in the distance—the mountain, or high place, on which stood the ancient acropolis. As we came nearer, we stopped to ask a local man how one would ascend it. He told us we could take a cable car or we could drive up the Akropol Cad. That was the name they gave to the narrow winding road with steep inclines and sudden turns. "Some call it the 'road of death,'" he said, laughing. Since we had a car, we took the Akropol Cad.

"We're on the road of death to the Throne of Satan," I said. "Doesn't sound promising."

Lara didn't laugh but remained quiet. I believe she was praying.

It was late afternoon when we reached the summit. The view was stunning—a sweeping panorama of the plain below, the city of Bergama, a vast fertile valley, fields and olive groves, distant mountains, and the blue shimmering of the Aegean Sea. And then there was the acropolis itself, the remnants of ancient buildings, the temples of the gods—walls, columns, capitals, foundations, and facades. But we had no idea what was what or how to find the Altar of Pergamon.

On the summit in the distance stood a man watching us. He was middle-aged, clean-shaven, pleasant-looking, with neatly trimmed dark hair, and wearing a long dark coat. He approached us.

"You seem lost," he said. "Can I help you?"

He was fluent in English, but with what I took to be a Middle Eastern accent. I assumed he was Turkish.

"We're just looking," I said.

"Is there anything specific you might be looking for?"

"The Altar of Pergamon," said Lara.

"The Great Altar," he said. "I can show it to you."

"Are you a tour guide?" I asked.

"No," he replied, "I'm a custodian. I watch over the site. Come."

We followed him through the ruins. He didn't stop to speak of them, as he knew we were focused on seeing the Altar. But he would point them out as we passed by. "The Temple of Trajan," he said, "the Theater…the Temple of Dionysus…the Sanctuary of Athena."

He then led us over to a terrace of earth jutting out from the side of the acropolis. It was an open, rectangular surface overlooking the valley below, an ancient platform for the displaying of a monumental structure.

"The Altar of Pergamon," he said.

In the midst of the terrace were the ruins of a once colossal structure outlining the Altar's perimeter. And in the midst of the ruins were the remnants of the stone stairway on which the priests of Zeus would ascend to offer their sacrifices. Around the perimeter were scattered blocks of stone and column drums with which the Altar was once adorned. The three of us stepped onto the terrace and approached the ruins of the Altar. Lara and I stood there gazing at the ruins as strong gusts of wind swept across the terrace.

"So this is what you're looking for?" asked the man.

"What we're looking for is its meaning," I replied.

"Perhaps I can help you."

"I appreciate it, but I don't think you can."

"His Throne upon the Mountain," he said. "His Altar in the Midst."

Lara and I looked up.

"How did you know those words?" I asked.

"It's my job," he replied.

"You're one of them!"

"Which 'them' do you mean?"

"The 'them' who are seeking to stop whatever is supposed to be revealed."

"Quite the opposite," he said. "We're here to stop those who would stop the revelation."

"And who are the *we*?" asked Lara.

"Those who keep watch."

"And how do we know," she said, "that you're not on the other side?"

"If I were here to stop you, you would have already been stopped."

"Then why are you here?" I asked.

"To help you, Mr. Herzog."

"I never told you my name."

"You didn't have to."

"So how can you help us?"

"What comes after His Altar in the Midst?" he asked.

Lara took out her notepad and found it.

"For Ages Hidden...Unearthed."

"Yes," he said. "I don't believe that part has been told to you. You see, for most of the last two thousand years, the Altar was covered. The Throne of Satan was hidden in the dust. You could say it was God who buried it. More specifically, it was the coming of the Gospel into Western civilization, into the pagan world, that caused the Altar to be abandoned and covered in ruins."

"So then," said Lara, "the Christianization of Western civilization meant the disappearance of Satan's Throne."

"Yes," said the man. "And what would the disappearance of Satan's Throne mean for the world? It would mean that the power of the Enemy would be restrained. There would, of course, be evil, as there always was. But it was no longer the *reigning* power. It would no longer rule cultures and empires as it had in pagan times. The power of darkness, the dominion of the Evil One, would be restrained."

"And it all centers on this place," she said.

"But what then would happen," said the man, "if the Altar returned? What would happen if the Throne of Satan was uncovered, if someone were to dig it up?"

"It would mean that the darkness would no longer be restrained," said Lara, "that the power of the Enemy would no longer be held back."

"It would mean," said the man, "that the power of darkness would be unleashed on the world, the power to reign over kingdoms. It would mean the reverse of what happened at the beginning of the age. If the Christianization of Western civilization meant the disappearance of the Altar, then the reappearance of the Altar would mean...the dechristianization of the West."

"So it was unearthed," I said.

"Yes," said the man. "The Throne of Satan was unearthed. Otherwise you wouldn't be seeing even its remnants."

"Of course," I replied.

"So someone came here," said Lara, "and unearthed it?"

"A stranger. He came here from far away."

"Did he know what he was doing?" I asked.

"He had no idea. And so when the Throne of Satan was unearthed, everything was set in motion," he said. "That which was holding back the power of darkness was removed, and the powers of the Dark Angel were unleashed."

"What exactly was unleashed upon the world?" I asked. "What exactly happened?"

"That," he said, "is the next piece of the mystery, the next revelation, and it is not for me to tell."

"Then…"

"But I have something to give you."

He reached into his coat, pulled out a sheet, and handed it to me. It was an illuminated manuscript in the same style and in what appeared to be the same language as the first.

"Another manuscript," I said. "Is it also stolen?"

"Apprehended," he said. "You were told that others had other pages of the book?"

"We were."

"This is the second page."

"And how will we know what it means?" asked Lara.

"That you'll have to find out yourself."

"You don't make it easy," I said.

And with that, he began to walk away, back to the summit, and without looking back, said, "Goodbye, Mr. Herzog and Lara." Then, again without turning his head, he spoke a last parting word: "Godspeed."

It was an image of a castle, a chance glimpse of a television newscast, a city of domed buildings, an ancient bazaar, a room full of colored lamps, and a bearded man in a flat-topped red hat that would reveal the next mystery: the mystery of the dark kingdom.

PART II

KINGDOM

Chapter 9
THE MAN IN THE BAZAAR

We returned to the car.

"That didn't just happen," I said. "How could he have possibly known who we were? And how did he just happen to be there when we happened to come? And how did he happen to have that page?"

"Just go with it," she replied.

We didn't want to wait until we got back to Izmir to look at the manuscript, so we decided to examine it right there in the car on top of the mountain. Without being able to interpret its text, we focused on its image, a stylized symbol or icon. It appeared to be some sort of castle. At its bottom was a large open doorway. Inside the doorway was what appeared to be a throne.

"What do you think it means?" I asked Lara.

"I don't know. Looks like a castle with a throne in it. That wouldn't seem unusual."

"Maybe it has to do with a king."

"What king would be connected to the Altar of Pergamon?"

"I don't know. The king of Turkey?" said Lara. "A sultan?"

But nothing clicked. We had to translate the text. Its heavily stylized calligraphy, along with its ornamental markings, meant we couldn't rely on a cell phone or computer-generated translation. And Lara wanted to make sure every word was right. So that night, she manually transcribed the words of the page and, working with a translation program on her laptop, rendered the text into English. The next day, at lunch in a Turkish coffeehouse in Izmir, she opened her notepad and began to read me the translation.

"It has something of a title under the picture, the word 'Basileia.'"

"Which means…?"

"Kingdom. And then it says this:

The Altar Taken
The Throne Removed
The Seed Is Planted
In Colder Soil

The Altar
Of the Kingdom
Bears Its Fruit
And the Kingdom
Of the Altar
Is Born."

"So the castle represents a kingdom."

"But what does it mean?" she asked. "What kingdom?"

"And what planting of what seed?"

Suddenly, Lara was transfixed, gazing over my head. Her eyes were wide open, almost as if in shock.

"What?" I asked.

Mounted on the wall behind me was a television screen. It had been on the whole time, but we hadn't paid it any attention, as it was in Turkish.

"What is it?" I asked.

"My dream," she said. "It's what was in my dream!"

I turned around. On the screen were scenes from a Turkish bazaar.

"The bazaar...the old streets...the golden lamps...and it's all covered with arched ceilings. It's exactly what I saw in my dream!"

"Are you sure it's not just something similar to what you..."

"No. It's the exact place we walked through. We have to go there. It's the next key. It's where we'll find the answer."

"We can't just pick up and..."

"Yes, we can!" She took out her phone and began searching for bazaars in Turkey. "This is it!" she said as she looked at the images that came up. "It's called the Grand Bazaar. It's in Istanbul. The domed buildings in my dream...Istanbul is famous for its domed buildings! We have to go there."

She continued searching and scrolling.

"There are flights from Izmir to Istanbul. It takes less than an hour and a half. This is a divine setup. We have to go there...now!"

I was skeptical. But it was because of a dream that she had agreed to come with me in the first place. And we had nothing else to go on. So I went with it. I picked up my phone and managed to secure two seats on a flight to Istanbul that same afternoon. We rushed back to the hotel, packed our things, rushed out to the airport, and boarded a flight to Istanbul. So intense was Lara's sense of urgency that upon our arrival, we dropped off our luggage at our hotel and headed straight for the Grand Bazaar.

The Grand Bazaar was located inside Istanbul's old walled city. With over sixty covered streets and over four thousand shops, it was one of the largest and oldest covered markets in the world. And with its multitude of streets, it was—as Lara had seen in her dream—something of a maze.

"You have to trust me with this," she said, "and you have to let me lead you as I did in the dream."

I agreed. The bazaar, as in her dream, was an explosion of Middle Eastern sights, sounds, and fragrances—a sensory overload. As we walked through the maze of streets and shops, Lara provided me with continuous commentary.

"Look!" she said. "The golden lamps, the ceramic plates, the rugs, as in my dream…Listen…the sound of the instruments, the same sounds."

When we came to a cross street, she would pause, then turn left or right or continue straight depending on what she sensed. At times, she would close her eyes to concentrate, trying to remember the course she had taken in her dream. And then she stopped.

"Look," she said, pointing to her right. It was a wooden door. The door was framed by two painted pillars of brown, yellow, black, and red, as in her dream. "And look at that," she said, pointing. There, in the center of the door, was a small carved image of an eagle, as she described seeing on the wooden door of her dream.

"He's in here," she said.

"Who's in there?"

"I haven't the slightest idea, but that's what I said in the dream."

"Then let's find out," I replied.

I knocked on the door. It opened. Standing before us was an older Turkish man with a short but full white beard, a distinctive aquiline nose, and thick, rosy cheeks. He was wearing an ornately woven red vest and a fez, a flat-topped hat of red felt with a red tassel.

"Americans?" he asked. We nodded. "I'm Mr. Isik. Welcome to my store! Please come in!"

His store was something of a microcosm of the bazaar, with golden lamps; trinkets; painted ceramic plates, bowls, and vases; elaborate garments and embroidered fabrics; souvenirs; Turkish rugs and furnishings; and much more—all gently illuminated by a series of colored lamps. But there was no one there but us.

"I wouldn't have known it was a store," I said, "if you hadn't opened the door."

"I usually conduct my business by special appointment," he said. "So how did you hear of my store?"

"We didn't," said Lara. "We were just kind of led."

"Very interesting," he said. "So tell me what you're looking for."

"Do you deal in illuminated manuscripts?" I asked.

"Illuminated manuscripts," he repeated. "Can you give me a little more detail or show me a picture of what you're looking for?"

I took out the manuscript we had been given on the mountain and laid it on the counter before him.

"I'm sorry," he said. "I don't sell such things."

It made no sense. Why would we be led to that shop only to find nothing there? With nothing to go on, we thanked the man and turned to leave.

"But," he said, "I still might be able to help you…Mr. Herzog."

"You're one of them," I said.

"Come," he said. He led us into a back room with a red Turkish carpet on which rested a number of ornate cushions. He motioned for Lara and me to choose a cushion on which to sit. He closed the door, locked it, and joined us on the carpet.

"Now," he said, "shall we talk of the Altar? And what became of it? The planting and the kingdom?"

"Yes," I replied.

"Then let us begin."

There, in that dimly lit back room of a Turkish souvenir shop, the dark mystery of ages was opened to us.

Chapter 10

THE DARK KINGDOM

"THE THRONE OF Satan," he said, "it lay buried in the earth for ages. It should have never been disturbed. But then...he came."

"Who came?" I asked.

"The stranger, the disturber, the uncoverer."

"Do we know his name?"

"His name was Carl Humann. Had he known what he was about to unleash on the world, would he have done anything differently? Would he have laid down his shovel and spade? We will never know."

"Who was he?"

"An engineer. As a young man he was stricken with tuberculosis. So he decided to move to a warmer climate. So he came here."

"To Turkey."

"It was then the heart of the Ottoman Empire. He came here to Istanbul. He worked with the empire in the building of roads and in various projects of surveying and mapping. His work on those projects led him to travel the land. One day in the mid-1860s, in the midst of his travels, he came to Pergamon. He ascended the ancient high place and saw its ruins. I believe you know of it."

"We were just there," I said.

"The ruins impressed him. He believed they were of great significance. So drawn was Humann to that place that he would write in his diary, 'I could not resist the urge, to visit Pergamon again.'[1] And so he returned again and again. He even set up a residence there to use as his base for further study of the ancient site. While in Pergamon, he came across strange images on stone plates or fragments—a god, a giant, an ancient man. To Humann, it indicated there was much more lying in the dust of Pergamon. He would set out to uncover it.

"While visiting Istanbul, Humann happened to encounter a famous archaeologist, Dr. Ernst Curtius. Humann told him of his discoveries and convinced him to come to Pergamon to see for himself. So Humann led Dr. Curtius to the ancient ruins. He showed him some of the ancient images on the stone plates as evidence of what was hidden in the ruins. His encounter with Dr. Curtius would prove critical in the unearthing of the ancient Altar.

"Shortly after showing Dr. Curtius the ruins, Humann sent two ancient pieces of stone from Pergamon back to his homeland in Europe. He didn't yet know it, but the two pieces he sent were from the Altar of Pergamon, from the Throne of Satan. It was the beginning. After centuries of lying in the dust, the Throne of Satan would be uncovered. It would ultimately lead to the Altar's unearthing and to its being moved to another land."

"The Altar Taken," said Lara. "The Throne Removed."

"Yes," said the man, "in its unearthing, the Altar would be taken apart, piece by piece. The pieces would then be shipped across the world. And there, in Humann's homeland, they would be received, restored, and pieced back together. The ancient Altar would then be reconstructed in another land."

"What would it mean?" asked Lara.

"What would it mean to unearth the Throne of Satan?" asked the man. "It would mean the resurrection of an ancient darkness, the reawakening of an ancient force, and the reempowering of an ancient entity. What would it mean?" he asked again. "It would mean calamity...for the world."

"And what about its moving?" asked Lara. "What would it mean to move the Throne of Satan?"

"It would mean that the evil would be given a new resting place; the darkness would find a new home. It would mean that a new land would become the center of his workings in the world. And as from the throne comes the kingdom, so if one moves the throne to another land, then the kingdom will follow. So the land that received the Throne of Satan would also receive his kingdom."

"The Altar of the Kingdom Bears Its Fruit," said Lara, repeating the words of the text. "The Kingdom of the Altar Is Born."

"And the kingdom of Satan is what exactly?" I asked.

"The kingdom over which Satan especially reigns," he replied, "an empire ruled by evil."

"And so a kingdom of Satan would somehow appear in the modern world?" I said.

"Yes, a modern kingdom," he said, "a modern nation ruled by the ancient evil...a modern people infused by a pagan darkness...possessed by the resurrected evil."

"A pretty heavy concept," I replied.

"And a heavier reality," he replied. "What would you expect to happen when you unearth and transfer the Throne of Satan? You would expect something dramatic to begin, something dark to be set in motion."

"How would it happen?" asked Lara.

"Step-by-step," he replied. "The nation that received the Altar would undergo a transformation, a metamorphosis. Its inhabitants would be subject to a dark phenomenon, that of satanization. That nation would become the instrument of the Evil One, a vessel to accomplish his purposes in the world."

"Sounds like science fiction," I said. "It doesn't sound real."

"But it is real."

"You never told us where," said Lara. "Where was the Altar taken? What land?"

"The land was called *Germany*," he replied. "The Altar of Pergamon was taken to Germany. And so it became the new home of Satan's Throne."

We would now be shown the next manifestation of the mystery—what would happen when the ancient Altar was moved to its new home and how it would transform the world.

Chapter 11
CONCEPTION

"GERMANY!" I SAID as a multitude of thoughts began flooding my mind.

"So Carl Humann was German," said Lara.

"Yes."

"And Dr. Curtius?" she asked.

"He was also from Germany. It was Germany," said the man, "that initiated everything. It was Germany that dug up the Altar and unearthed the Throne of Satan. And it was Germany that transported it across the world that it might be erected on its soil."

"In colder soil," said Lara. "The Altar Taken, the Throne Removed, the Seed Is Planted in Colder Soil."

"And it was Germany," said the man, "that would piece it together so that it would again manifest to the world for the first time in thousands of years."

"When everything began," said Lara, "when Humann came to Pergamon, when he uncovered it, when he transported it, did any change take place in Germany?"

"Yes," said the man, "as when one sows seed into soil, one couldn't then see all that it would bring forth, but it was then that it all began to germinate. And in time, the whole world would know it."

"So what happened in Germany?" I asked.

"It was more than what happened in Germany," he replied.

"What do you mean?"

"Germany, as you know it, did not exist. There was a German language, a German culture, and German lands. But Germany did not exist as Germany, not as a nation, and had never existed."

"So," I said, "when Carl Humann came to Pergamon…"

"There was no Germany. Humann was German and came from the land that would become Germany. But it didn't exist."

"Then where was he from?" I asked.

"From Prussia. Prussia was a German state and kingdom, the most powerful of German states. It was in 1864 that events were set in motion that would lead to the Altar's unearthing as Humann set out to visit its ancient ruins. It was that year that a dramatic transformation began in Europe, one that would alter the history of the world. In 1864, Prussia, under Otto von Bismarck, entered into war with Denmark and emerged victorious. The war would strengthen Prussia's military power, increase its political standing, and expand its territory.

"In 1866, Humann made a return visit to Pergamon. It is recorded that during that visit, he came upon an ancient stone relief. It would turn out that the relief was a dislocated piece of the ancient Altar. So 1866 marked Humann's coming into contact with an actual piece of Satan's Throne and would mark the beginning of his own transition from a traveling engineer into the archaeologist who would unearth the long-hidden object.

"That same year, another series of events was set in motion in the Germanic lands as Prussia declared war on Austria and again emerged victorious. The war reshaped the political map of Europe. It would lead to Prussia's organizing twenty-two northern German states into the North German Confederation with a federal constitution and a new parliament to be called the Reichstag. The war took place in the summer of 1866, the same summer of Humann's return to Pergamon.

"The most critical year in the Altar's return to the world was 1871. It was then that Humann led Dr. Curtius to the ancient ruins and showed him the images on the ancient stone plates. And it was that same year that Dr. Curtius arranged for Humann to send two of the Altar's ancient pieces from the ruins of Pergamon to Berlin."

"So then 1871," I said, "was the year that marked the beginning of the transference...the moving of the Altar from Pergamon to Germany."

"Not the official or complete transference—that would come later—but the initial transference, the sending of its first two pieces. And it was that same year that would witness another critical event of incalculable consequences for the history of the world. It was 1871 that marked the end of the wars that began in 1864 and the completion of the transformation. The last of those wars was waged between Prussia and France, the Franco-Prussian War. The conflict allowed Bismarck to unite the southern German states with the northern confederation. And again Prussia emerged victorious.

"In the last days of the Franco-Prussian War, while Paris was still under siege, German princes gathered in the French Palace of Versailles. There they issued a proclamation heralding the birth of the German Empire.

Later that year, its constitution would come into effect. It was the birth of the nation that the world would come to know as Germany."

"So," said Lara, "it all happened at the same time."

"The ancient Altar and the nation of Germany," he said, "they both came into the world at the same time...They both manifested to the world in 1871."

"The Altar of the Kingdom," said Lara. "The Kingdom of the Altar."

"With the throne," he said, "comes the kingdom, and with the kingdom the throne. And so as the Throne of Satan returned to the world, the nation of Germany was born."

"And that was just the beginning," I said, "wasn't it?"

"Yes. Germany, having been born with the Throne, would now begin transforming into the kingdom."

"Of the Enemy," said Lara.

"Of the Dark Angel. Germany would undergo a metamorphosis, transformed step-by-step until it became the vessel of the plans and purposes of the Dark One. Through Germany he would bring war to the earth. Through Germany, he would bring death and destruction to millions. From the kingdom of the Altar, he would shake the earth and leave it in ashes. He would alter the course of world history. And it all began in 1871, the year of the Altar's discovery and its first unearthing."

"And yet there was more," he said. "In the year that the Altar began its return to the world, something else was set in motion...something else would come into the world."

Chapter 12

THE SIGN

"AT THE TIME Germany was born," said the man, "one could not have foreseen where it would all end. But a sign was given of what was to come.

"It began with a businessman from Germany who became obsessed with the works of the ancient Greek writer Homer. He believed that the places mentioned in the ancient Greek stories were real. His name was Heinrich Schliemann. In the *Iliad,* Homer wrote of the ancient city of Troy. In the nineteenth century, many historians believed Troy to be a myth. Schliemann set out to prove them wrong by finding its ancient ruins and unearthing them.

"His search led him to a site in Anatolia along the Dardanelles Strait, at the meeting place of Europe and Asia. It was known as the Hisarlik mound. Digging deep into the mound, Schliemann found the ruins of a civilization dating back thousands of years. Schliemann had discovered the city of Troy, and the discovery would catapult him to world fame.

"In his excavation of Troy, Schliemann would uncover something else...an ancient symbol. It appeared on pottery shards, sculptures, and round spindle whorls. He was able to dig up almost two thousand variations of that same ancient symbol. As the news of Schliemann's discoveries spread around the world, so did the symbol. The sign had been known of beforehand, but it was Schliemann's discovery that brought it into the world's consciousness, particularly in Europe and especially in Germany.

"Schliemann himself believed that the ancient symbol was connected to German civilization and thus that German civilization was connected to ancient Troy. Further, he believed that the sign bore witness to an ancient civilization that joined together Germany, India, Greece, and others. Schliemann's findings and theories were picked up by German nationalists who used the symbol to identify themselves and their movements. The sign that Schliemann unearthed would become known in Germany as the *Hakenkreuz,* or the hooked cross. It would become known throughout the world as the *swastika.*

"It was Schliemann's discovery that especially joined the swastika to the German belief in the Aryan race. The connection would be taken up by

Adolf Hitler, who would make it the symbol of Nazism. Hitler would give it the red, white, and black imagery by which it would become known across the world."

"So the swastika," I said, "and the Altar of Pergamon were both unearthed by the same people, the Germans."

"Yes," he replied, "and in the same land, the Ottoman Empire, and in the same region, on the coast of the Aegean Sea."

"When?" asked Lara. "When did Schliemann find the swastika?"

"The year of the swastika was 1871."

"The same year as the Altar of Pergamon!" she said.

"Yes. As the first pieces of the ancient Altar were being crated and sent to Germany, the swastika was unearthed in the same land and being prepared to be sent back to Germany. So the Throne of Satan and the sign that would embody its evil entered the world together."

"And Germany," I said. "It all happened in the year of Germany's birth."

"Yes," he replied. "A kingdom for a throne and a sign for the kingdom. They all came into the world together, the dark trio of resurrections—the unearthing of Satan's Throne, the birth of Germany, and the resurrection of the swastika. It was all set in motion by the hand of the Dark Angel. And yet nothing could have prepared the world for what was coming."

And the revelation was over. We rose from the carpet, and the man, Isik, walked us over to the front door.

"I told you I didn't sell illuminated manuscripts," he said. "But that doesn't mean I can't give them away." With that, he handed Lara a sheet.

"The third page?" I asked.

"Yes, and the second manifestation. I know my shop doesn't have everything, but I always hope that my customers find what they're looking for."

We left the store and headed down the labyrinthine streets of the Grand Bazaar. The next mystery would take us across the world and into an even more ominous mystery—the raging of a dragon.

PART III

FURY

Chapter 13

THE DRAGON'S LAIR

We were about halfway through the bazaar when I noticed it.

"Keep walking," I said. "Don't look back. I believe we're being followed. There's a man in back of us who's been in back of us from the time we left the shop. Let's take the next side street."

So we did. As soon as we turned, we saw an alleyway and quickly hid ourselves in it. We saw the man pass by us, looking in all directions, wondering where we had gone. I decided to deal with it head-on. I told Lara to stay where she was as I stepped out into the street about thirty feet behind the man. He appeared to be in his late forties or early fifties, with close-cropped black hair, a neatly trimmed mustache and beard, almond-shaped eyes, and an aquiline nose. I assumed he was Turkish.

"Why are you following us?" I shouted.

He turned around and began approaching me.

"For your protection," he said with an accent. "But you don't make it easy."

"Our protection? Who are you?"

"My name is Kazim Yarikan. I work for an intelligence agency that specializes in terrorism. We've been following you and the woman since your arrival in Bergama."

"Why?"

"To track an association of interest," he said, "a homegrown organization from this region. I would describe it as clandestine, somewhat mystical, militant, and, as far as you're concerned, dangerous."

"What does it have to do with us?"

"We've been tracking them, and they've been following you. You didn't realize it, but they've been watching you, tracking your steps."

"Why?"

"I don't know why. But for some reason, you're of interest to them. Maybe it's because of the people you've been meeting here, maybe because of something you know or something you have. Do you have any idea what it might be?"

"No," I said. But, of course, I did have an idea. "What else can you tell me about them?"

"Not much more than that, except that we have every reason to believe they pose a threat to you and to the woman. Be very careful in your travels. They have a wide reach and members throughout the world. Here," he said, giving me his card. "If there's anything—anything of concern, anything questionable, anything suspicious, or if you have any questions, anything at all—contact me."

"Are you going to keep following us?"

"Yes, through the bazaar, but we'll try to be less conspicuous."

I turned to go back to Lara. I was about fifteen feet away from him when I heard him say, "Good night, Mr. Herzog." I returned to Lara, and we resumed our walk through the bazaar.

"So who is he?" she asked.

"He said he was an intelligence agent and was following us for our protection."

"Protection from what?"

"He didn't give a lot of details, but I think we can guess."

"The ones from whom the pages were taken."

"I'm sure."

"So they want them back?"

"I believe it's more than that. The man who gave me the first page said they served the plans and purposes of 'the Dark One.'"

"The ones who threw him out of the window."

"Those ones, yes."

"So what do we do?"

"We try not to get thrown out of windows."

She was quiet for the rest of the walk, looking very concerned. Leaving the bazaar, we took a taxi back to our hotel.

"Let's look at the page," I said.

So she took it out. The color of the page, the text, the layout, and the stylization all matched that of the previous pages. The only thing we could hope to make sense of at that point was, again, the image. It was a dragon, a red stylized image of a dragon. It was standing upright, hands outstretched, mouth open, and breathing fire.

"It looks like something out of medieval heraldry," said Lara, "something you'd see on a royal crest or a coat of arms."

"Maybe it's identifying a house, a dynasty."

"I think it stands for something deeper than that," she said.

The next day, we met for breakfast at one of Istanbul's traditional cafés.

Lara brought her notepad. She had translated the text below the dragon and now read it to me.

"The title reads 'Fury,' and this is the text:

The Beast Aroused
Of Ancient Rage
The Deadly Fire Given
In Dragon's Lair
By Water's Edge
He Waits
For the River Child
To Make of Them
An End."

"The Beast Aroused," she said. "The Dragon."

"And the Deadly Fire," I said, "would be the fire that comes from the Dragon's mouth. But how does that help? We already knew that from the image."

"But the fire is *given,* not just breathed. What does that mean? And who is the River Child…and the one he seeks to make an end of?"

"I don't know."

"We don't have enough to know where to go next."

"So let's stay in Istanbul until we do. Maybe you could have another dream?"

"I'll work on it," she said with a wry smile.

We were three days in Istanbul before it happened. She called me from her hotel room in the middle of the night to tell me—she had a dream.

"I was walking through the streets of a city," she said. "I don't know what city, but I knew it was in Europe. I was looking for something, but I didn't know what. As I walked, I noticed a bridge stretched over a little river, across which people were walking. I turned to join them.

"Lining the sides of the bridge were white statues, Greek- or Roman-looking statues, in pairs. I heard a great commotion in the distance. So I stopped in the middle of the bridge and looked over its railing toward the source of the noise. A woman on my left did the same. 'It's coming,' she said.

"Then I saw it: a gigantic red dragon walking up the city street alongside the river. It was swaying its head back and forth, agitated, angry, raging, and speaking another language, which I knew was German. As the people listened to its voice, they began following it. It made its way to the bridge and began crossing over, with multitudes following behind it. I knew that the most dangerous thing about the dragon was the words coming out of its mouth. 'He's coming,' said the woman at my side, 'to his home, the new dragon's lair.' And the dream ended. I know where we have to go," she said.

"Where?" I asked.

"To Germany. The city had to have been in Germany."

"But how do we know where in Germany?"

"Berlin. That's where they sent the Altar. We have to go to Berlin."

"Where in Berlin?"

"To the bridge with the statues."

"How do we know for sure it exists?"

I went to my laptop to see if there was such a place in Berlin, a bridge spanning a small river open to pedestrians and lined with pairs of Greek- or Roman-looking white statues. It existed. It was called the *Schlossbrücke*, or the Palace Bridge.

The next day, we boarded a plane for Berlin. It would be there that the dark mystery of the dragon and his ancient fire would be revealed.

Chapter 14
THE WOMAN ON THE BRIDGE

We landed in Berlin and arrived at our hotel. The following day, we took a taxi to what we believed was the site of Lara's dream. We stepped out of the taxi and began walking along the river. Lara stopped and stared at it from a distance.

"Is it the place?" I asked.

"It is," she said, pointing into the distance. "There's the bridge, the statues, just as I saw them."

"Find the place where you were in your dream."

She walked about halfway across the bridge, then turned to gaze out at the river and the streets that lined it. I joined her there and gazed out with her.

"This is where I was standing when I saw the dragon approach and cross over and where the woman told me the dragon was coming home."

"And is this the river," I asked, "of the River Child?"

"I would think so."

"So what does it all mean? And what does it have to do with the Altar?"

There was a woman standing to our left. She appeared to be in her early thirties, Mediterranean- or Jewish-looking, with long, dark, wavy hair. We didn't notice her until she spoke.

"Excuse me," she said with a German accent. "I couldn't help overhearing you ask about the Altar of Pergamon. Do you know where you are?"

"What do you mean?" I asked.

"Do you know what this bridge leads to?"

"No."

"It leads to the Altar of Pergamon."

"Where?"

"This," she said, pointing to the other side, "is Museum Island. The Altar is contained in a museum that was built to house it."

At that, Lara turned to me and said, "It's her."

"Who?"

"The woman in my dream."

"How do you know?"

"It's her voice—it's her."

I decided to take a risk and ask her. "Are you one of them?"

"One of whom?" she replied.

"One of those who happen to be waiting for us in the exact places at the exact moments we happen to get there?"

"I am," she said. "Cross the bridge with me."

I had, by this point, figured that the people we were encountering in each place, who knew our names and who seemed to know our footsteps before we took them, were part of some intelligence network, some agency, some organization that, no doubt, had us under its surveillance. And they were somehow connected to the Altar. And they were *for* us, or at least *for* having the mystery revealed to us. And now it was the woman with long, dark, wavy hair. We followed her across the bridge.

"I'm sorry," she said. "I didn't introduce myself. My name is Yaira. You were speaking of a dream. Would you mind telling me what you saw in your dream?"

So Lara told her.

"You know the Scriptures?" she asked.

Lara nodded yes, while I said no.

"There is a vision in the Scriptures," she said, "in the Book of Revelation, of a dragon and a woman. The dragon is red, and the woman is crowned with twelve stars around her head. The woman gives birth to the Messiah.[1] The dragon wars against her, pursues her, hunts her down, and—according to the Greek word used—persecutes her.[2] The dragon hates the woman and rages against her. Who is the dragon?"

"Satan," said Lara.

"And who is the woman?"

We didn't answer.

"There is only one entity that gave birth to the Messiah and is still in the world today," she said. "Israel, the Jewish people. So what would that reveal?"

"That Satan," said Lara, "wars against the Jewish people, the nation of Israel."

"Yes, he pursues them, persecutes them, and hunts them down."

"That would explain a lot," I said, "why they're the most hated and persecuted people in history."

"But why does the Dragon hate the Jewish people?" asked Lara.

"Because he exists," said the woman, "to war against the purposes of God. And the children of Israel, the Jewish people, exist to fulfill God's purposes, to bear witness to the world that God exists. So that would mean there would be war. He would seek their destruction."

"To Make of Them an End," said Lara. "That's what it meant."

"If the Dragon could destroy the Jewish people," said the woman, "he could bring the purposes of God to an end."

We finished crossing the bridge and entered Museum Island. The woman led us onto the Lustgarten, a large open area of manicured grass with a fountain in its center.

"In my dream," said Lara, "a dragon came to this place raging, speaking to the people in German. What exactly did it mean?"

"The Altar," said the woman, "is the Throne of Satan. Satan is the Dragon. So the coming of a dragon represents the coming of the Altar and everything it stands for."

"The coming of Satan to Germany," I said.

"The Throne of Satan to Berlin," said the woman. "So what then would we expect to happen?"

"Something satanic," I replied.

"Something satanic, yes," she said. "A deadly combination for the Jewish people. The satanic hatred for that ancient people would now focus on and indwell the nation and people of Germany. The Devil's ancient hatred for the children of Israel would take control of that nation."

"The Ancient Rage," said Lara. "It was the Enemy's ancient hatred, his rage against the Jewish people."

"Yes, that which comes out of a dragon's mouth. But in your dream, what was it that came out of his mouth?"

"Words...German words."

"The dragon's fire manifested as German words, and the words became the vessels of that fire."

"The Deadly Fire Given," said Lara. "It was the passing of the Dragon's hatred for the Jewish people to another nation."

"And so Germany," said the woman, "would become the most deadly vessel of the Dragon's rage. And thus, it was no accident that of all nations in the world, it was the one that received the Altar, that restored the Throne of Satan, that became the most satanically driven of nations—and satanically driven against this one particular people. So the Germans became obsessed with the Jewish people, and as the Dragon's fire inflamed them, they set out to bring God's ancient people to an end."

"To Make of Them an End," said Lara.

"So it all follows where the Altar rests," I said. "What about the *time* of the Altar?"

"The time?" asked the woman.

"The time the Altar was discovered and unearthed, the time it was transferred, and when its first pieces arrived here in Berlin. Was the timing part of the mystery?"

"Come," she said. "I will show you."

She then led us over to the Altes Museum, where she would reveal the mystery of timing and the days of the Dragon's rage.

Chapter 15

THE ANGEL'S FURY

THE FRONT OF the Altes Museum consisted of a monumental colonnade of eighteen Greek Ionic columns, each topped with a stone eagle. We slowly walked through it, frequently stopping along the way as our guide opened the revelation.

"As long as the Jews have been in the world," she said, "they've known what it was to be hated. But in modern times, that hatred took on a new form. It would be known as *anti-Semitism*."

"Isn't that what has always been?" I asked.

"No. *Anti-Semitism* is a modern word that speaks of a unique modern manifestation of the ancient hatred—a most intense, virulent, and deadly manifestation. In older times, the Jews were hated for their beliefs, their religion, their faith. But anti-Semitism speaks of an ideology of hatred for the Jewish people based on race, blood, existence. The Jews were to be hated because of who they were. The new hatred was noted for its multitude of conspiracy theories and its blaming of virtually every evil in the world on this single people. And do you know what was critical in the rise of anti-Semitism?"

"Tell us," I said.

"The birth of Germany. Germany was founded on what was called *volksgemeinschaft*, or ethnic nationalism, the belief that Germans were joined together by a shared blood and ancestry. The idea cast the Jews as outsiders having no legitimate place within the German nation, a separate 'race' as opposed to the race of the German people. Anti-Semitism, in the form we now know it, would not have arisen without the birth of Germany. And so it was born on German soil. And what happened when Germany was born?"

"The Altar returned to the world," I said.

"And so the foundation year of the Altar's return was also the foundation year of modern anti-Semitism. In 1871, the Throne of Satan and his ancient hatred came together in the land of Germany."

"What happened to the Altar *after* 1871?" I asked.

"The Altar's discoverer, Carl Humann, did some unofficial exploration on the Pergamon acropolis and tried his best to draw attention to his findings, pushing for an excavation of the site, but with little success.

But everything changed when a German archaeologist named Alexander Conze was appointed the director of the Berlin Collection of Classical Antiquities. Conze examined the stone fragments that Humann had sent to Berlin. Studying the writings of ancient authors, Conze came to the realization that the fragments were part of the Great Altar of Pergamon.

"Up to that point, no one realized it. So Conze made contact with Humann, and together they lobbied the Ottoman government to grant permission for Germany to dig up and unearth the Altar. Permission was granted. Before the decade was over, the first major excavation of the Altar had begun. And so Germany would unearth the Throne of Satan."

"Sounds ominous," said Lara.

"What was ominous," said the woman, "was what happened to Germany when it began uncovering the Throne of Satan. The same year Germany set out to bring the Altar back into the world, Germany would bring something else into the world. As the excavation began in Pergamon, a new movement was born in Germany. It was that year that would mark the birth of anti-Semitism. The same year that they put their shovels into the ancient dirt to unearth the Altar, the world's first anti-Semitic political party was born. It was the birth of that party that would officially bring anti-Semitism into the German parliament and legitimize and establish it in the nation's mainstream and political culture. The event would herald the birth of a multitude of anti-Semitic organizations and movements and would foreshadow the rise of the Nazis.

"The first shovel broke the earth around the Altar in 1878. The first anti-Semitic party began as well in 1878. As German archaeologists removed the dust from Satan's Throne, the satanic madness began to stir in their homeland. Germany had only been in existence seven years when the ancient evil began officially germinating in its soil."

"And what happened to the Altar?" I asked.

"They had come to Pergamon not only to unearth it but to take possession of it, to remove it from its ancient sanctuary. So for the first time since its creation, for the first time in over two thousand years, the Altar was moved—the Throne of Satan was transported away from Pergamon to Berlin, Germany."

"So if the Altar was removed," said Lara, "what was it that we saw when we stood there on the high place of Pergamon?"

"The remaining foundation stones," she replied. "But what the ancients saw of the Altar—its carvings, its facade, its images, its gods and goddesses—all that was taken to Berlin."

"How?" I asked. "How did they do it?"

"The Altar's immense blocks were lifted out of the ground by ropes and wooden beams. The blocks were then put into wooden crates and carried in animal-drawn carts down the steep trails to the plain of Bergama."

"Sounds like an Indiana Jones movie," said Lara.

"Indiana Jones?" said the woman.

"The movie."

"I've never seen it," she said.

"It's like what you're describing," said Lara, "a Middle Eastern archaeological excavation, led by Germans...and involving an ancient object connected to the supernatural."

"Except," I said, "with Indiana Jones it was connected to the other supernatural, to God. This is the dark side."

"It was the Ark of the Covenant," said Lara. "And another difference, the Ark wasn't an altar."

"But it was," said the woman. "The Ark is actually the Altar of God."

"In the movie," said Lara, "they try to take the Ark back to Germany because they believe it's going to give the nation supernatural power."

"In the movie," I said, "the Ark of the Covenant struck down the evil...but the Altar is joined to the bringing forth of evil."

"So what happened then?" asked Lara.

"The crates were brought to the ports, where they were loaded onto ships that carried them across the Aegean Sea, to the Mediterranean, and to Western Europe, where they were transferred to rail wagons for Berlin."

"All that," I said, "to bring the Altar of Satan to Germany. What could possibly go wrong?"

"When Humann sent back the first pieces, they represented samples. But these were different. They weren't samples. These represented the Altar's total unearthing and the beginning of its transference to another land. What might you expect to happen?"

"Something evil," said Lara.

"It was just as the first pieces of the Altar's transference arrived on German soil that a new word was birthed in Germany. The word would embody the hatred that had just come into the world—the word was *anti-Semitism.*"

"It never existed before that?" I asked.

"It was waiting for the Altar," she said. "So it is no accident that the word *anti-Semitism* was born in Germany. The Devil's rage had to be planted in the same soil that received his Throne. And it was no accident that the word made its appearance before the world in 1879, the same year that the first pieces in the excavation of Satan's Throne arrived in Germany. The man who first penned the word did so in an anti-Semitic pamphlet and would go on to found the League of Anti-Semites. He had actually committed it to paper in 1878, the year when the unearthing began. But the pieces would appear in Germany the following year…and so would the word."

"Again, like a movie," said Lara. "They disturb an ancient object, and an ancient curse is unleashed."

"Except for one major difference," I said. "The movies are fiction. This isn't…It's real."

"And real were the consequences," said the woman. "With the Throne's unearthing and transference, its ancient darkness would be unleashed upon the world."

We didn't realize it then, how close we were to the ancient object behind our quest. But in a few moments, we would behold it.

Chapter 16
THE ALTAR

"Where exactly," I asked, "did they put the pieces of the Altar?"

"Some they put on display right here in the Altes Museum."

"Can you take us in to see it?"

"You won't find it here," she said. "The Altar now sits in a different house. But I can take you there."

She led us out of the colonnade and across the island. It was just a few minutes' walk. The sun had now set, and the sky was darkening.

"They're closed," she said, "but I can get you in."

"How?" asked Lara.

"I have some connections that give me special access."

"Why did they move it from the Altes Museum?" asked Lara.

"The old museum wasn't made to hold something of the Altar's massive size. So a new building was constructed to contain it."

We came to the building.

"This is the Altar's house. It was even named after the Altar. They call it the Pergamon Museum."

"The Altar's new home," I said, "the Dragon's Lair."

She led us through a side entrance. There was no one inside but us. Though several of the museum's hallways were dark, she led us through them as if knowing the place so well she didn't need light. She led us out to the Pergamon Hall in which the Altar rested. But we couldn't see it yet, as we were still standing in the dark.

"Stay here," she said as she left to find the lights.

The lights came on. They weren't made to illuminate the room. They appeared to be auxiliary or emergency lights. As a result, our surroundings were only dimly lit. But it was enough for us to see it there in the center of the hall—the Altar of Pergamon. The dim illumination only intensified its mystical appearance.

Rising almost forty feet from the ground, it was colossal, more like a temple than an altar—a strange U-shaped temple adorned by an ancient marble frieze three hundred and sixty feet long. Slowly, we approached it.

When we stood on the acropolis of Pergamon, we couldn't quite visualize its size. But now, standing at the foot of the Altar's massive stairs, Lara and I felt dwarfed by its magnitude.

"And they brought all this on carts?" I said.

"What you see on the Altar's exterior," said the woman, "are the sculptured images of the Gigantomachy frieze—gods, goddesses, giants, and mythological beings."

She led us around the Altar's perimeter as she identified the images that adorned it: the god Zeus hurling his thunderbolts down at his enemies, the goddess Athena dragging a giant from the earth, Artemis with her bow, Apollo wearing his quiver of arrows, Poseidon holding his trident, the sun god Helios, the moon goddess Selene, and the others—the hybrid creatures, the lions, the serpents, the sea monsters—an explosion of gods and mythological beings. The Altar stood as a colossal embodiment of the pagan world in which it was birthed.

She then led us back to the front and center of the Altar's steps. We gazed upward at the mountain of ancient marble before us.

"Imagine," she said, "being there in ancient times, seeing the priests of Pergamon ascend the stairs to the sounds of flutes and drums in worship. In their hands are baskets of grain, offerings of wine, and animals to be slaughtered and offered up as sacrifices to the gods. At the top of the stairs, they approach the raging flames of the Altar's inner courtyard. The sacrifices are slain, the offerings are presented, and their smoke ascends into the sky."

We didn't go up the Altar's steps. It was enough to just stand there and take in its immense form.

"There is," said the woman, "a word that is appointed to be read and recited in every synagogue of the world on the Jewish Sabbath, a passage of Scripture. Every week, a different scriptural passage is appointed to be read on that particular Sabbath day. The Scripture is, of course, of ancient origins…but there are no accidents."

"You mean," I said, "it could relate to the time of its appointed reading?"

"At times, it could," she said. "The unearthing of the ancient Altar commenced on Monday, September 9, 1878. Carl Humann was the one overseeing it. That first week of the Altar's unearthing concluded on the Sabbath. And on that Sabbath, all over the world, including Germany and Turkey, Jewish people read and chanted the appointed Scripture."

"And what did it say?" asked Lara.

"It spoke of an altar," she said.

"An altar," I repeated.

"An altar built on a mountain," said the woman.

"As in the Altar of Pergamon," I said.

"What kind of an altar?" asked Lara.

"An altar connected to curses."

"A cursed altar?" I said.

"An altar connected to the going forth of curses."

"As curses go forth," I said, "from the Altar of Pergamon."

"What kind of curses did the Scripture speak about?" asked Lara.

"Curses," said the woman, "that bring calamity and disaster on Israel, the Jewish people, particularly through the hand of an enemy—an enemy who would oppress them and bring terror upon them...an enemy who would come to them as an eagle swooping down on its prey."

"Like the eagles on top of the Altes Museum?" asked Lara.

"The national symbol of Germany," said the woman, "was an eagle."

"And all that," said Lara, "was in the Scripture appointed at the start of the Altar's unearthing. And its unearthing would mark the beginning of the calamity that was coming on the Jewish people of Germany and the world."

"And so it was," said the woman, "that as the Altar of curses was being unearthed and the word of the altar of curses was being proclaimed throughout the world, the curses and calamities that were to fall upon them were set in motion."

I felt an unease being there. I don't know if it was what I knew about the Altar or the Altar itself, but I sensed an evil. The woman led us out of the museum. It was now night. She wished us well and parted from us. But it was not the end of the revelation she had opened. It would not be complete until the mystery of the River Child was opened to us.

Chapter 17

THE MONSTER'S BIRTH

As we walked toward the Palace Bridge to depart from Museum Island, we realized we had no idea what to do or where to go next. Up to that point, every encounter had ended with our being given the next page of the book. But our time with the woman left us nothing more to go on. We took a taxi to a hotel in Berlin, where we withdrew to our rooms for the night. The next morning, we met in a Berlin café for breakfast.

"I guess we'll have to just wait here," I said, "until we get some idea where to go next."

Lara didn't say anything. She just sat there, smiling.

"What?" I asked. "What is it?"

Still she didn't say anything.

"Did you have a dream?" I asked.

Her smile grew larger.

"You did! What did you see?"

"It was different from the others," she said, "shorter. I was overlooking a river, standing on the edge of a town or city that, again, I knew was European. But it wasn't like Berlin; it was rural. Suddenly, something shot up out of the water. At first, I couldn't tell what it was. It was a giant fish with a man on its back, riding it as one would ride a horse. They were both shimmering with light. They were both golden, as if statues of gold, but alive and moving. They flew in and out of the water and then toward me. They paused, hovering in the sky above me. The man signaled to me, but I couldn't discern what it meant. Then they flew away into the distance and disappeared."

"And this is going to help us?" I asked.

"Actually, it will. This morning after I woke up, I went online searching for a statue of a man on a fish. I came up with a number of them but found only two in Germany. And only one matched what I saw in my dream."

"Where is it?"

"In a place called Simbach am Inn. It's a town in southern Germany. It sits on a river, as in my dream. And there's a bridge over the river; that's where the statue is, by the bridge."

"I guess that's where we're going," I said.

So we rented a car and headed for the town of Simbach. It took us over six hours to get there, but we left early enough in the morning to arrive by late afternoon. And there it was—the man on the fish, a bronze statue plated with a gold finish and standing at the edge of the river by the bridge. We drove up to the statue, got out, and examined it. It was a unique object, but it didn't give us anything to go on. We spent the rest of the day driving around Simbach and searching online for anything about the town that could be of some significance but came up with nothing. We found a hotel and stayed the night.

The next morning, over breakfast, I asked Lara, "In your dream, when the man riding the fish disappeared into the distance, in what direction did he go?"

"I have no idea."

"Was it upstream, downstream, or across?"

"Across."

"I believe that's the key," I said. "The man was signaling you to join him as he went across. We have to cross the river."

So we drove across the bridge and into the town on the other side.

The river formed part of the German-Austrian border. So we were now in Austria. After driving through the town, we decided to get out and walk its streets. We headed to the Stadplatz, the town's old central square.

"That man," said Lara.

"What man?"

"Over there...sitting outside the café with the cell phone. He was there in Berlin on the Palace Bridge with his cell phone, watching us. It's him, and he's watching us again."

"So he drove hundreds of miles just to watch us? How do you know it's the same man?"

"It's him."

When the man saw both of us looking at him, he turned away.

In the midst of the town square was the *Fischbrunnen,* or Fishers' Fountain, with a statue of a "Savior" figure on an octagonal base. It was as we approached it that I saw her. She was standing on the other side of the base.

"It's her," I said, "the woman on the bridge who showed us the Altar."

We approached her. Lara looked back to the café, but the man was gone.

"You made it," said the woman. "I'm glad."

"Can you tell me," I said, "how you all manage to always be there when we just happen to arrive?"

"Actually, you were late," she said. "But it's all right."

"How do you do it?"

"You could call it a trade secret."

"Why are we here?" asked Lara.

"For the final revelation I'm to give you."

She began walking away from the statue, leading us through the streets of the town.

"So where did we leave off?" she asked.

"The digging up and the transferring of the Altar," said Lara.

"It took years for Humann to unearth the Altar and ship each piece to Germany. The excavation that had commenced in 1878 was officially completed in 1886. So it took them eight years. It was then that the pieces were first displayed in Berlin. But they were *pieces*," she said, "the components of what the Altar once was. And many of those pieces were found scattered away from the Altar's foundation. So they had never been brought together since ancient times. But that would change.

"The goal had never simply been to recover the Altar's pieces and fragments but to reassemble them so that the ancient Altar would stand again in its entirety on German soil as it had stood on the high place of Pergamon. In the late 1880s, Otto Puchstein, a German classical archaeologist famed for his work on Greek and Roman artifacts, began examining the ancient pieces. He would undertake the massive project of reconstructing the ancient Altar.

"So Puchstein began the painstaking work of piecing together the thousands of stone fragments into their original positions. It would mark the beginning the Altar's reconstruction in the modern world. For the first time since ancient times, the Altar began manifesting in its original form but in a land far away from its ancient resting place in Pergamon."

"But what," I asked, "does the Altar's reconstruction have to do with where we are now?"

"This is an old town," she said, "with origins dating back to the Middle Ages—a most critical town. It was here, in 1885, that a government official, after the loss of his first and second wives to disease, married his household servant. Soon afterward, she bore her first child and called him Gustav. While still an infant, Gustav died of diphtheria. Her second child was a girl named Ida. Ida would also die of diphtheria as an infant. Her third child, Otto, would die shortly after his birth.

"It was her fourth child, born in this town, who became the first of her children to survive past infancy. It was a boy. And so he would become especially precious to her. She called him Adolf. Her fourth child was Adolf Hitler.

"The name of this town is Braunau am Inn, Hitler's birthplace. *Braunau* means the place of springs or fountains. *Am Inn* means on the River Inn. It's the river you crossed to come here."

"The River Child in the text," said Lara. "It's Adolf Hitler."

"Yes."

"I thought it was referring to the river we crossed to get to the Altar."

"That was a different river," she said. "Please read me the text."

So Lara took out her notepad and began reading. "In Dragon's Lair, by Water's Edge, He Waits for the River Child to Make of Them an End."

"It is the Dragon who waits," said the woman, "the Enemy. He waits in the Dragon's lair, by his Throne, by the Altar. The waters are the River Spree, which lines Museum Island. He waits for the one through whom he will deal the deadly blow to his ancient enemy, the Jewish people.

"Look," she said, pointing to the three-story building that was now directly in front of us. It was an unremarkable-looking building—old, pale yellow or muted beige, with nothing to distinguish it from the others. One would pass it by without the slightest idea that anything significant had happened there.

"It was there," she said, "that the former servant girl, Klara, would give birth to her beloved son Adolf."

"Such an ordinary-looking building," I said. "You would never think it was the house in which such a monster was born."

"The child who became a monster," said the woman.

"But what," asked Lara, "would that have to do with what you told us at the beginning? What does the Altar of Pergamon have to do with the birth of Adolf Hitler?"

"Though it would be years before the German public would see the reassembled version of the Altar of Pergamon, its first reconstruction was begun by Otto Puchstein in 1888. It was in 1888 that Puchstein first conceived the Altar's finished form, the year of the Altar's conception."

"And why," asked Lara, "is that significant?"

"Because 1888 was also the year of the conception of Adolf Hitler. They were both conceived together. As the Altar was being pieced together and formed, so was Adolf Hitler formed in his mother's womb."

"When was Puchstein's initial work on the Altar's reconstruction completed?" I asked.

"In 1889," she replied.

"And Hitler was born…"

"In 1889."

"So then," said Lara, "1889 was the year of the two appearings: the first appearing of Satan's Throne in its original form since ancient times…and the appearing of Satan's vessel, the newborn Adolf Hitler."

The woman handed us the next manuscript and then, after wishing us well, departed. We were left standing there in front of Hitler's birthplace, trying to take it all in.

We drove back to our hotel, anxious to see what the next page would reveal. The meaning of that page would be revealed to us in a very different land, and its mystery would shake the world.

PART IV

DESTROYER

Chapter 18

A GAME OF CHESS

LARA TOOK OUT the page and examined it as I drove.

"What's on it?" I asked. "What does it show?"

"It looks like a broken pillar," she said, "an ancient classical pillar lying horizontally on the ground, broken in two."

"Could it be the ruins of the Altar?"

"But what would that tell us? That the Altar was left in ruins? We already know that."

"Then what?"

"I don't know."

That night, in her hotel room, she translated the text and the next morning showed me the results.

"The title is the Greek word 'Apoleia.' It means destruction or devastation."

"Ruins," I said. "The broken pillar is a symbol of destruction."

"I believe so," said Lara. "And this is the rest of it:

He Who Makes
The World to Shake
Who Turns the Earth
To Wasteland
Kingdoms
Into Raging Camps
Prepares the Vessel
Of His Wrath
The Two Lands
In Their Joining
The Die Is Cast
The Spark Ignites
The Many Fires
The World They Knew
Aflame."

"It's not about the ruins of the Altar," I said. "It's about the ruins of the world, a great devastation."

"OK," she said, "but where does that get us? The last revelation left off in 1889. What great devastation happened then?"

We drove back to Berlin. With its international airport, we could go anywhere once we had something to go on. About halfway through the drive, Lara fell asleep. It was then that I came to the realization that we were being followed. Keeping a good distance behind us was a black BMW sedan. It had been there through much of the journey, following us through several turns and many miles. There were two men sitting in the front seat, each wearing sunglasses. They never passed us. If I slowed down, they slowed down; if I sped up, so did they, but never enough to catch up to us. They just kept the same distance from our car throughout the drive.

When she woke up, I knew something had happened.

"You had a dream," I said. "I know it. Tell me."

"I did," she said. "We were in a city in some sort of a valley surrounded by blue mountains, walking its streets. I noticed the domes of mosques, but also churches. We walked into an open square in the midst of the city. In the center of the square was an ornate drinking fountain with a stone octagonal base and waterspouts on each side. On top of the base was an elaborately carved wooden structure, and on top of that, a light green dome. Around the fountain were cafés, tables, benches, and open seating areas. The square was filled with people and pigeons.

"There was a man sitting by himself at one of the small outdoor tables. I'm saying 'a man,' though I couldn't make out a form. It was more like a presence and like light. But somehow I knew him. He stood up from the table and called to us. He wanted us to follow him. We did. He led us through the city and along a river until we came to the beginning of a bridge. Then there was an explosion—a massive explosion—a flash of bright light, and everything went to white, and the dream ended."

"And what do you make of it?" I asked.

"We have to find the city."

"You said the square was filled with people. Were they speaking English or another language?"

"Another language."

"And what did it sound like?"

"It sounded Slavic to me."

"A Slavic city with mosques and churches. I'm guessing it's in the Balkans."

With that, Lara took out her cell phone and began searching for it, typing in every distinctive feature she could remember. It took about fifteen minutes.

"I have it!" she said. She held up the phone to show me a photograph of the octagonal drinking fountain she had just described.

"It's called the Sebilj Fountain. And it's in a place called Baščaršija Square."

"Where?" I asked. "What country and city?"

"Bosnia," she replied. "And the city is Sarajevo."

When we arrived at the hotel, I told Lara about the black BMW, then called Kazim Yarikan, the man I had met in Istanbul who had warned us we were being pursued.

"Those who are following you," he said, "will look for patterns, habits, predictability. Change things up. Continually alter your routine. Take different routes, ones you haven't taken before or that you wouldn't have taken. Make yourself unpredictable."

Going forward, we would seek to do that inasmuch as it was possible.

The next morning, we embarked for Sarajevo by plane. After arriving and checking into our hotel, we headed to the city square. It was just as Lara had described—cafés, outdoor seating areas, people, pigeons, and the fountain. Lara surveyed the surroundings to see if she could find anything of significance with regard to her dream.

"That man," she said, "over there, sitting by himself at the table. I wonder if it could...Why don't you go up to him?"

We couldn't see his face, as he was turned away from us. I walked around and in front of him. He was an old man with a large white mustache and a Greek fisherman's cap. On the little round table at which he sat was a chess set. Its pieces were arranged as if a game were underway between two opponents. But it was just him.

He noticed me staring at him.

"Would you like to play a game?" he asked with a Slavic accent.

"I never learned how," I replied.

"I can show you."

"I don't think I'd have the time to learn."

"Then would you have time for me to show you something else?"

I approached him. "Are you one of them?" I asked.

"Are *you*?" he replied.

"I guess it depends on what you mean by 'them.'"

"Exactly," he replied. "My name is Zoran. And you are Mr. Herzog. Please sit down and invite your friend Lara to join us."

So I motioned to Lara, and we joined him at his table, sitting on the opposite side of the chessboard.

"You want to know the meaning of the third mystery, yes?"

"Yes."

"The words on the page, how do they begin?"

Lara took out her notebook and began to read, "He Who Makes the World to Shake, Who Turns the Earth to Wasteland."

"Do you know where that comes from?" he asked. "From Isaiah the prophet, from the same prophecy that speaks of Lucifer and his fall from heaven: 'Can this be the one who shook the earth…who made the world as a wilderness and destroyed its cities…?'[1] You see, the Devil by nature is a destroyer…*the* Destroyer. He exists for the purpose of bringing that which exists out of existence…to nullify reality, to destroy the image of God, life, creation, the world. So how would he do that? That which he would destroy, he divides; he places it in conflict. And what do we call the most intense of conflicts, Mr. Herzog?"

"War."

"So with his Throne of Satan unearthed and returned to the world, he would seek to unleash his power of destruction…through war. He would seek to bring upon the world the greatest calamity ever wrought by the hand of man…a destruction so colossal that even those who were to wage it could never have imagined it."

"The First World War," I said. "It had no precedent; they couldn't imagine what was going to happen. But that came years after the Altar's unearthing—decades."

"Mr. Herzog," he said, "you don't know how to play chess. But if you did, you would know that those who master the game are those who anticipate the greatest number of future moves and countermoves, and then strategize, plan, and act in accordance with that knowledge. They make their first move in view of their last move—and every move in between—to victory or defeat."

"And what does that have to do with…"

"The Devil is a chess player. He sets in motion his plans long before the time of their fruition. He positions and moves the pieces years before his strategy is manifested. So it was with the mass destruction he would bring on the earth. Long before he shook the world through that war, he was moving its pieces into place and setting it in motion."

"But what," I asked, "would this have to do with the Altar?"

"Everything," he said. "The greatest of calamities and destruction to fall on the modern world was joined to the Altar from its beginning. The Throne of Satan was brought back to the world...and it all began."

So we sat there in front of the chessboard as he revealed to us the secret and dark origins of the calamitous events that would shake the world.

Chapter 19

BIRTH OF DESTRUCTION

"An altar requires blood," said the man, "and so blood would be spilled. To bring about the shedding of blood and mass destruction, the Destroyer would need an instrument, a vessel...a pawn." At that, the man lifted a pawn from his side of the board, a black pawn, and moved it forward. "You already know the pawn," he said. "It is the power that came into the world with the Altar."

"Germany?" I replied.

"Yes. The power that began its coalescing at the same time that Carl Humann's path began converging with the Altar."

"The Prussian wars," I said, "through which Germany was born."

"And so according to the mystery, the nation born with the Altar would become the central vessel in bringing the Enemy's destruction upon the world."

"But how did the birth of Germany lead to the First World War?" I asked.

"The Enemy would have to make sure that the newborn nation was imbued with a spirit of war and destruction. And so it was."

At that, he moved a black knight forward on the chessboard.

"Germany was born in a state of war. Its birth was announced in the midst of its war with France. Its victories in the Prussian wars would foster the belief that the German army was invincible and that military force was the most effective tool of foreign policy. The army became a central foundation stone in the new nation's government and a critical element of German culture and identity. Thus, Germany became an increasingly militaristic nation and predisposed to the idea of initiating war for its own advantage. And the year that it all crystallized in the nation's birth..."

"Was 1871," I said, "the year of the Altar?"

"Yes," said the man, "1871, the year when the connection between the Altar and Germany was forged, was also the seminal year in the birth of German power and ultimately of World War I. Before 1871, what we call Germany was a patchwork of small states. But in 1871, it was transformed into the strongest land power in Europe. That change would alter and destabilize the European balance of powers, and in so doing, set off a chain of events that would lead to the First World War.

"Germany's growing power and militarism would, in turn, provoke rivalries, distrust, and militarism in other nations—an arms race. All these would explode at the outbreak of the First World War."

At that, he began moving chess pieces from the white side to face the black pieces in the middle.

"What is it that drives war?" he asked.

"Conflict," I replied.

"So to bring about his planned destruction, the Dark Angel would have to sow seeds of conflict. And so he did. The same war that gave birth to Germany—the Franco-Prussian War—would sow the seeds of the coming world war. After defeating France, Germany imposed harsh terms on its vanquished enemy. France would be forced to give up territory to Germany, namely the strategically important provinces of Alsace-Lorraine."

At that, he removed some of the white pieces from the board.

"It was a most humiliating blow. France was forced to render massive and crippling payments to Germany for war damages. Further, German troops were stationed on French soil to ensure that those payments were made.

"Germany's humiliation of France led to a growing French-German animosity. It gave birth to the French *revanchist*, or revenge, movement. The revanchist movement aimed at retaking the territories it lost in the Franco-Prussian War, namely Alsace-Lorraine, as well as exacting revenge on its enemy. And this too would lead to the First World War. The Devil had moved his chess pieces into place. And when did it all begin? When Germany defeated and imposed its harsh conditions on France. It all happened in 1871.

"So then all these causes and triggers of the First World War were set in motion in the year of the Altar and the sending of its first pieces to Germany. And so it was no accident that the same power that received those first pieces of the Altar would become the central player in bringing that calamity to the world. Now, what was it that the Destroyer must do to bring destruction?"

"Divide," said Lara.

"So to set the stage for the calamity, Europe had to be divided into two opposing camps. The one was called the Dual Alliance, with Germany and Austria-Hungary as its core members, which in the war would become known as the Central Powers. The other was called the Triple Entente, with France, Britain, and Russia as its core members, which in the war would become known as the Allied Powers. It was these alliances that turned Europe into a powder keg on the verge of explosion at the slightest spark. It was all set in motion with the forging of the Dual Alliance. It was that alliance that triggered the rest and ultimately led to the war."

With that, he moved two black pieces to the center of the board and then three white pieces to face them.

"Kingdoms," said Lara, quoting the text, "into Raging Camps."

"When did Germany forge the Dual Alliance?" I asked.

"The Dual Alliance was formed in 1879, the same year in which the Altar's transference to Germany began, when the first major shipment of that transference arrived in Berlin. And in that arrival, Germany became the appointed vessel to set in motion the greatest destruction in human history—for an altar requires blood, and the Throne of Satan requires destruction."

He would now lead us to the place that altered the history of the world and there reveal to us the ancient secret that lay hidden behind it.

Chapter 20
THE DANGEROUS PIECES

"Let us walk," said the man as he rose from the table. Lara and I did likewise.

"The Throne of Satan is linked to authority and power. If the gaining of that throne meant the rising of the power that came into its possession—Germany—what would its loss mean?"

"What do you mean?" I asked.

"One power gains the Altar; another loses it. What would happen to the one that loses it? It would lose its power. It would decline. As goes the Altar, so goes the world. The Altar was in the possession of the Ottoman Empire. Germany then took possession of it. And what happened to Germany?"

"It began to rise," I said, "as a major world power."

"As for the Ottoman Empire, when did it begin losing the Altar?"

"When German excavators began digging it up," I replied.

"And when did that digging up begin?" he asked.

"In 1878."

"And so it was 1878 that marked the turning point for the Ottoman Empire. The same year in which the empire began losing possession of the Altar, it began a dramatic and accelerated decline."

"What happened," I asked, "to cause its dramatic decline?"

"In 1878, the Ottoman Empire suffered a major military loss. A congress was convened in Europe that same year to determine the empire's future. The treaty it put forth would take away vast territories that had long been under Ottoman rule. So the same year that inaugurated its loss of the Altar inaugurated as well its loss of empire, starting with its land.

"And as Germany was the nation that took away its Altar, so Germany was the nation that led the congress that took away its land. And more specifically, as it was Berlin that directed the removal of the Altar, so the event that initiated the fall of the Ottoman Empire was the Congress of Berlin, and the treaty that sealed it was the Treaty of Berlin."

"So," said Lara, "is it the Altar that follows the world...or the world that follows the Altar?"

"The Altar is a marker on time and space concerning the plans, the works, and the purposes of the Enemy. It is also the embodiment of that which moves and alters the course of human history. It is both. The Altar follows the world, and the world follows the Altar."

After taking us through the cobblestone alleys that bordered the square, he led us alongside a river—narrow, fast-flowing, and lined with stone walls: the River Miljacka.

"What happened," I asked, "to the lands that were taken from the Ottoman Empire?"

"They would give birth to nations—Serbia, Montenegro, Romania, Bulgaria…But it was one land in particular that would become the most critical of lands in view of what was coming. You're standing in it," he said. "Bosnia."

"How did it become the most critical place?"

"In the year of the Altar's unearthing, 1878, the land of Bosnia was taken from the Ottoman Empire. It was given to be occupied by one of Germany's allies, Austria-Hungary. In 1908, Austria-Hungary began permanently annexing Bosnia into its territory. The annexation sparked the Bosnian Crisis. Serbia, another one of the nations born of the broken pieces of the Ottoman Empire, was enraged, as was Russia. The crisis led Austria-Hungary to form a closer alliance with Germany. It intensified nationalism, fostered the birth and growth of radical organizations throughout the Balkans, destabilized the region, helped ignite the Balkan Wars of 1912 and 1913, hardened national enmities and alliances, and convinced the key players that the next conflict would require major military force. In other words, it set the stage for the explosion that would take place the following year."

"The First World War."

"The Dark One had moved all his pieces into place," he said. "Only a spark was needed to ignite the calamity."

"The Spark Ignites," said Lara, "the Many Fires."

We came to a little stone bridge that crossed the Miljacka River. There he stopped.

"It's the bridge in my dream," said Lara.

"It's called the Latin Bridge," he said. "What happened here by this bridge would change the world. It was June 28, 1914, when the archduke Franz Ferdinand, heir to the throne of the Austro-Hungarian Empire, was being driven through the streets of Sarajevo in an open motor car, along with his wife, Sophie. The motorcade took a wrong turn, and the archduke's car stalled right here by the bridge, where a nineteen-year-old

Bosnian Serb, Gavrilo Princip, was waiting. He fired two shots; one killed the archduke and the other, his wife. He said he did it to free Bosnia from Austrian control. But he was only a pawn in the Enemy's hand. And it turned out that behind the plot to assassinate the archduke was a secret organization named the Black Hand.

"And then it began. Austria-Hungary declared war on Serbia, and Russia entered the war on behalf of Serbia; Germany declared war on Russia, then on France, and then invaded Belgium. Then Britain declared war on Germany, and Austria-Hungary declared war on Russia, and Britain and France declared war on Austria-Hungary. And what would become the First World War and the greatest destruction ever brought upon the world by the hand of man had begun."

"That was the explosion," said Lara, "that ended my dream."

"And yet, it was all set in motion years before when the pieces were moved into place on the chessboard. It all began as the Throne of Satan returned to the world and was brought to Germany. The aging empire lost the Altar and, at the same time, its lands in the Balkans. That loss would, in turn, destabilize the region, and those dangerous pieces would usher in the global calamity, with the Altar's new possessor, Germany, as its central agent."

"The entire *world* became destabilized," I said.

"What would you expect," said the man, "when you move the Throne of Satan? Nothing less than the shaking of the world."

He would now open up his last mystery—that of a strange and mystical man who, in his journeying, would prepare the way for an evil that, like the war, had no precedent in human history.

Chapter 21

THE WIZARD

WE WALKED ON from the bridge to what the Sarajevans called the Yellow Fortress. The Ottomans built it in the early eighteenth century to defend the city against invaders. It was somewhat octagonal and made up of countless golden or yellow stones, thus its name. It was a cannon fortress and military lookout point.

In the middle of the fortress was something of a park, with soil, some grass, trees, and several tables and chairs to accommodate visitors. The man led us over to one of its ledges, where we could take in the view. It was a beautiful panorama with Sarajevo's red-tiled roofs set against the gentle blue mountains that formed the backdrop. As sunset approached, the city took on a golden glow beneath a pink and orange sky.

"Such a beautiful city," he said, "to have brought about such a calamity. And so came the destruction, spanning the globe, from Europe to the Middle East, Africa, and Asia, and bringing in its wake famine, disease, and slaughter. By the time it was finished, the war had caused thirty million casualties, with sixteen million people having lost their lives. And at the center of it all was the Throne of Satan.

"Of the three Central Powers at the start of the war in 1914, two of them had possessed the Altar, Germany and the Ottoman Empire. Both had been involved in the Altar's unearthing, and now both were involved in the start of the global calamity."

"The Two Lands in Their Joining," said Lara, reciting the words of the manuscript. "It was the two lands of the Altar, the Ottoman Empire and Germany."

The man led us over to a table around which we sat down.

"By the war's end," he said, "Europe was devastated. The three Central Powers that had begun the war were no more. The Austro-Hungarian Empire had fallen. The German Empire had fallen. And the centuries-old Ottoman Empire had collapsed and was soon to be brought to its end. You see, the Enemy destroys his own, even his own vessels of destruction.

"From seed comes fruit," said the man, "and from fruit, more seed and more fruit. So it is with evil. And so the fruit of the calamity, the First

World War, would contain the seeds for future calamities. The one evil would give birth to others."

"How?" she asked.

The man pulled out a little black cloth bag he had kept in his pocket and emptied some of its contents onto the table before us.

"This is my collection of special pieces," he said, "unique players, pawns, hand-carved out of stone."

He placed a somewhat strange-looking pawn in the center of the table. It was multicolored and slightly misshapen.

"It was the joining of the two lands," he said, "the two possessors of the Altar, Germany and the Ottoman Empire, that was most dangerous. What I'm about to tell you concerns one of the little-known and mystical joinings of those two lands.

"He was born in Germany in 1875 and named Adam Glauer. He would develop a deep fascination with the Ottoman Empire and, shortly after the turn of the century, would undertake a journey there. There he lived for several years. He returned to Germany, got married, then divorced, and then returned to the Ottoman Empire, where he became an Ottoman citizen. It was there that he took on a new identity, calling himself Rudolf von Sebottendorff. When the First Balkan War broke out, he enlisted in the Ottoman military. He would later return to Germany.

"But it was during his years in the Ottoman Empire that Sebottendorff became captivated with and then enmeshed in Turkish mysticism and the occult."

"And by *occult,* you mean…"

"The word literally means hidden, concealed, covered over. It is the dark realm of spirituality…and thus, the domain of the Dark One. Sebottendorff became a devotee of occult knowledge and practices. He soon became convinced that he had discovered what he called 'the key to spiritual realization.'[1]

"As the First World War drew to its end, Sebottendorff endeavored to take the occult knowledge and practices he had come upon in the Ottoman Empire and bring them back to Germany. He founded an occult organization called the Thule Society. The Thule Society was obsessed with mysticism and the belief in an ancient Aryan race from which the German people were said to be descended. Though his beliefs were strange and esoteric, he was able to attract a following."

The man then placed a number of black pawns behind the multicolored one.

"In order to influence the future of Germany, his occult creation—the Thule Society—decided to form a political arm, a party that would implement its beliefs and aims in the German political realm. And so the society gave birth to what it called the *Deutsche Arbeiterpartei*, or the German Workers' Party."

"And what happened to Sebottendorff?" asked Lara.

"Sebottendorff would move on from the society he had founded." The man then removed the multicolored pawn from the table. "But he had fulfilled his purpose. He prepared the way. He had given birth to the Thule Society. And that which the Thule Society had given birth to, its political arm, would become known to the world...as the *Nazi Party.*"

"The Nazi Party," I said, "born of an occult society!"

"Born of the Dark Angel," he said, "and Sebottendorff was his pawn. And again, it was in the joining of the two lands of the Altar that the evil was birthed into the world. Carl Humann came to the Ottoman Empire and there acquired the Altar and sent it back to Germany. Rudolf von Sebottendorff likewise came to the Ottoman Empire and there acquired his occult knowledge, brought it back to Germany, and in the process gave birth to the Nazi Party. So the first land of the Altar sent its gift to the second—the Throne of Satan and the birth of the Nazi Party."

The man then took out one more piece from the bag, a pawn of black stone, slightly misshapen or damaged, and placed it on its side, as if struck down in the game.

"The war had one more casualty. Lying in bed in a military hospital in a small town in northeastern Germany was a German soldier who had been wounded in the war. A gas attack had left him temporarily blinded. While hospitalized, he was given the news of Germany's defeat. It filled him with rage. He would later state that it was in that moment that he received his 'calling.'[2]

"The German soldier was Adolf Hitler. His calling, as he would see it, was to become the leader of Germany. But it would not come to pass until a fateful encounter. After recovering his sight, he would enter a beer hall in Munich in which a small political gathering was taking place. It was a meeting of the organization born of Sebottendorff's occult Thule Society, the German Workers' Party, which would now give birth to the Third Reich."

The man then raised up the black pawn and placed it in front of the others.

"Hitler was another pawn in the Devil's hand. And now the one evil would give birth to the next."

If there could be a still darker or more sinister revelation than what we had just been shown, it was what was now about to be revealed. And it would be a child who would reveal it.

PART V

POSSESSION

Chapter 22

CHILD OF NUREMBERG

There in the Yellow Fortress, the man handed us a sheet, the next page of the book and the fourth mystery. He wished us well, and we parted. After dinner, Lara and I sat down in the hotel's lounge to look at the page. Its image was that of a dark figure, a robed man, standing on top of what appeared to be an altar. His hands were stretched out and upward. If the object was an altar, if it stood for the Altar of Pergamon, then who would be standing on top of it? A priest? A king? That was as far as we got in trying to decipher it. Then Lara changed the subject.

"Tell me," she said, "why did you become an unbeliever? What was it that made you lose faith in God and become so cynical?"

"That doesn't have anything to do with the mystery," I said.

"I'm pursuing another mystery."

"My grandfather, my father's father, was a survivor of the Holocaust. I don't talk about it much. I can remember as a child hearing him speak of the horrors he witnessed—not to me, but to others. They didn't know I was listening. That was it...what caused me to become a cynic. I couldn't fathom how there could be such evil in the world and, on the other hand, a loving God.

"And beyond that, it happened to the Jews, the 'chosen people'—His own people. How could there be a God of the Jews and a Holocaust in the same universe? I couldn't fathom it. But what was even more unfathomable to me was that my grandfather still believed in God after everything he had seen. How could he still pray? How could he still keep the holidays and the observances? That's why. That's why I became an atheist and, more than that, an opponent of such faith. I would devote my life to fighting against it.

"And what about you? Why do you believe? I assume it's because you were born into it. It's your religion."

"No," she replied. "It's not religion. I grew up knowing about God. I was taken to church on holidays. I prayed at times. It was religion, but it wasn't what the Bible speaks about. It didn't change my life."

"And what happened?"

"When I was a teenager, I got into things I shouldn't have gotten into."

"You, Lara Winter, the paragon of virtue? I can't believe it!"

"And in the middle of a bad drug episode, when I thought I was losing my mind and overdosing, I cried out to God. And He heard me."

"A drug episode? How do you know God heard you?"

"The episode ended, just like that, in a flash. That's when I began searching. And I found Him. And it changed my life. It's not about religion or what you were born into. It's what you choose. It's what you receive...a new birth."

"Interesting," I said. "I guess we each have our own mysteries. And now we have a new one to open."

We said good night and went to our rooms. That evening, she translated the text into English. The next morning at breakfast in a Sarajevan café, she told me what she found.

"The title reads 'Possession,'" she said. "And then it says this:

The Possession
Possessed
The Builders
Building
For the Altar
A Temple
For the Throne
A Kingdom
For the King's Rising
At the Time of Revelation
The Unholy of Holies
His Rage
Upon the Throne."

"The Possession Possessed," I said. "The Altar now comes into Germany's full possession. And so the Builders can now build a permanent building to house it. For the Altar, a Temple. The woman who showed us the Altar in Berlin told us that they built a museum specifically to house the Altar."

"It fits," said Lara, "but what about the Unholy of Holies, and the King's Rising, and the Rage upon the Throne? What does it mean?"

"Perhaps you could sleep on it," I suggested. And she did. But the next morning when we met for breakfast, there was nothing new to report, no dream. But later that day, she texted me, suggesting we go for dinner, as she had something to show me. So we did.

"This afternoon," she said, "I fell asleep in front of the television."

"And you had a dream. And you were shown the next place."

"I'm not sure," she said. "It didn't seem to be about a place. This one was different."

"What did you see?"

"Him," she said. "I saw Hitler. It was night. He was standing in front of thousands and thousands and thousands of people. All around them were shafts of light shooting up into the night sky, pillars of light. He stood above the multitude on a square stone platform. He began to speak. They were mesmerized, entranced by every word. He started out low in volume and slow and measured in his pacing. Then he grew louder and louder and more and more intense and impassioned until he drove himself into a frenzy and the people with him."

"Sounds like a Hitler speech," I said. "Did you see anything else?"

"No, except that my attention was drawn to a boy in the crowd. He was different. He didn't fit in. He didn't belong with them. While everyone was in a frenzy, he just stood there with a troubled expression on his face. That was it."

"How does that tell us where to go next? And what kind of clue is Hitler? It was more about an event than a place."

"But events take place in places," she said. "So where would that have taken place?"

"In Germany."

"Then we have to go back to Germany."

"And then what?"

"I don't know," she said. "We'll see."

So we arranged for a flight back to Berlin. Upon arriving, we checked into a hotel and waited and waited. With nothing more to go on, we decided to go for a walk through Berlin. We figured it was possible that we might happen to encounter someone on our walk that we were supposed to encounter, but nothing happened. Then it hit me.

"Maybe," I said, "your dream wasn't telling us just to go back to Germany. Maybe it was telling us to go to the place *in* Germany, the specific place where Hitler gave that speech."

"But Hitler gave many speeches," said Lara. "How would we know where he gave that one, or if he gave it at all?"

"Tell me again, what did you see in that dream?"

"Mass crowds at night, a raised stone platform, beams of light shooting in the sky."

I took out my cell and put in her description along with "Hitler speech." I went through the search results.

"And I think I have it," I said.

"That was quick. Where?"

"Nuremberg. What you described was Hitler giving a speech in Nuremberg at the annual gathering of the Nazi Party, the Nuremberg rallies. That's where we need to go—Nuremberg."

The next day, we rented a car and headed for Nuremberg. It took us about four hours to get there. You could still see the medieval walls that once enclosed the city, the stone towers, and the cobblestone streets. At the same time, it was impossible not to think of Nuremberg's associations with the Third Reich.

We reached the grounds that once hosted the mass gatherings of the Nazi Party. The first impression was of its colossal scale, its near-endless expanse. The second was that of contrast, the roaring thousands who once occupied the grounds and the silence and emptiness that now filled it.

We began walking across the grass of Nuremberg's Zeppelin Field, on which Hitler's rallies took place. Lara and I were both silent, pondering the significance of where we were. We didn't know what we were looking for but figured the best way was just to keep walking and looking. There were others similarly walking the field. I took them to be tourists or natives of Nuremberg. One of them was taking photographs with his cell phone—not of Zeppelin Field, but of us. I stopped and stared directly at him. He lowered his cell phone and casually walked away.

Stranger than that was a small figure standing in the distance: a child, a boy. Lara was the first to notice him.

"Look," she said. "He's all alone. There's nobody with him, no parent... What's he doing there by himself?"

We walked over to him. He had blond hair and blue eyes and was, I imagine, around eight years old.

"It's him," said Lara softly to me, "the boy in my dream at the rally in Nuremberg. It's him."

"Do you speak English?" I asked.

"I do," said the boy.

"Where are your parents?"

"I am here by myself," he said with a German accent.

"Do you need help?" asked Lara.

"No," said the boy.

"What are you doing here?" I asked.

"Waiting…for you."

"No," I said. "Don't tell me you're one of them."

"Because I'm a child?" he asked.

"Who would use children?" I said to Lara. "Who would send a child out by himself…and for something that could involve danger?"

"I'm not in danger," he said. "And it is *you,* Mr. Herzog, who need *my* help."

At that, Lara turned to me and said, "Just go with it."

"Yes," said the boy. "What else do you have to go with?"

I didn't reply.

"Now," said the boy, "may we begin?"

As we stood there on the grass with the boy on Nazism's most sacred ground, the mystery of the king, the temple, and the throne would be revealed to us.

Chapter 23
THE TEMPLE

HE DIDN'T SPEAK like a boy, not like any boy I had ever heard speak.

"Where do you find altars?" he asked. "In temples. Therefore, Germany would set out to build the Altar a temple, a house."

"In the form of a museum," I said.

"Yes, a house, a shrine, in which the Altar would be lifted up and hallowed, where people would gaze at it in wonder, a temple fit for an altar."

"And when did they build it?"

"On the eve of the twentieth century. They began building it in 1897. It wasn't the one you saw on Museum Island. It opened in 1901. It was only the first house, but it was a major step in the nation's veneration of its new possession."

"The Possession Possessed," I said, quoting the text.

"But it was not a fitting house for the possession. It was too small. It only allowed the Altar to be displayed in pieces or sections. And the building's foundation was found to be faulty. So the Altar's sections were displayed there for seven years before they closed it all down in 1908 and razed the building to the ground.

"Germany would now set out to build the Altar a permanent sanctuary, a much larger house, a temple worthy of such a hallowed object. They began building it in 1910. But the war put a halt to the project. After the war, the construction resumed. It was during the 1920s that the Altar's new house began to rise. And it was during that same time that the Altar was reconstructed, not in sections but as one piece.

"It was a monumental task...and historic...not just for Germany but for the world. The opening of the new house would mark the Altar's first permanent home since it stood on top of the high place at Pergamon. It would also mark the first time the Altar would appear fully reconstructed as a whole, in one piece, for the world to see—the first time since it stood in ancient Pergamon."

"On the page we were given," said Lara, "it reads, 'The Builders Building, for the Altar, a Temple, for the Throne, a Kingdom.' What does it mean?"

"The Altar," said the boy, "is not just an altar; it's a throne, the Throne of Satan. I know you know that. So while Germany embarked on building a temple for the Altar, the Evil One would embark on building a *kingdom* for the Throne."

"What kingdom exactly?" asked Lara.

"A kingdom of darkness," he said, "of the Evil One. At the same time the house began rising for the Altar, a kingdom began rising for the Throne. A throne has to do with kings, governments, and power. So the mystery would involve a rising to power and the possessing of a government."

"The King's Rising. What does that mean?" asked Lara.

"A throne is made for a ruler," he replied. "The Throne of Satan is made for a satanic ruler. So there would come a satanic ruler."

"Adolf Hitler," I said.

"Yes," said the boy. "As the Throne of Satan was being prepared, a satanic king was rising."

"We were shown," I said, "the parallel between Hitler and the Altar, how, when the Altar was first pieced together, Hitler was conceived, and, in the year when the Altar's configuration was complete, Hitler was born."

"The parallel didn't end there," said the boy. "As a king is connected to the throne, so the two would rise together.

"The year 1907 was critical for the Altar. It was in that year that the plans for the building of its permanent house were first submitted. That same year, 1907, would be a turning point in the life of Adolf Hitler. It was in 1907 that his mother, Klara, to whom he was deeply attached, died of cancer. And that same year, his dream of becoming a great artist was crushed as he was rejected by the Vienna Academy of Fine Arts, altering his life's course. And it was in that same year that he moved to Vienna. Vienna was a cauldron of anti-Jewish hatred, It was there, in the midst of the cauldron, that Hitler, destitute, aimless, and embittered, was exposed to anti-Semitic writings, beliefs, and ideologies. He would later write that it was his time in Vienna that formed his worldview and his hatred for the Jews.[1]

"The First World War would interrupt the construction of the Altar's house. So too it would interrupt Hitler's life. At the war's end, the building of the Altar's house would resume. And at the war's end, Hitler's rise to power would begin as he entered the political realm and began building the Nazi Party.

"It was in the 1920s that the construction of the Altar's house fully resumed. It was the decade that marked the rising of its temple. So too it was the decade that marked the rising of Adolf Hitler and the Nazi Party.

"As a throne is built for a king, so the Throne of Satan was being prepared for the coming of a satanic king, just as the satanic king was being prepared for the Throne. As the Throne of Satan was being raised up in Berlin, Hitler's rise to power could only culminate when he too came to Berlin, to the city of the Throne. And when the two came together, the mystery would be sealed."

"But it wasn't just a king being prepared," said Lara. "You said it was also the kingdom. How was the kingdom being prepared?"

"That was also connected to the Altar," said the boy, "but it involved a hidden realm."

He would now open that hidden realm and speak of a much more mystical rising.

Chapter 24

THE POSSESSION POSSESSED

"LET US WALK," he said. So we walked with the boy through Zeppelin Field.

"I think you have something confused," he said, directing his words to me. "The Possession Possessed, you believed it was speaking of the Altar and its possession by Germany."

"And it wasn't?"

"Not primarily," he said. "Germany did come to possess the Altar. But the words speak of another kind of possession. The Dark One is also a possessor. And as Germany came into possession of the Throne of Satan, the Throne of Satan came into possession of Germany."

"So the title of the page," said Lara, "'Possession,' refers to the possession of Germany itself."

"Yes."

"Sounds like something out of *The Lord of the Rings*," I said. "The one who possesses the ring becomes possessed by it."

"Yes," said Lara, "except *The Lord of the Rings* is fiction and fantasy, and what happened to Germany and to the world was real."

"How did it come about?" I asked.

"When the Altar was moved to German soil, something strange began happening to the nation."

"Something strange," I repeated. "Like..."

"The occult," he said. "Germany began opening itself up to the occult, to the dark realm of the spirit world, to witchcraft and spells, to the invoking of the dead and the summoning of dark powers, to spirits, secret rites...demonic spirituality...and satanic indwelling. So as Germany came into contact with the Throne of Satan and then received it onto its native soil, the satanic realm began taking hold of Germany.

"And as it was the 1870s that saw the Altar's discovery and the preparation for its transference to Germany, so it was the 1870s that saw the preparation for the occult revival of Germany. Occult articles and books were published, others were translated into German, occult societies were founded, and occult doctrines began proliferating.

"And then as the Altar was unearthed and moved to Berlin in the late

1870s and the 1880s...at that exact time, the revival of the occult began exploding throughout Germany."

"The Altar was moved to Europe," I said, "to the West. So was there any occult revival in Europe or the West?"

"Yes," he replied, "but in other places, it was more of a passing fad. But in Germany, it took deep hold. It became entrenched in German culture. The spreading and proliferation of occult beliefs, practices, and societies continued into the 1890s and then into the twentieth century.

"As the Throne of Satan came to rest in its new home, the nation began undergoing a dark metamorphosis. The ground was being prepared, and the people were being readied for what was coming. The satanic Throne would herald a satanic kingdom, a demonic Reich.

"And then something else happened," said the boy. "As the Altar was brought to Germany, another movement began to germinate. It would be called the *völkisch Bewegung*, or the people's movement. Like much else, its origins could be traced to 1871."

"The year of the Altar's discovery," I said.

"The birth of the German nation set in motion a search for true German identity, what was German and who was not. So the völkisch movement became a breeding ground of anti-Jewish hatred. It also became the cauldron of anti-Christian hatred, as it sought a pure German ideal from the nation's pre-Christian and pagan past and in a mythical Aryan origin. And as it was with the occult revival, so it was that when the Altar was brought to Germany, the völkisch movement began infusing German culture.

"And then a stranger thing happened. The völkisch movement began coalescing with the occult revival, and the occult revival with the völkisch movement. It could be seen incubating from the late 1880s onward and into the twentieth century. Mystical societies began forming that joined German identity with occultism, secret rituals with virulent anti-Semitism, the call for a greater Germany with the worship of gods and spirits. It was a dark and dangerous mixture."

"And a satanic mix," said Lara. "The occult, hatred of the Jews, the völkisch hatred of Christianity, paganism...it all sounds satanic."

"Yes," said the boy, "the spirit of the Dark Angel began taking possession of the nation. And it all crystallized with the birth and rise of Nazism."

"And that too came from the German occult," I said, "with the Thule Society."

"How long did the occult revival continue?" asked Lara.

"After the war," he said, "in the 1920s, it exploded again and further saturated German culture. It happened in the same decade that saw the rising of Hitler and Nazism and the house of the ancient Altar."

"So when did it end?" asked Lara.

"When it bore its fruit," he replied, "when it produced the Third Reich. And even then, it didn't end but took the form of a satanic kingdom. It was no accident that the Nazis took up the symbols of the German occult revival—the swastika; the two lightning bolts of the SS, Hitler's elite paramilitary force; and many others. They were all birthed in the same dark cauldron as was the Nazi Party itself. And from that same occult revival would also come an expectation and a prophecy that a ruler would arise and lead the German people to rule the world."

"They were being possessed," said Lara. "It was all being prepared for his rising."

"Yes," said the child, "for an Altar, a Temple, and a Kingdom for a Throne...and now a King for a Kingdom...the Possession Possessed."

"And one more thing was needed," he said. "The child that was born with the Altar would have to come together with the Altar that was resurrected for the child. And in their coming together, the dark kingdom would be born."

Chapter 25
THE TURNING

"It has an ominous feel," I said, "how so many things came together at the exact time in the exact place—the uncovering of the Altar, the birth of Germany, the beginning of modern anti-Semitism, the occult revival, German nationalism and militarism, the birth of Adolf Hitler...how all the pieces fell into place to bring about what happened."

"I don't know that the pieces fell into place," said Lara, "as much as they were pieced into place."

We walked by the series of massive blocks of stone, the towers that once lined the fields of Hitler's Nuremberg rallies.

"Where," I asked the boy, "was the occult revival centered?"

"There were three major centers," he said, "Vienna, Munich, and Berlin. Hitler spent his formative years in Vienna. And then he went to the other occultic center, Munich, where the Nazi Party was born and where Hitler became its leader. And the mystery would only be complete if he went to Berlin, the third occult center and the city of the Altar.

"But in 1928, it didn't look as if that would happen. Hitler and the Nazis suffered a major setback. In the general elections, the party received just 2.6 percent of the vote and, out of almost five hundred seats in the Reichstag, the German Parliament, only twelve. Hitler and the Nazi Party appeared set for an irreversible decline into irrelevancy. But events beyond Hitler's control would dramatically alter his prospects."

"And what was happening to the Altar at that time?" asked Lara.

"As the decade of the 1920s approached its end, the twenty-year project of the Altar's construction inside a permanent house approached its completion. The time drew near for its revealing. In the spring of 1929, an advance glimpse of the nearly finished Altar was given to a group of archaeologists, a dress rehearsal for the grand revealing."

"So then," said Lara, "the Throne of Satan was almost ready, but the satanic king was not."

"Yes," said the boy, "after the 1928 elections, Hitler's prospects for ruling Germany were more distant than ever. But then something happened. In the autumn after that first glimpse of the Altar was given, and less than a year before its grand revealing, the New York stock market crashed and ushered in the Great Depression. The German economy likewise collapsed. Extreme crises open the door to extreme remedies.

"The grand opening of the Pergamon Museum and the Altar's grand revealing happened in the autumn of 1930. And as worshippers once came to gaze on it in ancient times on the Pergamon acropolis, now multitudes of Germans came from all over to gaze upon the Altar in its new temple and displayed in one piece for the first time since ancient times. It was a critical milestone and turning point in a history that had spanned ages.

"But those same days marked another critical milestone—the turning point in the rise of Adolf Hitler, the Nazi Party, and Germany. It was then that a dramatic change took place in the German general election. The Nazi Party, which had won less than 3 percent of the vote and 12 seats in the Reichstag, now won 107 seats. It had multiplied nearly ten times what it had won just two years earlier. Suddenly, what had been a fringe political party was catapulted into becoming the second-largest political party in Germany. The die was cast, and it would now be only a matter of time.

"The turning point in the Altar's history and the turning point in Hitler's rise to power took place not only in the same year but less than twenty days apart. The Throne of Satan was lifted up before the German people, and so too was his vessel, his satanic king. The satanic Throne and the satanic king were converging.

"And something else was birthed in that turning point," said the boy. "The Devil's fury against the children of Israel began erupting across Germany. The Nazis' private army, the storm troopers, began attacking Jewish people on the streets of Germany—destroying Jewish property, vandalizing Jewish shops, establishments, and synagogues—while anti-Semitic leaflets proliferated to further spread the hatred. That autumn marked the beginning of the Nazis' systematic 'eruptions' of street violence against the Jews of Germany. It was a foreshadowing of what was coming and a dress rehearsal for *Kristallnacht*, the Night of Broken Glass. And it all exploded in that autumn of 1930, when the ancient Altar was unveiled and the Throne of Satan exalted in its new temple.

"And it was only the beginning. When the Altar was revealed to Germany, the number of Nazi storm troopers was around seventy-five thousand. Within one year, it had tripled to over two hundred and twenty thousand. Less than a year later, its numbers were approaching four hundred and fifty thousand, and the following year, around two million. So too as the Altar was being prepared to be revealed, membership in the Nazi Party was around one hundred thousand. The year after its revealing, the number of Nazis exploded eightfold to over eight hundred thousand members and the following year to over a million. The Nazi Party had been transformed in a metamorphosis that began in the autumn of the Altar.

"Two years after the autumn of the Altar's revealing, Hitler's fringe organization had become the largest political party in Germany. And then, in January 1933, Hitler was appointed chancellor of Germany. In a short time, Germany would be turned into a Nazi state.

"What began when Carl Humann sent the first pieces of Satan's Throne to German soil had now come to fruition. The Throne had produced its kingdom. The child born with the Altar had now come to power in Berlin, the city in which the Altar rested.

"The satanic king had come to the Throne of Satan to rule the nation. And the nation had been transformed into a satanic kingdom. Those who had come to possess the Throne of Satan had now, by Satan's Throne, become possessed."

"But there was another mystery that lay behind what happened to Germany that went back thousands of years to the Throne of God."

Chapter 26

THE UNHOLY OF HOLIES

THE BOY LED us to the front of Zeppelin Field, toward the place where Hitler stood before the awed masses of Nuremberg.

"And now," he said, "I must reveal the mystery of the revealing."

"You speak in riddles," I said.

"All the mysteries," he said, "focus on an object, a dark and unholy object, the Devil's Altar. But the Devil is a mimic. He takes the things of God and inverts them. So as there was an altar of Satan, there was an altar of God."

"In the Temple," I said.

"Yes," he replied, "and more than one: the Altar of sacrifice, the Altar of incense, and the Altar of altars...the Ark of the Covenant."

"The Ark of the Covenant," said Lara, "as in Indiana Jones."

"Who is Indiana Jones?" said the boy.

"He's from the movies," said Lara. "He's an archaeologist who uncovers ancient objects, including the Ark of the Covenant. And the Nazis try to take it for themselves, for Hitler, to use its power for evil."

"The Ark," said the boy, "was the most holy vessel in the Temple, the golden housing for the tablets of the Commandments, the central vessel in the covenant between God and Israel."

"But how," I asked, "was it an altar?"

"Its function as an altar only manifested one day of the year, on the holiest of days, Yom Kippur, the Day of Atonement. It was the only day the High Priest could enter into the Holy of Holies, the only day when man could stand before God. On that day he would sprinkle the sacrificial blood on the mercy seat, the Ark's golden covering. And through that act, Israel's sins were ceremonially washed away, and atonement was made between man and God—salvation. It was a symbolic act, a shadow of a coming sacrifice, a future atonement, the forgiveness of sins, and redemption. So the Ark of the Covenant was the most holy of altars and so was kept in the most sacred of places, the Holy of Holies, for the most holy of days, Yom Kippur, when it served as the most holy Altar of God."

"So we have the Altar of Satan," said Lara, "and the Altar of God. What does the one have to do with the other?"

"The Altar of Pergamon was revealed to Germany and the world with the opening of the Pergamon Museum on October 2, 1930."

"And...?" I said.

"October 2, 1930," said the boy, "was *Yom Kippur*. The Altar of Satan was revealed on the day of God's Altar...On the day of the Most Holy, the most unholy of objects, the 'Unholy of Holies,' was opened to the world."

"And they didn't know when they planned it?" I asked.

"The Enemy knew," he replied. "Yom Kippur was the only day that the Altar of God could be revealed...the only day the High Priest could pass behind the veil that concealed it."

"So on the day that God's Altar was revealed," said Lara, "the Altar of Satan was revealed as his Altar."

"Do you know what *reveal* means?" asked the boy. "It means to remove the veil. So it was on Yom Kippur that the veil was moved out of the way and the Temple of God was opened for man to enter its innermost sanctum."

"And on that day in Germany," I said, "the Altar of Satan was revealed and its temple opened to Germany and the world."

"Yes," said the boy. "Now I have a question for *you*. If the Altar of Pergamon is also called the Throne of Satan, then what about the Altar of God?"

"Is it a throne?" I said.

"It *is* a throne," he said. "The Altar of God, the Ark of the Covenant, *is* the Throne of God."

"How?" asked Lara.

"On the Ark were two golden cherubim. God promised to dwell there. So it is written that the Lord *sits enthroned* between the cherubim. It was a symbol, of course, of His Throne in heaven. But on earth, His presence dwelt in the Holy of Holies and on the Ark of the Covenant. Do you remember what the Enemy said at the beginning? 'I will exalt my throne above the stars of God....I will ascend....I will be like the Most High.'[1] He seeks to take the things of God and turn them against God's purposes. That's why it all happened on the holiest day of the year. It was the sign of the Dark Angel and of his ultimate goal to replace the Throne of God with his own."

"So he exalted his Altar," said Lara, "on the day of God's Altar...and exalted the Throne of Satan on the day of the Throne of God."

"Yes," said the boy. "It was always about the changing of thrones. And that's what Hitler sought to do in Germany, to exchange the Throne of God for the Throne of Satan. And if that was not ominous enough, it would be even more ominous for one particular people whose most holy day was desecrated by the Throne of Satan."

"The Jewish people," said Lara.

"And the Day of Atonement," he said, "was the day of their redemption. So what would the Evil One do but turn their day of redemption against them…to bring about their destruction?"

"And that," said the boy, "brings us to one last mystery, one so large you would miss it if you weren't looking." He then led us to a massive object that stood in the distance and a mystery so unreal that if I didn't know better, I would have thought it was made up. But it was real.

Chapter 27

THE MAN ON THE ALTAR

"LOOK," SAID THE boy as he pointed into the distance.

Before us stood a massive edifice of pale limestone, long, rectangular, and framed by a colossal set of stairs. The scale of the object was overwhelming, even from a distance.

"That is the Zeppelin Tribune," said the boy. "It was built for Hitler as his reviewing stand and speaking platform for his massive Nuremberg rallies. Do you see that boxlike structure in the middle? That's where the monster stood and spoke to the masses."

"Is it the same as it was back then?" I asked.

"No, it was much bigger then. It stretched to the left and to the right, with massive columns. What remains is just the centerpiece, the smallest part. It was then even more colossal.

"Nuremberg was the symbolic heart of Nazism, the ground of its rituals, its symbols, and its liturgies. And the Zeppelin Tribune was the focal point of Nuremberg. So that object was the symbolic heart of Nazism."

"And what is the mystery?" I asked.

"Do you know what you're looking at, Mr. Herzog?" he replied.

"I guess not. What am I looking at?"

"You're looking at the Altar of Pergamon."

"What do you mean?"

"Soon after coming to power, Hitler commissioned his architect, Albert Speer, to come up with a massive rostrum to serve as the center of the Nuremberg rallies and from which he would stand enthroned above the multitudes and speak. In his search to find inspiration for such a massive project, Speer would be led to the Altar of Pergamon."

"How do we know for sure," said Lara, "that it came from the Altar of Pergamon?"

"Speer himself admitted it. These are his own words:

> I struggled over those first sketches until, in an inspired moment, the idea came to me: a mighty flight of stairs topped and enclosed by a long colonnade, flanked on both ends by stone

> abutments. Undoubtedly it was influenced by the *Pergamum altar.*"[1]

"Of all the objects in the world," I said, "Hitler's platform was a re-creation of the Altar of Pergamon! It seems too unbelievable to be true."

"But it is true," said the boy. "The central symbolic structure of Nazism was the re-creation of the Altar of Pergamon."

"So the object linked to his rising," said Lara, "became the object on which he was lifted up, the platform of his power."

"Hitler, standing on top of the ancient Altar," I said. "It's crazy."

"The ancient Altar," said the boy, "but on a massive scale. The Altar of Pergamon multiplied many times over. The massive columns that stood on each side of the centerpiece and that were capped with two massive wings were the colossal version of the columns and wings of the ancient Altar. And the massive staircase leading up to the edifice was the colossal version of the ancient staircase that led up to the Altar and on which the worshippers ascended to offer up their sacrifices."

"Only now," I said, "it was Hitler standing there."

"The ancient worshippers," said the boy, "ascended the steps to their god, but Hitler descended the steps as if a god come down."

The boy now led us closer to the podium on which Hitler stood.

"So what I saw in my dream," said Lara, "Hitler speaking at Nuremberg, it was this. He was speaking to the multitude from a colossal Altar of Pergamon."

"And the image," I said, "on the page, the dark-robed figure standing on top of the altar, it wasn't a priest; it was Hitler standing on top of the Altar."

"Or maybe it was a priest," said the boy. "Maybe Hitler was a priest, a priest of darkness."

"It's the completion of what was from the beginning," said Lara, "what came to Germany in wooden crates from Pergamon. It's as if it was destined to become the centerpiece of the Third Reich."

"And of the mystery of Adolf Hitler," said the boy. "Remember, he was joined to the Altar from his birth. And so now he returned to it. It was destined to become his platform."

"So of all the nations in the world," I said, "it just happens to be Nazi Germany that builds a colossal version of the Altar of Pergamon as its hallowed podium...and it just happens to be Adolf Hitler standing on top of it."

"And not just the Altar," said the boy, "but *Hitler's platform was the Throne of Satan.*"

"So of all the nations of the world," I said, "it was Nazi Germany that built the Throne of Satan as its sacred centerpiece."

"Why would they do that?" asked Lara.

"Nazism was a form of paganism," said the boy. "They had turned away from God, spurned His Word, rejected the faith. They didn't realize it, but it was all part of the mystery. When one turns from God, one will turn to something else. Remember, the Altar disappeared when the Gospel of God came in. But now, in the turning away from God, the Altar returns, and the result is Nazi Germany and Hitler standing on the colossal Altar."

"So," I said, "when Hitler was railing to the masses, he was railing from the Throne of Satan. You couldn't make this up."

"His Rage upon the Throne," said Lara. "It was Hitler's rage on that platform."

"It was the Dragon's rage," said the boy, "raging through the raging of Adolf Hitler. Germany had exchanged the Throne of God for the Throne of Satan. And now they were ruled by it. A throne for a kingdom and a kingdom for a throne. So it is no accident that the most satanic of kingdoms would have as its sacred rostrum the most satanic of objects, the Throne of Satan, on which the satanic king would rule them."

"And he raged," I said, "as a man possessed."

"And through him," said the boy, "the possession of a nation."

"It was all leading up to this," said Lara.

"Yes," said the boy. "As Hitler entranced them from that stone platform, the mystery manifested—*the nation that thought it could possess the Altar was now by the Altar possessed.*"

"But it was not the end of the mystery," said the boy, "for a kingdom ruled by the Throne of Satan will become not only a most evil thing but a most dangerous and deadly thing. And the evil that manifested in this place would not stay in this place. No. It would manifest before the entire world."

PART VI

CATACLYSM

Chapter 28

GUARDIANS OF THE THRONE

THE BOY HANDED Lara a sheet of paper, the next page and mystery from the book. Then he said goodbye.

"Are you going to be all right?" asked Lara.

"Yes," he replied, "just as I was before you came."

We left the Zeppelin Field and headed back to our car. The boy stayed behind by the Zeppelin Tribune. We stayed the night at a hotel in Nuremberg and the following day headed back to Berlin. Of course, we couldn't help looking at the page the boy had given us. It had an image of an altar surrounded by what appeared to be lightning bolts, stylized and radiating outward.

On the drive to Berlin, we shared our thoughts. I wondered if it had to do with Zeus, since he was associated with lightning bolts. Lara, on the other hand, wondered if it had to do with the Bible's description of Satan falling like lightning from heaven.[1] But since Lara had not been able to translate the text, we couldn't go much further.

It was early evening when we arrived in Berlin. I was waiting in the hotel lobby for Lara to join me for dinner, sitting on a couch, looking over the page the boy had given us.

"Are you from out of town?" said a man sitting on a nearby couch. He appeared to be in his late fifties. He spoke with a European accent, but I couldn't place it. I took him to be some sort of corporate executive on a business trip.

"I am," I replied.

"I am as well," he said. "And what are you in Berlin for?"

"Business."

"What kind of business?"

"It has to do with ancient artifacts."

"That is a coincidence," he said, "as I am also interested in ancient artifacts. Do you mind if I join you?"

"Sure," I said, not wanting to be rude. But I placed the page face down on the couch so that its image and text were hidden from view.

"Are you here in Berlin because of perhaps one artifact?"

"That could be."

His expression and tone now changed.

"I would be very careful if I were you," he said.

"What do you mean?"

"It is not wise to embark on a journey when you don't know where it will lead…or to open that which was never meant to be opened."

I placed my hand on the page.

"You have no idea what you're dealing with," said the man, "or how much danger surrounds you. There are others who have an interest in such artifacts and who would stop at nothing to remove any obstacle to their purposes. Why would you risk your life and the life of the one who accompanies you? And for what? Because you're curious? Bring this all to an end before it's too late…and before it destroys you."

He then placed his fingers on the page.

"And it is certainly not wise to be in possession of stolen property. The rightful owners of such things could not possibly be happy about your having what belongs to them. Or did you think we were not aware of who you are…and exactly where you are? I wouldn't spend much more time in this city, Mr. Herzog."

At that, he stood up. At the same moment, a second man who had been sitting on the other side of the lobby also rose to his feet, and then a third man from the corner of the lobby did likewise. The three of them then walked out the hotel's front entrance together.

I took out my cell phone and called Lara. "Stay in your room," I said. "I'll explain as soon as I can." I called our contact in Istanbul—Kazim—and told him what had happened.

"Don't stay another night in that hotel," he said. "Find another one—one you've never been to and in which you would not normally stay. Make sure no one follows you there. And when they assign you a room, ask for a different one."

I told Lara what had happened. We gathered our things and headed out to another hotel.

The next morning, we went out for coffee in one of the city's cafés. While we were waiting to place our order, a young woman came in the door and sat down by our table. She appeared to be of college age, with long blond hair and a knapsack, which she took off and laid on the seat beside her. She looked at us and smiled.

"Are you from America?" she asked with a Slavic accent.

"Yes," said Lara. "And you?"

"I'm from Poland," she said.

"Are you studying here in Berlin?" asked Lara.

"I am. And you? What are *you* doing in Berlin?"

"We're also kind of studying," said Lara.

"Studying what?"

"You could call it archaeology."

"Archaeology!" said the woman. "I'm an archaeology major! Excuse me, I don't want to impose, but would it be all right if I joined you? I'd love to hear what you're doing in the city, and I never want to miss an opportunity to practice my English."

"Join us," said Lara.

She grabbed her knapsack and moved to our table.

"My name is Alaina. I'm from Gliwice in southern Poland. Now tell me, how has archaeology brought you to Berlin?"

"There's an object in Berlin that has our interest," said Lara.

"The Altar?" she said.

"How did you know?"

"It's a major site here," she said. "But that's not how I know. I know because I'm here to help you."

"You're one of them?" asked Lara.

"I am."

"How do we know?" I said. "How do we know who is who? Last night, I met a man who wanted us to end the journey. How do I know you're not one of them?"

"Because of what I have to show you and give to you."

"Tell us who the others are," I said, "those who are against us."

"They call themselves the Keepers of the Altar. They claim to be descended from the priests who kept the Altar in ancient times."

"The priests of Zeus?"

"Yes, but agents of the Dark One. They also call themselves the Guardians of the Throne. They passed down their mission from generation to generation—to guard the Altar while it rested. But once it was unearthed and the Enemy's purposes were set in motion, they committed themselves to safeguarding those purposes and ensuring their fulfillment, all the while keeping their activities and the Altar's mystery hidden from the world."

"And those who would hinder or expose their activities?" I asked.

"They would eliminate them."

"The book," said Lara. "Tell us about the book."

"It's their scripture," she replied, "their testament. As the Bible records the purposes of God and His workings in the world, so they would create a book to record the purposes of the Dark Angel and his workings in the world, as manifested in the Altar. They began writing it soon after the Altar was unearthed and continued through the nineteenth century, the twentieth century, and even now. They used mystic verses that they would understand, but that would be hidden to others. The book was not for others to read."

"Or to have," said Lara.

"They're quite dangerous," said the woman. "They're all over the world. And they use every means at their disposal to fulfill their mission. Beware of them." She paused. "Please, don't rush. Finish your coffee. Then we'll begin."

The next of the Altar's secrets and the next evil to be unleashed would concern the greatest cataclysm in human history.

Chapter 29
THE SORCERER SPEAKS

WE FINISHED OUR coffee, and the woman led us out of the café and to the streets of Berlin.

"I never shared what I found," said Lara.

"You were able to translate the page?" I asked.

"Last night." She took out her notebook and began reading it to me as we walked. "It's titled 'Kataklusmos,' or 'Cataclysm':

The Sorcerer Speaks
The Fire Summoned
And Death Comes
Like Lightning
The Evil Born
Of Mirrored Hall
To Bear a Darker Spawn
The World in Cataclysm
Into the Earth
The Child Falls
The Possessed Now
Dispossessed."

"Do you want to know what it means?" said the woman.

"Please," I replied.

"You came here from Nuremberg," she said, "and you were told of Hitler's podium, the massive re-creation of the ancient Altar. Yes?"

"Yes."

"It was no accident that he spoke on an altar, for an altar requires blood. And so it was there on that Altar that Hitler would call his nation to prepare for war. There, on the Throne of Satan, he called Germany to prepare for the shedding of blood. And as the Altar on which he stood was colossal, so too would be the scale of blood it required and of the destruction he invoked.

"The construction of the colossal Altar of Pergamon began in the year 1935. It was that same year that Hitler began openly preparing for war, introducing military conscription and announcing that Germany would begin rearming. And when he first stood on the colossal re-creation of the Altar in 1937, the tone of the Nuremberg rallies changed, becoming increasingly militaristic, more and more geared toward war. It was in the very first rally in which Hitler stood on the colossal Altar at Nuremberg that the Nazis performed a full-scale war game involving live ammunition and air-ground attacks before the awed multitudes. And shortly after that rally, Hitler convened a secret meeting with his leaders in which he outlined his plans for war.

"At the next rally, in 1938, Hitler's ragings from on top of the Altar were the most brazenly militaristic yet. It would be called the Rally of Greater Germany. It would herald Germany's invasion of the surrounding nations. It was during the rally that Hitler threatened to invade Czechoslovakia. By the time of the next rally, 1939, there was no rally, as Germany had made its move and the Second World War had begun.

"You know," she said, "the Enemy is a destroyer. The first global destruction, the First World War, wasn't enough. So he would bring a second, a world cataclysm of destruction that would exceed that of the First World War, a calamity that was nearly unfathomable even to those who had witnessed the first.

"So as Hitler stood on the colossal podium and called for Germany to prepare for war, the Enemy was preparing to bring upon the world a megacalamity, a megadestruction, and a megacataclysm worthy of the mega-Altar. And so all the destruction, all the millions who would be killed, it was all invoked on top of that colossal Throne of Satan."

As we walked the streets of Berlin, the woman would show us the mystery behind the greatest cataclysm in world history and how it had also begun with the ancient Altar's return to the world.

Chapter 30

THE HALL OF MIRRORS

"I believe," said the woman as we walked through the city, "that you were told of how the Enemy's works contain the seeds of his future works. So it was that the first calamity, the First World War, would sow the seed of the Second."

"How?" I asked.

"At the end of the war, France was committed to inflicting severe punishment on Germany. It would do so through the Treaty of Versailles. The treaty forced Germany to take sole responsibility for the war, to pay 132 billion gold marks in reparations, to severely restrict its military force, to be stripped of land, to endure occupation, and to suffer national humiliation.

"But what it did was to foster a bitter resentment among the German people, a fierce German nationalism, a widespread yearning to restore German power and greatness, and a desire to inflict revenge on France and its other enemies. The reparations destabilized the German economy and led to severe economic hardship. The loss of German territories, about 13 percent of its land and 10 percent of its people, further damaged its economy, increased national resentment, and destabilized the region.

"The Treaty of Versailles opened the door for the rise of Adolf Hitler and the Nazi Party. Hitler vowed to undo its terms, rebuild the German military, regain its lost territories, and restore German power, greatness, and glory. It was the Treaty of Versailles that led to Hitler, and Hitler's defiance of the treaty that led to the Second World War.

"Hitler would rebuild the German military, militarize the Rhineland, annex Austria, and invade neighboring countries to regain lost land and then land that never belonged to Germany—all in defiance of the Treaty of Versailles. One of the nations he invaded was my homeland," she said, "Poland. It was that invasion that triggered the Second World War.

"So the root of the Second World War can be found in the Treaty of Versailles. But could there be more to the story? What about the Treaty of Versailles itself?"

"What do you mean?" I asked.

"What were the roots and origins of the Treaty of Versailles?"

"I don't know."

"It was born out of the Franco-Prussian War. You were told what happened at the end of that war?"

"Yes," said Lara, "Prussia imposed a devastating peace settlement on France. France was forced to pay massive war reparations to Germany, to accept German occupation, and to give up its territories in Alsace-Lorraine."

"Yes," said the woman. "And so the Treaty of Versailles was France's revenge on Germany for what Germany inflicted on it at the end of the Franco-Prussian War. So the Treaty of Versailles inflicted massive war reparations on Germany, French occupation on German land, and the giving up of German territory, specifically that of Alsace-Lorraine.

"And do you know why France insisted on signing the treaty in Versailles?"

"Why?" I asked.

"Because it was in Versailles in 1871 that the German leaders proclaimed the birth of Germany to humiliate France. And they proclaimed it in the Hall of Mirrors."

"The Mirrored Hall," said Lara.

"So now France," said the woman, "would exact its revenge on Germany in the same Hall of Mirrors. So if the origins of the Second World War went back to what France did to Germany at Versailles in the Hall of Mirrors at the end of the First World War, and if that went back to what Germany did to France at Versailles in the Hall of Mirrors at the end of the Franco-Prussian War, then when were the seeds of the Second World War sown?"

"In 1871," I said.

"And what was 1871?"

"The year of the Altar's return to the world."

"Yes," said the woman. "The seeds of the Second World War, the most destructive calamity in world history, were sown in 1871, when the Throne of Satan returned to the world."

She would now reveal to us the mystery of the lightning and how the nations of the world would be transformed by the Altar and drawn back to it.

Chapter 31

MOTHER OF CATACLYSMS

WORLD WAR II was triggered," she said, "because of what happened in Gliwice, Poland."

"Your hometown," said Lara.

"Yes. Back then, it was called Gleiwitz and was part of Germany. Hitler claimed that Polish soldiers had taken over the city's radio station to broadcast anti-German messages. But the truth was, it was Nazi agents dressed as Polish soldiers who took over the station on Hitler's orders. It was Hitler's excuse for invading Poland and triggering the Second World War. On the page of the book marked 'Cataclysm' is an image. What did you see in it?"

"An altar," I said, "with lightning bolts radiating out of it."

"And what did you make of the lightning?"

"Lightning was connected to Zeus," I replied.

"And to Satan," said Lara.

"Yes," said the woman, "and to Hitler. The Nazi agents who took over the radio station to start the Second World War were SS agents. The sign of the SS was two lightning bolts. Hitler's invasion of Poland, which triggered the war, was called…"

"The *blitzkrieg,*" I said, "the lightning war."

"And so where did it all come from," she asked, "the war that came upon the world like lightning?"

"From Germany," said Lara.

"From the land of the Altar. And where specifically?"

"From Berlin," I said.

"Berlin was the center of the Third Reich, the seat of Hitler's power and the place through which Hitler and the Nazis ruled Germany and hoped to rule the world. And Berlin was the seat of the Altar of Pergamon. So it is no accident that of all the places on earth, it was the city of Satan's Throne from which the most destructive of calamities would come upon the world."

"So the Second World War," I said, "was invoked from the colossal Throne of Satan at Nuremberg and was brought upon the world from the actual Throne of Satan, Berlin, the seat of the ancient Altar."

"The Evil Born," said Lara, reciting the words of the text, "to Bear a Darker Spawn, the World in Cataclysm. What is the Darker Spawn?"

"The devastation that came upon the world in the First World War," said the woman, "had no precedent. But the devastation that came upon the world in the Second World War transcended even that. It would bring destruction not only to Europe but to Asia, to Africa, and to the Pacific. It would reduce major cities, from one end of the earth to the other, into ruins. It would bring death to an estimated seventy million people. It would transform the world and irrevocably transform human history.

"Once again, the city of Satan's Throne was at the center of mass destruction. And the entire world was now reeling in the wake of its evil.

"Then, at the war's end, the world would be drawn back to the Throne that had devastated it. The Red Army and the Western Allied Forces now converged on Germany, the land of the Altar. And it would only be when Berlin, the city of the Altar, was conquered that the war in Europe could be brought to an end. The great powers would then converge on the ruins of the city of the ancient Throne. They had no idea of the connection or of its mystery, and yet they were all drawn to it.

"The same city that had given the order to unearth the Throne of Satan, the same city that had taken possession of it, had now shaken the earth, devastated nations, altered the course of world history, and shed the blood of millions."

"And yet it was what happened *underneath* the city," said the woman, "that would provide the final word." She would now reveal it to us—in a parking lot.

Chapter 32

THE DISPOSSESSED

SHE LED US to a quiet residential area and to a parking lot lined with red-roofed apartment buildings. There was nothing about it that would strike an observer as anything other than ordinary.

"This is what I saw!" said Lara.

"When?" I asked.

"In my dream last night."

"You didn't tell me you had a dream."

"Because I didn't think there was anything significant about it. I saw a parking lot."

"And…?"

"And nothing. I just saw a parking lot. I didn't think it meant anything."

I turned to the woman. "But it *does* mean something, doesn't it?"

"The Devil destroys his own," she said, "his own followers, his own worshippers, his own children. Those whom he uses to bring destruction are, in the end, destroyed by having been used. When they've served their purpose and he has no more use for them, he discards them. And so Nazi Germany was used for his purposes. And now it was destroyed. Berlin was especially used. And now it lay in ruins. The Nazis were used. And now they were gone."

"And Hitler…?" I said.

"He was especially used," she said. "He was especially joined to the Altar and the Throne of Satan from his birth, and the two were glorified together.

"But early in the war, with Allied bombing striking Berlin, the Nazis disassembled the Altar and hid it inside a bunker within the city in order to protect it. As Hitler's destiny had been joined to the Altar from the beginning of his life, so it would be joined at the end. As the Altar was transferred into a protective bunker in Berlin, so at the war's end, Hitler himself would be transferred into a protective bunker in Berlin. The Altar's shelter was called a *hochbunker*; Hitler's was called the *Führerbunker*."

"Into the Earth," said Lara, "the Child Falls."

"Yes," said the woman, "the child of the Altar fell into the earth. And do you know where it happened?"

"No," said Lara.

"Right here," she said. "It happened right here."

"In this parking lot?" asked Lara.

"Here, beneath this parking lot and beneath these buildings. It is here that lie the remains of the Führerbunker, the last seat of Hitler's power."

She then led us over to a sign erected in the midst of the parking lot that testified to that fact. It was there under the pavement that Adolf Hitler would spend his last days on earth. And the sign was the only visible evidence that he had.

"He had served his purpose," said the woman. "He had brought destruction to the earth. And his ability to bring any further destruction was at its end. So the Enemy had no more use for him. And so his power would be removed. His life would end under the city of the Altar."

"What about the other Altar of Pergamon," I asked, "the colossal one that stood at Nuremberg?"

"That one had been crowned with a giant swastika. The swastika was so massive that it was described as being the size of a house. Its placement on the colossal Pergamon Altar symbolized the union of the two, the Third Reich and the Throne of Satan.

"In late April 1945, the Allies arrived at Nuremberg. They came to Zeppelin Field and to the colossal reproduction of the Pergamon Altar. There the engineers of the Seventh Army placed explosives by the colossal swastika and blew it up. The act represented not only the end of Nazi Germany but the separation of the Altar from Nazism, the removal of the satanic Throne from the Third Reich.

"At the same time, Berlin was under siege. Hitler, in his underground bunker, was given the news that his orders to launch a counterattack against the invading army had been disregarded by his commanders. It was the breaking point. It was then that Hitler's illusion that he could save Berlin and the Third Reich from the Allied Forces fell apart. His reaction would be described as a breakdown, a collapse.

"It was on that day that, for the first time, Hitler declared that all was lost and that rather than fleeing Berlin, he would stay in the city and commit suicide. From that day on, he became sullen and withdrawn, and the aura of death permeated the bunker. It would now only be a matter of time, a short amount of time, until the end.

"The day the massive stone swastika was removed from the Altar of Pergamon's platform at Nuremberg was April 22, 1945. The day of Hitler's collapse in Berlin and his surrender to his fate was April 22, 1945. As the swastika was removed from the colossal Altar, as the Altar was being severed from Nazism, the dark fire that had inflamed its leader was removed. He lost the will to go on. Eight days later, he was dead.

"Just before his death was the Sabbath. And so the Jewish people throughout the world recited the words of the Scripture appointed for that day. The passage for that Sabbath ended with a word of warning concerning blasphemers and murderers. The blasphemer and murderer were to be put to death. Hitler was both a blasphemer and a murderer. And now he would be put to death.

"He had fulfilled his purpose as a vessel of darkness. Cities now lay in ruins, and millions of lives had been taken. And now the city where it had all begun and where the Throne of Satan had stood also lay in ruins. And under the ruins, inside his stone bunker, the one who had brought so much destruction to the world would now bring about his own destruction. And yet in another stone bunker in the same city lay the Altar, the Throne of Satan, the vessel of evil, hidden away from view that it might endure.

"So the life of the child bound to the Altar from birth came to its end on April 30, 1945."

"The Possessed Now Dispossessed," said Lara. "Hitler, possessed by the Altar, was now discarded, and the Altar was now dispossessed of him."

"Yes," said the woman. "But it was not the end."

"What do you mean?" I asked.

"The Altar survived the destruction," she said. "And it would pass into the hands of another."

"I have this to give you," said the woman as she handed us the next page. "I must warn you…It is an especially deep mystery."

"More so than this?" I asked.

"More so than this," she said. "It would be best to prepare yourselves."

PART VII

SACRIFICE

Chapter 33
THE STRANGER ON THE TRAIN

WE RETURNED TO our hotel and looked at the page. The image was again of an altar, but there was a lamb on top of it. That night, Lara translated the text and read it to me the following day at lunch in a local café.

"The word on the top of the page is 'Sacrifice.' And this is the text:

The Altar Prepared
The Offering Chosen
The Dark Priesthood
Waiting
By the Perpetual FIre
Burning
In the Holy Place
The High Priest Ministering
The Final Sacrifice
Offered
Ashes, Ashes
They All
Fall Down."

"It's consistent with the image," I said. "It sounds like the description of an ancient rite of sacrifice, a priesthood, an offering, ashes. But what would an ancient sacrificial ceremony have to do with the modern world?"

We had no idea what it was trying to say. The only thing left was the hope that Lara would have a dream. We stayed in that hotel, having no idea where else to go. But the dream didn't come, not in those first few days and not in that first week. By the second week, we questioned if it would come at all. And then, at the end of the second week, it came. I wondered, then and now, if we were being given that time of waiting that we might prepare ourselves for what was going to be revealed.

She told me at breakfast the morning it happened.

"I know where we're supposed to go," she said.

"You had a dream."

"I was on a train. I walked to the front where the engineer would sit, but there was no engineer; the train was running by itself. I was taking in the scenery: forests, farmland, small towns and red-roofed villages, and wide-open fields and plains. Then the landscape changed—fewer fields, more fences, and then watchtowers. Ahead of me was a long brick building that stretched across the track with an opening through which ran the rails.

"It was then that I realized where I was. I recognized the site from old photographs. I was at Auschwitz."

"Auschwitz," I repeated. "The next place is Auschwitz?" I became silent. I never would have imagined that our journey would take us to a concentration camp, much less the most infamous of all the camps. A chill came over me.

Auschwitz was in Poland. It had long been converted into a memorial for visitors and tourists. Because of Lara's dream, we decided we would go there by train. The next day, we headed to the Berlin Central Station and boarded the train for Katowice, Poland. From Katowice, we would take a second train to the city of Auschwitz and from there go to the camp. The ride to Katowice was by far the longest part of the journey, about six hours.

It was a classic European compartment train with private cabin seating. Each cabin had six seats, three on one side facing the three on the other side. In our cabin it was just Lara and me. But an hour or so into the journey, at one of the stops, a man joined us, taking his seat on the opposite side of the cabin. He gave us a polite greeting, then took out a newspaper and began reading it. He was middle-aged, thin, and of a deeply serious, even somber, demeanor. His face was long and weathered, with a long crease running down each cheek. His hair was dark, wavy, and slightly disheveled.

It was about an hour after he entered the cabin that he spoke.

"If I may be so bold to ask," he said in a European accent I couldn't place, "are you here on business?"

"More of a mission," I replied.

"A mission? To where?"

"A historic site."

"Don't tell me you're going to Auschwitz?"

"We are."

"And here we are in the same cabin!" said the man. "I too am going to Auschwitz. And you could say I too am on a mission."

"What kind of a mission?" asked Lara.

"A mission," said the man, "to help you."

"You're one of them?" I said.

"I am, Mr. Herzog." He paused for a moment while Lara and I glanced at each other. "Now, the revelation I am to give you is of much weight. Are you sure you're ready for it?"

"I believe we are," I replied.

"We have a long ride ahead of us, but I see no reason we can't begin now."

At that, he sat up in his seat, leaned forward, and began.

"When the Allied soldiers approached the death camps of the Third Reich, they had already been through the most destructive war in human history. And yet nothing could have prepared them for what they were about to see. There are those who say they can believe in God but not in the Devil. But the Holocaust is a glaring testament to the Devil's reality. Such things cannot be accounted for by natural explanations, nor can the rise of Adolf Hitler and Nazism. Satanic phenomena are of satanic origins.

"It is no coincidence that of all the peoples on earth, this most ancient and satanic of hatreds was directed against the Jewish people, the people of God and against whom the Enemy most especially rages. And it was long in coming. The seeds of his fury were sown years before in the soil of the newborn German nation, just as the first pieces of his Throne arrived in that land. And now the seeds had come to their fruition. What happened in those camps, it all went back to the Altar."

And then it began, the mystery we were told to prepare for. But there was no preparing for what was about to be revealed.

Chapter 34

THE SCAPEGOAT

"AN ALTAR REQUIRES a sacrifice. So what will the sacrifice be?"

"The people the Enemy especially wars against," said Lara, "the Jewish people."

"And so he would seek to make the Jewish people his sacrifice. And so the ancient will be connected to that aim. You were told of the day that the Altar was revealed in Berlin?"

"On Yom Kippur," said Lara, "the Jewish Day of Atonement."

"Yom Kippur is the day of the scapegoat."

"What's a scapegoat?" I asked.

"On Yom Kippur, the sins of the people were symbolically placed on the head of a goat. The goat would then depart or escape out into the wilderness—thus, the scapegoat. It was a representation of God's removal of the nation's sins. But as the Enemy inverts and desecrates the things of God, so he would take the holiest of things and invert them so that what was meant to bring life would now bring death."

"What does that mean?" I asked.

"It means he would seek to turn the people of the scapegoat, the Jewish people, into the scapegoat themselves. In other words, the nation that was symbolically saved by the scapegoat will now become the scapegoat nation, to its destruction. And as the sins of Israel were cast upon the scapegoat, now other nations and peoples will cast their sins upon the Jewish people and nation."

"Like Germany," I said.

"Yes. Like Germany. And so the Germans cast their sins on the Jews, accusing them of every kind of evil, dehumanizing them, demonizing them. And so the revealing of the Altar to Germany on Yom Kippur, the day of the scapegoat, was the sign that the Jewish people would become the national scapegoat. And so it was then as well, in the autumn of 1930, that the Nazi Party would be catapulted to national power, for they would officiate over the scapegoating of the Jewish people.

"But that brings us to the other part of Yom Kippur, the offering up of the sacrifice. Yom Kippur is, as well, the day of the Altar and the sacrifice. For the sacrifice had to be offered up on the Altar.

"The fact that the Dark Angel revealed his Altar on the day of God's Altar, Yom Kippur, was the sign of a coming sacrifice. And as the people of the scapegoat now became the scapegoat, so the people of the sacrifice would now become the sacrifice."

"The scapegoat nation," I said, "would then become the sacrifice nation."

"Yes," said the man, "the Yom Kippur nation."

"And the sacrifice," I said, "was..."

"The Holocaust," he replied. "Where was the ancient Altar?"

"In Berlin," said Lara.

"And so the Holocaust would begin in Berlin. It was there in Berlin that Hitler set it in motion from his chancellery. And it was there in the Berlin suburb of Wannsee that the Final Solution was implemented. It had to be so that the city of the Altar would begin the offering of the sacrifice."

"What about the other Altar," I said, "the Altar of Nuremberg?"

"That too would be part of it. It was from Nuremberg, the city of the colossal Altar, that the Holocaust was also set in motion. It was from there that the Nuremberg Laws went forth in 1935, the same year that marked the beginning of the construction of the Great Altar there. The Nuremberg Laws stripped the Jewish people of their citizenship, framed the Jews as a threat to Germany, separated them from the rest of the nation, and paved the way for their destruction. It was again from the Altar that the sacrifice was set in motion.

"It was all there from the beginning," he said. "When the first pieces of the Altar arrived in Germany, the Holocaust was there. For the nation that houses the Throne of Satan will end up fulfilling his will. And the nation that possesses the Altar will end up performing the sacrifice."

And then he was silent, letting us absorb what was told to us. He would resume the revelation when we arrived at Auschwitz, where he would reveal an even deeper mystery.

Chapter 35

THE BURNT OFFERING

THE TRAIN PULLED into the station at Katowice. We then boarded the second train for the much shorter ride to our final destination, the city of Auschwitz. By "we," I mean me, Lara, and the man who had joined us. Upon arriving, we left the train and headed for the exit.

"You know," he said, "the camp is only about a mile from here. We could walk there."

And so we did. I called for a taxi to take my and Lara's luggage to our hotel. The man, though, came with no luggage. We kept our valuables with us, and the pages of the book I kept in my inside coat pocket. We walked on the outskirts of the city along a paved and mostly level path. And then we arrived.

We could see the outline of the camp's guard towers in the distance. In front of us were two lines of old, rusted rails surrounded by gravel and an open expanse of grass. There, on the rails, were two wooden freight cars, from another era, alone and motionless.

"This was called the *Judenrampe*," said the man, "or the Jews' Ramp. Here the Jewish people would be taken off the trains and sent to their fate. You want to see how real the Devil is? You want a glimpse of his nature? There it is.

"As his nature is to nullify existence, to twist the works of God against their purpose and to destruction, so he inverted the sacrifice of God, that which was to bring redemption to the children of Israel, to now bring their destruction.

"The most foundational of Israel's sacrifices was called the *olah. Olah* means to ascend, to go up. It spoke of the *whole offering*, the offering that was wholly consumed by fire and which then ascended in smoke to the heavens, the *burnt offering.* It is the mystery behind the Holocaust.

"The Nazis were driven by the Altar to offer up a sacrifice. The sacrifice they offered was a twisted version of the sacrifice ordained for the Jewish people. That which was lifted up here in Auschwitz and in the other concentration camps was the olah, the *burnt offering* and the *offering of fire.*

"As the camps of the Holocaust were born of the Altar, they became themselves altars of burnt sacrifices. And as the ancient sacrifices were brought to the altar as lambs to the slaughter, so now the Jewish people were brought as lambs to the slaughter on the satanic altars of Nazism.

"It is recorded in the Bible that a fire burned in the midst of the camp of Israel, and by it the whole offerings were consumed.[1] So in the Devil's Holocaust, a fire burned in the midst of the concentration camps, in their crematoriums, and by it their offerings were consumed. In the ancient ordinance of the burnt offering, it is written:

> And the fire on the altar shall be kept burning on
> it; it shall not be put out.[2]

"So it was a continual fire that burned at the altar of sacrifice."

"The Perpetual Fire," said Lara, "Burning in the Holy Place."

"And so it was part of Holocaust lore that the fires of Auschwitz never went out. And as the olah offering was so named because it ascended in smoke into the heavens, so the satanic sacrifices of the Holocaust ascended in smoke into the skies."

"What about the Altar of Pergamon?" I asked. "Was it connected specifically to the burnt offering?"

"Yes. The Altar of Pergamon was an altar of burnt offerings. And the place on which Hitler stood and from which he spoke on the Altar's colossal replica at Nuremberg would, on the ancient Altar, have placed him in front of the sacrificial fire. And what was he doing there in Nuremberg on that Altar but kindling the fire for the sacrifice."

"That's what you meant," I said, "when you said that it was all there from the moment the Altar touched German soil. It was specifically an altar of *burnt offerings*. And so the nature of the Altar determined the nature of the sacrifice and the calamity. The Altar that stood in Berlin required a burnt offering, and so Germany would offer it up. And thus, the Holocaust."

"Yes," said the man, "and yet the mystery goes even deeper than this."

Chapter 36

THE ALTAR OF THE HOLOCAUST

GERMANY NOW POSSESSED the Altar of Pergamon. But who possessed it from the start? Who built it?"

"The ancient Greeks," said Lara.

"It was a Greek altar of *burnt* or *whole offerings.* Do you know how to say 'burnt' or 'whole' offering in the language of those who actually built the Altar of Pergamon?"

"I wouldn't know," I replied.

"The ancient Greek word for *burnt* is *caustos.*"

"Caustos," I repeated.

"And the ancient Greek word indicating that the sacrifice was entirely consumed is *holos.*[1] Caustos…holos."

"Caustos…holos," I repeated. "And…?"

"Holos caustos…" said the man. "*Holocaust.*"

"Holocaust!" I said.

At that, Lara put her hand over her mouth.

"The Holocaust!" I said again.

"Yes," said the man. "The word originally didn't speak of calamity—but of an offering, a ceremonial offering, a sacrifice lifted up on the altar. So the Holocaust wasn't only implied from the beginning when the Altar came to Germany—*it was actually there.* The Altar of Pergamon, the Altar of Satan, the Altar that stood in Berlin was the Altar of the Holocaust. So the Holocaust was all there from the beginning.

"And when Hitler raged at Nuremberg, he was raging on top of the Altar of holocausts…a colossal altar that would require a colossal holocaust. And so it was from Nuremberg, the ground of that massive holocaust Altar, that the Holocaust was set in motion by the passing of the Nuremberg Laws. The altar determines the nature of the sacrifice. And as the Altar of Pergamon was Greek, so the word that would mark the calamity that came upon the Jewish people would not be German but Greek.

"Do you know what the very first language was into which the Hebrew Scriptures were translated? Greek. The translation was called the Septuagint. And in that first translated version of the Bible, do you know what the word for *burnt offering* is?"

Lara and I didn't answer.

"*Holocaust*," he replied. "The word is *holocaust*."

"The word *holocaust* is in the Bible!" I said.

"In the ancient translation, the word *holocaust* spoke of the sacred offering that redeemed the children of Israel. So the Dark Angel took it and turned it against the Jewish people through the Holocaust. When I told you of the Scripture that ordained the continual burning of fire inside the camp...the ancient translation of that Scripture begins with these words:

> *This is the law of the holocaust.*[2]

"And do you remember the Scripture that was appointed to be read in September of 1878, when they began digging up the Altar?"

"'The altar of curses," said Lara.

"Yes, but it was more than that. The Scripture appointed for the start of the unearthing specified that it would be an altar of burnt offerings. And in the Greek translation of the Bible, it was an altar of the holocaust.

"And the day in 1930 on which the Altar was finally revealed in its entirety to Germany and the world?"

"Yom Kippur," I said, "the Day of Atonement."

"On that day, there is a Scripture appointed to be read and chanted throughout the world. It is Leviticus 16. And do you know what appears in the ancient translation of that Yom Kippur Scripture? The word *holocaust*. And it appears in that Scripture *not once but four times*. In one of those verses, it reads,

> And he shall...offer his *holocaust* and the *holocaust of the people*.[3]

"So on the day that the Altar of Pergamon was revealed to the world, the Jewish people were chanting the ancient Scriptures that spoke of the holocaust."

"So the Altar of holocausts," I said, "was revealed in Germany on the day of the holocaust...to usher the Holocaust into the world."

To every altar is a sacrifice, and to every sacrifice is a priesthood to offer it. He would now reveal to us the mystery of the dark priesthood.

Chapter 37
THE DARK PRIESTHOOD

The man motioned for us to follow him away from the Judenrampe. But I couldn't move. Lara came over to me.

"Come," she said, "we have to follow him."

Still I was frozen, staring at Auschwitz and the Judenrampe. She stood there with me, silent, waiting for me to come. The man waited in the distance as well, also silent. Then she spoke.

"He was here?" she asked.

"Who?"

"Your grandfather. He was here at Auschwitz?"

"He was."

"You didn't mention it all this time."

"It's not something I talk about much. I can see him there being unloaded off the train with the others like cattle, having no idea what awaited them."

"I'm so sorry," she said.

"But he survived."

"I know. But still, he was here."

"This is where my faith in God was taken away. It was this place that told me that the Good did not exist."

"No, Ariel," she said. "This place doesn't prove that God doesn't exist—it only proves that evil does. Evil doesn't disprove the Good; it just wars against it. That's what this journey's about. That's what we've seen. All this…it's satanic. And the satanic testifies that Satan is real. But if Satan is real…then God is real."

We stood there silently a little while longer, then turned to follow the man away from there. The path was flat but at times uneven, a vast expanse of grass, gravel, and the remnants of rail lines. There was little noise except from the wind, so one felt strangely separated from the world. We soon approached Birkenau, the second and largest of the camps that made up Auschwitz, with its endless rows of brick chimney ruins where wooden barracks had once stood. And then we saw it, the long red-brick entrance building with its central tower and its rectangular opening that led into the camp.

"That's it," said Lara. "That's what I saw in my dream."

"That," said the man, "is the Gate of Death. In the latter days of Auschwitz, it was through that opening that the trains would pass, carrying their passengers into another world, an entranceway into hell."

We never actually went into the camp, but we approached its infamous entrance building and then stopped. The railroad tracks were still there in the grass field, still converging into the gate.

"In the book," said Lara, "it says, 'The Altar Prepared, the Offering Chosen, the Dark Priesthood Waiting by the Perpetual Fire…' The Offering Chosen. Is it speaking of the Jews?"

"Yes," he replied, "the Offering Chosen and the offering of the chosen."

"But what is the Dark Priesthood?" she asked.

"You cannot have an altar," said the man, "without a priesthood. Someone has to offer up the sacrifice. That someone is the priest. The priests of Israel were called the *cohanim,* the sons of Aaron, the brother of Moses. They ministered in the Temple of Jerusalem, kept the Holy Place, presided over the holy days and the appointed times, and offered up the appointed sacrifices. The priesthood was passed down from Aaron and his sons to their sons, from generation to generation."

"And what about the Altar of Pergamon?" asked Lara.

"Its ministers were of a pagan priesthood, most prominently, the priests of Zeus. There they offered up sacrifices to the 'king of the gods' and the other deities of his pantheon."[1]

"And the Altar was also connected to Satan," said Lara. "Its sacrifices could be called satanic offerings."

"They could," he replied, "as behind the gods of ancient paganism were spirits…dark spirits."

"And what about the Nazis?" she asked.

"The Nazi Party espoused pagan ideals, pagan imagery, and even pagan gods," he said. "As for Hitler, he despised Christianity and the God of the Bible."

"So would the dark priesthood be the Nazis?" she asked.

"You could say that," he replied, "but the mystery goes still deeper. Among the most powerful leaders of the Third Reich was Heinrich Himmler. Himmler was steeped in mystical and occult beliefs and practices. He was also the head of the SS, the most feared of Nazi organizations. Himmler envisioned the SS as the closest thing to a Nazi priesthood. And as a priesthood is to uphold and guard the sacred, so Himmler set up the SS to uphold and guard the racial and ideological purity of Nazism.

"Every SS officer was expected to renounce Christianity and partake in pagan ceremonies prescribed by Himmler himself. And as priests officiate over sacred rites and ceremonies, so the SS were appointed to officiate over summer and winter solstice celebrations and other pagan and occult rites and ceremonies. They were indeed Nazism's dark priesthood.

"But the ultimate priestly act required an altar. It is at the altar that the priest must minister."

"And Nazism," I said, "had the Altar."

"Yes, and from that Altar, many others, the altars of the Holocaust."

"The concentration camps," said Lara.

"And so as the priests must minister at the altar, so those who operated the concentration camps, the dark altars of Nazism—they were the dark priesthood."

"And if the SS," said Lara, "were the priests of Nazism, then…"

"Yes," he replied, "then they would be the ones to minister at its altars. And that is exactly what happened. Himmler sent his SS to the concentration camps. It was his Nazi priesthood that administered and oversaw the lifting up of the burnt offerings of the Holocaust.

"The SS was the Dark Angel's inversion of God's priesthood, the priesthood of Aaron. As the sons of Aaron entered the priesthood through a sacred ceremony, so the SS entered their priesthood through occult and pagan ceremonies.

"As the Aaronic priesthood oversaw the preparation of the sacrifices of God, so the SS oversaw the preparation of the Holocaust sacrifice, the Jewish people, separating them, displacing them, and bringing them to the altars. And as the priests of Aaron were charged with keeping the fire burning in the camp of the Lord, so the SS were charged with keeping the fire burning in the camps of their Holocaust.

"But the mystery of the priesthood goes still deeper," he said. "In the Book of Exodus, it is recorded that when God brought the Israelites out of Egypt, He gave them this calling:

> And you shall be to Me a kingdom of priests and
> a holy nation.[2]

"Israel was called to be a 'kingdom of priests.' As priests are mediators, so the Jewish people were called to be God's mediators in the world, bringing God to the world and the world to God. But the Holocaust was the Enemy's attempt to annihilate them through the hands of his own priesthood. And so the Holocaust was a war of priesthoods, a satanic priesthood seeking to destroy the priesthood of God."

"To turn the priests," I said, "into the sacrifices."

"Yes," he said. "Do you know what the first sacrifice of the Holocaust was?"

"I don't know," I replied.

"Though the systematic mass killing of the Final Solution would be implemented years later, the Nazis opened their very first concentration camp in March 1933, just weeks after taking power. It was called *Dachau*. Dachau would serve as the prototype and model for all concentration camps, the first altar of the Holocaust.

"It was intended, at first, to be an internment camp in which the Nazis could imprison their political enemies. But as their foremost enemies were the Jews, Jewish people were among the first to be rounded up and sent there. One of those rounded up was a twenty-one-year-old German Jewish university student named Arthur, in the midst of preparing to go to medical school. He was arrested in Nuremberg in late March and taken to Dachau.

"In early April, he and three other prisoners of Dachau were singled out from the rest, taken outside, and shot. It was the first killing of the Holocaust. All four of the victims were Jewish. But the very first one to be killed, the very first victim of the Holocaust, was Arthur.

"Arthur's last name was Kahn. The name *Kahn* comes from ancient Hebrew. It means priest. It signifies that Arthur Kahn was a descendant of Aaron, the brother of Moses. It signifies that he was a priest. So the very first death in the Holocaust was that of one born of the ancient biblical priesthood. And strangely, another one of those first four victims was also named Kahn. And so the first sacrifice of the Holocaust, the Enemy's dark offering, was a priest of God."

"The priests of the Enemy," said Lara, "sacrificed a priest of God."

"Do you know what the first sacrifice Israel offered up as a nation was?"

"No," I replied.

"It was offered up on Passover—the Passover lamb, the beginning of all sacrifices. Heinrich Himmler sent the SS to Dachau to take charge of the first concentration camp on April 11, 1933. The day was significant. It was Passover. The next day, the dark priesthood offered up their first sacrifice, the priest of Israel. It was still Passover. So as God initiated Israel's redemption on Passover, so the Devil initiated Israel's destruction on the same day. And as it was Passover that began the sacrifices of Israel, so it was Passover that began the sacrifices of the Holocaust."

Lara and I were left speechless. I thought what he told us was the end of the mystery. It would have been more than enough. But the mystery would now go deeper still.

Chapter 38

THE HOLY PLACE

We were still standing there on the spot where we had stopped in our approach to Auschwitz's Gate of Death.

"I have a question," said Lara. "The page from the book reads, 'The Perpetual Fire, Burning in the Holy Place.' If the perpetual fire is that which burned in the concentration camp, how could it be called the 'Holy Place'?"

"First," said the man, "keep in mind the source. The words are being written from those who side with the Altar, with the Enemy, and against God. Everything is reversed; the holy is unholy, and the unholy is holy.

"Second, those who worshipped at the Altar of Pergamon in ancient times would have viewed the Altar as a holy object. And the place in which it rested they would have seen as a sacred chamber, a sanctuary, a holy place.

"And yet there is more to the mystery," he said. "In the Bible, the burnt offering could not be offered up in any place but only in the place specifically ordained. In the Book of Leviticus, it is written of the priest's offerings:

> And he shall slay the lamb in the place where he shall kill the sin offering and *the burnt offering, in the holy place*...[1]

"'The burnt offering, in the holy place,'" he repeated. "The Hebrew word used to describe the appointed place is *kodesh*. It means consecrated, hallowed, holy, and sanctified. It refers to the sanctuary of God. The burnt offering could only be sacrificed in the place that was consecrated, holy, and sanctified—kodesh—to God.

"When the Israelites journeyed through the desert, the kodesh, or holy place, was the Tent of Meeting, or Tabernacle, and there the burnt offerings were sacrificed. When they came to Jerusalem, the kodesh, or holy place, was the Temple. And there in the Temple sanctuary, the offering was slain and then placed on the Altar of sacrifice, where it would be consumed to ascend in smoke into the sky. In the days of Israel's departure from God, it was recorded that the people defiled and abandoned the Temple of God, and had not

> ...offered burnt offerings in the holy place.[2]

"The burnt offering is again joined to the holy place. It comes down to two Hebrew words: olah, for the burnt offering, and kodesh, for hallowed, consecrated, the place of the holy."

"And why is that significant?" I asked.

"Olah and kodesh," he said again. "What would happen if we translated those two words into other languages?"

"What do you mean?" I asked.

"What if we translated them into the language of those who possessed the Altar of Pergamon? What would we get?"

"I still don't get what you mean."

"Starting with the first word, in the language of the first possessors of the Altar, what would that be?"

"The word *olah,*" said Lara, "in Greek?"

"Yes."

"Olah," I said, "in Greek...is holocaust."

"And the second word, *kodesh,* the 'holy' or 'holy place,' what if it was translated into the language of those who took possession of the Altar...?"

"Into German?" said Lara.

"Yes, and into the language of the land in which they carried out their dark sacrifice...Here."

"Poland?" I said.

"Yes, what would happen if you translated the word *kodesh*, or holy, into a word that is both German and Polish?"

"I wouldn't have any idea," I said.

"Then I'll tell you," he said. "The word *kodesh,* which describes the consecrated and sanctified place where the burnt offering must be offered up, in one German-Polish word..."

He paused for a moment, looking at us, not sure if we were ready. And then he said it.

"*Auschwitz.*"

We were both stunned and, for a moment, speechless.

"*Auschwitz!*" I repeated. "*Auschwitz*...the holy place?"

"Auschwitz," he said, "is the name of the city in which the Nazis' most infamous concentration camp stood. Auschwitz is the German version of the city's Polish name, Oświęcim. *Oświęcim* comes from the Slavic word *oświęcić*. *Oświęcić* means to consecrate, to hallow, to sanctify, to make holy. It is a Slavic equivalent of the Hebrew word *kodesh*.

"So according to the ancient ordinance, the burnt offering must be offered up in the place marked by the word *holy*, *consecrated*, and *sanctified*. And so the Jewish people were offered up...in Auschwitz, the place named *Holy*."

"It's too much," I said.

"And the Scripture," he said, "*Olah b'Kodesh*, the Burnt Offering in the Holy. In the language of the Altar's two possessors, it translates to 'the *Holocaust in Auschwitz*.'"

"It's..." I couldn't finish my words.

"And so," he said, "as the perpetual fire burned in the Holy Place, so the perpetual fire burned in Auschwitz. And as the sacrifices ascended from the Altar in the Holy Place of God's sanctuary, so the Devil's sacrifices ascended from the altar of Auschwitz."

"It was all a satanic inversion," said Lara.

"Yes, just as was the revealing of the Altar of Pergamon on Yom Kippur, the holiest of days, a satanic inversion. And do you know what was offered on Yom Kippur, that most holy day of the Hebrew year?"

"What?" I said.

"The Burnt Offering in the Place of the Holy."

"*The Holocaust*," I said, "*in Auschwitz*."

He paused before speaking again. He felt we needed time to digest what had been revealed to us. And we did. When we were ready, he began opening his last mystery.

Chapter 39
THE FINAL SACRIFICE

"THE HIGH PRIEST Ministering, the Final Sacrifice Offered," said Lara. "What does it mean?"

"The one who presides over the dark priesthood," said the man, "is the high priest. The one who presided over the Nazi priesthood, the SS, in their execution of the Holocaust was Heinrich Himmler. But above Himmler was Hitler. The ultimate high priest of the Holocaust was Hitler. It was he who was most especially joined to the Altar. It was he who initiated the Holocaust, who prepared the sacrifice, who separated the Jewish people, who scapegoated them and led them to the Altar. Hitler was the high priest who oversaw and officiated over the Holocaust. And what would be left at the end of the high priest's ministering, after the offering of the burnt sacrifice?"

"Ashes?" said Lara.

"Yes, ashes," said the man. "And what was left at the end of Hitler's ministry? Ashes. Everything was in ashes—Berlin, Germany, Europe, and beyond…and, of course, the countless ashes of the Holocaust."

"And what was the Final Sacrifice?" asked Lara.

"The final sacrifice was Hitler himself. As the Devil destroys his own, and his Altar consumes those who serve it, so Hitler had to offer himself as the final sacrifice."

"When he killed himself in the bunker," said Lara.

"Yes, but it was more than that. He served the Altar of *holocausts*, of *burnt offerings*. So he would be required to offer himself as a *burnt offering*. So he ordered that after he killed himself, his body was to be set on fire and burned. And so it was."

"But he wouldn't have done that," said Lara, "for the purpose of becoming a burnt offering."

"No, of course not," said the man. "He did it because he didn't want his body to come into the hands of his enemies. Nevertheless, the ancient mystery was fulfilled. As the high priest of the Enemy's Altar, Hitler had to become himself a burnt offering.

"Think about it: When Hitler stood on top of his most exalted platform, his colossal podium at Nuremberg, it was based on the ancient Altar of burnt offerings. So he was standing, as it were, on top of an altar of burnt offerings—it was a sign of his destiny...to become one of them.

"I told you of the Scripture that was appointed to be read on the Sabbath before Hitler's death—that the blasphemer and murderer would have to be put to death. But it said more than that. It said, 'So it shall be done to him.'[1] It's the law of reciprocity. You reap what you sow. And more specifically, whatever you do to the children of Israel, the Jewish people, will in specificity be done to you. Hitler had taken the lives of millions of Jewish people. So it was fated that he would take his own life. He had consigned millions of Jewish people to the fire of the crematoriums. So it was his destiny that he himself would be consigned to the fire."

"In other words," I said, "he had caused the Jewish people to become an offering of fire, a holocaust, so now *he himself would become a holocaust.*"

"Yes," said the man. "And that passage of Scripture that was appointed for the last Sabbath just before Hitler's death contained the words 'offering by fire' and 'burnt offering' no less than twelve times.[2] And what appeared in the Greek version of that appointed Scripture was the word *holocaust.*"

"We were told," said Lara, "that after Hitler's death, the Altar passed into the hands of another. Can you tell us who?"

"It is not for me to tell you that. But I can tell you this—according to the mystery, the Altar would pass into the hands of another just after it passed out of the hands of Adolf Hitler. By a twist of fate, the Altar would come into the hands of its new possessor *on the very next day...the day after Hitler became a holocaust.*"

Had the journey ended right then and there, I could have spent the rest of my life pondering what had been revealed to us. I had no idea another mystery—an entirely different mystery but just as colossal, just as calamitous, and just as world-changing as what had been shown to us up to that moment—was about to begin.

PART VIII

CONTAGION

Chapter 40

THE BLACK GATE

LARA AND I stood there in silence at the Gate of Death, the man allowing us more time to take in what we had been shown. Then he handed me a paper, the next page of the book.

"This will be the beginning of an entirely other realm of the mystery. I wish you success in your mission."

Those last words he said without moving, signaling us that it was time to go, but he would not be going.

"You're not coming?" I said.

"I've already taken much of your time," he said. "And you haven't even gotten to your hotel yet."

We tried to convince him to go with us, but he politely refused. Reluctantly, we left him there and began heading back to the area where we could find a taxi. While we were still close enough to hear his voice, he said, "Take care of yourselves."

We caught a taxi and headed to our hotel. The ride was short and yet long enough to allow us to glimpse the page we had just received. But we were so overwhelmed by what had been revealed that we didn't even think of looking, or feel that we could. Normally—if anything on our journey could be called normal—we would wait until we knew what our next destination was before checking out of our hotel. But in this case, we felt it best to leave the city of Auschwitz the following morning and head back to Berlin the same way we came, by train.

We were both exhausted and, on the first part of the journey back, napped on the train. Upon waking, I asked Lara if I could see the page. She took it out. The image was something of a circle, but with spikes radiating out of it all around.

"I don't know," I said. "It looks like a sun or star."

"I don't believe it is," said Lara.

"You did the translation?"

"Yes…and I had a dream."

"Tell me."

"The title of the page was made up of more than one Greek word. I translated it as 'Contagion.' And this is the text:

The Crimson Seed
On Ancient Soil
Sown
The Child of Sages
Turning
Speaking Words
Of Fallen Angels
The Fire Passed
The Embers Dying
The Rising Throne
Empowering
The Sword
Is Given
To Strike
The World."

"And do you have any idea what it means?" I asked.

"No. Do you?"

"No. Tell me the dream."

"I was walking through a Roman city, an ancient Roman city. It was in a valley, surrounded by low hills and next to a river. I came to a company of Roman soldiers. They were standing around a strange-looking stone building. It was several stories high with what appeared to be two stone towers built into it, along with a multitude of stone windows or openings, and, at its base, two stone archways.

"'What is this place?' I asked one of the soldiers.

"'This is the dark portal,' he said, 'the gateway of darkness.'

"'And what are you doing here?'

"'Guarding against that which would come through it.'

"And that was it."

"Why don't we do a search," I said, "for the place you saw in your dream? I would start with 'dark portal' and see what we get."

She took out her laptop, and we began searching "dark portal," then "dark gateway," then "dark entrance," and then "dark gate." We found that there was no shortage of such words in fantasy stories and video games. And then it hit me.

"They were Roman soldiers," I said. "Roman soldiers speak Latin. Let's do the search in Latin."

So I asked Lara to type in two Latin words: *porta,* for portal or gate, and *nigro,* for dark or black. That's when we found it.

"This is it!" said Lara. "That's what I saw in my dream. It's called the *Porta Nigra*, the Black Gate. It was a Roman structure, built in an ancient Roman city called Augusta Treverorum. Later, the city became known as Trier. Trier is known as the oldest city in Germany. It's surrounded by low-lying hills and sits next to the River Moselle. The Porta Nigra, the Black Gate, is still standing and is one of Trier's main landmarks."

"Well," I said, "we know our next destination."

For most of the remainder of the ride back to Berlin, we were still pondering and reeling from what had been shown to us. We spent the night in Berlin and the next day set out for Trier.

Though Trier is in Germany, getting there from Berlin involves a long journey. We decided it would be best to go by train. There were no direct routes, so we went first to the city of Cologne and from there to our destination. We arrived in Trier at night.

The next day, we met at the hotel restaurant for a late breakfast. We came dressed for the day, planning to go from there to the Black Gate. Just as we were about to leave, I realized I had left my cell phone in my hotel room.

I headed back to the room. The door was open. The cleaning crew was inside. They shouldn't have been since I had left a Do Not Disturb sign on the doorknob. I asked them why they were there, but they signaled that they didn't speak English. I ushered them out. It was then that I noticed the drawers of my night table and my dresser had been opened, as if someone had been searching for something.

I headed back to the restaurant and then with Lara to the front desk. We had to make sure that our rooms would be secure. We told the receptionist what had happened. He apologized.

"Is it customary for the cleaning crew to go through the drawers of the dressers and night tables?" I asked.

"We do have to make sure nothing's left there," he said.

"Before we check out?"

"No. That should not have happened."

I then described for him the two cleaners who had come into my room, a man who appeared to be in his forties and a woman in her thirties.

He looked troubled.

"We don't have any men in our cleaning crew."

I rushed back to my room and went up and down the hallway, but they were gone. How they knew we were at that hotel and that I was in that room, how they managed to be there and get in, we couldn't answer. It was an unwanted sign of the power and reach of what we were dealing with and what was working against us.

I called Kazim and told him what happened.

"Find another hotel, and until you're out of that one, don't say anything in your room you wouldn't want others to hear, in case you're being monitored."

So we did. By the time we settled into the new hotel, it was afternoon.

The Black Gate stood in the middle of the city as part of Trier's ancient Roman center. When you first see it from a distance, it appears almost shadowlike, a strange ancient edifice, darker than the buildings around it and seemingly out of place, more like a fortress than a gateway. As Lara and I approached it, we couldn't help but be impressed by its massive scale, as it dwarfed nearly everything around it.

We stood there at the gate for several minutes waiting for someone or something—a next step, a lead, a clue that would give meaning to our journey there. And then it happened. He came as a tourist. He approached the site as if for the first time, taking pictures of the ancient gate from virtually every angle. I would guess he was in his mid-forties—black hair, high cheekbones, and piercing green eyes.

"Quite a site," he said to us. "Almost two thousand years old! The Romans knew how to build to last. But its upkeep has been questionable. It wasn't always like this. Do you know why it's called the *Porta Nigra*, the Black Gate? Because of the elements—the smoke, the pollution, and the weathering—they've all darkened it. It used to be much lighter. And yet the name fits. It *is* a dark gate. All of Trier is a dark gate…a gate of darkness. For it was here in Trier that a great darkness entered the world."

"He sounds like the Roman soldiers in my dream," said Lara in a whisper.

"Come," he said, "and I'll show you the darkness that entered through."

I looked at Lara. She nodded to me as if to say she believed we could trust him. The man led us down one of Trier's main pedestrian streets, passing shops, cafés, and varied historic buildings.

"Your accent," I said, "is it French?"

"It is," he said. "You know, Trier is very close to France."

The streets began to narrow into one of the city's quiet residential sections. The buildings here seemed older.

"There," he said, pointing to a pale and modest house sandwiched between two buildings. For a small structure, it had no shortage of windows. I counted twelve on its facade facing the street.

"This is a most significant house," he said. "This is the house in which was born the man who ushered in the darkness."

"Who?" I asked.

"This is the house of Karl Marx."

"It all began in Germany," I said.

"Yes," said the man, "the same land from which came the world's greatest evils, the First World War, the Second World War, the rise of Adolf Hitler and Nazism, the Holocaust, and the death of millions. So too the mystery ordained that communism and the darkness that would fall on millions would come from this land."

"It all began here by the Black Gate," said the man. "And in its birth, one can find the fingerprints of the Dark Angel…even his words."

Chapter 41

THE SATANIC VERSES

"The Crimson Seed," said Lara, "on Ancient Soil Sown. Crimson, or red, is the color of Marxism...and the ancient soil is Trier, Germany's most ancient city."

"Yes," said the man. "And just three years before Marx's birth, Trier became part of the Kingdom of Prussia, the same kingdom that was critical in bringing Germany into existence."

"The Child of Sages Turning," said Lara, "what is that about?"

"Marx," said the man, "was born of a long line of rabbis, of sages. When Trier was incorporated into Prussia, his father, an attorney, had to convert to Protestantism in order to continue practicing law."

"So then was Marx brought up in the Christian faith?" I asked.

"Yes."

"Did he believe?" asked Lara.

"His own words," said the man, "would testify that he did. When Marx was seventeen years old, just days before graduating from the Trier Gymnasium, he wrote an essay called 'The Union of Believers with Christ According to John 15:1–14.' His words are permeated with what appears to be sincerity, thoughtfulness, and reverence. He wrote:

> The history of peoples and a consideration of individuals prove the necessity of union with Christ....Our hearts, reason, history, the word of Christ, therefore, tell us loudly and convincingly that union with Him is absolutely essential...that only He can redeem us...this love for Christ...causes us to keep His commandments by sacrificing ourselves for one another...who could fail to be uplifted and comforted by this assurance which the Savior Himself proclaims?"[1]

"Wow," I said, "Karl Marx said all that? So what happened?"

"Marx wrote those words in 1835. By the very next year, 1836, a change had begun. It was that year that Marx moved to Berlin, the city destined to house the Throne of Satan.

"That's where a metamorphosis took place. It was there that Marx attended university and there that he encountered the teachings of the German philosopher Georg Hegel. Hegel viewed history as a series of conflicts by which society evolved. Marx became an adherent of Hegel's theories and in 1837 joined the Young Hegelians. The Young Hegelians were particularly hostile to God, the Bible, and Christianity. The association completely transformed him. By the end of his time in Berlin, Marx had become radicalized, an atheist, and a hater of God."

"So the Karl Marx we all know," I said, "came into existence in Berlin."

"And something else happened during Marx's time in Berlin, at the start of his time of transformation, something strange. He began writing strange words, dark poems and stories, dark mystical verses, as if someone else was speaking through him. While Marx was in Berlin, he wrote these words:

> So a god has snatched me from my all...
> Nothing but revenge is left to me...
> I shall build my throne high overhead,
> Cold, tremendous shall its summit be."[2]

"Sounds like something the Devil would say," said Lara.

"Rather," said the man, "like something he already said. In Isaiah's prophecy, the Dark Angel declares,

> I will exalt my throne above the stars of God.[3]

"Compare that to the words of Karl Marx:

> I shall build my throne high overhead."[4]

"The Words of Fallen Angels," said Lara, "as in the text."

"He speaks of lifting up his throne," I said, "on a *summit*...a summit as on the high place of Pergamon. And he wrote those words in Berlin, the same city in which the Throne of Satan would be lifted up."

"And who," said the man, "would write of taking revenge against 'that being, that enthroned Lord'?"[5]

"A fallen angel," said Lara.

"And why does that fallen angel exist?" asked the man.

"To nullify existence," said Lara, "to destroy what is."

"Yes. Now listen to the verses that came from the pen of Karl Marx:

> ...though I bring the world to ruins—
> The world which bulks between me and the abyss

I will smash to pieces with my
enduring curses....
The world will dumbly pass away,
And then sink down to utter nothingness,
Perished, with no existence."[6]

"Doesn't sound like the words of a man," said Lara, "but of a spirit."

"Or the words of a spirit speaking through a man. And through the words of Karl Marx, death and destruction would come to millions...the goal of the Dark Angel. So Marx would write of wandering a ruined world in triumph:

Like unto a God I dare
Through that ruined realm in triumph roam.
Every word is Deed and Fire,
And my bosom like the Maker's own.[7]

"Or," said the man, "as in the words of Lucifer,

I will be like the Most High."[8]

"He will feel equal to the Creator," I said, "by destroying the world."

"Satanic verses," said Lara.

"Now listen as he speaks of a weapon he says he was given and who he says gave it to him:

The hellish vapours rise and fill the brain
Till I go mad....
See this sword?
The prince of darkness
Sold it to me."[9]

"The Sword is Given," said Lara, "to Strike the World. So Marx writes of a sword given him by the prince of darkness, Satan. Is it possible that Marx was consciously influenced...?"

"By the Enemy?" said the man, "One historian described him as having 'the devil's view of the world and the devil's malignity' and that sometimes 'he seemed to know that he was accomplishing the works of evil.'[10] Friedrich Engels, who would become Marx's collaborator, once described him as a 'monster' who 'rages without ceasing, as if ten thousand devils had caught him by the hair.'[11]

"Marx would indeed strike the world with a sword. And how many millions would be killed by it? His glorification of destruction and his Luciferian viewpoint would become a strange feature of Marxist ideology. And throughout his life, he was known for quoting the words of the demon Mephistopheles in the story of Faust."

"So Marx's inspiration came from a demon?" I asked. "What words?"

"'*Everything that exists deserves to perish.*'"[12]

"And yet," said the man, "we would not be speaking of Karl Marx today if it weren't for a twist of events that would transform a nearly forgotten movement into a global phenomenon, which would then shake the world. And as it was with the rise of Hitler, so with the rise of Marxism and communism—behind it all was an ancient altar and the Throne of Satan."

Chapter 42

DARK REBIRTH

THE MAN LED us away from the house and back in the direction of the Porta Nigra, but now to a different destination.

"Less than seven years after his days as a student in Berlin, Marx was commissioned by a small organization of German workers and intellectuals to write a pamphlet that would outline their tenets and goals. The organization was called the Communist League, and the pamphlet would be called the *Manifesto of the Communist Party*. It was at the time the *Manifesto* was released at the start of 1848 that revolutions seeking the overthrow of the ruling governments broke out across Europe. Marx sought to fan the flames of the revolution by founding a newspaper to advocate for radical change. But the revolutions were crushed, and Marx was exiled from Germany and moved to London.

"In London, he lived in obscurity. He had no leadership position, no organization, no movement, and no real followers. A few years after Marx moved to London, the Communist League dissolved. He became isolated and almost entirely disconnected, even from other socialist circles. His political and philosophical writings went largely unread. He lived in poverty, writing for the *New York Tribune* in order to survive and known more as a journalist than a political theorist. Even his partner, Engels, would describe him in this period as living in almost complete isolation and unknown to the public."

"Is that what the words meant," said Lara, "the Fire Passed, the Embers Dying? The fire and embers of the movement?"

"Yes," said the man. "The revolution had failed, and Marx had withdrawn. He was a marginal figure of a marginal movement and on the verge of being completely forgotten. Had the story ended there, the world would never have known the name of Karl Marx. He would have been nothing more than an obscure footnote in the assigned reading texts given to students of German political theory... But then came the Altar..."

"What do you mean?" I asked.

It was just then that we came to a pedestrian square. In the middle of the square was a massive statue, bronze, imposing, about twenty feet high. It was him: Karl Marx.

"The statue," said the man, "was given to the city of Trier by those representing a totalitarian state of over one billion people to honor their patron saint. You see, something happened that would transform this strange, isolated, impoverished, marginal, and mostly forgotten man into the leader of a movement that would alter the history of the world. It happened in my land. It was called the Paris Commune."

"The Paris Commune," I repeated. "What was it?"

"It was a revolutionary government," he said, "that for a brief time ruled much of Paris in the nineteenth century. It began as an uprising against the ruling government. It consisted of socialists, anarchists, workers' activists, and others opposed to the French government. It is considered the first radical, working-class government in modern history. It lasted less than seventy-five days before it was crushed. But it would change the world."

"How so?" I asked.

"It revived revolutionary socialism, which had for decades stagnated. It electrified radicals across Europe, radicalized workers, and aroused new interest in communism and Marxism, relaunching both movements.

"And even though he had no part in it, Marx would claim it as his own and as a vindication of his ideology that it was possible for workers, or the proletariat, to overthrow governments. He would call the Paris Commune 'the most glorious deed of our Party'[1] and a 'new point of departure of world-historic importance.'[2]

"Suddenly, Marx became the central voice of socialism and revolution. Before the Paris Commune, Marxism was a minority stream even within socialism, but after, it would become its dominant ideology. The Paris Commune made it appear as if Marx's theories could actually be translated into reality.

"Marx would use the Paris Commune to advance his agenda, penning a booklet titled *The Civil War in France*. It would be widely read, see multiple printings, and sell out upon its release. In it, Marx would revise, alter, intensify, and radicalize his ideology. Marx would now declare that the revolution could not work through the existing state. The revolutionaries would have to bring the state to destruction.

"In *The Civil War in France,* Marx would frame the Paris Commune as a model to be used for socialist revolution. In the twentieth century, the booklet would be read and studied by Marxist revolutionaries around the world. It would serve as a guide for what to do and not do to successfully bring about socialist revolution. As a result, millions and millions would come under the rule of communism."

"All that," I said, "from a pamphlet."

"The Paris Commune was the event that changed the trajectory of Marx's life, of Marxism, of communism, of social revolution, and of world history. After the commune and Marx's writings concerning it, socialist parties began forming and proliferating across Europe. Marxism was transformed from a theoretical proposition pondered by a small group of intellectuals into a global movement. It would alter the course of nations, bring much of the world under totalitarian dictatorships, and lead millions of others to their graves."

"And all that from a failed uprising," I said.

"Failure depends on one's goal," he said. "If there was a different goal, then it didn't necessarily fail."

"What different goal?" I asked.

"That goal of the Enemy. The uprising accomplished exactly what it was meant to accomplish. Do you know what triggered the Paris Commune?"

"No," I replied.

"Germany," he said.

"Again, Germany," I replied.

"It happened because of the German war against France."

"The Franco-Prussian War," I said.

"It was Germany's shattering of France that devastated the French government, the German siege of Paris that radicalized the Parisians, and the German terms of surrender it imposed on France that all converged to open the door to the uprising of the Paris Commune."

"And it was that same war," said Lara, "and those same terms that led to the First World War and then to the Second."

"Yes," he said, "and that same war led to the birth of Germany, and the birth of Germany to German militarism and German anti-Semitism, and German militarism to the Second World War, and German anti-Semitism to the Holocaust. And all these began when the Throne of Satan returned to the world.

"The Paris uprising that would resurrect a forgotten movement erupted in the year of the Altar's return to the world. And the pamphlet that Marx wrote concerning it that would guide mass revolutions and bring millions under the darkness of totalitarianism, that too was written in the year of Satan's Throne, the Devil's year."

"It's amazing," I said, "the greatest of evils to come upon the world, evils as different as Nazism and communism, and yet all going back to the same thing."

"And back to the same land," he said. "And it was in that land that another resurrection would take place...that of a sword given to strike the world."

Chapter 43
MANIFESTO

"NOTICE," SAID THE man, pointing to the statue, "what Marx is holding."

The statue's right hand was raised to his chest, but his left hand was holding a book.

"A book," I said. "Which book?"

"The creator of the statue wouldn't say. He kept it open. Marx's power was in his writings. It was his books that would alter world history, the first being the *Manifesto.* Do you have any idea how many people read the *Manifesto* before 1871, the year of the Altar's return?"

"No," I replied.

"It was published in February 1848. The number of copies printed has been estimated at eight hundred."

"Eight hundred?" I replied. "That's nothing."

"It was printed in German and aimed primarily at German émigré workers. Other printings had similarly minuscule numbers. In all the years leading up to 1871, only a few thousand people had read it, primarily German political exiles, members of the Communist League that would soon disband, and a handful of radical intellectuals. Even Marx and Engels rarely mentioned it. By 1871, it was a largely forgotten pamphlet that appeared to be consigned to oblivion. But in the year of Satan's Throne, everything changed. The return of the Altar brought with it the return of the *Manifesto.*"

"How?" asked Lara.

"With the Paris Commune, interest in socialism and Marxism exploded. Marx's writings on the revolt, *The Civil War in France,* made him famous. Suddenly, people wanted to read his earlier writings. But something else happened that would change the course of the *Manifesto,* and then the world. And it would take place in Germany, the land that was *just then* receiving the first pieces of Satan's Throne.

"It would be called the Leipzig High Treason Trial. In March of 1872, the German Empire decided to put three men on trial for high treason. They were charged with opposing the Franco-Prussian War and supporting the Paris Commune. To prove the defendants' revolutionary ideology, the prosecution decided to read from Marxist texts. They sought to show that the defendants aligned with Marx's revolutionary ideology and that their support for the Commune was part of a larger Marxist conspiracy. So they read into the record passages from the *Manifesto* Marx had written for the Communist Party.

"The trial was widely reported. It catapulted Marxism into national headlines. It made Marx's *Manifesto* politically relevant and helped shift German socialism to Marxism. Suddenly, people throughout Germany were hearing of communism, of Marx, and of the *Manifesto.* Interest in the forgotten pamphlet exploded. Up to that point, the *Manifesto* had been suppressed in Germany and, for the most part, unobtainable. But the trial changed all that. Now it was openly discussed and quoted from. The explosion of interest convinced Marx and Engels to release a new edition of the communist treatise. So what the trial sought to eradicate, it ended up resurrecting.

"The new edition of the *Manifesto*, written in German, gained a much wider readership than any previous version and would become the basis of all its future translations. By the mid-1870s, the book had become the foundational text of the socialist movement and was being read by tens of thousands of people. But it was just the beginning.

"It would end up being translated into over one hundred languages. Its print runs would now reach into the hundreds of millions and would be deemed the second most widely read book in history after the Bible. It would ignite uprisings and revolutions throughout the world. It would cause the overthrow of governments and the birth of communist regimes across the earth. It would bring into existence the most colossal totalitarian regimes in world history and place millions of lives under its dominion.

"And it all began in the land of the Altar and at the very moment that the Altar first touched that land. The *Manifesto* had come into the world in German and then, even more importantly, had been resurrected in German. It was from that resurrection that the *Manifesto* went forth to the world. It was fitting that it came forth in the tongue of the kingdom that had come to house the Throne of Satan.

"Everything was paralleling what was happening with the Altar. As Carl Humann came upon its first pieces and forged its connection to Germany, the resurrection of Marxism was set in motion through the Paris Commune and the writing of Marx's book *The Civil War in France.*

But the following year, 1872, was just as important. It was then that the Altar's first pieces arrived on German soil, and it was then that the *Manifesto* was resurrected to world-altering repercussion.

"But it wasn't just a reprint. Something had changed. Up to that moment, the book was titled *Manifest der Kommunistischen Partei,* or *Manifesto of the Communist Party.* But when it was resurrected in 1872, its name was changed. For the first time, it would be called *Das Kommunistische Manifest,* or *The Communist Manifesto.* From then on, that would be its name, and by that name, it would alter the world. And so it was in the Devil's year, just as the first pieces of the Altar arrived on German soil, that *The Communist Manifesto* was officially born and, in German, entered the history of the world."

He led us back to the place where he first appeared and there handed us the next page and departed. The next mystery would take us on a journey to a very different land—but one likewise joined to the Altar and one that would likewise shake the earth.

PART IX

REVOLUTION

Chapter 44
THE ANGEL IN THE SQUARE

On the way back to the hotel, we looked at the image on the page.

"It's almost the same," I said, "as that on the first page—except it's upside down."

It was a stylized depiction of a castle or palace, but upside down.

"On the first page," said Lara, "it stood for a kingdom, a nation, the birth of Germany. So I would think that this would represent an upside-down kingdom or nation. The birth of an upside-down kingdom?"

"Let's see what you get."

The next morning, Lara was late for our breakfast meeting. She arrived, out of breath, with her notepad.

"Sorry I'm late," she said. "I was working on it."

"The translation."

"That too."

"What else?"

"The dream."

"Tell me."

"First, the words on the page, they translate to this:

The Eastern Wind
With Crimson Seed
To Foreign Soil
Of Youth Inflamed
Child of the Unearthing
The Contagion Sent
A Journey Sealed
The Kingdom Come
A House
Of Revolution."

"And what is it titled?" I asked.

"The Greek word is 'Kinesis.' It can mean movement or change.

But it's also used to mean revolution. I believe that's what it means here—Revolution."

"That would go," I said. "Revolution would follow Marxism."

"And it goes with the dream."

"Tell me..."

"I was standing in the midst of a gigantic open square. In front of me was a massive building, ornate, a kind of Baroque palace. Its facade was white and pale green, and it was filled with a multitude of columns and statues stationed on its roof like sentinels. Then I heard the noise of a multitude. The noise grew louder and louder as if they were drawing closer to the building. And then I found myself engulfed by the multitude. They were angry, and they were pressing forward. They appeared to be from the past, from a century ago or more. They stormed the massive palace.

"Then I was led to look up. Above the crowd was a glowing angel. He was standing on top of a tall column overlooking the people and holding or supporting a large cross, the cross being much taller than his body. The people didn't seem to have any idea he was there, standing over them as they rushed the building. And that was it."

"And what did it mean?" I asked.

"I went online to search for angels holding crosses, angels on columns, and buildings of white and green. And then I found it...an angel holding a cross much larger than its body, on top of a tall column, in the middle of an immense square, overlooking a massive green-and-white palace. The angel is a statue on top of what is known as the Alexander Column."

"Where?"

"In Russia. In St. Petersburg. The building I saw was the Winter Palace, the place from which the tsars ruled the Russian Empire."

"And the multitude," I said, "was storming the palace as part of a revolution."

"Yes."

"So we're going to Russia."

"We're going to Russia."

The journey to Russia would require visas, which neither of us had. Even with an expedited process and the help of the museum, it took us over a week to get them, during which time we stayed at our hotel in Trier. Once we obtained them, we headed by train to Frankfurt. Lara had napped for much of the way but woke up at one of the stops. As people began boarding, she turned to me.

"Did you see what just happened?" she said in a hushed voice.

"No. What?"

"The man who just came on. When he boarded the train, he signaled to the man sitting in front of us, then just kept on walking to the back of the car. As he passed us, I turned around and saw him signal to another man who was sitting behind us, and he signaled back."

"Maybe they're friends."

"And they just happen to be sitting separately in our car, signaling to each other without saying a word?"

"They can't be everywhere, Lara."

"No?"

Needless to say, there would be no more napping for the remainder of the ride.

From Frankfurt, we flew to St. Petersburg. We landed at Pulkovo Airport and from there took a taxi to our hotel. The feel of the city was distinctly different from that of Western Europe. We were in Russia. The atmosphere was subdued, somber, and as if everyone and everything there were complicit in keeping some long-hidden secret. We passed by the low, austere, gray apartment buildings from the Soviet era and then passed rivers and bridges. As we drew nearer to the city center, the architecture changed. The buildings became more ornate—some with columns, many with intricately sculptured facades—and more colorful, with pale greens, yellows, light blues, and whites.

We arrived at our hotel, checked into our rooms, and retired early, exhausted from our travel. The next day, we headed out to the Winter Palace. The streets that took us there were relatively narrow and lined with the classical facades of old and ornate buildings. Suddenly, everything opened up into a vast, symmetrical expanse. It was the Palace Square.

"This is what I saw," said Lara. "This is the open square."

The square was so immense that it didn't seem to matter how many people would try to fill it; it would still look vast and spacious, and they would appear dwarfed by it. There, in the distance, was the ornate green-and-white, massive Baroque complex that housed the Russian tsars, the Winter Palace.

"And there it is," said Lara, "the angel."

The angel was standing in the midst of the square on top of a massive red granite column that had to be at least a hundred and fifty feet high, with a giant cross in his arms. There were people walking through the square, separated by its vast expanse. We approached the column, close enough to view its details but far enough to still see the angel on its pinnacle.

"So that's the angel you saw?" I said.

"Yes, except it was alive and glowing white."

I didn't notice her standing there when we approached the column, but she was there now, to our right, and likewise gazing up at the angel. She was an older woman, thin and elegantly dressed in a dark purple scarf and a long dark burgundy coat. Had it been an earlier time, I would have taken her to be a member of the Russian aristocracy.

"Do you see that at the angel's feet?" she said in a Russian accent. "It's a serpent. That's the meaning of the sculpture. Do you see what the angel is doing? He's crushing it, the power of the serpent, by the power of the cross. The serpent is a representation of the Devil. It's about the crushing of Satan's power."

It was that last sentence that especially caught our attention. Lara and I glanced at each other.

"Do you know who we are?" I asked.

"Of course. Would I be here if I didn't? You are Mr. Herzog, and you are Lara Winter. My name is Svetlana."

"Do you have something to show us?" I asked.

"I do."

She led us toward the Winter Palace, then stopped.

"This building is older than your nation," she said. "It has over a thousand rooms, almost two thousand doors, and just as many windows. Here the tsars ruled the largest nation in the world, one-sixth of the earth's land mass, too big a prize to be resisted. So he came to make it his own."

"Who?" I asked.

"Him," she replied. "He who takes possession of that which is not his, the possessor, the thief. And it was here that he took possession of it."

It would now be revealed to us how the Throne of Satan transformed the largest nation in the world into a satanic kingdom.

Chapter 45
THE EASTERN WIND

"Now let us speak of what happened here," she said. "According to Marx's theory, it would be the highly industrialized societies of the capitalist world that would give birth to communist revolution. It would be carried out by the proletariat, or working class, as it sought to rid itself of capitalism. None of that happened. In the places where communist revolution was supposed to arise, it didn't. And where it was not supposed to arise, it did.

"Russia was not a highly industrialized capitalist society, but rather agrarian and economically underdeveloped, with a small industrial working class and an enormous peasant population. According to Marxist theory, the revolution should not have happened here."

"In other words," I said, "the Marxist revolution in Russia disproved Marxism."

"You could say that."

"The Eastern Wind," said Lara, "with Crimson Seed to Foreign Soil. To the east of where the Altar is would be the east of Germany, as in Russia. So the crimson seed, the gospel of Marxism, would be carried to the land of the east, Russia."

"Marx's two most famous works," said the woman, "were *The Communist Manifesto* and *Das Kapital*. While *The Communist Manifesto* is considered the introduction to Marxism, *Das Kapital* is considered its bible, its foundational and fundamental text.

"When *Das Kapital* was published, it was largely ignored. Marx would complain that it was a bourgeois 'conspiracy of silence.'[1] But a few years after its first publication, its first translation was made."

"Into...?" asked Lara.

"Russian," said the woman. "And it wasn't only a Russian translation; it was a Russian publication produced by a Russian publisher inside Russia."

"And what happened?" I asked.

"In Russia, *Das Kapital* became a bestseller. The Russian print run was several times larger than the original German print run, and while it took years for the original German version to sell out, the Russian translation sold out in just weeks.

"The impact of *Das Kapital* in Russia was pivotal in helping produce a generation of radicals who would bring communism to this land. One of them, Georgi Plekhanov, would found the first Marxist organization in Russia in 1883."

"During the years of the Altar's unearthing," I said.

"Yes," said the woman, "it all happened with the return of the Altar. And it all began at the beginning of the Altar's return. *Das Kapital* first appeared in Russia in 1872, the same time that the first two pieces of the ancient Altar arrived in Europe.

"It was a milestone. The Russian version of *Das Kapital* not only represented the first translation of the Marxist bible into any language but was the very first Marxist writing ever to be published in Russia. It would start a process that would ultimately transform the world's largest nation into the first communist totalitarian state.

"As the first pieces of the Altar arrived on German soil, the first writings of the German contagion, in the form of *Das Kapital*, would take root on Russian soil."

"But there was another player in Russia's dark metamorphosis," she said, "without which it would never have happened, certainly not as it did. And yet he, like many others, was an unwitting pawn in the ancient game."

Chapter 46

THE REVOLUTIONARY

Vladimir Ilyich Ulyanov was born to a Russian family in Simbirsk, Russia, hundreds of miles east of Moscow. He would become known as Lenin. He came into the world at a most critical time concerning the mystery. He was born at the time of the Franco-Prussian War."

"The war," I said, "that would lead to the birth of Germany."

"And the Paris Commune," said Lara, "and the reviving of Marxism, and the First World War."

"And now," said the woman, "with the birth of Lenin, it would be connected to another evil. And yet one would never have suspected that a child of such origins would become the chief catalyst and agent of so great an evil.

"He was raised in a prosperous, upper-middle-class family with connections to the Russian nobility. His father was an official in the tsar's imperial government. But in the midst of Lenin's teenage years, a series of twists and turns would transform him into the radical figure the world would come to know.

"1886 marked the completion of the Altar's unearthing and transference to Germany. That same year, 'Pergamon Fever,' a surge of fascination with the ancient Altar, took hold of the German public. And that same year, 1886, a series of turning points in Lenin's life and a dark transformation began.

"In January of 1886, when Lenin was fifteen years old, his father suffered a cerebral hemorrhage. The hemorrhage was fatal. The event removed a major stabilizing influence from Lenin's life. He became withdrawn and increasingly skeptical and defiant of authority, from the authority of the tsar to that of the church. He would grow progressively more rigid and intolerant in his beliefs and more combative in promoting them. It would also open the door for his radicalization, his embrace of extreme doctrines, and his subsequent renouncing of faith in God.

"In the year that completed the Altar's transference to the West, a dramatic change took place in Lenin's older brother, Alexander Ulyanov. He joined a socialist revolutionary party and terrorist organization and in March of 1887 was arrested for his involvement in a plot to assassinate the tsar. In May, he was executed. His execution has been cited as a central catalyst in driving Lenin into revolutionary politics. His radicalization was now fully underway.

"In 1889, for the first time since ancient times, the Altar was pieced together in Germany. That same year, the pieces of a different mystery began coming together—Marx and Lenin. It was in 1889 that Lenin came upon the writings of Marx, initiating the beginning of his conversion to Marxism, a convergence that would alter the history of the world."

"And it was the same year," I said, "that Adolf Hitler came into the world."

"Yes," said the woman, "as the Throne of Satan was reconstructed, the two evils were born, each one to lead to the coming of a satanic kingdom."

"And there would be another one born," she said, "who would rule over the satanic kingdom of Marx and Lenin and bring it to its dark apogee."

Chapter 47

CHILD OF THE UNEARTHING

THE WOMAN LED us through a small archway to the side of the Winter Palace and through a narrow passageway that opened up to a view of the Neva River.

"This is why the tsars came here," she said, "because of this river. It opened Russia to the West. And it played a part in the Marxist overthrow of the Russian government.

"But it was far away from here, in the land of Georgia, that a peasant girl named Ekaterine was born. She grew up in deep poverty and worked as a domestic servant and laundress. She married a shoemaker named Besarion. She would give birth to two sons, both of whom died in infancy, before giving birth to her third and only surviving child, a son, to whom she became especially devoted."

"Sounds like the story of Adolf Hitler," I said, "a child born to a poor servant girl after the deaths of her first children—the first of her children to survive past infancy."

"It does," she said. "His mother dreamed that he would become a priest. He was named Ioseb Jughashvili. He would become known to the world as Joseph Stalin. As with Hitler, his father was a brutal man who often beat him. Hitler's father died while he was still a youth. While Stalin was a child, his father abandoned him."

"The origins of monsters," I said.

"Neither of them had to be," she said. "They chose it. Ironically, it was while studying to be a priest at seminary that Stalin came across the writings of Marx and Lenin, and other radical literature."

"The Crimson Seed is carried," said Lara, quoting the text.

"It was those writings that began his transformation into a radical Marxist," she said. "He would be expelled from the seminary and would become a full-time Marxist agent, seeking to foment revolution and overthrow the tsar. As a Bolshevik revolutionary, he would organize bank robberies, kidnappings, and bombings, killing dozens of innocent people for the sake of funding the party.

"Once in power, Stalin would take the Marxist state, the satanic kingdom, to darker depths than that which even Lenin had envisioned. He would murder those who were his enemies and those who were not. He would set up forced labor camps, initiate mass executions, mass famine, the Great Purge, and the Great Terror. He would oppress millions, starve other millions, and still other millions he would brutally murder."

"And is there a connection between Stalin and the Altar?"

"The unearthing of the Altar after ages hidden in the dust began as Carl Humann dug his shovel into the ground of the Pergamon acropolis. The year was 1878.

"The child who would become the monster known as Joseph Stalin entered the world in the same year, 1878."

"The Child of the Unearthing," said Lara.

"Yes," said the woman. "The unearthing began in the latter part of 1878. Not long after the first shovel was pushed into the ancient ground, the baby Joseph Stalin was born."

"And the Scripture that was appointed for the week the unearthing began," said Lara, "the Scripture that spoke of the altar of curses—Stalin was part of the Altar's curse."

"So the two great monsters of the modern world," said the woman, "Hitler and Stalin, were each joined to the Altar. One came into the world at the beginning of its unearthing, and the other at the completion of its reassembling. Each child was joined from birth to the Throne of Satan, and each was destined to rule his kingdom."

She would now lead us to a very different site to reveal the secret story of a hidden journey and its dark contagion.

Chapter 48

THE SEALED TRAIN

SHE LED US along the Neva River's broad and granite-lined bank, the site of the tsars' imperial parades and of revolutionary gunfire, then across a low, ornate, iconic bridge of cast iron and granite called the Trinity Bridge. Finally, we came to a large open square.

There, in the midst of the square, was Lenin. He was made of bronze and standing on a black granite pedestal, his left hand raised and pointing forward as if in the middle of a speech. Altogether, he stood thirty feet off the ground.

"This is Lenin Square," she said. "And this is one of the first monuments ever made to commemorate him."

"What happened to him?" asked Lara. "The last you told us, he had just come into the writings of Karl Marx."

"He became a radical Marxist and moved here to St. Petersburg. Here he began organizing the Marxist underground, unifying its scattered study groups into a coordinated movement, shifting it from theory to political action, and working to agitate workers toward revolution. He was arrested for his activities and sent into exile in Siberia. After Siberia, he fled Russia for Western Europe, where he spent most of the next two decades in political exile. And then came the First World War.

"In 1917, Lenin was living in a small apartment in Switzerland, rarely going outside except to the public library where he would spend his time reading of past revolutions. He was now in his late forties. And it appeared as if history had passed him by."

"Sounds like Marx," said Lara. "Just when it seemed as if his works would be forgotten, everything turned."

"Yes," said the woman, "as if an unseen hand was turning events in the direction of a dark purpose. So it would again. The war caused Russia to suffer catastrophic military defeats, food shortages, bread riots, economic collapse, and mutinies. Finally, the tsar was forced to abdicate."

"But Lenin was still in Switzerland," said Lara, "so the tsar wasn't overthrown by the communists?"

"No. Lenin and the communists never overthrew the tsar. The tsar was overthrown by others. The communists never overthrew tyranny."

"Then what did they overthrow?" asked Lara.

"Democracy. They overthrew democracy. They cut off a democratic Russia at the moment of its birth."

"I don't understand," said Lara.

"That's why you were brought here," she said, "and the reason for the statue."

"Come," she said as she led us over to the building at the end of the square. It had a white rectangular facade with a large clock tower in the middle and the sterile appearance of a Soviet-era edifice.

"This," she said, "is Finland Station. It's a railroad terminal. It was this station that changed the world. Shortly after the tsar's abdication, Lenin and a group of his comrades, also living in exile, boarded a train in Switzerland that was especially prepared to take him on a fateful journey to the east. He would be transported through Germany to the Baltic Coast, to Sweden, to Finland and from Finland to here, Finland Station, St. Petersburg. When the train arrived, thousands of his supporters were waiting to greet him.

"He was escorted to an armored vehicle on top of which he stood and delivered one of the most famous speeches of the revolution. That's what that statue is commemorating. His speech was a radical call to arms, in effect, charging his listeners to overthrow the Provisional Government and fight for 'worldwide socialist revolution.'[1] Even some of his Bolshevik followers were shocked at his words. It was the opening act of the Bolshevik Revolution and a critical turning point in Russian history.

"The Provisional Government would conduct its sessions in the Winter Palace that year, laying the foundation for democracy in Russia. It had planned to hold national elections at the end of the year, but the elections would never take place. On November 7, 1917, Lenin's Bolshevik army stormed the Winter Palace and overthrew the Provisional Government.

"The largest nation on earth would now become a communist dictatorship under the rule of Vladimir Lenin and would soon be known as the Soviet Union. But that was only part of the story. The other part was the real story."

"So tell us the real story," I said.

"When all this was happening, where was the Altar?"

"In Germany," said Lara. "In Berlin."

"The Throne of Satan was in Berlin. So is it possible that the evil of communism, the Soviet Union, and, from that, the communist totalitarianism that would spread across the world in the twentieth century all originated from the Throne of Satan?"

"Tell us," I said.

"The train that took Lenin to St. Petersburg didn't just happen to be there. It was all arranged by another power."

"Which power?"

"Germany, the German government. Germany was behind it all. Germany planned it, approved it, and executed it."

"Why?" asked Lara.

"Because Russia was Germany's enemy in the war. And so the German high command sought to use Lenin to cause Russia to become destabilized and so neutralize its war effort. The German Foreign Ministry was involved; so were the German General Staff and German intelligence. And it was all overseen from Berlin, the city of the Altar. It was all directed from Satan's Throne.

"Berlin issued special orders to the border guards that no passports were to be checked, no one was to be stopped, and the carriage that contained Lenin was to be treated as 'sealed' as an extraterritorial domain. Thus, it would be known as the 'sealed train.' To further safeguard Lenin's passage, Germany stationed police and military personnel so the train would not be stopped or interfered with. Further, the journey required the train to come to Berlin before being sent on to Russia."

"So the evil again came from Berlin," I said, "from Satan's Throne."

"A Journey Sealed, the Kingdom Come," said Lara. "It was the journey of the sealed train, and the Contagion Sent—that was Lenin."

"Yes," said the woman. "In fact, Winston Churchill would liken Lenin's journey to the sending of a *plague bacillus* to Russia."[2]

"Was it fate?" asked Lara. "Was Lenin destined for that train?"

"There is destiny," said the woman, "but everyone has a choice within it. As for Lenin, he came into the world in 1870. Do you know what also came into the world in 1870? Finland Station. The child for the station...and the station for the child."

"And the Russian patient," I said, "succumbed to the infection."

"Yes, the results of the plan would far exceed Berlin's greatest hopes. In less than a year after Lenin's arrival in St. Petersburg, Russia had withdrawn from the war. And in the process Germany had brought into being the world's first communist state and the prototype for future communist revolutions by which millions and millions would be placed under totalitarian dictatorships."

"So even that," I said, "the birth of the Soviet Union and communist revolution, it all came from the city of Satan's Throne, the same city that would soon give birth to the Third Reich, the Second World War, and the Holocaust. The city of evil."

"It's not the city of evil," said the woman. "It's the *Throne of evil* within the city. And what would you have expected, Mr. Herzog, of the one who said, 'I will exalt my throne above the stars of God...I will be like the Most High'...and of him who makes 'the earth to tremble,' and 'the world as a wilderness'?[3] Would you have expected anything less?"

The woman would now tell us of the Devil's paradise.

Chapter 49
THE DEVIL'S PARADISE

LENIN WAS OBSESSED with the year of the Altar's return to the world. It was because of the uprising that had taken place that year, the Paris Commune. He studied it over and over again."

"Why obsessed?" asked Lara.

"He saw it as the model for everything he was attempting to bring about: communist revolution and a communist state. In the summer of 1917, just before he led the Bolshevik Revolution, he wrote *The State and Revolution,* the foundational text of Leninism. It would be used not only in the formation of the Soviet Union but in the revolutions and totalitarian regimes of communist China, Vietnam, and Cuba, among others.

"And he based it on what happened in 1871, the uprising of the Paris Commune. It was from that year that his doctrines of violent revolution; the destruction of the state; the elimination of all opposition parties; the dictatorship of the proletariat; the ruthless suppression and destruction of all 'counterrevolutionary' forces, movements, and people; and the violent campaign for world revolution were born. All those evils were birthed in 1871, when Satan's Throne returned to the world.

"In fact, the Soviet Union itself was set up in Lenin's vision as a modern incarnation of the Paris Commune. The Commune had instituted a governing council of workers and radical activists and called for the establishment of smaller workers' councils. Lenin wanted that for his communist state. Do you know what the word for *council* is in Russian?"

"No," I said.

"*Soviet,*" said the woman. "The word is *soviet.*"

"The Soviet Union..." said Lara.

"Yes. So the Soviet Union also went back to 1871, the year of the Altar. And the connection between the Soviet state and the year of the Altar's return was sealed in what happened to Lenin after his death."

"*After* his death? What happened?" I asked.

"They took his body and wrapped it in a flag created in 1871 in the Paris Commune—a witness in red to communism's mystic bond to Satan's Throne."

"The image on the page," said Lara, "was of an upside-down kingdom. What does that mean?"

"Revolutions turn kingdoms upside-down. Satan turns all things upside down. Lenin would lay the cornerstone for an upside-down kingdom. In it, oppression was called 'freedom,' brainwashing 'enlightenment,' and deception 'truth,' or *pravda*.

"In the name of liberation, he would unleash a campaign of mass terror against his own citizens, declaring entire classes of people 'enemies of the state,' to be imprisoned, tortured, and killed.

"He would provide the rationale and create the apparatus that would be used to annihilate millions across the world. He would usher in the Marxist utopia of labor camps, gulags, and endless corpses. He would open the gates of a darkened heaven, the Devil's paradise, and kingdoms born of the satanic Throne."

We would be led to our next destination and the next mystery by a mysterious man, revered by those who knew him, but who had been dead for centuries. It would be through him that we would be shown how the course of the modern world was changed in an instant by the mystery of the Altar.

PART X

TRANSFERENCE

Chapter 50

THE HOLY FOOL

SHE HANDED US the next page, wished us well, and departed. We looked at it right there at Finland Station. The image was similar to the one on the previous page and even more similar to that on the first page. It was a palace-like building with a large opening in which stood what appeared to be an altar. But it was also different; the towers on the palace-like building were each crowned with an onion-shaped dome.

"It's definitely Russian," said Lara.

"A Russian castle?"

"More like a Russian church, like a Russian Orthodox cathedral."

We headed back to our hotel in the center of St. Petersburg. The next morning, we met for a late breakfast in one of the city's coffee shops. While waiting for our meal, Lara took out her notebook and read her translation of the page.

"It's titled 'Transference.' And this is the text:

The World in Ruins
The Kingdom Fallen
The Hidden Throne
Uncovered
Now Passes to Another
The Changing of the Guard
The Winds of Spring
Blow Through the Earth
To Seed
The Deadly Harvest
Kingdoms Birthing
Kingdoms
Powers Birthing
Powers
The Mantle
Of the Dragon
Given."

"Did it come with a dream?" I asked.

"It did," she said, "and I know where we're going next. And it was right there on the page."

"So what was your dream?"

"I was on a boat," she said, "on a river. The boat touched the shore, and I stepped out onto a gigantic square. As I walked the square, I came across a thin, barefoot man, dressed in rags. His hair was disheveled, his eyes were piercing, and his face was long, narrow, and bearded.

"'Have you come to my house?' he asked.

"'I don't even know who you are,' I said. 'Who are you?'

"'They call me a saint,' he said, 'but I am only a fool crying out.'

"'And what do you cry out?' I asked.

"'The evil has come into the house.'

"Right after he said those words, the dream ended."

"And you know what it means?" I asked.

"I looked up Russian saints, and I found that there was one who walked around barefoot in rags and was known as a holy fool. He was a prophetic figure who rebuked the evil of the tsar Ivan the Terrible."

"The evil in the house," I said.

"I searched the Internet and found a Russian icon with his image on it. It matched the man I saw in my dream."

"And who was he?"

"He was called St. Basil the Blessed."

"And how does that help us?"

"He asked me if I had come to his house. His house is the Cathedral of St. Basil the Blessed, the most famous church building in Russia. It's the image on the page. We have to go there."

"Where?"

"Moscow…in Red Square, right next to the Kremlin."

The next day, Lara and I headed out from St. Petersburg to Moscow to go to the house of the holy fool.

It took us about four hours on the high-speed Sapsan express train to travel the four hundred miles between St. Petersburg and Moscow. We arrived at Leningradsky Station, an old and historic railway terminal in the heart of Moscow, a striking contrast to the modern train it served. We headed to our hotel, rested for the night, and the next morning set out for St. Basil's Cathedral.

The streets of central Moscow were noticeably wide, as if built for massive parades. We passed by ornate buildings from tsarist times with balconies and arches and elaborate facades of pale yellows, reds, and creams mixed in with buildings from the Soviet era and modern skyscrapers. As we approached our destination, we could see the red-brick towers of the Kremlin's walls and the golden domes of its cathedrals rising above the trees. We walked through the arched Resurrection Gate and into Red Square.

As in Lara's dream, it was a vast expanse. At the end of the square, in the distance ahead of us, was the Cathedral of St. Basil the Blessed. It was an eruption of shapes and colors, its intricately adorned red towers crowned with onion domes of gold or swirls of blue, white, and green stripes. It seemed out of place, as if from another world, something one might expect in a fairy tale or in a dream from one's childhood. Its shape matched the image on the page.

As we walked the stones of Red Square toward the cathedral, we noticed something else that looked out of place: a man sitting on the pavement in front of the cathedral's facade. We assumed he was homeless.

"He looks like the man on the icon," said Lara.

"St. Basil?"

"Look," she said as she held out her phone to show me an image of St. Basil's icon.

The man on the pavement was thin, with a long and narrow bearded face.

"There is a resemblance," I said, "but on the other hand…"

"What?"

"He's dead."

"I know," she said. "He's been dead for five hundred years."

"In that case, he looks remarkably well."

"What do you think?"

"I think it's a coincidence…or maybe…it's like GPS."

"What do you mean?"

"In order to pinpoint a specific position or location, you need more than one coordinate. We were supposed to come to St. Basil's Cathedral. That was one coordinate. And if he's the one we're supposed to meet, then the fact that there happens to be a resemblance to St. Basil could be the other coordinate."

We approached the man.

"Excuse me," I said. "You wouldn't happen to be named Basil, would you?"

Lara looked at me as if shocked that I would come right out and ask that.

"My name is Yaroslav. You were looking for someone named Basil?" he said with a strong Russian accent.

"Sort of," I said.

"You've come to his house," he said. "But St. Basil hasn't been here for years."

"You wouldn't be able to help us, would you?" I asked.

At that, the man rose to his feet.

"It is possible, Mr. Herzog, that I could."

And now through this unlikely homeless-looking man, the mystery of what became of the Altar, a mystery that changed the history of the world, would now be revealed to us.

Chapter 51

THE CHANGING OF THE GUARD

"THE RISE OF the kingdom," said the man, "that had begun with the Altar's return to the world was now approaching its end."

"The rise of Germany," I said.

"In the autumn of 1944, American and Allied forces had broken through France and the Low Countries and were now closing in on Germany. Allied bombing was destroying German transportation networks and decimating German cities. In the east, the Soviet Red Army was closing in, having pushed through Poland and having entered German territory. By January 1945, German forces were in full retreat."

"And Berlin…?" I said.

"The Battle of Berlin began in mid-April. It took only days for the Red Army to break through German defensive positions and encircle the city. And just days after that, the city that had begun the most destructive war in world history had fallen and lay in ruins. Germany surrendered. And the war in Europe was over."

"And the Altar?" I said.

"From the moment the Altar was uncovered and returned to the world, it had only changed possession once."

"From the Ottoman Empire," said Lara, "to Germany."

"Yes," said the man, "and now would come the second. It would pass into the hands of another. And with the passing of the Altar comes the passing of its mystery. And since the Altar is a throne, its passing would mean the transfer of power."

"A throne of evil," I said.

"Yes, so the mantle of evil would likewise pass to another. And another would become the Enemy's principal vessel on earth…the new capital of evil."

"So what happened to the Altar?" I asked.

"The Altar had been in Germany's possession since the late nineteenth century. When Hitler became Germany's master, the Altar came under his control. He became its ultimate possessor.

"In April 1945, the two, Adolf Hitler and the Altar, were each hidden in a protective bunker in Berlin. When Hitler lifted the gun to his head and pulled its trigger, he ended his life and his possession of the Altar. Now it could pass to another. Now another could become its master.

"And so it was on the very day after Hitler killed himself that the Altar passed into the hands of its new owner. The soldiers who invaded Berlin came upon the bunker in which the Altar was hidden. They opened the bunker and found it. It was on that day that the second transference took place. The Altar passed into the hands of another."

"And the soldiers who found the Altar," said Lara, "they would have been of..."

"The Red Army," said the man. "The Altar now came into the possession of the Soviet Union."

"That would mean a transfer of power," I said.

"In taking possession of the Altar, the Soviet Union would become darkly empowered. The mantle of evil passed from Nazi Germany to the Soviet Union."

"And as the Altar is an instrument of death," I said, "the Soviet Union would succeed Germany as a kingdom and instrument of death."

"The Soviet Union," said the man, "and the entire kingdom of Marx in all its forms and regimes."

"When," I asked, "did Joseph Stalin rule the Soviet Union?"

"He was ruling it at that very moment," said the man, "at the time of the transfer."

"And he was the one," I said, "whose birth was especially connected to the Altar's return."

"Yes, the one who came into the world just as they began to unearth the Altar."

"And now," said Lara, "he was the ruler of the Soviet Union. So he was now in position to receive it."

"He had come into the world with the Altar," said the man, "and now he was to become its possessor. As the absolute ruler of the Soviet Union, he was now the Altar's new master."

"The Hidden Throne Uncovered," said Lara, "Now Passes to Another, from one power to the other and from one master to another, from Adolf Hitler to Joseph Stalin."

"Yes, Stalin would replace Hitler as the Altar's new ultimate possessor."

"Each of their births," said Lara, "was linked to the Altar's return to the world. And each at the height of their powers was destined to possess it."

"Or," he said, "to be possessed by it."

"Two of the most evil monsters in world history," I said, "and they each just happened to possess the same object, the Throne of Satan."

"And with the passing of the Altar," said the man, "the world would be changed."

There was more to what happened in the spring of 1945 than a change of possession and more to what would happen to the world.

Chapter 52

MYSTIC CARGO

As we walked through Red Square, we came to the Spasskaya Tower, a red-brick clock tower built in the age of the tsars but crowned with a red five-pointed star from the days of the Soviet Union. It was there we stopped.

"Had the soldiers of the Red Army left the Altar where it was, it still would have marked a new epoch, the changing of the guard," said the man. "The Altar's ownership had been transferred, and it was now under the sovereignty of the Soviet Union, Moscow, and Stalin. But it wasn't only that.

"How many times was the Altar of Pergamon actually moved from one place to another?"

"In what time period?" I asked.

"In the Altar's entire history," he replied, "in two thousand years."

"I don't know," I replied.

"Only once," he said. "Only once was it actually moved from one location to another, when Carl Humann transported it from Pergamon to Berlin, Germany...only once in all of history." He paused. "But it was to happen once more.

"The Red Army did not leave the contents of the Altar undisturbed. Under orders from Moscow, they took its marble pieces out of the bunker and packed them into wooden crates. The crates were then loaded onto train cars.

"It was a massive operation involving hundreds of Red Army soldiers. And now in the year that was both critical and pivotal for world history, in 1945, the Altar of Pergamon, for the second time in its two-thousand-year history, was moved, this time from Germany to the Soviet Union. The Throne of Satan passed from the Third Reich to the Marxist state and from the sovereignty of Berlin to that of Moscow. As Berlin had directed its transference from Pergamon, now Moscow would direct its transference from Berlin. The Altar was taken to the same city that had turned Russia into the Soviet Union—St. Petersburg, now renamed as Leningrad."

"So what happened to the Soviet Union," I asked, "when the Altar changed hands?"

"It was already an evil power," said Lara. "So how was it affected by coming into possession of the Altar?"

"The joining of the Altar to Germany marked the beginning of Germany's rise to world power. So the joining of the Altar to the Soviet Union would now mark the rise of the Soviet Union to unprecedented heights of world power. It was the same year that the Red Army came into possession of the Altar that the Soviet Union was transformed into a superpower.

"In 1945, the Soviet Union possessed the largest standing army the world had ever seen. And in that same year, the year of the transference, its power would begin rising to an entirely other level. By force, manipulation, intimidation, and violence, it would become the head of nations, a kingdom over kingdoms, a ruler of rulers. Only one other power on earth was comparable—America.

"Its transformation from an evil power to an evil superpower meant that it would now reproduce and multiply its evils throughout the world, in every nation it was able to control or influence. What would we expect of a power that came to possess the Throne of Satan? We would expect it to spread darkness across the world. So that is exactly what happened. And against what specific people or nation does the Devil especially wage war?"

"The people of Israel," I said, "the Jewish people."

"So what would we expect to happen if the Soviet Union came to possess the Throne of Satan? We would expect it to become an especially anti-Jewish, anti-Israel, anti-Semitic power. We would expect it to wage war against the Jewish people. And that too is what happened. The Soviet Union now replaced Nazi Germany as the Jewish people's most powerful enemy on earth. In the late 1940s, under Stalin's directives, it began persecuting the Jewish people within its borders. Jewish leaders were purged and executed. There were even signs that Stalin was planning a second Holocaust, halted only by his sudden death.

"As for Israel, the Soviet Union would become its archnemesis. It would arm Israel's enemies and work for its destruction. Beyond that, it would become the world's most powerful disseminator of anti-Semitic propaganda, spreading anti-Jewish conspiracy theories and anti-Semitic hatred throughout the world. The power that possessed the Throne of Satan would become his mouthpiece.

"But as the Enemy wars not only against the Jewish people but against those who follow the Word of God and against the message of the Gospel, so now, with the Throne of Satan, the Soviet Union would become the most powerful enemy of God and the Christian faith on earth. It would disseminate its anti-God and anti-Christian ideology and hatred across the world. And as the dark head of nations, it would bring hundreds of millions of Christians under the heel of state-sponsored persecution.

"That which was implemented within its borders would now be reproduced in nations throughout the world. The Gospel would be banned. Children would be brainwashed against faith. Churches would be shut down, converted, or burned to the ground. And Christians would be imprisoned, tortured, and executed. The new seat of Satan's Throne would now wage war against God and His people throughout the world."

With a throne comes dominion. We would now be shown the massive repercussions of that connection as it touched the world.

Chapter 53

THE CONTAGION LOOSED

"When the Ottoman Empire lost the Altar," said the man, "it lost as well, and at the same moment, its territories and headed for oblivion. On the other hand, when Germany gained the Throne, it began its rise to world power as a satanic kingdom. At the height of its power, when it took over much of Europe, do you know what its possessions included? Lands that once made up the Ottoman Empire."

"So in losing the Altar," I said, "the Ottomans lost the lands of their empire. And in taking the Altar, the Nazis would take lands of the empire that had lost the Altar."

"Yes. And so it was with Germany. The very day after the Nazis lost the Altar, they lost Berlin, and after that, Germany, and all the lands they had seized in the war—their empire. And when the Soviet Union gained the Altar, what do you think happened? It began expanding, spreading, taking possession of other lands—the lands of Eastern and Central Europe.

"It would be called the Soviet or Eastern bloc. But most of the lands now under Soviet dominion held something in common. Bulgaria was formerly part of the Ottoman Empire. Romania was formerly part of the Ottoman Empire. Albania was formerly part of the Ottoman Empire. Serbia was formerly part of the Ottoman Empire. Bosnia was formerly part of the Ottoman Empire. Montenegro was formerly part of the Ottoman Empire. Macedonia was formerly part of the Ottoman Empire. Kosovo was formerly part of the Ottoman Empire. Even Hungary was, at one time, part of the Ottoman Empire."

"So the power that possessed the Altar," I said, "came into possession of the Altar's empire."

"As if the Altar," said Lara, "was re-creating its empire."

"Or," said the man, "as if the Throne was re-creating its kingdom. And yet the borders of the dark kingdom would extend much farther than this. The Altar would empower not only the Soviet Union but the contagion by which it was birthed, Marxism.

"You see, it was not only the Soviet Union that possessed the Altar—but the Marxist world and Marxism. The Throne of Satan was now bonded to the Marxist contagion. And in that dark bonding, the contagion was empowered and would spread beyond the Soviet Union, beyond Eastern Europe, even to the ends of the earth.

"After the Soviet Union came into possession of the Altar, communism began powerfully advancing through Asia. In 1948, communist forces took over North Korea and, in 1954, North Vietnam, and then Laos and Cambodia. But the crown jewel of the Marxist kingdom came into being just four years after the communist world took possession of the Altar, as an army of Marxist revolutionaries took over the world's most populous nation—China.

"In the late 1960s, in the form of Marxist-Leninism, the contagion spread to Africa. In 1969, the People's Republic of the Congo became the continent's first Marxist state. Then came Ethiopia, then Benin and Mozambique. The contagion even spread to the Western Hemisphere, to America's doorstep, as Nicaragua, Bolivia, and Venezuela came under the rule of Marxist-leaning governments, and as the islands of Cuba and Grenada were taken over by Marxist-Leninist revolutionaries.

"Those leading the uprisings were following the Marxist-Leninist principles of revolution, deriving from the Paris Commune in 1871. So the revolutions that in the twentieth century overtook much of the earth went back to the year of the return to the world of Satan's Throne.

"With the Throne of Satan in its possession, the kingdom of Marxism would, at its peak, *rule over one-third of the world's population.* And as the Devil is a murderer, it would lead to the murder of tens of millions of people. In its expanse and in the multitude of its murders, the Altar's new masters would exceed even those of its former Nazi possessors. For no matter what the kingdom, the Altar required the shedding of blood and the Throne of Satan, destruction."

The man had one more revelation to open, that of a mystery that began as the Altar materialized on German soil, but which manifested to the world on the very ground on which we now stood.

Chapter 54

THE HIGH HOLY DAY

He led us farther up Red Square until we came to a red-and-black angular building, a stepped pyramid.

"What's that?" I asked.

"That," he said, "is Lenin's Mausoleum. It's where his body, embalmed and preserved, was put on public display. It was the nearest thing to a communist shrine. And it was on top of that building that the leaders of the Soviet Union—Stalin, Khrushchev, Brezhnev—would stand reviewing the parades and massive displays of Soviet power that rolled through Red Square."

"I've seen pictures of it," I said.

"The May Day parades," said Lara.

"It was the only Soviet holiday," I said, "that I had any idea of."

"As it was for most," said the man. "Do you know when it began?"

"No," said Lara.

"It began in the late nineteenth century. And it didn't begin in Russia but in Paris. May Day was adopted as the official holiday of the international socialist and Marxist world. It would soon become the *central* holiday of the Marxist world and socialism's high holy day.

"With the emergence of communist nations in the twentieth century, May Day became a state holiday, celebrated in the Soviet bloc nations of Eastern Europe, in Cuba, in Vietnam, in China, and throughout the world.

"But it was in the Soviet Union that May Day's communist association found its most powerful expression. Even before the Revolution of 1917, Russian workers used May Day as an instrument of protest and revolutionary agitation, often leading to violent repression. Thus, in Soviet mythology, the holiday took on a legendary aura. But after the revolution, the Soviets turned May Day into an enormous celebration with massive parades and displays trumpeting Marxist ideology and the Marxist state.

"After the Second World War, with the Soviet Union's capture of the Altar and its transformation into a superpower, May Day took on even more significance as it was used to showcase Soviet power, not only to the Soviet people but to its allies, to its adversaries, and to the world. The parades of May Day now displayed military hardware, space technology, and nuclear weapons, interspersed with giant banners of Lenin and Marx. It was the Soviet Union's greatest spectacle and the most-viewed Marxist event in the world. And it happened right here in Red Square, with its leaders standing on that building to oversee it."

"But how does it relate," I asked, "to the mystery?"

"It was prophetic."

"What do you mean?"

"When is May Day?" he asked.

"May 1," said Lara.

"Do you know when it was that the Altar was transferred from Nazi Germany to the Soviet Union...when the Red Army came upon it in its bunker in Berlin? It was May 1. It was May Day. Communism and the communist world came into possession of the Altar on May Day. It was the day that altered history."

"But they were celebrating it for years," said Lara, "decades before the soldiers of the Red Army opened the bunker that day."

"Yes," said the man. "That's the point. They were celebrating the day they would take possession of the Altar years before it happened."

"But they didn't do it knowingly," I said.

"Not knowingly. But nevertheless, they did it. It was prophetic. They didn't know it. But he did."

"The Enemy," said Lara.

"The Dark Angel."

"And *after* that day?" I asked.

"They were still unknowingly celebrating the day they found the Altar and came into possession of Satan's Throne."

"What year was it," I asked, "that May Day became the official holiday of Marxism?"

"1889."

"1889," I repeated. "The same year that Lenin came upon Marx."

"And the same year," said the man, "that the Altar was reconstructed for the first time since ancient times."

"So the year the Altar was rebuilt," I said, "the Marxists adopted a holiday that would foretell the very day they would come to possess it."

"And the same year," said Lara, "that Hitler was born."

"Yes," said the man, "in the last days of April."

"Leading up to May Day," said Lara.

"And so again," he said, "Hitler led up to that critical May Day of 1945, as he took his life the day before May Day, when the Altar passed to another."

"So," I said, "the Marxists adopted May Day in the year of Hitler's birth...and then fulfilled it in the year of Hitler's death...on the day after his death."

"The Winds of Spring," said Lara, "the winds of May Day. They Blow Through the Earth to Seed the Deadly Harvest."

"And do you know what else May Day is?" asked the man.

"No," I replied.

"A high holy day."

"Of what?" asked Lara.

"Of the satanic calendar...a high holy day of Satan."

"And so," I said, "on the central holy day of communism and a high holy day of Satan, the Throne of Satan passed into the possession of the communist world!"

"Yes," said the man, "and then taken to its new house."

"'*The evil has come into the house,*'" said Lara. "In my dream those were the words of St. Basil."

"Then," said the man, "I guess St. Basil was right."

The next journey would involve a serpent, a gate, a wall, and a little girl, and would open a mystery of superpowers and of the world itself that began with an ancient name, the ancient name of the Devil.

PART XI

DIABOLOS

Chapter 55
THE SLITHERER

"YOU LOOK LIKE him, you know," said Lara. "Like St. Basil."

"Others have told me that," said the man. "But, of course, we only have his icons to tell us what he may have looked like."

"Of course," said Lara.

He began leading us away from Lenin's tomb. Then he stopped and turned to us.

"Now, you will be careful," said the man. "Your journey comes with many dangers, with evil in many houses. Stay alert. Stay aware of your surroundings. Stay vigilant."

He then handed us the next page of the book, wished us well, and departed. We walked back to St. Basil's Cathedral and around its side. There, hidden in a cluster of trees, we looked at the page.

The image on the page was simple, less an illustration and more a symbol: two horizontal dashes, one on the right and one on the left, with a space between them. And running vertically through the space in between the dashes was what appeared to be the letter *S*.

"S," I said. "So what does it stand for?"

"Soviet?" said Lara.

"Socialist?" I said.

"Stalin?"

"Satan?"

"Wait," said Lara. "If it's consistent with the other pages, then it would have to be Greek."

"A Greek word," I said, "beginning with the letter *S*?"

"Only the letter *S* isn't Greek. It does have the *S* sound, but it's represented by a different letter—sigma."

"Maybe," I said, "it's best to sleep on it."

We headed back to our hotel. The next morning, we went for breakfast in one of Moscow's many coffeehouses. Lara had the translation and, as I had hoped, a dream.

"Are you ready for the title?" she said.

"Ready."

"'Diabolos.'"

"*Diabolos*," I said, "like diabolical?"

"The word *diabolical* is connected to it."

"Isn't it used to speak of the Devil?"

"Yes. In Greek, it means the accuser or the slanderer. As the Devil is the Accuser, he's the Diabolos."

"But every mystery on this journey has had something to do with the Devil. So how does that help us?"

"We have more than that to go on," she said. "This is the text:

The Serpent Speaks
His Ancient Spell
And Casts Them
Through
The Curtain Falls
The One Is Two
As to the Throne
So Too the World
All to the Brink
All to the King
Of Separation."

"The serpent," I said, "would go with Diabolos, but what does the rest of it mean?"

"I didn't tell you my dream. I was walking the streets of a city when a snake appeared on the ground in front of me. It was large, thick, at least six feet long, and black with blue and red stripes running down the length of its body. I followed it as it writhed and slithered along on the sidewalk. The street then opened up into a square, a plaza of light-colored stones. At the end of the plaza stood a lightly colored stone structure, like something from a Greek or Roman temple, with several classical columns joined at their tops by a larger horizontal stone band. In the dream, I didn't recognize it, but as soon as I woke up, I realized what it was.

"I continued walking behind the snake in the direction of the structure until it stopped. Then, as would a cobra, it lifted the front part of its body off the ground, as if to stand. It turned around to face me. And then it spoke, and with a German accent: 'Shall I go through it?' I didn't answer. It turned back around, lowered itself to the ground, and resumed its slithering to the stone structure, then slithered through it, passing in between the two central columns that formed the gateway.

"As it passed through the columns, the structure began to shake violently. Then it broke in two, half of it parting to the one direction and half parting to the other. And it wasn't just the structure; the plaza itself was now parting to the one side and to the other. Everything was now parting as the divide grew larger and larger. And the dream ended."

"That was it," I said. "The image on the page, it wasn't a symbol—it was a picture. The *S* was the snake slithering. And the dashes on each side represented that which it passed through."

"I believe that's right," she said.

"And what about the object, the structure? You said you realized what it was as soon as you woke up. What was it?"

"It was the Brandenburg Gate."

"In Berlin," I replied. "We can't get away from it."

"No," said Lara, "I believe we're destined."

But there were others who didn't believe that we were destined to make our next journey. They would seek to persuade us otherwise.

Chapter 56

THE ELEVATOR PEOPLE

It was the day of our departure for Berlin. Lara and I were to meet in the hotel lobby, then head out to the airport. I was there, but she was not. I decided to go up to her room to find out what had happened. I took the elevator, came to her room, knocked on the door, but there was no answer. I went back to the elevator and headed back down.

There were two reasons for Lara's delay. The first was that she had been late in getting ready. The second was of a more ominous nature. When she stepped into the elevator, there were three people inside: a woman and two men. The woman stood to her right, the two men in back. The elevator began its descent, but halfway down, it came to a sudden stop in between floors. The three were unfazed by it, as if they had expected it to happen.

Then without turning her head but maintaining her gaze straight ahead, the woman spoke in an accent Lara couldn't place.

"Do you hope to someday have a family?"

"What?" said Lara as she turned to the woman, who did not turn in response but kept her gaze fixed straight ahead as she spoke.

"Do you hope to become a mother someday?"

"Why would you ask me that?"

"Because if you do not give up this pursuit, you never will. You won't live to see it happen."

Lara turned around so that she could see all of them. She backed away to the elevator wall, where the floor buttons were.

"You know what happened," said the woman, "to the one who started all this, the one who gave the first page to your friend? Sadly, he is no longer with us. He found it impossible to hide from us. All the precautions he hoped would protect him proved woefully inadequate. He could not escape his fate and his unfortunate accident."

Lara said nothing but slowly slipped her hand into her purse, searching for her pepper spray while silently praying for help.

"She believes her God can save her," said the woman. "Is that what you believe, Lara, that your God can protect you from this? Did not the others trust in their gods? And where are they now? Their gods were unable to save them. Neither will your God be able to save you. You see, the darkness is so much greater than the light. It's everywhere. The light cannot overcome it but can only be extinguished by it. Do you believe that, Lara?"

Just then, everything went dark. Lara started banging against the elevator wall, hoping to hit an emergency button or sound an alarm. After about twenty seconds of darkness, the lights came back on, and the elevator resumed its descent. The three just stood there as before, facing the elevator doors as if nothing had happened, or nothing that wasn't supposed to have happened.

"You know what they say, Lara," said the woman as the elevator neared the lobby floor, "'Thieves don't live long.'"

As the elevator doors opened, Lara rushed out. Once she was far enough away, she looked back at the elevator. The three were still there. The doors closed, and the elevator began descending to one of the floors below the lobby.

It was just then that the elevator I had taken down reached the lobby floor. The doors opened, and we saw each other. She took me over to one of the lobby's secluded corners to tell me what happened.

"How dangerous are these people," she said, "that they could do that…that they could make that happen…? And if they killed the man for having that one page of the book, what will they do to us for having several? And he knew the danger, but still he couldn't stop it. What do we do?"

"We'll figure it out," I said.

"Yes, if we can manage to stay alive in the meantime."

Toward that goal, we decided to skip breakfast and quickly head out to the airport. What awaited us in Berlin was a mystery of primeval origins, and yet that lay behind the most dangerous events of modern times.

Chapter 57

THE GIRL IN THE RED COAT

We headed to the airport, boarded the plane, flew to Berlin, and checked into our hotel. I don't believe we had ever been so cautious, so attentive to our surroundings, or so paranoid, and with good reason. We spent much of the next day in our hotel, processing what we had seen and been shown thus far. I called Kazim in Turkey to tell him what had happened. He went over with me all the precautions he had given up to that point, then gave me several more. I went over them with Lara. By the time we left our hotel, it was afternoon. We headed for the Brandenburg Gate. We walked on the *Unter den Linden*, or the Under the Linden Trees Avenue, so named for the trees that still line the boulevard. We approached the open expanse of the Parisian Square.

"This is the plaza I saw in my dream," said Lara.

It was now dotted with locals and tourists strolling through or standing for pictures.

"And there it is," said Lara, pointing into the distance to the end of the plaza, "the Brandenburg Gate."

It stood over sixty feet high and over two hundred feet wide and reminded me of an ancient Greek temple or Roman victory arch. It was as we approached that gate that we noticed her. She was wearing a red coat and sitting on the stone pavement to the right of the gate's last column. She appeared to be around seven years old with a light complexion, piercing blue eyes, deep red lips, and long, thick, wavy blond hair. In her right hand was a pencil, and across her lap was what appeared to be a notebook one would use in elementary school.

"Look," I said. "The girl sitting there…There's no one with her. I'm wondering…Let's go over to her."

So we did. She seemed too absorbed in her book to see us coming. But as we stood over her, she looked up and smiled.

"Is anybody with you?" asked Lara. "Your parents?"

"No, I'm here by myself," she said with a German accent. "But I'm allowed to come here as long as I stay in this one place. Are you from America?"

"We are," said Lara.

"Oh, good!" she said. "I'm doing my homework. Maybe you can help me with a math problem. What is one minus one?"

"Zero," I said.

"I would have said two," she said.

"No," I said, "one minus one is zero."

"Why did I think it was two?" she said.

I wondered then if I was mistaken and this was just a young girl who wasn't particularly good at math.

"Please sit down with me," she said.

So Lara and I sat down with the girl on the pavement by the gate.

"I'm Ilka," she said. "Can I tell you a secret?"

"We'd love to hear it, Ilka," said Lara.

"It's about the Devil," she said.

At that, Lara and I looked at each other.

"Do you know where the name *Devil* comes from?" she asked. "It comes from *Diabolos*...the *Diabol*, the *Devil*."

Lara and I again exchanged glances. I was not mistaken. And like the boy in Nuremberg, the girl at the gate did not speak as a child.

"And do you know what *Diabolos* means?" she asked.

"The Accuser," said Lara, "the Slanderer."

"Yes, but it's deeper than that. It comes from two ancient words: *bolos,* which means to cast, and *dia,* which means through. So the Devil is the one who *casts through*. And when you cast through, you separate, you divide. The Diabolos, the Devil, is the one who divides and separates. The Devil is the Divider.

"He divides everything...God from us, man from woman, people from people, worlds from worlds. And do you know why? Because when you divide, you can destroy. Divide nations against nations, and you have war, death, and destruction."

"So the Devil is the Divider," I said, "because he's the Destroyer. He divides in order to destroy."

"Yes," said the girl, "a house divided against itself cannot stand."[1]

"That's what the symbol meant," said Lara, "the image of the serpent. It was passing *through*. It was dividing the lines."

"What he wills to destroy," said the girl, "he divides."

"And do you have something to tell us about this place?" I asked.

"I do," she said. "It's another secret. But I think you already have an idea."

She looked around as if to make sure no one else could hear it when she told us her secret. And then in a hushed but tense voice, she said, "This city, Berlin…is his throne, the throne of the Diabolos. It was from here that he tried to destroy the world, more than once. And from here he would try again, in a different way. As he's the Diabolos, so he would divide.

"The division of Berlin was sealed on May 2, 1945, the day it fell into the hands of the Red Army."

"The day after the Red Army found the Altar," I said.

"Berlin was the city of the Diabolos, so it would become the divided city and the symbol of division for the entire world. It was all part of a plan much bigger than the city…a plan of destruction…a diabolical plan."

She would now reveal that plan, how it would unfold, and how it would change the entire world.

Chapter 58

THE DIABOLICAL WORLD

"THAT WHICH IS divided loses its unity, its oneness," said the girl. "And when you lose your oneness, you become two. You see, one minus one can equal two. So now there would be two Berlins—one under American and Western dominion, West Berlin, and the other under Soviet and Eastern dominion, East Berlin. But it wasn't just the city. As goes the throne, so goes the kingdom. The Throne was in Berlin and the kingdom…"

"Was Germany," said Lara.

"After dividing the city, the Diabolos would now divide the nation. Germany would now be *cast through*—dia bolos—broken apart. So now there would be two Germanies in the world: one allied with America and the West, West Germany, and the other allied with the Soviet Union and under communist totalitarian rule, East Germany. But the plan of the Diabolos was larger than that."

"In my dream," said Lara, "as the serpent passed through the Brandenburg Gate, the gate broke in two. The ground—everything—broke in two."

"And so," said the girl, "the division that began in the city of the Altar would spread far beyond the borders of Germany. Before the end of the Second World War, the Soviet Union had joined with its Allied partners in guaranteeing the European nations liberation from Hitler, free elections, national self-determination, political freedom, and national sovereignty. But at the end of the war, the agreement was broken.

"By intimidation, manipulation, force, and repression, the Soviet Union would impose communist totalitarianism on the nations of Eastern Europe. The Red Army would replace the German army as an occupying force. Communists would be placed in key government positions; voters would be intimidated and elections rigged to ensure communist victory.

"As in the Bolshevik Revolution in Russia, democratic forces would be rapidly and thoroughly crushed. Democratic and opposition leaders would be denounced, arrested, exiled, or executed. As in Russia, secret police began operating throughout Eastern Europe to intimidate, terrorize, and crush any dissident activities. And as in Russia, the Communist Party would impose totalitarian control over each nation.

"The division that began in the divided city now stretched across the entire European continent. In 1946, just one year after the war's end, the British leader Winston Churchill gave a speech in Fulton, Missouri, in which he said, 'From Stettin in the Baltic to Trieste in the Adriatic, an iron curtain has descended across the continent.'[1]

"It was from that speech that the words *Iron Curtain* would come into being to describe the division of Europe, which had placed millions under the darkness of communism. And yet the Iron Curtain was just another manifestation of the dia bolos, the casting through, of the Divider. And as with all the other evils that came upon the world, it would again come from Berlin and through the power that came to possess the Devil's Throne in this city on May Day."

"In my dream," said Lara, "the snake had red and blue stripes. Was that significant?"

"Red," said the girl, "for the communist world and blue for the Western or Free World."

"And when everything in my dream broke apart, it was about more than Berlin, more than Germany, and more than Europe."

"Yes. The breaking apart that began in Berlin would continue to spread across the world. When the communist revolutionary Mao Zedong declared in 1949 that China would now be ruled by a 'people's dictatorship,'[2] the Diabolos had succeeded in dividing China into two and in bringing half a billion people under totalitarian rule and into the division that was now encircling the globe.

"The history of the world was once again following the mystery of the Altar. The division of Berlin had now spread to Europe, Asia, Africa, Latin America, and even to the islands. The nations of the world found themselves in one camp or the other, or in the shadow of the two camps. Never before had the entire world been so *cast through* into two worlds. And it all went back to Berlin.

"And what was the diabolical plan? If he could divide the world, he could destroy the world. From division comes conflict; from conflict and from war comes destruction. So the Diabolos would divide the world for the purpose of destroying it."

"The Cold War," said Lara.

"Think about it," said the girl. "What were the two sides that made up the Cold War? The side that possessed the Altar, the Throne of Satan, and the side that did not. But then what were the two sides that made up the First World War? The side that possessed the Altar and started the war, and the side that did not. And what were the two sides of the Second World War? The side that possessed the Altar and started the war, and the side that did not. You see, the mystery is behind it all. It's all part of the same war.

So in the Cold War, it was the side that possessed the Altar that sought to spread a godless and evil ideology and dominion throughout the world. And the side without the Altar sought to stop that from happening.

"And wherever the Enemy brought the division, there would be conflict or war for that region and, potentially, for the world. He divided Korea in two and brought the Korean War. He divided Vietnam in two and brought the Vietnam War. And he divided the world in two to ignite a third world war that he might destroy the world.

"And how do you divide something in two?" she asked. "With an instrument of division, as in a sword. And wasn't it Karl Marx who wrote, 'See this sword? The prince of darkness sold it to me.'[3] Now the kingdom of Marx possessed the sword that the prince of darkness had given it. And the words of Karl Marx, which he quoted from the demon in *Faust*, would now for the first time come to the verge of fruition: 'Everything that exists deserves to perish.'"[4]

The Altar of Pergamon would be moved once more, from one land to another. We would now be told of it and how that moving would set in motion a crisis that would bring the world to the edge of calamity.

Chapter 59

THE FLASH POINT

THE SUN HAD set, and the sky was darkening. The Brandenburg Gate was now illuminated by floodlights shooting up from its base, glazing it in a warm yellow glow that caused it to stand out against the deep blues and reds of the early evening sky.

"You know that in all its thousands of years of existing," said the girl, "the Altar of Pergamon was moved just two times."

"Yes," I said, "from Pergamon to Germany and from Germany to the Soviet Union."

"And each time," she said, "it was the beginning of something colossal and of something that would end up bringing death and destruction." She looked down at the pavement, pausing before speaking again.

"But it was moved a third time."

"From the Soviet Union to where?" I asked.

"To its adopted mother city, Berlin—East Berlin."

"So," said Lara, "the Altar was brought back to what was now the world's dividing point and the ground from which its division was birthed."

"Yes," said the girl. "The Soviet Union put the pieces of the Altar in crates and loaded them onto freight cars. It took hundreds of freight cars to do it. The Altar was carried back to Berlin and to its house on Museum Island, within a mile of the line that split the world in two."

"Why?" I asked. "Why would the Soviet Union give it away?"

"First," she replied, "it was a political act. And second, they didn't really give it away. Remember, East Germany was a satellite of the Soviet Union and under its dominion. It was an occupied land with massive Soviet military forces stationed inside its borders. It was Moscow that had the ultimate authority over East Germany, controlling its economy, its political realm, and virtually everything else of note.

"The Altar was still in the possession of the communist world, and the Soviet Union was still in control and in possession of East Germany. And East Berlin was even more absolutely under the dominion and authority of the Soviet Union. The city was controlled by Soviet troops under the authority of the Soviet Union. The Altar was housed in East Berlin under Soviet control.

"So the Altar's dominion did not change, but its location did. But that alone would have massive repercussions. To move the Throne of Satan back to the city of Berlin would mean that Berlin would again become the focal point in the Enemy's purposes. And since Berlin was now the city of the world's division, it was now the division itself that would become empowered—and the potential of that division to bring mass destruction."

"When," I asked, "was the Altar transported to Berlin?"

"It happened in the autumn of 1958," she said.

"And did anything significant happen in 1958," asked Lara, "anything having to do with the city of Berlin?"

"Something of great significance," said the girl. "In the years since the birth of East Germany, there had been no major conflicts between the superpowers over Berlin. But all that would change. It would change just after Nikita Khrushchev consolidated his power to become the Soviet Union's premier. Troubled by the mass exodus of people from the communist world to the West and the role of West Berlin in that exodus, and furious over West Germany's rearmament, he issued an ultimatum to America and its Western allies.

"He demanded the West surrender its claim on Berlin and evacuate the city. He gave America and its allies six months to get out. The West rejected his demands and began preparing for the possibility of war. There was talk among American officials not only of waging war over Berlin but of the possibility of using nuclear weapons."

"Which," I said, "would have ushered in a third world war."

"That was the Dark Angel's plan…the destruction of the world over the city of his Altar…and right after the Altar had been returned there."

"And how long," asked Lara, "did the crisis go on?"

"That which would come to be known as the Berlin Crisis would go on into the following year. It would only subside when the Soviet Union's ultimatum expired in May of 1959."

"So the Altar was moved back to Berlin in 1958," I said, "and it just so happened that in that same year Berlin suddenly became the center of a conflict that almost brought the two superpowers to war and the world to nuclear war."

"Yes."

"When exactly was the Altar moved to Berlin?" I asked.

"In November of 1958," said the girl.

"And when did the crisis begin?" I asked.

"In November of 1958."

"The same year and the same month," said Lara.

"Yes," said the girl, "like clockwork."

"So after years of there being no major crisis over Berlin," I said, "as soon as they begin moving the Altar there, everything erupts. The Altar arrives in Berlin, and suddenly, the superpowers are drawn into a conflict, preparing for war and the possible use of nuclear weapons, and the entire world is drawn to the precipice of potential destruction. And it all once again centers on the city of the Altar, the Throne of Satan."

"The Throne of the Diabolos," said the little girl.

"But it wasn't over," she said. "It was only the beginning. The Berlin Crisis that began as the pieces of the Altar were brought back to the city was unresolved. And Berlin would continue to be the major focal point of the global conflict between the two superpowers. And the Enemy wasn't finished. The events that would now unfold would lead observers to call the city of the Altar the most dangerous place on earth."

Chapter 60

CLASH OF THE SUPERPOWERS

"In 1961," SAID the girl, "John F. Kennedy became president of the United States. In June of that year, Khrushchev and Kennedy met for a summit in Vienna specifically to address the issue and crisis concerning Berlin. Khrushchev now again demanded that the West withdraw from Berlin. The meeting left Khrushchev with the perception of Kennedy as weak and inexperienced. It would embolden him to go further.

"Just two months after that meeting, Khrushchev began the construction of an object that would become the symbol of the Cold War and the embodiment of the world's division—the Berlin Wall. They built it right there," she said, pointing into the distance, "right behind the Brandenburg Gate...a wall, the symbol of division and captivity, right next to a gate, the symbol of openness and freedom. So the Devil's Throne came to Berlin, and then three years later, the symbol of the Diabolos, the Divider—the wall—appeared. He had successfully divided the city, the nation, the continent, and the world. Now it would all manifest in the form of steel, concrete, and barbed wire."

"So what happened," asked Lara, "when the wall went up?"

"The Enemy would seek to use the divided city of his Throne to bring the world to destruction. America saw the building of the wall as a threat to the stability of Berlin and the postwar order. Kennedy mobilized American forces. He put the American military in Europe on high alert. He sent American troops into West Berlin to strengthen the West's position there and to be prepared for the possibility of war. He ordered over a hundred thousand guardsmen and reservists into active duty. He deployed military aircraft and tactical fighter squadrons to Europe, the largest jet deployment in the history of the American Air Guard and Air Guardsmen, with personnel specifically trained to deliver nuclear weapons. He moved American tanks and armored personnel carriers toward the wall.

"The conflict over Berlin would lead the world into still more dangerous territory. Kennedy and his advisers believed that the crisis was so dangerous that they had to begin preparing for nuclear war. The Pentagon produced the Berlin nuclear scenarios. Nuclear forces were strengthened, moved into position, and readied for war. On the other side of the wall and of the Iron Curtain, the Soviet Union began readying its own nuclear arsenal in Eastern Europe. Both superpowers were preparing for the prospect of nuclear war."

"So the world was being led to the edge of destruction," I said, "because of the city of the Altar."

"And over a wall," said Lara. "It doesn't make sense."

"But it does," said the girl. "What more likely place for the world to be brought to the edge of destruction than at the Devil's Throne? And yet the Enemy would bring the Berlin Crisis into even more dangerous territory.

"Two months after the beginning of the Berlin Wall, a United States official sought entrance into East Berlin at the crossing point known as Checkpoint Charlie. The communist guards refused to let him pass. The incident erupted into one of the most dangerous moments of the Cold War. American tanks rolled to the wall and to the checkpoint. The Soviet Union sent its tanks on the other side, toward the wall, to counter the American tanks.

"The two superpowers now stood face-to-face at the world's dividing line, each prepared for war. It was the only time in the Cold War that American and Soviet tanks actually faced each other, and at point-blank range. Both sides were ordered to shoot if fired upon. A single misstep could have triggered a cascading calamity. It was the closest that the world had ever come, up to that day, to the brink of nuclear war and destruction."

"And again...Berlin," I said, "Berlin...the mother of Germany and of German militarism, mother of anti-Semitism, mother of the First and Second World Wars, mother of Marxism in its cradling and of its resurrection, mother of Hitler's reign and the Third Reich, mother of the Holocaust, mother by implantation of the Soviet Union and communist revolution, mother of divisions and the dividing of the world, and mother of what was almost the destruction of the world. Quite a record."

"Quite a mother," said Lara.

"But it's not the city, Mr. Herzog," said the girl. "It's what came into the city, what the city received, and what rested here. What brought the world to the edge of nuclear war began in November 1958, just as the Altar was brought back to this place. And just one mile from the confrontation of American and Soviet troops at the wall stood the ancient Altar, the Throne of the Diabolos.

"And yet it wasn't over. For what was about to come would be even more ominous. And behind it all was the Altar's most dangerous of mysteries."

That most dangerous of mysteries would be revealed to us across the world in a desert of white sand and white mountains—in America.

PART XII

INFERNO

Chapter 61

LAND OF WHITE MOUNTAINS

THE LITTLE GIRL got up from the ground. We did likewise.

"And this is for you," she said as she handed us the next page.

"I must thank you for allowing me to practice my English and for trying to help me with my math. I hope it's been as enjoyable for you as it has been for me."

"Will you be going home now?" asked Lara.

"Yes."

"I wouldn't think it safe for a young girl to be walking alone at night in the city," said Lara. "Let us take you home."

"I'll be safe," she said. "I know the city. I know exactly where to go. I'll be safe. It is *you*, however, who must be careful, and *you* who must keep safe."

Before we could insist on taking her home, she left us and quickly disappeared from our view.

"Do you think she'll be all right?" I asked.

"I don't know," said Lara. "Let's go after her."

So we followed in the direction in which she departed. We searched for her for some time but never found her. Finally, we decided to have dinner. We chose one of Berlin's outdoor cafés. A few minutes after the waiter took our order, a second server came to our table with two glasses on a serving platter.

"This is one of Germany's favorite drinks," he said. "It's called Apfelschorle. It's a nonalcoholic beverage of apple juice and sparkling mineral water. It's a complimentary gift to you as our guests."

"Thank you," said Lara.

"Of course," he said with a smile before leaving us.

I got up from my chair to go to the restroom to wash my hands before eating. On the way I saw the waiter who had taken our order.

"Thank you," I said. "That was very nice of you."

"For the drinks?"

"Yes."

"That wasn't from us," he replied. "It was from your friend."

"My friend?"

"Yes, he told us he was your friend and wanted to surprise you with two drinks. He paid for the drinks and asked us to let him serve them to you. So we did."

I rushed back to Lara. She had lifted the glass and was about to drink. I put my hand around her wrist and gently lowered the glass to the table.

"What?" she asked.

"I believe the apples are bad," I said.

"The apples are bad? How would you…?"

"Let's get out of here."

So we left the café and headed back to our hotel. During the taxi ride, we caught our first glimpse of the page the girl had given us. Its image appeared to be that of a stylized flame.

"I'll work on it tonight," said Lara.

We decided we would not eat breakfast in a café or even at the hotel but would pick up some food from a store or from a random street vendor. So we had our breakfast that morning outside in a park. After eating, Lara took out her notebook and began sharing what she found.

"The title," she said, "was made up of several Greek words. They speak of a great fire. I would translate it as 'Inferno.'"

"That would certainly go along with the image," I said.

"And this is the text:

A Strange Fire
Kindled
To Consume
The Sacrifice
The Uncuttable
Cut
The Unbreakable
Broken
Children of the Priesthood
Keepers of the Flame
And of Another Desert
Death Is Born."

"So it has to do with fire."

"Yes," said Lara. "And how does that help us?"

"I haven't the slightest idea."

"What do you think cutting the Uncuttable means?"

"The Diabolos?" I said. "He's the Divider, the one who cuts through."

"But how do you cut the uncuttable?"

"I'm hoping you're going to say yes to my next question. Did this by any chance happen to come with a dream?"

"Well, as a matter of fact, it just so happens that it did."

"Go on."

"It wasn't long. I was walking through an arid, desertlike landscape colored with pale tans, rusty reds, and occasional streaks of white. The ground was made of hardened dry sand, with scattered stones and low desert shrubs. In the distance behind me was a white mountain range; in the distance ahead was a desert of white sand.

"I noticed the sound of people singing, chanting. I turned in the direction of the sound and saw what appeared to be some sort of ceremony of Indians."

"Indians from India or…"

"Native American Indians dressed in traditional Native American clothing—buckskin garments, headbands, feathered headdresses—dancing in a circle around a tall fire. As I came closer, I realized that it was a poplar tree. They were dancing around a burning poplar tree."

"How did you know it was a poplar tree?"

"I know what they look like, but in the dream it was just that I knew."

"And…?"

"That was it. The dream ended."

"The fire matches the words and image on the page. But what else do we have to go on?"

"I searched for a white mountain range and a white sand desert. In Spanish, 'white mountain range' is *sierra blanca*. The Sierra Blanca is a mountain range that overlooks the White Sands National Park."

"Where is it?"

"New Mexico."

"And the poplar tree?"

"The area is filled with poplar trees."

"And the Indians?"

"It's the land of the Mescalero Tribe. They have a reservation there. That's where we have to go."

So we set out on our next journey, one that would take us across the world to a land of white mountains and white desert sand, and where the mystery of the strange fire would be revealed.

Chapter 62

A STRANGE FIRE

We landed in Dallas and from there took a flight to El Paso, where we spent the night. The following morning, we rested, then in the afternoon set out in a rented car for New Mexico. It took us less than two hours from El Paso to see it.

"There it is," said Lara, "the White Sands."

It was to our left: a vast expanse of white sand dunes, their crests and valleys appearing out of place, like a snowscape in the desert sun. As we drove on, the color of our surroundings shifted from light tan to deep green. We had entered the Mescalero Apache Reservation. Dominating its horizon was the Sierra Blanca, the White Mountain Range. Driving up a winding mountain road, we made our way to Ruidoso, an oasis village of tall pines, forests, deer, bears, and cool mountain air in the middle of a desert. We stayed the night in two rented log cabins and the next day set out to find a landscape that matched that of Lara's dream.

We spent much of that morning driving around the area and finding nothing. Then we decided to head westward. It was only about twenty minutes after that that Lara became convinced we had come to the right place. The landscape was arid, with hardened sand and low desert shrubs.

It was about ten minutes later that Lara spotted a man sitting alone on the desert floor, far off the road in front of a circle of stones in the midst of which was a fire. We stopped the car, got out, and began walking toward him. As we approached, he looked up. He was middle-aged with a broad face, high cheekbones, copper-toned skin, and straight black hair down to his shoulders. He appeared to be Native American. I assumed he lived on or near the Mescalero Reservation.

"Are you lost?" he asked.

"That depends," I said.

"On what?"

"On who you are."

"I'm just the keeper of a fire," he said. "I don't know that I could be of any help to you unless…"

"Unless what?" I asked.

"Unless you're interested in fires."

Lara and I looked at each other and back at the man.

"I don't think we're lost," I said.

"Why don't you join me?" he said.

So we sat down alongside the man at the circle of stones.

"Shall we begin?" he asked.

"Let's," I replied.

"What have you learned of the Altar? What kind of altar is it?"

"An altar of burnt offerings," said Lara.

"An altar of burnt offerings, yes. And so those who came to possess the Altar in modern times would offer up burnt offerings. They would light a fire on the earth—the fire of war—to the consuming of lands, cities, and peoples. And have you been told what such things were called in the tongue of those who created the Altar in ancient times?"

"Holos caustos," said Lara. "Holocaust."

"And so the people who came to possess the Altar thousands of years later would not only light the fire of war but would seek to destroy a people by lighting the fire of a holocaust."

"Yes," said Lara. "It's been revealed to us."

"But the Altar of holocausts would bring forth another fire. The war that began in the city of the Altar of fire would end with the kindling of a new fire."

"A *new* fire..." said Lara.

"A much greater fire," he said, "the fire of atoms. The war would end with a fire kindled of atoms."

"Hiroshima and Nagasaki," I said.

"A strange fire," said the man.

"A Strange Fire Kindled," said Lara.

"The word *holocaust*," said the man, "is spoken of two things in the modern world. What are they?"

"The Nazi Holocaust," I said, "the destruction of the Jews."

"And...?"

"Nuclear holocaust," I replied.

"The Throne of Satan is an altar of holocausts. And so from that Altar would come the Holocaust of the Nazis and the nuclear holocaust that followed it, the holocaust of a strange fire."

"The inferno," said Lara.

He was stoking the fire with a leafless branch as he began opening the mystery of the Altar's other fire and how it came to be kindled on the earth.

Chapter 63

THE UNCUTTABLE

"What exactly does the word *holocaust* mean?" asked the man.

"Wholly consumed by fire," said Lara.

"What does the power of nuclear explosions allow us to do?"

"To wholly consume by fire," said Lara.

"What about the word *atom*? Do you know why an atom is called an *atom?* It comes from the Greek word *atomos,* which means it can't be cut…uncuttable…indivisible. The atom is called the atom because it was believed to be the most basic element of matter, one that could not be cut."

"The Uncuttable," said Lara. "It was talking about the atom."

"But in the late nineteenth century," said the man, "it was discovered that atoms contained still smaller components. So they were not the smallest of particles and perhaps not indivisible. In 1932, the British physicist James Chadwick discovered one of the atom's components, the neutron. Since the neutron is without an electrical charge, it could theoretically be used to penetrate the atom's nucleus without being repelled.

"Six years later, in December 1938, the chemists Otto Hahn and Fritz Strassmann, seeking to build on the work of Italian physicist Enrico Fermi, began an experiment in which they used neutrons to bombard uranium atoms. They expected that the neutrons would join the uranium atoms and produce heavier atomic elements.

"But something strange happened. Instead of finding heavier atomic elements, they found barium. Barium is an atomic element with a much lighter atomic mass than uranium, almost half as light. The findings shocked the two chemists. Hahn mailed the results of his experiment to his colleague and partner, the physicist Lise Meitner. Meitner showed the results to her nephew, Otto Frisch, who was visiting her for the holidays.

"In pondering Hahn's findings, the two realized what had happened. The nucleus of the uranium atom had split in two, producing two lighter nuclei. They identified the phenomenon as nuclear division. In order to describe it, Frisch drew on the division of biological cells and coined the term *nuclear fission.*"

"The Uncuttable Cut," said Lara, "the splitting of the atom."

"But it was what the cutting of the uncuttable would lead to that would prove to be the most ominous thing. Drawing on Einstein's equation

$E = mc^2$, Meitner and Frisch realized that the splitting of the uranium nucleus would release massive amounts of nuclear energy. Further, it was possible that the splitting of the atom would cause other neutrons to fire at other atoms and set off a chain reaction, igniting an atomic explosion. Upon hearing the news, physicists across the world began repeating the experiments seeking to produce the same result, nuclear fission—and they did.

"With that," said the man, "the world entered the Atomic Age of nuclear weapons and the power to unleash a holocaust of unimaginable destruction. For the first time in human history, man would have the capability of bringing the world to an end. Do you know where Hahn and Strassmann split the uranium atom?"

"No," I replied.

"Berlin," said the man. "It all happened in Berlin...in the city of the Altar. The Altar of holocausts required the fire of holocausts, and so it was there that the fire was kindled. And so the city of the holocaust Altar would give the world two holocausts—the Holocaust that would fall upon the Jewish people and the holocaust that would fall upon the earth. Both holocausts were foreshadowed in the same year, 1938: the first holocaust in Kristallnacht in November of that year, the second, in the splitting of the atom the very next month."

"And so that too," said Lara, "it was all there from the beginning when the first pieces of the Altar arrived in Berlin from Pergamon...The same city that was given the Altar of fire and holocausts would give the world the fire of nuclear holocaust."

"Yes," said the man, "and that the fire that now threatened to destroy the earth would be ignited at the Destroyer's Throne."

We would now be told of a different and contrary mystery, one that would ensure that Hitler would never acquire the power of nuclear destruction—a mystery even more ancient than that of the Altar.

Chapter 64

KEEPERS OF THE FLAME

"SO," SAID THE man, "the most destructive force ever unleashed on the world came into being because the atom was divided. And who is the Divider? The Diabolos. And it wasn't only that the atom was divided in Berlin but in Nazi Germany.

"When Hahn and Strassmann split the uranium atom, they did so under the Kaiser Wilhelm Institute for Chemistry. The institute was an integral part of the Third Reich. So the power to destroy the world was birthed under Adolf Hitler. It would be within his grasp. Do you realize how close the world came to seeing the Enemy's strategy fulfilled? Had Hitler developed the first atomic bomb, it could very well have meant the world's destruction.

"And when was the atom split in Berlin? At the very end of 1938, on the eve of the year Hitler would begin the Second World War. Do you think that if he had acquired the power of nuclear destruction, he would not have used it in waging that war?

"The splitting of the atom in Berlin set off a race to build the first atomic bomb. To achieve that goal, Hitler established the *Uranprojekt*, or Uranium Project, overseen and directed from the city of the Altar. But Hitler's plans to acquire that power would be thwarted by a mystery that began long before the creation of the Altar of Pergamon."

"How would a mystery from ancient times," asked Lara, "affect the development of nuclear weapons?"

"The Altar of Pergamon was not only an altar of burnt offerings but a satanic inversion of the Altar that stood in the Temple of God. You were told of the law of burnt offerings as given in the Scriptures?"

"The law of holocausts," I replied. "Yes."

"And what did the law of holocausts require?"

"That the fire of the Altar was to be kept burning."

"And who was it that was to light and keep that fire?" he asked.

"It would have had to have been the priests," said Lara.

"And what did God call the children of Israel to be?"

"A holy nation," said Lara.

"And a 'kingdom of priests,'"[1] he said, "a priestly nation. And it was for the priests to light and keep the fire. So Israel, as the priestly nation, was called to kindle and keep the fire of burnt offerings, the fire of holocausts. Is it possible then that the children of the priestly nation would also be the kindlers, the igniters of the other fire—the fire of nuclear holocaust?"

"The Children of the Priesthood," said Lara, "that's what it meant."

"Who was it that kindled the nuclear fire?" he asked. "The man who, in the early twentieth century, came up with the theory and the equation that would predict the immense energy that nuclear reactions would release was the Jewish patent clerk Albert Einstein. The man from Copenhagen who developed the model of the atom and helped America unlock nuclear power was the Jewish scientist Niels Bohr.

"The man who first conceived of a self-sustaining nuclear chain reaction in the early 1930s and the possibility of an atomic bomb was the Jewish physicist Leo Szilard. The Austrian whose work with Otto Hahn proved essential in the splitting of the uranium atom was the Jewish woman Lise Meitner…"

"The one," said Lara, "who first identified nuclear fission."

"Yes. And the reason Hahn had to mail her his results was that she had fled Germany for Sweden to escape the Nazis. The man from Austria who helped Meitner break that mystery and who coined the term *nuclear fission* was the Jewish scientist Otto Frisch.

"The German who demonstrated that the making of an atomic bomb was possible and practical was the Jewish physicist Rudolf Peierls. The Hungarian who came up with the design for nuclear reactors in the production of plutonium was the Jewish physicist Eugene Wigner. The Austrian overseer of the Theoretical Physics Division of the Manhattan Project, America's endeavor to produce the first atomic bomb, was the Jewish physicist Victor Weisskopf.

"Other prominent contributors to the Manhattan Project included the American Jewish physicists Richard Feynman, Rubby Sherr, and Joseph Hirschfelder; the Polish Jewish physicist Joseph Rotblat and the Jewish mathematician Stanislaw Ulam; and the Hungarian Jewish physicist Edward Teller, who would also become known as the father of the hydrogen bomb. And the most critical and central figure in the Manhattan Project, the man who oversaw and directed it, the father of the atomic bomb, was the Jewish theoretical physicist J. Robert Oppenheimer."

"The Children of the Priesthood, Keepers of the Flame," said Lara.

"It was no accident," said the man, "that they were all born of the priestly kingdom, the kingdom charged with kindling and keeping the fire. And so they became the kindlers of the fire of the atomic age."

"Without them," I said, "the history of the world..."

"Would have had a very different outcome," said the man. "America would not have become the world's first nuclear power. Did you notice how many of these came from Europe, from Germany and Austria? Hitler could have gained the power of nuclear destruction. But his war against the children of Israel caused German science to lose its Jewish physicists, chemists, and theorists who could have otherwise enabled it to attain nuclear capabilities. But they fled for their lives to the West and to America. And so it was not Nazi Germany but America that became the world's first nuclear superpower. It was these same refugees who, upon hearing of the splitting of the atom in Berlin, warned the West of the danger that would come to the world if Hitler came into the possession of nuclear weapons.

"The memorandum that would lead both America and the United Kingdom to begin pursuing the development of the atomic bomb was written by the Jewish scientists Otto Frisch and Rudolf Peierls. And before that, the letter that first warned President Franklin Roosevelt of the danger of Nazi Germany acquiring nuclear weapons and urging America to pursue it first was written by the Jewish physicists Leo Szilard and Albert Einstein.

"And so," said the man, "from the mystery of the one Altar, the power to destroy the world almost fell into the hands of Adolf Hitler. But from the mystery of the other Altar, it was kept from him and given to another."

"And the world wasn't destroyed," I said.

"Yes," he replied. "That too."

We would now be given the last mystery of the strange fire and the poplar tree.

Chapter 65
THE POPLAR

"WHY WERE WE brought *here*," I asked, "to be shown these things?"

"You don't know?" he said. "You don't know where you are?"

At that, he rose to his feet and motioned for us to do likewise.

"You are in the land where it all happened, where it all began. Look," he said, pointing into the distance. "There, just beyond the White Sands, is Trinity."

"Trinity," Lara repeated.

"The ground on which the first atomic bomb was tested, the site of the world's first nuclear explosion.

"It was there at 5:29 in the morning on July 16, 1945, that a blinding flash turned the predawn darkness into that which was brighter than noon. It was there that the first mushroom cloud in world history appeared and went up seven miles into the sky. The blast was so powerful that it shattered windows over one hundred miles away. And it was there that the world irrevocably entered the age of nuclear destruction."

"I can't imagine," said Lara, "what it was like for those who were there to witness it for the first time."

"Even many of those who devised that bomb stood there in stunned silence. That is *where* it happened. And do you know *when* it happened? It happened during the ancient biblical days appointed for sorrow and lamentation, the nine days of mourning at the start of the month of Av.

"The Sabbath leading up to the day of the explosion was called the Black Sabbath, as it is the most sorrowful of Sabbaths in the biblical year. And it is appointed that on that day, the words of the prophet Isaiah are to be read, words of judgment. And in that appointed passage are four allusions to the ancient cities of Sodom and Gomorrah."[1]

"The cities that were destroyed," said Lara, "by fire from the sky."

"The appointed word," he said, "speaks of cities 'burned with fire.'"[2]

"What do they mourn for," asked Lara, "on those days?"

"Destruction," said the man. "Calamitous destruction."

"Of what?" I asked.

"The destruction of their world. In 586 BC, the armies of Babylon destroyed the Holy City, Jerusalem, and the nation of Judah. Their world ended in fire. Centuries later, in AD 70, the armies of Rome would do the same, and the city and nation would again be brought to an end by fire. The two destructions happened at the same time of year, the same week and days. And so it was during those days of mourning over the two destructions of fire that the most powerful of fires, and the most unimaginable of fires, was unleashed on the world."

"I had a dream," said Lara, "where I saw Native Americans dancing around a burning poplar tree. Does that mean anything?"

"This," he said, lifting up the branch he had been using to stoke the fire, "is the branch of a poplar. Do you know how to say 'poplars' in Spanish?"

"No," said Lara.

"*Los alamos.*"

"Los Alamos," she repeated.

"Los Alamos," I said, "the name of the place where the first atomic bomb was built."

"Yes," said the man. "And it *was* all there from the beginning. When those two ancient pieces of the Altar of holocausts first arrived in Berlin from Pergamon, it was a sign that from that city would come two unimaginable holocausts, that which brought destruction on six million Jews and that which threatened to bring destruction on the world. And just as the first holocaust was completed in 1945, the second holocaust was kindled."

"But it would not be enough for the Enemy that such a power had come into the world or that it had the potential for bringing the world to an end. He would seek to make it happen. And had he succeeded in his plans, if what almost happened actually had happened...you wouldn't be here today. You wouldn't exist."

"What do you mean?" I said.

"It is not for me to tell you," he said. "It is not my charge."

But the answer would be waiting for us on the shores of a veiled and secret-laden tropical island.

PART XIII

ABYSS

Chapter 66

THE PASTEL CITY

THE MAN WALKED us back to our car and then, before we parted, handed us the next page.

"Will you be all right?" I asked. "Do you need a ride?"

"I'll be fine," he said, "I know this land well."

As we drove off, the man waved, then headed back to the fire. Lara began studying the page.

"So what does it look like?" I asked.

"Like two castles or palaces with a circle between them. The circle is a black spiral swirling into the center."

"The two castles, I would say, represent two kingdoms."

"And the spiraling circle?"

"I don't know."

Our journey was short. We had decided that there was no point in returning to El Paso when we had no idea where we were going next. So we headed back to our cabins in Ruidoso, the mountain village on the Sierra Blanca. The next day, Lara and I met in an outdoor seating area by our cabins for our morning meeting. She took out her notebook and read her translation of the page:

"The Dark Angel
Calling
Down His Fire
To the Earth
Powers
To the Island
Of Destruction
And a World
To the Edge
Of the Abyss
While Hidden
Lie the Arrows
Of the Lightning
Of the Gods."

"OK," I said. "The Dark Angel I think we can identify. But the Abyss, the Island, the Lightning of the Gods…I have no idea. Was there a dream to go with this?"

"Not yet."

The dream would come three days later. Lara came to breakfast that morning with a slightly mischievous look on her face.

"It happened," I said. "You had a dream, and it revealed to you the place where we're going next."

"You could at least let me surprise you occasionally."

"All right, surprise me."

"I was walking through a city of pastel-colored buildings—faded yellows, oranges, pinks, blues, and greens—with wrought-iron balconies draped with laundry. The air was thick with the smell of coffee, sea salt, and the smoke of cigars seeping out of the buildings. There were palm trees everywhere. I knew I was in the tropics. And from the music that spilled onto the streets, I knew I was in Latin America. By the way the people were dressed and the cars, which seemed to be from the 1950s but were new, I concluded that the vision was not of the present but of the past.

"I noticed a child standing on the sidewalk ahead of me, a little girl. She couldn't have been more than four or five. She was wearing a wide-brimmed yellow hat and a turquoise dress. She took my hand and began leading me through the streets. The city began darkening, and just as it turned to night, the little girl led me into a massive open plaza. Overlooking the plaza was a large white tower with a large white statue in front of it. The plaza was filled with people, tens of thousands of them, in rapt attention to a man who was addressing them in Spanish.

"'They have no idea what's coming,' said the girl.

"'And do you?' I asked.

"'I do,' she replied.

"At that, the little girl was pulled back away from me into the crowd. I couldn't tell what was pulling her, and I couldn't stop it. 'Remember!' she cried out. 'Remember this when you come here,' and then she disappeared into the crowd. And the dream ended."

"And what do you make of it?"

"I searched the Web to see if I could identify the place. I looked for the plaza, the white tower, and the statue—and found them. The tower was a monument to the Cuban hero José Martí. The white statue was of him. It was Revolution Plaza. I was in Havana."

"We're going to Cuba?" I asked.

"I believe we are."

"How do we even get in? It's not the most open of places."

"I'll contact the museum and see if they can arrange it."

So she did. For two weeks, we waited there in Ruidoso to hear back from her contacts at the museum. Finally, the word came. The museum was able to obtain permission for us to go to Cuba for the purpose of "educational activities" and "research." One could argue it was true.

It was our last night at Ruidoso. We had come back to our cabins from an early evening walk. As I entered my bedroom, my attention was drawn to a Bible on my night table. It was a hotel Bible that had formerly been placed inside the top drawer of the night table. What caught my attention was the fact that it was open, and I hadn't opened it. Further, a verse on the opened page was highlighted in yellow and read:

> I will ascend into heaven,
> I will exalt my throne above the stars of God.[1]

It was the vow of Satan to lift up his Throne above the Throne of God. They were in my room. In that remote mountaintop village in the middle of a desert, they had found where I was staying and were able to get inside. We felt it was too late to check out of those cabins, so we each slept with heavy furniture moved in front of our doors.

The next morning, we drove back to El Paso, then set out for Miami. From Miami, we boarded a plane to Havana, Cuba. The veiled island would open up for us a secret of ancient origins that almost brought the world to an end.

Chapter 67
THE DESTROYER'S PAWN

CUBA IS ONLY about ninety miles off the coast of Florida. But we might as well have stepped into another world and another age.

Havana closely matched what Lara had told me she had seen in her dream: the pastel-colored buildings, the wrought-iron balconies, and the palm trees—a city frozen in time, stuck in the days of the Cuban Revolution, with buildings from the 1940s and 1950s and cars from the same era. And it appeared to be crumbling from decades of neglect.

The day after our arrival, we headed for Revolution Plaza, the central setting of Lara's dream. It wasn't filled with multitudes of people as in the dream; only scattered pedestrians dotted its expanse. We walked the plaza, looking, as covertly as possible, for a sign, a clue, something to go on. But there was nothing.

"You're not expecting to find the little girl in your dream?" I said.

"You never know," Lara replied.

"She was how old, did you say—five, four? I don't think they'd be using them that young. There have to be laws against it."

"She told me to remember. There had to be a reason."

"You don't even know that she was real."

We continued walking, but still there was nothing.

"Something I've been wondering about," I said.

"What?"

"The end."

"Of our journey?"

"When we come to the last page, what then? What are we supposed to do with all this? And what am *I* supposed to do? Everything changed when that stranger showed up to hand me that piece of paper. That skeptic who was so sure of himself and who doubted the existence of anything he couldn't see with his eyes or reason with his mind...I'm beginning to doubt that he exists anymore...And if he doesn't exist, then what do I even go back to?"

"I would think," said Lara, "to something better."

Finally, we gave up the search and headed back across the plaza and then to our hotel. As we passed the tall white tower and the statue of the José Martí Memorial, Lara stopped.

"Look," she said. Sitting on the slope of the grass on which the tower stood was a woman, perhaps in her late sixties or early seventies, with black hair down to her shoulders.

"Look at her," said Lara again. "She's wearing a yellow hat."

"There have to be a lot of yellow hats in Cuba."

"And a turquoise dress. That's what the little girl was wearing."

"But she's not a little girl and hasn't been one for some time."

"We have to go to her."

If the woman saw us coming, she gave no sign of it but just sat there staring intensely out into the plaza. It was only as we came close that she looked up.

"Do you need some help?" she said in a voice that was weathered, husky, and yet warm. Her English was eloquent and yet delivered in a pronounced Spanish accent. She had an air of dignity about her and gave the impression that she had seen and endured much.

"Can you help us?" said Lara.

"With what?"

"A mystery."

"About what?"

"An altar."

"Why don't you join me?"

So we sat down on the grass by the towering white monument in Revolution Plaza.

"Would you by any chance be speaking of an ancient altar...an altar of evil?"

"Yes."

"The Altar of Pergamon?"

"Yes."

"What was the last you were told of it? Where did they leave off?"

"The Altar was sent back to Berlin, and just then Berlin became the center of a global conflict that almost brought the two superpowers and the world to war."

"When did they send it back to Berlin?" asked the woman.

"In 1958," I replied.

"When in 1958?"

"November."

"So everything began in November of 1958, and it ended up bringing the world to the point of war."

"Yes," said Lara.

"The Enemy was seeking the world's destruction," she said. "But he needed one more puzzle piece. He found it here. The island was in turmoil. A band of guerrilla fighters led by the rebel leader Fidel Castro was engaged in an armed struggle against the island's dictator, Fulgencio Batista. The revolution had been largely contained in the island's mountains for two years. But then everything changed."

"When?" I asked.

"In 1958. The year the Altar was returned and the year that began the Berlin Crisis. And not just 1958. The turning point of the Cuban Revolution came specifically in November of 1958, when the Altar was brought to Berlin, to the dividing line of the Cold War.

"It was in November 1958 that the Batista regime began to collapse. And it was in November that Castro's forces had taken over most of Cuba's Oriente and Las Villas provinces, splitting the island in two. And it was then that Castro's victory and Batista's defeat assumed the air of inevitability. After November, just one month would pass before Batista would flee the island and Castro would take over, soon to become its new dictator.

"So in November of 1958, the Altar was brought to the dividing line of the Cold War. And that same year and that same month, that dividing line spread into the Western Hemisphere and to the island at America's doorstep. And the Cold War began entering its most dangerous phase.

"All the pieces—America, the Soviet Union, Berlin, Cuba, and Castro—were being set into position. You must know that the Devil plays chess. He sets his pieces on the board years, decades, before he puts them into play."

"That's who it was in my dream," said Lara. "It was Castro who was addressing the people in this plaza."

"He was one of the Enemy's most important chess pieces," said the woman.

"How so?" I asked.

"He was placed on the board for that moment as a pawn."

"For?"

"For many things. But most importantly, to bring about the destruction of the world."

"And when the moment came, it would usher in the most dangerous event in human history."

Chapter 68

EDGE OF THE ABYSS

"It began in Berlin," said the woman, "as all these things do. It was the armed confrontation between the two superpowers at the wall that began driving the world to what could have been its end."

"How?" I asked.

"The Berlin Crisis led the superpowers to increase their nuclear deployments. It emboldened the Soviet premier, Nikita Khrushchev, to challenge American power. As the United States stationed its forces in West Berlin, so now the Soviet Union would station its forces at America's doorstep, Cuba. Khrushchev believed that by doing this, he would gain leverage to drive the West out of Berlin. Though it was unspoken, Berlin was again at the heart of world conflict.

"Castro's revolution and his anti-American and pro-communist stance had opened the door for Khrushchev to make a dangerous move. Not long after the confrontation at the Berlin Wall, Khrushchev began considering placing nuclear missiles in Cuba aimed at the American mainland. By the summer of 1962, with Castro's consent, the Soviet Union began secretly transporting troops, equipment, and missiles to the Caribbean island. By October, thousands of Soviet troops, technicians, and support equipment had arrived there, along with nuclear ballistic missiles and nuclear warheads able to strike major American cities in minutes."

"The Dark Angel," said Lara, "Calling Down His Fire to the Earth."

"In mid-October 1962, an American spy plane took photographs of Soviet ballistic missile sites under construction in western Cuba. The photographs were shown to President Kennedy. Kennedy then went on television to address the American people, informing them of the crisis and of his decision to place a naval blockade on Cuba while demanding that the Soviet Union immediately remove the missiles. Soviet ships carrying missile parts were already on their way to the island. Two days after Kennedy's ultimatum, they would approach the line of quarantine in the American blockade."

"And Powers," said Lara, "to the Island of Destruction."

"The United States and the Soviet Union stood one step away from all-out nuclear war. American forces were placed on DEFCON 2, meaning that nuclear bombers were now airborne and ready to strike at a moment's notice. For thirteen days in October 1962, the world stood at the brink of destruction, and its people in fear of instantaneous annihilation. The slightest miscalculation on either side could have brought the world to its end. Kennedy was being urged to invade Cuba, while Castro was urging the Soviet Union to launch a nuclear strike on America. Had either one of those things happened, it would have meant the destruction of entire cities and the instant death of millions."

"And a World," said Lara, "to the Edge of the Abyss."

"Yes," said the woman. "In his televised speech on the crisis, Kennedy would tell the nation that the world had been brought to 'the abyss of destruction.'"[1]

"That's it," said Lara. "The image on the page. The two castles, the two kingdoms—one was America; the other was Russia. And the circle in between them, with the spiral winding to the center, represented the abyss spiraling into oblivion."

"It was the time of the Destroyer," said the woman, "the closest the world had ever come to the end of history. People rushed to stores and supermarkets, stripping them of canned foods and emergency supplies. Others fled their homes and cities in search of refuge. Still others scouted emergency fallout shelters to hide themselves and their families from the coming destruction. Schools throughout the nation ran practice drills in which the children hid under their desks in the hope of being protected against nuclear explosions. Families stocked their fallout shelters with food. And some parents bought metal dog tags to simplify the identification of their children's bodies.

"And they had no idea that their lives and their world were almost brought to an end because of the mystery of an ancient altar and the Throne of Satan. It all began when they moved that Altar back to Berlin, and then it kept progressing, step-by-step, up to that moment."

"Carl Humann," I said. "He should never have set foot in that place."

"The power that now almost brought the world to destruction," said Lara, "was birthed in the city of the Altar when they split the atom."

"And the power that triggered it," I said, "the Soviet Union, was birthed through Karl Marx, who said, 'Everything that exists deserves to perish.'"[2]

"'I bring the world to ruins,' he wrote," said the woman, "'the world which bulks between me and the abyss.'[3] And yet long before that, the prophet wrote of him who began it all, the one who shakes the earth, who causes kingdoms to tremble, who seeks to turn it all into a wasteland.[4]

"He almost destroyed it," said the woman. "He almost destroyed it all. They were that close. And if it had happened, everything you now see—the grass, the flowers, the blue sky—would be gone...or would have never come into existence...And all who now live—those who walk this square, the children playing in the distance—none of them would exist...and all because of an ancient mystery, an altar, and the Throne of Satan. That's how real it is. That's how real *he* is, Mr. Herzog, not a red-caped man but the Destroyer. That's the reality of evil.

"And the two of you, you would never have come into existence. You see, long before you came across this mystery, long before you even knew of its existence, your lives were already joined to it...just as are the lives of everyone who lives on this planet."

"And yet," said the woman, "there was another mystery behind the events that almost brought the world to an end in 1962—a deep secret that the American president and Soviet premier kept hidden from the world."

Chapter 69

THE ANCIENT MATRIX

"WOULD YOU LIKE to see the ocean?" she asked.

"I don't see why not," I replied.

"It's a bit of a walk, but pleasant."

We got up from the grass and followed the woman out of the plaza and through the streets and neighborhoods of Havana to the ocean. The closer we came to the water, the saltier and breezier the air became. And then the buildings opened up to reveal the Malecón. The Malecón is Havana's protective seawall and coastal promenade, along which one could see fishermen, strolling couples, street musicians, and men, women, and children sitting along the seawall, as the three of us decided to do. We sat down and, from the edge of the Malecón, gazed out into the vast blue expanse of the Caribbean Sea.

"It was in these waters," she said, "that the American ships stood ready to confront the Soviet ships approaching with nuclear missile parts as the world stood on edge."

"And what happened?" I asked.

"Well, not to spoil the ending," she said, "but they didn't blow everything up. The world didn't end."

"That's good to hear," I said.

"After bringing the world to the brink of destruction, the Soviet Union backed down and agreed to remove its missiles.

"But it was another place, far away from here, that the secret story behind the crisis unfolded. The leaders of both superpowers kept it hidden for as long as they could. And yet behind the hidden story was another hidden story, and behind their secret lay an even deeper secret, hidden even from them.

"The most dangerous moment in world history, when did it begin? What was the specific event that set it all in motion? What led Khrushchev to place those missiles in Cuba?"

"Tell us," I replied.

"What happened in Berlin at Checkpoint Charlie would set the stage for it. It was just months after the confrontation that Nikita Khrushchev was in the Crimea on the shores of the Black Sea. His attention was drawn to the nuclear missiles America had placed on the other side of the sea, aimed at the Soviet Union and so close that they could wipe out the communist state in a matter of minutes. Khrushchev believed it was time that America learned what it felt like 'to have her own land and own people threatened.'[1]

"It was those nuclear missiles on the other side of the Black Sea that led Khrushchev to come up with the plan to place nuclear missiles on Cuban soil at America's doorstep. So it was there that the crisis that almost brought the world to an end began.

"And yet even this had its roots in Berlin in the wake of the showdown at the wall, when the two superpowers embarked on a massive nuclear buildup with an accelerated production of nuclear missiles and new deployments of those missiles and weapons.

"It was from the Berlin Crisis that Kennedy decided to place nuclear missiles at Russia's doorstep, on the other side of the Black Sea. It was in October 1961 that the US placed its missiles there, in the very same month of the superpower showdown at the Berlin Wall. And though they were never fired, those missiles would prove to be the most dangerous weapons in the entire Cold War, for it was their very presence that brought the world to the edge of nuclear destruction."

"And what was the secret behind the secret?" asked Lara. "What was it that even the superpowers didn't know?"

"When Khrushchev pondered those missiles on the other side of the sea and got his inspiration to place missiles in Cuba, he had no idea that it was all connected to an ancient mystery."

"How?" asked Lara.

"The land on the other side of the Black Sea was Turkey."

"The land of the Altar!" said Lara.

"Yes," said the woman, "the nuclear missiles were all stationed in the ancient home of the Altar, of Satan's Throne."

"The vessels of destruction," I said, "in the land of the Destroyer."

"And yet it was even more than that. The missiles were all stationed on Turkey's western coast in the region of Izmir."

"Izmir," said Lara. "The biblical Smyrna from the Book of Revelation. We were there."

"And it was more than that," said the woman. "For out of all the many provinces of Turkey, *Izmir is the ancient resting place of the Altar of Pergamon. The crisis that almost destroyed the world began in the land of the Altar of Pergamon.*"

"And the Altar's foundation is still there," I said, "on the high place of Pergamon. So that which almost destroyed the world came from the land of Pergamon."

"It's unbelievable," said Lara.

"The entire world," I said, "was almost brought to an end from the Throne of Satan!"

"The missiles that almost destroyed the world," said the woman, "were stationed on the ground of an ancient kingdom."

"Which one?" asked Lara.

"The Kingdom of Pergamon."

"The destruction of the world from the Kingdom of Pergamon!" said Lara.

"Those missiles," I said. "How far were they stationed from the Altar?"

"Some stood as close as fifty miles from the Altar's foundation. Some were as close as forty, some as close as thirty. And some stood just twenty miles from the high place of Satan's Throne."

"It's too much," said Lara.

"So that which the Book of Revelation identified as the place 'where Satan dwells,'"[2] said the woman, "would become the place that brought the world to the brink of a nuclear holocaust and the abyss of total destruction…the destruction of the world from the Kingdom of Pergamon."

"And yet," said the woman, "there is even more to the mystery. For behind the missiles that almost brought the world to an end…was an ancient god."

Chapter 70

LIGHTNING OF THE GODS

SHE PAUSED, GAZING silently out into the waters, giving us time to process what we had heard. The ocean wind had grown more intense and was now buffeting our hair and clothes. Finally, Lara broke the silence.

"You said that they hid it from the world, the missiles in Izmir. Why?"

"To avoid destruction," she replied. "Khrushchev had given America two demands: first, that America pledge that it would not invade Cuba and, second, that it would remove its nuclear missiles from Izmir. Publicly, America accepted only the first demand. But privately, it agreed to the second—on the express condition that the Soviet Union would keep the connection of the missiles in Izmir to the Cuban Missile Crisis a secret. The Soviet Union removed its missiles from Cuba, and several months later, America secretly removed its missiles from Izmir."

"And the other mystery?" I said.

"The Altar of Pergamon," she said, "is the Altar of Zeus. And the Altar of Zeus is the Throne of Satan. Why is that?"

"As it was explained to us," said Lara, "the Scriptures state that behind the gods were spirits. In Hebrew, they were called the *shedim*, and in Greek, the *daimónia*, or demonic spirits. Zeus was the king of the gods and so the lord of spirits. The lord of demonic spirits is Satan. And so behind Zeus was Satan. Or, in other words, Zeus was one of his ancient masks. And so the Altar of Zeus is the Throne of Satan."

"And what kind of name is *Zeus*?" asked the woman.

"Greek," said Lara.

"Yes, it's what the Greeks called him. *Zeus* comes from the Indo-European root words *Dyeus Phter*, meaning Sky Father. The Romans also worshipped him. In the language of Rome, the Sky Father, Dyeus Phter, became *Iu Piter*...or *Jupiter*. The Altar of Zeus was the Altar of Jupiter, and Pergamon, the place where his sacrifices were offered up."

"So what would that have to do with the near destruction of the world?" I asked.

"Because the vessels that brought the world to the edge of destruction bore a name."

"What do you mean?" asked Lara.

"The missiles that triggered the most dangerous moment in world history bore the name of an ancient god."

"Which ancient god?" I asked.

"Jupiter," said the woman, "Zeus."

"How?" I asked.

"They were called the *Jupiter missiles.*"

"So they placed the missiles of Jupiter," I said, "in the land of the Altar of Jupiter."

"An altar of Jupiter," said the woman, "that required fire for its burnt offerings. And now came the missiles of Jupiter carrying the fire."

"Vessels of nuclear fire," I said, "in the missiles of Jupiter."

"Jupiter, or Zeus," said the woman, "was the god who would throw down lightning bolts, fire from the heavens, on his enemies. And do you know the Latin word for that which is thrown? The word is *missilis,* as in *missile.* The thunderbolts in this case were the Jupiter missiles...the missiles of Jupiter."

"While Hidden Lie the Arrows," said Lara, "of the Lightning of the Gods."

"So in the land of Pergamon," said the woman, "where the Altar of Jupiter stood—the vessel of fire, holocausts, and burnt offerings—now stood the missiles of Jupiter—vessels of fire, holocausts, and burnt offerings of another kind. And though they were never fired, they would shake the earth. And so once again from the mystery of the Altar came death and destruction, now to the point where it almost destroyed the world."

Again she paused, and again she gazed out into the waters of the Caribbean. And then she spoke.

"When the two of you began this journey, you had no idea what you would find or what you were getting yourselves into. You set out on the journey because the mystery fascinated you, you were drawn into it, and you couldn't dismiss it."

"I came," said Lara, "because I didn't have much of a choice."

"And there was a dream," I said. "Don't forget the dream."

"But what you found was a mystery far beyond anything you imagined, far more real and far more colossal...to the rising and falling of nations and powers, to the igniting of world wars, to global calamities and holocausts...a mystery that has altered the course of human history...and one that almost brought the world and everyone in it to an end.

"And that's why there are forces and agents of those forces that would stop at nothing to keep you from completing your journey and fulfilling this mission...because the stakes are that high...nothing less than the future of this world. And that is why you must not stop...No matter what happens, you must keep going...to the final revelation...and the completion of the journey...no matter what may come."

I didn't know how to respond to such words, nor did Lara. So we just sat there, the three of us on that stone seawall, gazing out toward the horizon as the wind gusted against us.

But it wouldn't be long before the weight of her words would come crashing down on us. And it would begin there in Havana before we set out on the next journey—the journey that would uncover the mystery of the last page.

PART XIV

MYSTERY

Chapter 71

A TASTE OF OLD HAVANA

WE GOT UP from the seawall. The woman handed Lara the next page of the book.

"It's the last one, the final page and a mystery of what was, what is, and what is yet to come."

She wished us well and departed. But before disappearing from our view, she turned around. "Remember what I've told you," she said.

"Remember," said Lara. "That was the last thing the little girl in my dream told me before she disappeared into the crowd."

"I believe she was referring to what she said about finishing the course," I replied.

"Do you realize how old she would have been," said Lara, "at the time of the revolution? Maybe four or five years old...*just like the girl.*"

"We don't even know that the girl was real," I said. "She was probably just a sign to lead us to the woman."

"I don't know."

We walked along the Malecón for a bit, then turned into a side street, the ocean wind now at our backs. The street was packed with people, with music blaring through the open windows of the apartments above us. Not long after turning into that street, Lara glanced behind us. She turned back ahead and said to me.

"I'm not saying it's definite," she said, "but there are two men who were walking behind us on the Malecón and who are walking in back of us now."

"Maybe they're just headed in the same direction."

"And maybe not."

I turned around and saw them, about thirty feet behind us, two men in black shirts, pants, and jackets. It could have been what I had just told Lara, but I was beginning to doubt it. Just then, a bus pulled up and stopped in between us and the two men behind us. A crowd of people got off. At the same time, a vendor pulled his cart across the sidewalk just as we passed him. I took it as our chance to break away.

"Let's go!" I said as I grabbed Lara's hand and we rushed onto a side street to our left, hoping to lose the two men. The street was quieter, with crumbling sidewalks and far fewer people. But the men again appeared in back of us and at the same distance. Then one of them crossed over to the opposite sidewalk while the other stayed behind us. The two walked in a perfect parallel line. It seemed as if they were trying to herd us into a corner.

I spotted a narrow passageway between two buildings. We turned into it and ran, with dripping pipes over our heads, garbage cans to our sides, and stray cats that darted out of our way as we barreled through. The two men likewise turned into the alleyway in pursuit. We spotted another alleyway and ran into it and then into a third. The two men did likewise.

Suddenly, everything opened up into a courtyard in the midst of the buildings. A family was eating dinner there over a small wooden table. As we ran across the courtyard, they stared at us in shock. I spotted an open stairwell. We sprinted onto it and up toward the roof. I looked back and saw the two men running into the courtyard beneath us.

We reached the rooftop out of breath but kept running, now through assorted water tanks, damp garments swaying on clotheslines, and clusters of pigeons that burst into the air in a flurry of fluttering wings as we charged into them. The building's rooftop was joined to that of another building, narrower than the first and with more water tanks, more pigeons, and more clotheslines. I glanced back. One of the two men was now running across the first rooftop. The other was running across a lower rooftop to our right.

We came to the rooftop's edge. There was another building and another rooftop, lower but not adjoined. Between the two buildings was an alleyway.

"What do we do now?" asked Lara in a panic.

"To stay here is certain death; to go forward is probable death. The second option has better odds."

"To go forward?"

"To jump. I'll go first."

"First?"

"We don't have a choice. This might be a good time to pray."

I realized that the end of my life could be seconds away, but there was no other choice, and there was no time to think about it. I backed away from the edge, then ran toward it and jumped as far as I could. I don't know if it was a miracle, but I made it.

I knew Lara was petrified. I shouted back to her, "You can do it! Come!" She backed up, ran to the edge, and jumped.

She didn't make it.

She was able to just grab onto the rooftop's edge. She held on for her life, suspended over the alleyway.

"Don't let go!" I shouted as I ran to her.

The roof's old masonry now began crumbling under her hand. Her grip was loosening. I grabbed hold of her one wrist and then the other.

"Don't let go!" she said.

For a moment, it felt impossible. But with my heart racing and with all my strength, I managed to pull her up over the edge. We sat there gasping, out of breath under the Havana sky, but not for long. We could now see the man on the rooftop behind us nearing its edge. We got up and began running. We found a fire escape and sprinted down its rusted steps as fast as we could. It brought us to a dark and narrow alleyway. We could now hear the hurried footsteps of our pursuer against the metal of the fire escape as he ran down after us. At one of the alleyway's ends, we could see light. We ran to it, knocking over more than one garbage can on the way. We came out onto a main artery: bright lights, stores, traffic, and crowds.

There was a bus into which a crowd of people was pressing to board. We merged with the crowd and pressed forward to get on the bus. We made it in just before the doors closed. It was then that the two men appeared on the other side of the bus doors. They stared up at us through the glass with a look of frustration and anger. I stared back at them and, as the bus pulled away, made sure to wave goodbye.

We just stood there, trying to catch our breath as the bus took us through the city. After a long while, I decided to break the silence.

"So," I said, "how did you enjoy your tour of old Havana?"

She didn't answer.

"Me, I appreciated the scenery, but I found the pace a bit excessive."

Our journey would now move to the revealing of the mystery of the last page.

Chapter 72

THE LAST PAGE

We were both quiet for the rest of the bus ride, pondering what had just taken place. When we got back to our hotel, I called Kazim and told him what had happened.

"You need to get out of Havana," he said. "The city is heavily monitored, and it's possible that some of those pursuing you may have connections with the Cuban government. There are small lodging places outside the city. Find one that's off the beaten path."

So we did. We spent the night at a small and modest lodging place outside Havana, barely a hotel. After settling in, Lara and I spoke of what had happened.

"Are you all right?" I asked.

"All right? I don't know, but I'm alive."

"It's what the woman told us," I said. "It's a sign of how big this thing is, how high the stakes are. That's why she told us we have to keep going no matter what. And we do. And we're at the last page. We're near the end. Are you still in?"

"I'm still in."

"Let's look at the final page."

So we did.

"Looks like an angel," I said.

"I don't know," said Lara. "It's not exactly a book in which I'd expect to find angels."

The image was of a winged being or creature and, as were all the other images, stylized, black, and iconic.

The next morning, Lara shared with me her translation.

"It's titled 'Mystery.' This is what it says:

The Curtain Lifts
The Players Fall
The Two Are One
And One Is All
So Comes
The Warring Creature
On Hoof and Wing

Herald
Of the Wakened God
The Shining Beast
To Take the Royal Child
What Kingdom Come
What Will Be Done
What Power Reigns
On Earth
But Not in Heaven."

"And what does it mean?" I asked.

"It's a mystery," said Lara.

That same day, in the afternoon, Lara decided to take a nap in her room. She had a dream. She would tell me at dinner.

"I was in a garden," she said. "The garden was filled with animals. In the distance I could see a wall. I was in Berlin. It was the Berlin Wall. On top of the wall was a crowd of people, and in the midst of the crowd, a white figure, womanlike and winged."

"The angel," I said.

"I don't believe it was an angel. I would call it a winged creature. It looked like a statue of white stone but moved as if it were alive. In the garden was a tall, monumental column. Suddenly, the creature flew up from the wall and landed on top of the column. I was now surrounded by thousands of people who had gathered there for some kind of mass event. The creature looked down at us and at the man who was speaking to the multitude from a podium below the column.

"The creature then flew from the column and over many landscapes until landing on a red-brick building in the midst of an ancient ruin. As it lifted its hands, the ruins were transformed into a living city. Then it flew off the red-brick building and landed on a massive stone arch, and, from there, to the top of an amphitheater, a massive white stone open-air stadium. There it stood, looking down inside the stadium and smiling. Then it was as if I was being moved farther and farther away until I saw a globe, the earth. But the size of the creature stayed the same. It was now standing on top of the earth. And then the dream ended."

"So we go to Berlin?"

"I believe so. That's where the vision began."

"Back to the Altar," I said. "Back to the Throne of Satan."

"I believe this will be our last time."

"Do you know where in Berlin?" I asked.

"In the dream I was in an animal garden. I looked it up on the Web. In German, the word for *animal garden* would be *Tiergarten*. The Tiergarten happens to be the largest park in the city of Berlin."

"To the animal garden then," I said.

And so began the journey to unlock the mystery of the last page, the only one that actually bore the name "Mystery." I believe it was because it would speak not only of the past and the present but of things that were not but were yet to come.

Chapter 73

THE CURTAIN LIFTS

We returned to the city of the Altar and, following the course of Lara's dream, headed for the Tiergarten.

The Tiergarten was a world unto itself, a hidden world in the middle of Berlin, with fields and meadows, ponds and streams, and walking paths with bicyclists, pedestrians, couples, families, and children. We chose to take one of those paths to begin our search, figuring from past experience that one was as good as any. It was a bright day, with sunlight pouring through the green leaves that formed a canopy high above our heads and flickering along the ground of our walk.

"Your first time in the Tiergarten?" asked a man sitting on one of the green wooden benches that lined our path. He was thin, with striking features: a sculpted face, high cheekbones, pale skin, piercing blue eyes, and unusually light blond hair. He appeared to be in his late thirties and was wearing all black.

"Yes," I said.

"How did I know?" he replied. "One can get lost here. Could you use some guidance?"

"We could," I said. "Are you the one to give us some guidance?"

"I am, Mr. Herzog," he said. "May I join you?"

He got up from the bench and joined us along the walking path.

"I have much to tell you. Why don't we begin with a question? What happens when the Altar changes hands?"

"Something happens in the world," said Lara.

"History changes," I said.

"You were told of the crisis that caused the wall to be built?"

"The Berlin Crisis," I replied.

"That's how the wall began. And this is how it ended. In May 1989, Hungary removed its border fences with Austria. That caused a breach to open in the Iron Curtain. Thousands of East Germans began fleeing through the opening to the West. Demonstrations broke out across East Germany demanding freedom. In October, the East German government began to collapse. On November 9, 1989, thousands of East Germans gathered at the border with the West. The guards, unprepared and unwilling to use force to stop them from passing through, opened the gates. It was the beginning of the end of the Berlin Wall. People began passing through, or climbing the wall, celebrating its end and dismantling it. The wall came down."

"That's what I saw in my dream," said Lara, "the people on top of the wall. They were celebrating."

"The division was over," he said. "The city of the Altar was one."

"The Curtain Lifts," said Lara. "The Players Fall, the Two Are One…"

"And a year later," said the man, "Germany was freed from communism. East Germany was dissolved. The two Germanies became one.

"When the Altar was moved back to Berlin in the late 1950s, it was still under the dominion and ultimate control of the Soviet Union. It was still the possession of the communist world. But on October 3, 1990, all that changed. With the dissolution of communist East Germany, the Altar came under a new dominion, the newly unified German Republic. The new Germany was not part of the communist bloc, nor under the Soviet Union. For the first time since the soldiers of the Red Army came to possess it in the spring of 1945, the Altar's ownership had changed. What would that mean?"

"The changing of history," I said.

"What specific change?" he said. "What happened to the Ottoman Empire after it lost possession of the Altar?"

"It entered into an accelerated decline and collapse," said Lara.

"As it lost the Altar," I said, "it lost its territories and, finally, its empire."

"And what happened when the Altar's possession was changed again, when it was taken from the Third Reich?"

"The Third Reich collapsed," I said. "Germany collapsed."

"So now it was the communist world that would lose the Altar, the Eastern bloc and the Soviet Union. So what would we expect to happen?"

"We would expect," said Lara, "the Eastern bloc, the Soviet Union, and the communist world to collapse."

"And so it did," he said. "As the Altar was removed, it all collapsed. Regimes fell; millions were set free. It was all part of the ancient mystery. What about the power that had especially possessed the Altar and ultimately was in control of it?"

"The Soviet Union?" I said.

"Yes."

"It would mean that the Soviet Union would collapse."

"And so it did. East Berlin collapsed, East Germany collapsed, and the

Soviet Union collapsed. When East Berlin and East Germany collapsed and disappeared, the Soviet Union was effectively cut off from the Altar. And so it would only be a matter of time before the Soviet Union also disappeared. That which many thought would never happen had now happened. One of the world's two superpowers collapsed and disappeared, virtually overnight."

"Just as Nazi Germany collapsed," I said, "when it lost the Altar to the Soviet Union, and as the Ottoman Empire collapsed when it lost the Altar to Germany."

"The lives of millions were changed," said the man, "and they had no idea that it was all joined to an ancient mystery. Once again, what happened to the Altar would change the world, and the altering of its ownership would signal the altering of history."

And yet the repercussions of the Altar's transference would be even larger than that. The ancient mystery would transform the world.

Chapter 74
THE COMING POWER

He led us onto a stone bridge over a narrow waterway. Halfway across, Lara said, "I have a question." The man stopped.

"Ask it."

"Losing the Altar, the Throne of Satan...wouldn't that be a good thing? Shouldn't it result in something good for the one who lost it?"

"Yes," said the man. "The Throne of Satan is linked to both power and evil. Therefore, its loss means not only the loss of power...but the lifting of evil. What happened when Nazi Germany lost the Altar?"

"It stopped being Nazi Germany," said Lara.

"Yes," he replied, "the evil that had been germinating in that land from the moment the Altar touched its soil now came to an end...and did so the very moment the Altar was removed. Thus began the process of denazification, the lifting of the evil.

"And what happened when the Soviet Union and the communist world lost possession of the Altar?"

"The Soviet Union," said Lara, "stopped being the Soviet Union, and the communist bloc stopped being the communist bloc."

"Again," said the man, "when they lost the Altar, it meant not only the loss of power but the lifting of evil. When the Altar was removed, the shadow of communism, totalitarianism, oppression, and persecution was removed with it. The Iron Curtain was lifted."

"Like the lifting of a curse," said Lara.

"What happens here," said the man, "in the city of the Altar, happens to the world. And so when the East-West division of Berlin was torn down, the East-West division of Germany was also torn down, and then the East-West division of Europe. The dividing had begun in the city of the Altar, and so it would end in the same city. The tearing down of the wall in Berlin would mean the end of an age."

"I have a question," I said. "Each power that possessed the Altar, when it lost the Altar, it fell, and another power rose, the power that took the Altar. So what power then is now to rise?"

"In the case of the Soviet Union," said the man, "its transformation into a superpower came almost instantaneously with its taking the Altar. In the case of Germany, though its rise was joined to its coming upon the

Altar, it would take decades to fully manifest. What it was to become was, until history revealed it, a mystery. So with the power that is yet to come, it is for a time a mystery."

"I have a question," said Lara. "If the world follows the Altar and its city, and the city went from being divided and bipolar into one, would that mean that the world would now likewise be moving from a divided state to a unified state, a one-world state?"

"Is that it?" I asked. "Is the coming power...a one-world state?"

"Note what happened," he said. "The fall of the Berlin Wall was followed by a massive wave of unification and integration. Within a year of its fall, Germany had reunited. And with the fall of the Iron Curtain, the former communist nations of Eastern Europe began integrating with the West. And the wave of unification and integration didn't stop there but went far beyond Europe.

"The fall of the Berlin Wall and the reunification of Germany ushered in the 1990s, the same decade that ignited a movement of global integration. As Berlin, Germany, and Europe began moving toward integration, so did the world. There followed an unprecedented explosion in international trade, investment, cultural exchange, global production chains, and talk of a *new world order*. The fall of the Berlin Wall was a microcosm of what would now manifest throughout Europe and the world—the breaking down of walls, the falling of borders and barriers throughout the world.

"And now a question for you," he said. "Who now possessed the Altar?"

"Germany," said Lara.

"More than Germany," he said. "The Altar's new possessor was not simply Germany. At the time of the transfer, Germany was part of a larger entity, the European Community. It was a new phenomenon, the voluntary integration and merging of modern nation-states into one larger entity. The Altar would ultimately come under the dominion of a supranational state. It was only one year after the reunification of Germany and the change in the Altar's sovereignty that European leaders gathered in the city of Maastricht in the Netherlands to lay the foundation for the political integration of Europe and a new European superstate to be known as the European Union. So the European Union was joined from its birth to the Altar of Pergamon, the Throne of Satan.

"How would a one-world global state come into being? Through the integration of nations. And Europe was at the forefront of that integration.

The Altar was now ultimately under the dominion of a new European political superstate. So as the discovery of the Altar in the ruins of Pergamon in 1871 marked the coming together of the German states to form a new world power, now it was Europe itself that had received the Altar and the European nations that were now coming together to form a new supranational entity and world power. Again, the world was following after the city of the Altar, the place of Satan's Throne, Berlin, this time in its unification. Even the virtual world was following it."

"What do you mean?" I asked.

"In the same year that the Berlin Wall came down, another wall—the barrier between peoples, nations, systems, media, communication, information, and knowledge—was about to likewise come down. 1989, the year that set in motion the fall of the Berlin Wall and the integration of East and West Germany, also set in motion the breaking down of the walls between people and nations and the integration of the world in another realm. It would be called the World Wide Web.

"The following year, 1990, saw the birth of the unified nation of Germany, with the unified city of Berlin as its capital. It was in that same year that the entity that would join the world together as one, the global Internet, was likewise born. Even more specifically, the unified Germany with its unified capital of Berlin came into existence in October of 1990. It was right after that, in the latter part of 1990, that the World Wide Web came into existence. The world again followed the mystery of the Altar."

"The Two Are One," said Lara, "and One Is All."

"Wouldn't the unification of the world be a good thing?" I asked.

"Was the unification of Germany in 1871 or that of the Union of Soviet Socialist Republics, the USSR, a good thing?"

"Is it then," said Lara, "that what the Enemy could not do by dividing the world, he would seek to do by uniting it?"

"Yes," said the man, "if the Enemy could unite the earth under his dominion…what then would become of the world?"

"When will it manifest?" I asked.

"There are no formulas for that. It took sixty years for the newborn nation of Germany to become the Third Reich. And what we now speak of involves the entire world. Rome wasn't built in a day, but that is the end goal. The kingdom of Satan comes not in a straight line but with many curves, detours, and setbacks—but it comes. And it comes not only in the emergence of a new world order but in the shaking, destabilizing, and dismantling of the old world order."

"The Web," said Lara, "it's not evil in itself, is it?"

"Not in and of itself," he replied, "but it can easily become a vessel of evil, and will be. In Hebrew, *w* is the letter *vav.* And so in Hebrew, the World Wide Web, or www, is vav vav vav. And in Hebrew, every letter has a numerical value. The numerical value of the vav is six. Thus, in the language of Scripture, the World Wide Web, www...is 666."

Lara and I were silent.

"Just something to think about," said the man.

Up until what was now about to be revealed, Lara and I had no idea that there was a connection between the Altar of Pergamon and an American president—but there was. And it would manifest as he made a visit to the city of the Altar and stood in the place in which we were now standing.

Chapter 75

THE VISIT

THE MAN TOOK us across the bridge and onto a walking path of open lawns, meadows, and flower beds.

"One of your presidents," said the man, "was connected to the Altar. It was in July 2008. At that time, he was running for the presidency and decided to pay a visit to the city of Satan's Throne. It was Barack Obama. He chose to address the people of Berlin from here in the Tiergarten. Hundreds of thousands of Berliners came to hear him speak.

"He spoke of Berlin's critical role in modern history and, unknowingly, of the Altar's mystery. He spoke of the city's part in the great calamities of the modern world, the place, he said, 'where the last war had ended, another World War could have easily begun.' He spoke of the Cold War that he said was 'born in this city.' He alluded to the conflict at Checkpoint Charlie that almost brought the world to destruction when, as he put it, 'The two superpowers that faced each other across the wall of this city came too close too often to destroying all we have built.' He spoke of the danger of nuclear destruction in what he called the 'further spread of the deadly atom,'[1] the 'deadly atom' that was born in the city of Berlin under Adolf Hitler.

"He spoke of the fall of the Berlin Wall and connected it to the unification of the world. 'When you, the German people, tore down that wall,' he told them, 'a wall that divided East and West...walls came tumbling down around the world....Markets opened too, and the spread of information and technology reduced barriers.' He would call the people of the world to look to the city of the Altar and stand as one.[2]

"Look," said the man as he pointed into the distance.

"That's the column," said Lara. "That's what I saw in my dream."

"It's the *Siegessäule*," said the man, "the Victory Column. That's where Obama stood in the Tiergarten to give his speech. And it was here in the same place, the Tiergarten, that the Nazis hid the Altar in its bunker. So Obama came to the city of the Altar and to the grounds that held Satan's Throne to give that speech as he called the world to stand as one.

"But his connection to the Altar did not end there. He returned to America to receive his party's nomination as its candidate for the presidency. But as he received the nomination and gave his acceptance speech, something strange stood on the stage behind him. It appeared to be an ancient structure. Most commentators identified it as Greek—a Greek religious edifice to the gods.

"The fact that those who designed it undoubtedly did so unaware of what they were creating made the manifestation all the more striking. It wasn't that they realized it, but the structure they created to stand behind Obama as he accepted the nomination for the American presidency *was a re-creation of the Altar of Pergamon.*

"Not only did it appear to be an ancient Greek religious structure, but it was filled with strange correspondences to the features and peculiarities of the ancient Altar: a long horizontal colonnade of Greek columns that made up most of the Altar's width; two rectangular columned structures at each end of the horizontal colonnade, just as with the Altar; seven spaces on the frieze of the two rectangular structures, as with the Altar; the enlargement of those two structures, simulating their forward positioning on the Altar; the converging series of steps leading up to its horizontal colonnade, as with the Altar; and on and on.

"And though they didn't realize what they were doing in creating it, Obama's platform was as much a re-creation of the Altar of Pergamon as the platform that Albert Speer had created for Adolf Hitler at Nuremberg. So now even the American presidential election and Obama's subsequent presidency were linked to the ancient Altar."

"So what does it mean?" asked Lara.

"The answer lies with her," he said.

"Who?"

"The creature," he said, pointing to the Victory Column. There, on the very top of the column, stood a golden figure, winged and helmeted.

"It's her," said Lara, "the winged creature I saw in my dream."

"Yes," said the man. "It is her...the one who holds a mystery as ancient as the Altar and a dark secret critical to the future of the world."

Chapter 76

THE WINGED CREATURE

EMBEDDED IN THE Altar of Pergamon are images of deities at war with giants. One of those deities fighting on behalf of the god Zeus is the goddess Nike. Nike was a warrior goddess, her name meaning victory. She became known as the goddess of victory in both war and peace, and as the champion of Zeus. In Rome, where Zeus was known as Jupiter, Nike was known by the Latin translation of her name, Victoria. That winged creature standing on top of the column is the ancient goddess Victoria…Nike."

"So it was her that I saw in my dream," said Lara. "She flew from the top of the Berlin Wall to the top of the column. She watched over the massive gathering here and over the speaker."

"So then Obama," I said, "called the world to stand as one under the gaze of the goddess."

"Yes," said the man. "And beyond being Zeus's advocate, the goddess would ride with him in his four-horse chariot, the *quadriga*. She would guide it forward. So in the days of war, it was not just Zeus, or Jupiter, who would be seen riding into battle, but Nike, Victoria.

"So now the Altar of Zeus was to be moved from Pergamon. Zeus was coming to Europe."

"So then," I said, "would the coming of Zeus to Europe involve the goddess?"

"It would," he replied. "And so as Zeus's charioteer and herald, the goddess would appear first to usher him in. So before the Altar of Zeus appeared in Europe, the ancient winged creature would begin appearing in Europe."

"So Comes the Warring Creature," said Lara, "on Hoof and Wing, Herald of the Wakened God."

"How did she appear?" I asked.

"The goddess's likeness began appearing in major cities across Europe and, most notably, in the city where the Altar of Zeus was to come—in Berlin."

"Where in Berlin?" I asked.

"On the Brandenburg Gate itself," he said. "If you look at the top of that gate, you'll see a figure driving a chariot; it's the goddess driving the chariot of Zeus. Later in the nineteenth century, in the spring of 1863, a massive nine-foot-high statue of a goddess was discovered and excavated on the Greek island of Samothrace. The goddess was Nike. It was eight years before the discovery and then the unearthing and transporting of Zeus's Altar to Europe that the image of Nike was discovered, unearthed, and brought to Europe.

"The year after that discovery, plans were made in Berlin to build a Victory Column to be crowned with a statue of Nike in her Roman form of Victoria. So Berlin became especially joined to the ancient goddess, placing her statue on top of both the Brandenburg Gate and the Berlin Victory Column. And it was just as Berlin began erecting the column for the goddess that Carl Humann arrived in the city of Pergamon, the city of the Altar. And by the time the column was finished and the goddess stood on its pinnacle, the first pieces of Zeus's Altar had arrived in Berlin."

"It's as if," said Lara, "the city had been marked from the beginning to receive the Altar."

"And as if," I said, "the two deities that moved together in ancient times now moved together to Berlin, first the goddess, then Zeus."

"The goddess," said the man, "was something of an omen, a sign of things to come, as she would play a central role in the transformation of Western civilization and the world.

"After his victory in the Battle of Actium, the Roman leader Augustus Caesar installed a statue of the goddess Nike, or Victoria, in the new Senate building. The image of the goddess was a sign and portent of Rome's transformation into an empire. The Roman Senate would thus convene and deliberate under the gaze of the ancient goddess. Every Senate session would be inaugurated with the lifting of offerings to the goddess at her altar. The goddess of victory was seen as critical in sustaining the empire's success and power.

"With the coming and ascent of the Gospel and the Christianization of the empire in the fourth century, there came increasing calls to end the offering of sacrifices to Victoria in the Roman Senate and for the removal of her altar. The result was a conflict and struggle. Pagan senators and leaders fought for the goddess and her altar while Christian senators and leaders called for their removal. It was a war for the future of the empire and Western civilization. And the focus of that war and that future was the winged goddess.

"In the end, the statue of Victoria was removed from the Roman Senate. It would mark the end of pagan Rome. So the goddess was again a sign and omen, this time by her disappearance, which would portend the disappearance of the gods, the end of a pagan civilization, and the dawn of a Christian one.

"So if the disappearance of Victoria signified the Christianization of Western civilization, then what would her reappearance signify?"

"The dechristianization of Western civilization," I said.

"And if the departure of Victoria portended the end of pagan Western civilization, what would her return portend?"

"The return of pagan Western civilization," said Lara.

"And so it was no accident," he said, "that the nineteenth century, which witnessed the most powerful and visible return of the goddess to Western civilization, was the same century that sowed the seeds of Marxism, fascism, and Nazism, the most potent and deadly anti-Christian and neo-pagan ideologies and movements in world history."

"And the return of the goddess," said Lara, "was now connected to the return of the god Zeus in the form of his Altar from Pergamon."

"It was all joined together," said the man, "just as the goddess was linked to the god. When the goddess disappeared from Western history, so did Zeus and his Altar. And as they had disappeared together, so now together they would return. And the Altar that disappeared as Western civilization turned to God and to the Christian faith now reappeared just as that same civilization was turning from both.

"And it was no accident that the same decade in which the goddess crowned this column and the first pieces of the Altar arrived in Germany saw the sowing, the birthing, or the resurrection of what would become the most deadly anti-Christian ideologies and movements the world had ever seen."

"What about Obama?" I asked. "What did he have to do with it?"

"The emperor and the Senate of Rome," he replied, "once ruled Western civilization under the image of the goddess Victoria. Now Obama stood under the image of that same goddess. Here was the man who would become the leader of the Western world now addressing the world under the gaze of the goddess."

"As did the emperors of Rome," said Lara.

"It was a sign of the dechristianization of Western civilization. It was no accident that Obama would become the first American president to be known for publicly declaring that America could no longer be called a 'Christian nation,'[1] nor that his presidency would be marked by a noticeable dechristianization of his nation's culture along with that of the West.

"When the Altar was in the possession of the Marxist world, the West—particularly America—stood consciously as the defender of Christian civilization against the godlessness of communism. But now the Altar had been transferred to the West. And in that transference, the West would begin a marked and dramatic transformation from what could still be called a Christian civilization into what was now a post-Christian civilization and, increasingly, an anti-Christian civilization. Nike, or Victoria, the charioteer goddess of Zeus, had returned, the sign of a pagan civilization and the harbinger of the dechristianization of Western civilization and all that it would mean for the world."

The sign of the goddess would lead us to yet another mystery and to a revelation that would be revealed to us in another land. But it almost never came, or rather, I almost never got there.

Chapter 77
THE NIGHT CALLERS

"My time here is finished," he said.

"So was that the last mystery?" I asked.

"My time *here* is finished; the mystery continues...elsewhere."

"Where elsewhere?"

"Where," he said, "is part of the mystery."

"What does the mystery concern?"

"What was and is to come," he said and then departed.

We headed back to our hotel, where we had dinner and tried to figure out where the *elsewhere* could be but came up with nothing. We headed up to our hotel rooms and said good night.

That night, I dreamed of the man who had given me the first page. I saw him sitting at my lecture, and then I saw his death. He was sleeping in his hotel room when two men in black clothes and black face coverings broke into his room and grabbed him. He tried to fight them off but couldn't. They brought him to the hotel window and rammed him through it to his death.

And then I saw Lara in the dream. She was standing in my hotel room in the dark.

"Wake up!" she said. "Wake up! They're coming!"

What happened next I couldn't make any sense of, at least at first. I was being grabbed, lifted out of my bed. I thought I was dreaming, but the dream was over. It was real. I couldn't see anything, as it was pitch-dark. When I realized it was real, I began thrashing, turning, striking out in every direction, and, for a moment, breaking free.

There were at least two people there in that room with me. Again they grabbed me and were trying to move me to another part of the room. Again I pushed back, turned, and punched in every direction. At one point, one of them lost his balance and went flying into the furniture. I struggled with the other, and we both crashed into the dresser. Then the other one pulled open the curtains that hung over the hotel room window. I could now dimly see my attackers. They were wearing black clothing and black face masks.

Again they grabbed me and tried to run with me toward the window.

The room was on the top floor. It was over a hundred feet to the street below.

"Time to fall, Mr. Herzog," said one of them as they tried ramming me through the window to my death, just as they had done to the man who had given me the page. And they almost did, but I managed to catch the wall with my feet and push back as hard as I could. The three of us were thrown back, off balance. And the struggle continued.

I managed to grab a lamp from the night table and hit one of my attackers with it. With each strike, the lamp broke to the point that its edge was now sharpened glass. The man let out a scream and withdrew. His partner then attacked me all the more furiously from behind, grabbing my neck in a chokehold. I swung the lamp in back of me. Its wires were now exposed so that when it struck his neck it caused a flash and an explosion of sparks. It stunned him, and he let go.

People were now banging on the door and walls, shouting and screaming. At that, the two men rushed to the door, pushed it open, and ran down the hallway. I turned on the light and made my way to the door. There, outside in the hallway, was a crowd of shocked people, some in pajamas, who had found it hard to sleep with all the activity going on in my room. In front of them stood Lara. She was the first to bang on the door and shout. She had a shoe in her hand.

"A shoe?" I said. "You were going to fight them with a shoe?"

"It's what I had," she said, "and it has a pointy tip."

"I appreciate that. Now, we should get out of here."

We gathered our things. By the time we were ready to go, the sun had risen. As we checked out, the front desk clerk, having no idea what had happened, asked us the customary, "Was everything to your satisfaction?"

"Not really," I said. "I had a problem with the wake-up service. I felt it was a little over the top."

The final mysteries of the last page would now be revealed.

Chapter 78

WHAT WAS AND IS TO COME

ON LEAVING THE hotel, I called Kazim and told him what had happened.

"From here on in," he said, "stay away from hotels in major cities or that are part of a chain. Look for small, independent, inconspicuous places, off the track. And avoid using credit cards to check in. Pay only in cash."

"And if they don't accept cash?"

"Offer to pay them more. It's worth your security."

So we searched for a lodging place outside Berlin. We found one, a private home that had been converted into a bed-and-breakfast, and they accepted cash. The next morning, Lara told me she believed she knew the place where we were to go.

"The revelation left off at the Victory Column," she said. "In my dream the winged creature flew from the Victory Column over many landscapes before landing in the next place. So the next place isn't near. The creature descended on an ancient brick building in the middle of a city of ancient ruins, then onto an arch, and then onto a stadium. I searched the Web to find a place that matched that description. And I found it."

"Where?"

"Rome."

"And the building?"

"It's the Curia Julia, Rome's ancient Senate building."

And so we began preparing for our next journey. Lara had friends whom she had known for years, an older married couple who had moved to Italy and were now living in Rome. She contacted them and asked if we could stay a few days with them while in the city. They said yes. So the following day, we boarded a flight to the City of Seven Hills.

The day after our arrival, we headed for the Roman Forum. The Curia Julia stood out from the white marble ruins for which the forum was known. It was a large rectangular brick building, stately but not majestic, very much intact and looking much newer than we had expected from such an ancient building.

In front of the Curia Julia was a tour group of about forty people listening intently as their guide spoke to them of its history. Their departure from the site revealed a solitary man standing by the building's main entranceway. It was the man from the Tiergarten. We approached him.

"I'm glad to see you figured it out," he said as he greeted us. "I believed you would. This is where the Roman Senate convened and in which stood the statue of the goddess, the place over which raged the controversy concering the empire's future. This is where the age of pagan Rome officially came to its end.

"Come," he said. "Follow me." He led us onto the *Via Sacra,* the ancient Sacred Way, a path of irregular stones lined with arches, foundations, and columns—the remains of ancient Rome. We passed the ruins of several ancient temples before stopping at the Regia, the headquarters of the Roman Pontifex Maximus, its chief priest.

"When the Book of Revelation identified Pergamon as the place 'where Satan's throne is,'[1] the Altar was then under the dominion of Rome. It was a fitting arrangement since both the Altar and Rome were especially connected to Jupiter, or Zeus. Jupiter was the empire's ultimate god and the one from whom it believed its power was derived.

"As you know, as the Altar's ruin and disappearance were connected to the Christianization of Western civilization, so its unearthing and reappearance were connected to the dechristianization of that civilization—but also to the rise and empowering of satanic movements and anti-Christian *states, powers,* and *governments.* Each power that came to possess the Altar sought to become a form of world empire...as was Rome, the Altar's ancient possessor. And so if the Altar's disappearance signaled the disappearance of a pagan empire, what would its reappearance signal?"

"The return of a pagan or post-Christian empire?" said Lara.

"Yes."

"Would that mean," I asked, "that the Altar's unearthing would be connected to some kind of resurrection of Rome?"

"In all of world history, one entity is made up of more nations derived from the Roman Empire than any other. Do you know which one?"

"Which?" I asked.

"The European Union. And do you know the name of the document that laid the groundwork for what would ultimately become the European Union?"

"No," I said.

"It was called the Treaty of Rome."

"So will the European Union bring about a resurrected Roman Empire?" asked Lara.

"Whether it is the bringer of what is to come or its precursor, that which must come...will come, one way or another. And at present, the Altar is under the ultimate dominion of that entity, that union."

"Why Rome?" I asked.

"Rome was the greatest of the ancient powers to have possessed the Altar. And it was under the dominion of Rome that the Altar's fires last burned."

"Will that which 'must come,'" asked Lara, "be called Rome?"

"Its name will not matter," he replied, "but its essence and nature. That which is coming will share the essence and nature of the ancient empire in a modern incarnation. And as with Rome, it will come as a universal empire."

"A one-world state," said Lara. "It's the one-world state you were alluding to...from the fall of the Berlin Wall."

"Come," he said. He then led us up the slope of a hill. On top of the slope stood a massive Roman arch.

"This is what I saw in my dream," said Lara, "the arch on which the winged creature landed."

"Which people, which nation is it," he asked, "that are especially hated and warred against by the Dark Angel and that he especially seeks to destroy?"

"Israel," said Lara, "the Jewish people."

"This is the Arch of Titus," he said. "Do you know what it celebrates? The destruction of Judea, the first-century embodiment of Israel. It was Rome that destroyed the Jewish state, that slaughtered its people, that took its survivors into captivity, and that began Israel's nearly two-thousand-year global exile from its homeland. It was no accident that the empire that possessed the Throne of Satan would become the vessel that would bring about the destruction of that nation. And what is it that you notice about every power that came to possess the Altar?"

"Each one became an enemy of the Jewish people or Israel."

"In possessing the Altar, Germany tried to exterminate the Jewish people. And in possessing the Altar, the Soviet Union tried to destroy the Jewish state. The Altar's modern possessors were continuing the war waged by its ancient possessor. And with Israel, the nation that Rome destroyed in ancient times, now back in the world..."

"It would be round two," I replied.

"Yes, but imagine if Israel faced a state that encompassed the world and was raging against it with a hatred greater and more demonic than that which inflamed ancient Rome, Nazi Germany, and the Soviet Union. And that is what is prophesied in the Scriptures—a world at war against the tiny Jewish nation."

"It seems as if we're getting closer," I said. "Most of the world's nations are already against Israel."

At that, he began walking away from the arch and down the gentle slope of the hill. We followed him. Then we saw it: a massive elliptical shell of pale white stone and concrete, with layers of walls on top of each other and countless arches—the ruins of the Colosseum. He led us closer but stopped short of the point from which we would no longer be able to see the entire edifice.

"It's the last place I saw in my dream," said Lara, "the last place on which the creature landed."

"The Dark Angel has another war," said the man, "another people he seeks to destroy. Who would they be?"

"Those who follow God," said Lara, "believers, Christians."

"And so the empire that once possessed the Altar erected places like this—theaters, amphitheaters, circuses, and stadiums, in which it staged spectacles to shed blood and throw Christians to wild beasts as the crowds cheered for more. And what is the other hatred that the possessors of the Altar hold in common?"

"Each one was," said Lara, "or became, an anti-Christian state. Each one warred against God and those who followed Him."

"Yes," said the man. "Each of the Altar's possessors became as Rome, an empire at war with God, at war with Christianity, and at war with those of faith, those who lived and stood for biblical values—just as had Rome in ancient times.

"What is the mystery of what is coming? Imagine a one-world totalitarian state that persecutes, imprisons, and kills Christians, that wages war against God, against His ways and His people, and does so even more than these? This too is the picture that Scripture gives concerning the last days. In that, all roads do lead to Rome. For far more dangerous than a pre-Christian civilization, a pre-Christian Rome, is a post-Christian one."

"And so what the Enemy failed to do in dividing the world and attempting to destroy it," said Lara, "he would seek to do by unifying it and possessing it."

"It was all there from the beginning," said the man. "As a throne requires a kingdom, so the Throne of Satan required a satanic kingdom. And so each of the powers that came to possess the Altar, the Throne, was or was to become a satanic kingdom."

"But now," I said, "the Altar is joined not to a single nation but to the merging and integration of nations, the unification of the world."

"And so what would happen if the Enemy could unify the world as his own?"

"What Kingdom Come," said Lara, "What Will Be Done, What Power Reigns on Earth, *but Not in Heaven.*"

"What kingdom come?" said the man. "A satanic kingdom. But it would not be a nation. It would be the world itself."

"I have one more mystery to show you," said the man, "the mystery of a princess, a beast, and an ancient abduction."

Chapter 79

THE WOMAN AND THE BEAST

"Come," he said. "Let me take you to the belly of the beast."

"The belly of the beast?" I repeated.

"Follow me."

He led us through the ruins of the forum on a walk that took us a little over ten minutes and ended on the top of a hill.

"You are now standing at the heart of ancient Rome. As the city was the heart of the empire, this hill was the heart of the city. This is Capitoline Hill. The ancients called it *Caput Mundi*, the Head of the World. It served as the city's political and spiritual center. It was named after the temple that stood here at its summit, the *Capitolium*. The Capitolium was the Temple of Jupiter, Rome's most important sanctuary, the center of its religion and worship."

"Zeus," I said. "Its center was the Roman Temple of Zeus."

"Yes," said the man. "Jupiter, Zeus, was central to Western civilization, the chief god of both the Greeks and the Romans, the supreme god of Western culture until the coming of the Gospel, until the Christian faith. And so the worship of Zeus was especially at war against the worship of God. And the Gospel prevailed. But if that same civilization, Western civilization, should ever turn away from God and reject the Gospel, then..."

"Then," said Lara, "would it be as if Zeus returned...in one form or another?"

"The Altar of Zeus did return," I said.

"And if the Altar of Zeus," said the man, "was connected to a religion that warred against God and the Christian faith in the ancient world...then in its return to the world, it would be joined to the movements and ideologies that war against God and the Christian faith but in the modern world."

"Marxism," I said. "Communism, Nazism..."

"What civilization," said the man, "has been at the center of Western civilization for most of the last two thousand years, the heir of Greek, Roman, and Christian civilization?"

"Europe," said Lara.

"And to where was the Altar of Pergamon taken after it was unearthed?"

"To Europe," I said.

"So in its return to the world, the Altar was specifically joined, or rejoined, to Europe. And yet there's more to the mystery. What I'm about to tell you," he said, "comes from an ancient myth, the origins of which go back ages before the birth of the Roman Empire."

"But it relates to the Altar?" I asked.

"Yes, inasmuch as the Altar relates to Zeus. The myth begins with a princess from the land of Phoenicia, a daughter of King Agenor. One day, the princess was gathering flowers with her companions in a meadow by the seashore. It was there that Zeus took notice of her and desired her. But in order to approach her without causing fear, he transformed himself into a bull—a white, shining bull, tame and nonthreatening, with small, gently curved horns. The princess and her maidens were drawn to the beast. They gathered around it and began touching it and decorating it with garlands.

"The princess decided to climb onto the animal's back. The moment she did, it abducted her, taking her to the shore, plunging into the waters, and carrying her away from her homeland and across the sea. The princess looked back toward the shore of her home, stretching out her arms, longing to return. The beast took the princess to the island of Crete, where it revealed itself to her as Zeus. Then he impregnated her. The princess bore three sons, each of whom would in some way become associated with death."

"And what," I asked, "does the myth of Zeus and the princess have to do with the mystery?"

"The name of the princess," he replied.

"Is what?" I asked.

"*Europa.*"

"Europa," I said, "as in Europe?"

"Not *as in* Europe," he said. "*Europa is Europe.* Europa is the exact name that Europe calls itself."

"How did it get that name?" asked Lara.

"From the myth," he said.

"Europe originated from a myth?" I said.

"Europe bears the name of the princess Europa, who was carried away by the beast."

"So Europe was already linked to Zeus," said Lara.

"Yes," he said. "And so the mystery of Europe was joined to the ancient god from the beginning."

"So then it's no accident," said Lara, "that the Altar of Zeus, the Altar of Pergamon, was moved to Europe and that Europe became its possessor."

"Yes," said the man, "as Zeus was joined to Europa, so the Altar of Zeus was joined to Europe."

"So it had to be brought to Europe," I said. "And Europe had to possess it."

"Yes," he replied. "So the Altar sits in Berlin but under the ultimate dominion of the European Union. For the first time in its history, the Altar sits under the dominion of a unified Europe…the Altar of Zeus joined to Europa."

"But Zeus carried away Europa," I said. "What would that mean?"

"Europe was once seen as the center of Christianity, a civilization that knew and worshipped God. But in the case of Europa, Zeus drew her away from that which she had once known and loved. So it was that as the Altar of Zeus came to Europe, Europe was drawn away.

"And as Europa was impregnated and gave birth to Zeus's offspring, so Europe was impregnated with a different kind of seed, that which would cause it to give birth to the darkest and most satanic offspring of the modern age. As Europa was carried away by Zeus, so Germany was carried away by the darkness of Nazism, and Eastern Europe and Russia by the darkness of communism. An entire continent was carried away by evil and the darkness of war and destruction."

"It's almost as if European civilization was destined to be carried away," I said.

"And that its being carried away," Lara said, "would be connected to Zeus…the Altar of Zeus."

"But remember," said the man, "European civilization is not bound by the waters that surround it. That civilization has spread to the world. America is one of its extensions. Do you know why Capitol Hill is called Capitol Hill?"

"Not because it's in the capital?" I said.

"No," said the man. "It is named Capitol Hill after Capitoline Hill and so is linked to the Temple of Jupiter. America is joined to European and Western civilization, as is Russia…and so now, in one form or another, is the world."

"So the carrying away of Europa," I said, "would mean…"

"The carrying away of the world," he said. "For the entire world has now been sown with the seeds of European civilization."

"Remember," said the man, "Zeus is a mask for the Enemy, just as the Altar of Zeus is the Throne of Satan. So it is the Enemy who drew Europe away and will seek to draw away the entire world.

"And so the Altar of Zeus passed to Europe, and then the European Union was born. It was the reunion of Zeus and Europa. And in the year when the European Union was born, a statue was erected outside the European Union Parliament building. The statue was of the ancient princess Europa. Later, another statue was erected outside the European Union Council building. Again it was Europa, this time showing her being carried away by Zeus in the form of a beast. And do you know what appears on the currency of the European Union? Europa, being carried away by the beast…Zeus.

"When the European Union set out to draft a constitution that would cite the origins of European civilization, it decided it would exclude any mention of Christianity or God. And yet in its imagery and symbols, it would declare another origin—a pagan one. It would identify as a pagan woman carried away by a beast. The civilization once known for its devotion to God was now being abducted by another god of a very different nature."

There was so much for us to take in. And that is what we now seek to focus on. We had no idea what was coming. But Lara and I were soon to enter the most dangerous part of our journey—and of our lives.

PART XV

REVELATION

Chapter 80

THE MAN ON CAPITOLINE HILL

"Do you have anything to give us?" I asked.

"A page?" said the man. "No, you've been given the last one."

"Then we have all the mysteries?" said Lara.

"Certainly not all."

"What other mystery then?" I asked.

"The mystery," he said, "of why you were given the mysteries."

"Why were they given to us?"

"That," he said, "will be for you to find."

"Can you give us any help?" I said.

"To whom much is given," he said, "much is required."

At that, he departed. As he descended Capitoline Hill, he passed a middle-aged man with short wavy hair and what I took to be a Mediterranean appearance. His features would not be out of place in a statue of an ancient Roman emperor. The two glanced at each other but said nothing.

Lara and I then began descending the hill. As we passed by the man, he spoke.

"So how did you like the forum?" he asked with a foreign accent.

"Interesting," I replied.

"You know of the blood that was shed here?"

"I've heard."

"The blood of Christians," he said. "And yet it was their own choice. You see, they were killed because they wouldn't give up their beliefs. It was their choice to die.

"And for what? For an idea? For a righteous cause? For that, they gave up their lives."

"For something greater," said Lara, "for something greater than their own lives."

"For a notion," said the man, "among countless other notions."

"They were martyrs," said Lara. "They gave their lives for their faith, for God, for the Gospel."

"For the Gospel," he repeated. "For a message? They gave up their lives for a message? Is that worth losing your life?"

"Are you thinking of any message in particular?" I asked, sensing that his words were about more than ancient history.

"Perhaps a message that one feels one must bring to the world because one believes it to be of great importance, a message one feels will expose the darkness and bring light…but a message that will end up bringing about one's death."

"Sounds threatening," I said.

"I'm just posing a question."

I turned to Lara and whispered, "He's one of them. Let's get out of here." So we left the man and resumed our descent. About half a minute later, we heard his voice from behind us.

"Is it worth it?" he shouted from Capitoline Hill. "Is it worth losing your life?"

It wasn't long after leaving the forum and stepping back into modern Rome with its cars, scooters, buses, tourists, and street vendors that my cell phone rang.

"Mr. Herzog?"

"Who's this?" I asked.

"You and I spoke shortly after Max Yildirim's death."

I recognized the voice.

"Detective Richter with the New York Police Department. I'm following up on our conversation. You told me that you didn't know who Mr. Yildirim was."

"I told you I never heard the name."

"Well, it turns out you did, in fact, know him. It turns out he met with you just before his death…and gave you a certain object. Would you like to tell me what that certain object was?"

"I would think you would already know," I replied.

"What I know, Mr. Herzog, is that you could very well end up like Mr. Yildirim. In fact, I believe you almost did."

"And how would you know that?"

"It stands to reason," he replied. "As it was written, '*Thieves don't live long.*'"

"You're not with the New York Police Department. Who are you?"

"Who am I? Strange that you should ask that since we just met."

"What do you mean?"

"On Capitoline Hill."

It was then I realized that, except for the change of accents, the voice of the "detective" and the man who had just spoken to us on Capitoline Hill was the same.

"You can't escape us any more than could Mr. Yildirim. Surely you'll share his fate. In your case, it could be said, '*Thieves don't live much longer.*' Is it worth it, Mr. Herzog?"

And then came a click, and the call ended. I called back the number, but there was no dial tone, no line, nothing.

We now had to figure out what to do. There were no more pages, no more clues, no more leads. We didn't want to impose any further on Lara's friends. We thought we would look for a place to stay outside Rome until we had some kind of direction. But when we told our hosts of our plans, they suggested something else.

"We have a cottage," said the man. "It's small but comfortable, with two bedrooms, a kitchen, and a living room. It's not far from the shore. It's yours to use for whatever you need and however long you need to use it."

We accepted the offer. Before setting out for the cottage, we transferred all our research, our notes, our pictures, and our recordings onto both of our phones and made several backups. We left our laptops with the couple and those items we believed we needed to safeguard. The pages of the book I kept with me in my inside coat pocket.

The cottage was on the Italian east coast facing the Adriatic Sea. It took us nearly three hours to get there. The cottage was humble, rustic, and charming. And the setting was beautiful, a short walk from the shore.

We looked forward to a time of rest in which we could figure out what we were supposed to do with everything that had been revealed to us. But something very different awaited us there.

Chapter 81

THE COTTAGE

On our first full day at the cottage, we explored our surroundings and spent some time on the shore. That night, in the cottage's living room, Lara and I discussed what our last guide had told us.

"So what is the mystery of why we were given the mysteries?" I said.

"He told us, 'To whom much is given, much is required.' We've been given much…the mystery behind the most cataclysmic events of our age…a mystery that shakes the world, alters its course, and holds the key to its future."

"And why was it given to us?"

"So we could expose it," said Lara. "So we could bring it to the world."

"But why us?" I said. "You, I can understand. But me? I'm the least likely person—the skeptic, the cynic, the debunker of faith."

"That's why," said Lara. "It's *because* you're the least likely person. It's *because* you were the skeptic. It means more coming from you. You're the perfect person."

"The perfect person?"

"We are the ones it was given to. Somehow we have to get it out…to the world. To whom much is given."

"Much is required," I said. "That's what I'm afraid of."

Just then the sea breeze blew through the cottage's open windows and through the living room.

"Lara," I said, "a question: If you knew before you said yes to going with me—if you knew all that would be involved, all that would happen, the dangers, the cost, everything—would you still have come?"

She thought about it for a moment. "Yes," she said, "I believe I still would have…And you, if you knew?"

"I'm glad I didn't know…But yes, I think I still would have come."

We were silent. The wind continued blowing through the cottage.

"It's been a long day," I said. "I think we should get some sleep."

I had trouble sleeping that night. The words kept echoing over and over in my mind: "To whom much is given, much is required." I couldn't stop dwelling on what it all meant and what it all would mean. The questions were always there in the back of my mind from the start of the journey.

Why was it all being revealed? Why to us? And why now? I could avoid dwelling on them during the journey because so much was happening. But now there was nothing else. Finally, I drifted off to sleep, exhausted.

It was early in the morning or late at night and still dark out when I woke up with the questions again filling my mind. I tried to get back to sleep but couldn't. I decided to go for a walk along the shore. I got up, got dressed, put on my coat, and headed for the door, careful not to make any noise that would wake up Lara, who was sound asleep in her room.

I made my way to the beach and walked along the shoreline until I came to a large rock on which I sat down. I must have been there on that rock for over an hour, dwelling on my questions and apprehensions. The sky was just beginning to lighten. And then it happened.

It was a sudden explosion. I turned around to face the direction of the sound. In the distance was a glow that shouldn't have been there and that wasn't there before—the glow of fire. And it appeared to be in the vicinity of our cottage. I ran as fast as I could. The closer I came to the cottage, the brighter the light. And then to my horror, I saw it: Our cottage was ablaze.

I wanted to run inside, but the doorway was engulfed in flames, and flames were shooting out of the windows. I ran around to the back where Lara's bedroom was. "Lara!" I shouted. "Lara!" Again and again, I shouted her name. But there was no response, no sound except that of the fire consuming the cottage.

Finally, I gave up. There was no way she could have survived it. I walked away from the burning cottage and found a patch of sandy ground on which to sit down. An overwhelming grief took hold of me, a deep, painful, bottomless sorrow. I couldn't fathom Lara being gone. I had been her nemesis, and yet she still agreed to go with me across the world to help me. We would never have admitted it, but against all odds we had become partners, even—almost—companions. I had come to depend on her, and without her, I wouldn't have made it. And now she was gone. In my entire life, I had never felt so empty and alone as I did then.

And then on top of the sorrow came the guilt. It was because of me that her life was placed in danger. If not for me, she would still be alive. The sorrow was painful enough, but with the guilt, it was shattering. I sat there in the radiance of the burning cottage and in the darkness of my thoughts. I don't know how long it went on for, but at the time it seemed endless.

There was a noise—a slight noise but distinct enough to stand out from the sound of the burning cottage—the voice of a woman weeping. I turned. There in the distance, in front of the burning cottage, was the silhouette of a woman sitting on the ground, as if she had collapsed there, crying. *It was Lara.* She was alive.

I got up from the ground and cried out, "Lara!" She looked up and realized it was me. Her mouth was wide open in shock, as were her eyes, even as tears still streamed down her cheeks. "Ariel!" she cried out. It was only the second time she had ever called me by my first name. Except for the moment she tried to comfort me in Auschwitz, she had either avoided using any name or called me "Herzog." She got up from the ground and cried out again, "Ariel!" Her face was still covered with tears but now filled with joy as well. She ran to me as I did to her. We embraced. That was another thing we had never done before and which, up to that moment, had been unthinkable.

"I thought you were dead," she said.

"And *you*—I thought *you* were dead!" I replied. "How did you get out?"

"I didn't," she said. "I wasn't in the cottage when the explosion happened. I was by the shore."

"Why?"

"I had a dream," she said. "In the dream I heard a voice saying, 'Wake up, Lara. Wake up.' It was your voice. You were standing by the sea. 'You need to wake up now,' you said, 'and come here.'

"I woke up, put on my clothes and my coat, and headed to the door. I was quiet so as not to wake you up. I walked to the shore. I didn't know why. So I just began walking along the shore, praying to know the reason I was supposed to be there. And how did *you* get out?"

"I just woke up and decided to go for a walk on the shore. We must have walked in different directions."

"I'm so glad you're alive, Ariel," she said with tears still streaming down her cheeks.

"And you, Lara. I couldn't imagine going on..." I didn't finish the sentence. There was a long pause. "I never thanked you."

"For what?"

"For everything. Without your help, without you, I never could have made the journey. Thank you for coming with me...for all your help...Thank you for everything."

She didn't say anything but appeared moved and surprised to hear me say that.

"They found us again," I said, "even here. And we were almost killed. They'll find us again, and next time they might not fail. You don't have to keep going. It's too dangerous."

"Do you want me to come with you?"

"I do. But I don't want you to get killed with me."

"You'd rather get killed alone? It's *because* of the danger that you shouldn't be by yourself. You have a better chance of being killed alone than you do with someone else. Anyway, we've come this far..."

"Are you sure?"

"I am."

"OK..."

"So now what?"

"First thing, we come up with a nice way of telling our hosts that the cottage they loaned us doesn't exist anymore."

We would soon embark on a journey that would take us back to the beginning and to a surprise, an unexpected revelation, and a danger no less great than what we had just survived, and to the moving of an ancient hand.

Chapter 82

NIGHT OF THE ALTAR

IT WASN'T LONG before fire trucks, ambulances, emergency workers, and curious onlookers arrived on the scene, along with police officers who made sure to question us. Who were we? Why were we there? Did we have any enemies who would seek to harm us? We didn't feel that telling them about a clandestine organization dedicated to satanic purposes, a certain ancient object, and mass destruction would actually help matters. So we kept our answers as short and vague as possible.

After the questioning, we left the town and headed down the coast in search of a safe place in which to spend the night. We found a small bed-and-breakfast inn overlooking the shore and offered to give the owners more than their asking price on the condition that we would pay in cash, stay there anonymously, and show no identification. They agreed. Upon our arrival, I called Kazim and told him of the explosion.

"They're desperate now," he said. "They would never have done something like that if they weren't. That makes this stage especially volatile and dangerous. They will be taking more and more risks in order to eliminate you."

"So what do we do?"

"Up to this point, I thought I could help keep you safe from a distance. But the situation is beyond that now."

"What does that mean?"

"You have to get out of there."

"Out of where?"

"Out of where you are and out of Italy."

"And go where?"

"Here," he said. "Here in Turkey, we have the resources to deal with the danger. We'll be able to safeguard you from the moment you arrive at the airport to the moment you depart. We can't ensure your safety from a distance."

"For how long?"

"Until things calm down and we can ascertain that it's safe."

He urged us not to delay but to leave right away. I told him we had just gotten to our lodging place and needed time to replace the items destroyed in the fire. We stayed there the following day, bought some luggage, and replaced what else we could. The next day, we headed to the airport in Rome, staying extra vigilant and, as instructed, making sure no one was following us. There we boarded a plane for Izmir. Kazim had given us the descriptions and names of the two security officers who would meet us at the airport. And they were there waiting for us when we arrived, right outside passport control. They looked the part: tall and stoic, in dark suits, with earbuds and dark sunglasses.

"Mr. Herzog, Lara Winter," said one of them, "we are here on behalf of Mr. Yarikan. Welcome to Izmir." They led us into a black limousine and began driving us to our destination, the two of them in the front seat and Lara and me in the back.

"Mr. Yarikan," said the driver, "insisted on seeing you as soon as you arrived."

"Where?" asked Lara.

"For purposes of security and your safety, the location is undisclosed."

"But you can tell *us*," she said.

"If we knew," he said. "We were only given the coordinates."

A little over an hour into the drive, Lara and I began noticing that the scenery was looking increasingly familiar.

"We're almost there," said the driver.

And then we saw it in the distance—the high place.

"Pergamon," I said. "He's meeting us in Pergamon."

"I guess it's appropriate," said Lara.

The car began ascending the Akropol Cad, the narrow, winding, treacherous road that led up to the top of the acropolis.

"We're back on the 'road of death,'" I said.

Lara was silent, just as she had been when I said those words the first time we ascended that road. Upon reaching the summit, the two men got out and opened the doors for Lara and me to exit the car. It was now early evening. The sky was filled with storm clouds and darkening. In the distance stood three figures. It was Kazim and two of his officers. They approached us.

"Welcome to Pergamon!" he said. "I'm glad you made it."

"You have a dramatic flair," I said, "meeting us here of all places."

"I knew we would have privacy here," he replied. "And I thought it was especially fitting to meet where it all began, at the Altar's ancient resting place…in view of everything. Speaking of where it all began, why don't we continue there? We have some important things to share with you."

He led us down the path to the terraced earth on which the Altar had stood in ancient times and where the stones of its foundation still rested. His two security officers walked by his side, while the two who drove us followed behind us. The wind was now strongly gusting across the terrace, as it had on our first visit there.

"Look at it," said Kazim, pointing to the Altar's foundation. "All because of this. A pile of ancient stones. So much trouble…so much conflict…because of this."

"The death of millions," I said. "The near destruction of the world."

"I don't mean that," he said. "I mean all the trouble it's caused you. And all the trouble it's caused us."

"What do you mean, the trouble it's caused you?"

"Having to keep watch over you," he replied, "having to track every journey, every move, every change of plan."

"You were tracking us everywhere we went?"

"Throughout," he replied.

"For our protection?"

"For protection? Yes. But not yours. For the protection of that which we were entrusted to protect."

"What do you mean?"

"You still don't understand? We are not *for* you, Mr. Herzog; we're *against* you. You know there are two sides to all this. And we happen to be of the other side. I am not your advocate. I'm your adversary."

It was the first shock we would receive that night—a night that was intended to end our lives—but it would not be the last.

Chapter 83
THE ARROWS

I LOOKED AT LARA. I knew her enough to realize that she was terrified but determined to put on a brave front. I surveyed the surroundings and our prospects for getting out of there alive. We were standing on the high place of Pergamon. We had no vehicle to get us down. There were three men in front of us and two behind us. We would never outrun them, and at least the two who drove us there were armed. Barring a miracle, there was no way out.

"I am of an ancient order," Kazim said. "The Keepers of the Altar...the Guardians of the Throne. We are the heirs of the priests who ministered in this most holy place. My involvement with you was not for your protection but for the protection of the Altar. It was to guard the mysteries and to ensure the fulfillment of his purposes."

"Whose purposes?" asked Lara.

"The one we serve and worship," he said, "the Dark Angel. We have been charged with ensuring that nothing disrupts or threatens the outworking of his plans. Unfortunately, your activities and your intentions to expose all this constituted a growing threat to the outworking of those plans.

"There were others," he said. "They tried to unlock the mysteries. But none came close to what you were able to do and find. None had so much revealed to them. And you didn't make it easy for us. On the other hand, you did help us by calling me throughout your journey and divulging information we otherwise would not have known. We tried to dissuade you. We tried to convince you that it wasn't worth losing your lives. You can't say you weren't warned, Mr. Herzog. But you wouldn't be dissuaded. You wouldn't stop. You left us with no choice. And so here we are."

"Here we are for what?" I said.

"Here we are in the place of the Altar. And as you well know, an altar requires a sacrifice. How does it feel to be part of the Altar's mystery...as the sacrifice?"

We could hear the rumbling of a distant thunder and see the flashes of distant lightning in the darkening skies.

"You were going to expose it. You were going to tell the world of the mystery. You were going to reveal to them how it altered everything—their history, their lives, their world. You were going to warn them, to prevent what is still to come. But it all ends here. We've come back to the place of the beginning to bring it all to an end. And to think, all those journeys, all that work, and all those revelations, and it will all come to nothing. No one will ever hear. No one will ever know."

At that, he signaled his men. The two who were in back of us grabbed our arms and began tying them behind our backs. The Altar had been surrounded by a protective fence, but a large section of the fence had been cut out, undoubtedly by Kazim's men for the sake of the night's proceedings. They led us onto the stones of the Altar's ruins, the two now standing at our sides and slightly in back of us, with Lara and me in between them as lambs prepared for the slaughter.

Kazim, meanwhile, was now standing at the end of the terrace overlooking a steep valley. His two men stood with him, one on each side, about ten feet apart. They bent down and picked up a dark cloth that was lying by their feet and clothed themselves with it. Each was now wearing a black hooded robe. If the scene was not menacing enough, the robes made it all the more so. The two who were standing with us on the stones of the Altar each took out a large knife, ornately decorated and of an ancient appearance. They were to be our executioners.

"Just a formality," said Kazim. "It's an accepted convention that altars require the shedding of blood. Now, shall we begin?"

At that, he turned around, away from us and toward the sky. His two men did likewise. He lifted his hands, as did they, and began speaking in another language. I couldn't tell if it was Turkish, ancient Greek, or something else. But it was as if he was chanting the words of an ancient liturgy.

I turned to Lara. "If you were thinking of praying," I said, "this would be a great time."

The chanting grew louder, as did the thunder rumbling in the distant sky.

"Yarikan!" It was the voice of a man shouting from the distance. The chanting stopped. Everyone turned to see where the voice was coming from. It was coming from behind and above us. There, overlooking the terrace, was the figure of a man in a long dark coat. It was the same man whom Lara and I had encountered on our first visit to the high place of Pergamon, the one who had told us he was the custodian, the one who watched over the site.

"Yarikan!" he again shouted. "What are you doing here on this ground?"

"The ground belongs to us," Kazim shouted back.

"You have no business here."

"But I do. I have urgent business. It will all be over in a moment."

At that, he signaled to the men on the Altar, who placed their knives across our throats. Lara and I looked at each other as if for the last time.

"Don't lay a hand on them," shouted the man.

"You can't stop it," Kazim shouted back.

"Release them," shouted the man.

"Make just one move," said Kazim, "and they'll be dead. You might as well sit back and enjoy the liturgy."

Just then, a lightning bolt lit up the sky, followed by a loud crack of thunder.

"Ah!" said Kazim with a look of delight on his face, "lightning and thunder, the sign of the ancient god! We can't keep him waiting."

At that, he lifted his hands as he had before, as did his two men, but this time they were turned away from the sky and facing us and the Altar. The man on the mountain above us now stretched out his hand in the direction of Kazim and began speaking in a language I couldn't understand. Kazim resumed his chanting but now in English, as if to make sure we understood what he was saying:

"Ancient of Nights
Who Is
And Who Is Not
The Unborn
The Uncreated
Angel of the Dark
Master of the Void
Come Rage
Against the Fabric
Of the Weaver
Come War
Against the All
Come Break
The Cosmic Mirror
That the Ancient Face

Be Blotted Out
That Which Is
Will Be as Not
And All
Will Be
As You."

The sky darkened, and the flashes of lightning grew more frequent, more intense, and seemingly closer. And it was all to Kazim's delight, as he was taking it all as a favorable sign. Lara's eyes were now closed, but her lips were moving. She was praying. So too was Kazim, but to a different god:

"Altar of Pergamon
Sacred Bringer
Of Death
Accept
What Is Given You
Consume
What Is Yours
Receive
The Sacrifice."

The word *sacrifice* was no doubt the signal for our slaying. The men on the Altar tightened their grip around their knives. It was then, for the first time since childhood, that I prayed. It was a short prayer, just one word: "*Help!*"

It was at that exact moment that help came and with a most dramatic arrival. A bolt of lightning struck the knife of the man standing to my side, causing it to fall out of his hand and him to fall backward onto the Altar's ruins. The same bolt struck the knife of the man at Lara's side and to the same effect. A second bolt then struck the edge of the terrace, just in front of Kazim, causing a crack to appear in the ground, which began to spread. The expression on Kazim's face changed from one of brazen assurance to that of terror.

Then came the third and final bolt. It struck Kazim and then the two men standing at his side. He began to violently convulse, as did his two men. Then as the crack at the edge of the terrace deepened, the ground underneath their feet began giving way, causing all three of them to fall backward. Their bodies now plummeted down from the high place of Pergamon to the valley below.

And then the storm subsided. Lara and I looked at each other. We were shaken, relieved, overwhelmed, and glad to be alive. Our two would-be executioners, who had fallen back on the ruins, had been knocked unconscious. But they soon awoke. Slowly, they got up from the ground, badly shaken. They looked around, trying to make sense of what had happened. Seeing no sign of the others and fearing for their lives, they ran away.

Soon after our two executioners fled the scene, a man appeared on the terrace. It was the "custodian." He untied our hands.

"You do realize what just happened?" he said.

Lara was in a state of awe, reluctant to speak. But then she answered him in a soft voice, just above that of a whisper, almost as if speaking only to herself.

"The Lord 'covers His hands with lightning,'" she said, "'and commands it to strike....The Lord thundered....He sent out His arrows and scattered...them.'"[1]

I was silent. There was nothing I could say in light of what had just taken place.

"It's been some time since we first met in this place," said the man. "I hear you've been keeping busy...but not out of trouble."

"It hasn't been dull," I replied.

"It's good to see you're still alive. We did believe you would be."

"We?"

"Those who helped you," he said, "and others."

"And now that we've made it," I said, "now that we've finished the journey, what do we do?"

"But you haven't finished, Mr. Herzog. You have one more journey to make. And for this one, you need to be prepared."

Chapter 84
REDEMPTION

"Mr. Herzog," he said, "you and Lara have been shown much concerning the darkness, but there is another side."

"What do you mean?" I replied.

"The light," he said. "The other side is the light. You've seen how real the darkness is, how it has changed the world. But if the darkness is real, so too must be the light. And you can't fight the power of darkness except by the power of light. You have been shown how real is the one you once scoffed at."

"Satan."

"If Satan is real, so too must be God. And if what the Scriptures reveal of Satan is true, then so too is what they reveal of God. And as real is the power of darkness, to the point of altering history, even more real is the power of God. You were told of the meaning of the name *Satan.*"

"The Adversary," I said, "the Opposer."

"You can only oppose that which exists. And if your existence is based on opposition, then it is dependent on the existence of that which you oppose. You see, the nature of evil is parasitic. It can only exist by warring against the Good. You can have good without evil, but you cannot have evil without good. Life can exist without murder, but not murder without life. Laws can exist without transgressions and crime, but crime and transgressions cannot exist without laws. And truth can exist without lies, but lies cannot exist without truth. So you see, the existence of evil does not testify *against* the existence of God but *for* it."

"What is God?" I asked.

"Everything Satan is not. What do you know of Satan?"

"He's the epitome of evil."

"And so God is the epitome of good. And if Satan is the embodiment of hatred, then what is God?"

"The embodiment of love."

"And what is love? It is the joining of oneself to another, the giving of oneself for another, and the putting of oneself in another's place. So if God is love, what would He do?"

"Become one with another?" I said. "Put Himself in the place of another?"

"And if the other is us, then what would be the greatest manifestation of love but God becoming one with us, with you?"

"You mean Jesus?"

"The greatest love would be that God would put Himself in our place. And if Satan is the Destroyer and the taker of life…"

"Then God would be the giver of life."

"And so He would give Himself, His life, for us to death, that those who were dying would be given life. He who is all good would die for our evils, our sins, that we would be saved. You know what the name *Satan* means. Do you know what the name *Jesus* means?"

"No."

"It's a translation of His real name, His Hebrew name, *Yeshua.* It means 'God is salvation.' You were shown the mystery of Satan's Altar, the Altar of darkness…but there is another altar."

"What other altar?"

"The Altar of light…the Altar of altars. You see, an altar is that on which a sacrifice is slain. And so the Altar of altars is that on which the Sacrifice of sacrifices was slain. The Altar of altars is that on which God was sacrificed. What is the cross but the Altar of God's love, the antithesis to the Altar of Satan? The Altar of Satan brings evil, but the Altar of God nullifies evil; it washes it away…It cleanses us from sin. The Altar of Satan brings death from life, but the Altar of God brings life from death, resurrection, a new beginning from an empty tomb and from the end, a new birth. Mr. Herzog, you have learned the mystery of the Altar of Pergamon, the Altar of darkness. But you must now learn the mystery of the Altar of God."

"How?" I asked. "I'm not a religious person."

"It's not about religion," he said. "It's about the heart. It's about a relationship. It's about you and God. It's what you choose. It doesn't come from being born of religion. God is Spirit. Therefore, His children are not born of flesh or culture or religion. The children of God are born of the Spirit. And so one cannot enter the kingdom of God, one cannot be saved or see heaven…unless one is born again."

"How?"

"By receiving the love of God that was given on that Altar…the Sacrifice, the Lamb of God…Jesus…Yeshua."

"It's not my heritage."

"But it *is* your heritage. It is everything your heritage is about: the

Atonement, the Passover Lamb, the Messiah. It's the fulfillment of all things…even of your life. You were shown the mystery of the Dark Angel's Altar that you might overcome it. It is only by the Altar of God that you can overcome the Altar of Satan and, for that matter, the power of sin and evil and guilt and the past and darkness and hell."

"How does one receive it?"

"By opening your heart…by receiving His love, His cleansing, His forgiveness, His sacrifice, His life, His power of resurrection, His salvation…by receiving Him into every part of your life, by putting your faith in Him and following Him, by living in His presence and letting His presence live in you. And it can begin here and now…even with a simple prayer…from your heart…to God."

"On the Throne of Satan?"

"You can come to God in any place and at any time. But what better place than this for the overcoming of darkness?"

At that, he departed, ascending the summit and leaving me to myself. Lara also left, but before leaving, nodded to me and smiled, as if to assure and encourage me.

Many of those who make their peace with God do so at the altar of a church sanctuary. That night, I made my peace with God in a pagan sanctuary, at an unholy altar, and before the Throne of Satan.

We were now about to embark on the last journey.

PART XVI

RETURNINGS

Chapter 85

HOLY GROUND

I REJOINED LARA AND the man on top of the summit.

"Did you make your peace with God?" he asked.

"I believe I did."

"Then I believe you're ready."

"For?" I asked.

"For the last part of the journey and the last revelation."

"Can you tell us where?" asked Lara.

"On holier ground than this."

He led us over to the road that would take us down. There was no car. The two men had driven away—and with our luggage. Again we would have to replace it.

He walked us down from the high place and, at the end of the descent, departed. We walked on from there to the center of the town, where we found a hotel and spent the night. The next morning we both had a sense of peace, to the point that we felt it safe to find a random Turkish coffee shop and have breakfast there.

"So where do you think we're going?" I asked Lara.

"The man told us we were going to holier ground," she replied. "We're going to the Holy Land."

"You believe we're going to Israel?"

"No," she said, "I know it."

"You had a dream."

"I did," she said with a smile.

"Please go on."

"It was similar to the one I had at the beginning."

"Of the Turkish bazaar?"

"I was leading you into a walled city. The stones of its walls were pale brown or pale gold, as was much of the city. We walked down the descending road of a Middle Eastern marketplace, in some ways similar to the Turkish bazaar—filled with colors, trinkets, lamps, Middle Eastern fabrics, and small wooden sculptures and figurines. After reaching the bottom, we turned to the right and walked through a stone passageway, wider than the marketplace and more peaceful. It took us into a different part of the city, with bearded men in long black coats, women in colorful scarves and head coverings, and little children playing on the stone streets and squares. And then as in the first dream, I led you down streets and alleys until we reached a door. Over the door was a small lion carved in stone. I turned to you and said, 'It's here.'"

"How do you know it's Israel?"

"The men and women were Jewish—Orthodox—the stone was Jerusalem stone, and the walls were the walls of the Old City. It's Jerusalem. Our last journey is to the Holy Land."

We spent one more full day in Turkey, once again replacing our luggage, clothes, and other essentials. The following day, we flew to Tel Aviv and from there took a taxi to the city many believe is the center of the world and the meeting place between heaven and earth: Jerusalem.

We found a hotel in the new city, spent the night, and the next day made our way to the walled city, Old Jerusalem. Lara wanted to make sure that we entered through the same gate she saw in her dreams. It took a while, but then we found it. It was the Jaffa Gate.

As we passed through the gate, we could see in the distance ahead of us the Shuk, the Arab marketplace, which we entered. As in Lara's dream, it was filled with sound and color, golden trinkets, olive wood figurines and sculptures, and Middle Eastern fabrics. And as in her dream, we were walking down a descending road. Soon after reaching the bottom, we made a right turn and, as in her dream, the atmosphere changed as the path widened and became more peaceful. We were now walking through the Cardo, the heart of the ancient city.

And then, as in her dream, the Cardo opened up into a different part of the city, with children playing in the streets, bearded men in long black coats, and women in colorful head coverings. It was the Jewish quarter of the walled city. She led me down golden-stone streets and alleyways until she came to a stop outside a door. Carved into the stone above the wall was a small lion.

"It's here," she said. "Whatever we're supposed to find, it's here."

I knocked on the door. There was no response at first. But then it slowly opened. Standing there in the darkly lit room was a man who I would guess was in his mid-fifties to early sixties, with black-and-gray hair, a matching beard, and a long black coat. He had to have been Jewish and, I would have guessed, Orthodox, except that his beard was cut short, his coat was different from those I saw the Orthodox Jewish men of the city wearing, and, most strikingly, his head was uncovered—no hat, no skullcap. Except for the coat, he looked to me like what I imagined an ancient prophet of the Bible would have looked like and carried an air of authority as I imagined they had as well.

"You were wanting to see me?"

"I believe so," I said.

"My name is Meir," he said. "Please, come in."

The room was its own world, illumined with the light of oil lamps and filled with a variety of exotic Middle Eastern items—golden utensils, antique books, and ancient-looking artifacts of clay and stone.

"This isn't a store," said Lara.

"No, but I don't suppose you came here to buy souvenirs. Please sit down."

In the middle of the room were three chairs and a small table between them, as if it had all been set up for our coming.

"You've been shown much," he said, "but not about the beginning."

"What do you mean?"

"The origins of the mystery."

At that, he got up from his chair, walked toward an alcove, and came back holding a large golden lampstand, which he placed on the small table between us.

"This is a menorah," he said. "You may know it from the festival of Hanukkah. It is with this that it all began."

It was then in that dimly lit room that for the first time the mystery's origins would be revealed to us.

Chapter 86
ORIGINS

"YOU WERE TOLD," said the man, "of Lucifer's vow in the Book of Isaiah: 'I will ascend into heaven. I will exalt my throne above the stars of God. I will also sit on the mount of the congregation.'[1] So the Enemy's goal is to replace the Throne of the Holy One with his own. But the Throne of God is in heaven. And yet He has, as well, a throne on earth. It's here in Jerusalem, the *Beit Mikdash*, the Temple, the Throne of His resting. So where would the Enemy seek to set up his Throne on earth to replace the Throne of God? Here in Jerusalem, on the Temple Mount, the sanctuary of God."

"'I will also sit on the mount of the congregation,'" said Lara. "God was worshipped on the mount of the congregation, the Temple Mount."

"So the Enemy would use a vessel of evil named Antiochus Epiphanes, who would ascend the mount and desecrate the Temple, turning it into a pagan sanctuary. And do you know how he desecrated the Temple? By erecting an altar. And do you know what altar?"

"No," I replied.

"The Altar of Zeus."

"The Altar of Zeus," I said, "as in the Altar of Pergamon?"

"The same, except this one actually stood in Jerusalem in the Holy Place. But the Dark Angel was behind them both. It was that object of desecration, the Altar of Zeus on the Temple Mount, that would ignite a war, the Enemy's kingdom against the kingdom of God. Antiochus would launch a persecution against the Jewish people. He slaughtered those who followed the ways of God. He burned the scrolls on which the Scriptures were written. He was seeking to wipe out Israel's faith and blot out the name of God. And it appeared as if he would succeed, except that God had other plans.

"An unlikely people named the Maccabees rose up in resistance. They fought back, and miraculously, they won. They ascended the holy mountain to the defiled Temple, cleansed it, and rededicated it to God. The rededication was commemorated in the holiday of Hanukkah, the Festival of Lights."

"And what happened to the Altar of Zeus?" asked Lara.

"They destroyed it and removed its stones from the Holy Place."

"And this has to do with the mystery we've been shown?" I asked.

"I would say so," he replied. "Antiochus had a friend, a close associate, an ally. His name was King Eumenes. Do you know what he was king of?"

"No," said Lara.

"Pergamon," said the man. "Eumenes was the king of Pergamon. He was the one who erected the Altar of Zeus on Pergamon's high place. And it all happened at the same time. In the days when his ally Antiochus set up the Altar of Zeus in the Holy Place and was defeated, Eumenes set up the Altar of Zeus in Pergamon. For behind it all was a spiritual war. The Enemy had tried to set up his Altar on the holy mountain, his Throne in the place of God's Throne. But it was taken away. So he would find another mountain, another high place, and would set up the same thing, the Altar of Zeus, but he would make it larger, colossal. There he would establish his Throne—in Pergamon.

"So you see, the Altar of Pergamon was birthed in the midst of spiritual war, the kingdom of Satan warring against the kingdom of God. And so from its inception, it was part of the Enemy's war against the purposes of God, against the people of God, against the Jewish people, and against all who uphold God's name and will."

"And that's why," I said, "the Altar was connected to the rise of anti-Semitism, to Hitler, the Nazis, and the Third Reich, to communism, Lenin, Stalin, and the Soviet Union, to the persecution of Christians and the Holocaust. It was all a continuation of the war in which the Altar was born."

"I have told you the mystery of the Altar's origins," he said. "Now I will tell you the mystery of its return."

Chapter 87

THE OTHER KINGDOM

SHALL WE GO for a walk?" said the man.

He led us outside and through the streets of the Jewish Quarter of the Old City of Jerusalem, through narrow alleyways and open squares, and past stores and synagogues, as he opened up the mystery of the Altar's return.

"The Enemy's war against the kingdom of God would continue with the rise of the Roman Empire. In the year AD 70, the armies of Rome came to the Holy City and destroyed the Temple, the city, and the nation. It was that destruction that ushered in two thousand years of Jewish exile from the land—two thousand years of persecution and sorrows. It all began as the armies of Rome reduced this place to ruins…and they did so under a sign…the sign of Jupiter…Zeus."

"The god of the Altar," said Lara.

"The mask of the Enemy," said the man. "It was under the emblem of Jupiter, or Zeus, and in his name that the nation of Israel was destroyed.

"But it didn't end there. In the following century, Rome would seek to obliterate the connection between the Jewish people and Israel, their ancient homeland. They renamed the land *Palaestina*, or *Palestine*, after Israel's ancient enemies, the Philistines. And they planned on building a temple of Jupiter on the site of the Temple of God in Jerusalem. It was the Enemy's declaration of victory. He had taken possession of the Holy City, the Throne of God.

"But the war would not end there. From Jerusalem, the city of God, the Gospel would go forth to the world, starting with the Roman Empire. The first of Messiah's followers, the early Christians, would be persecuted, imprisoned, and killed by the Romans, who did so under the authority of their chief god, Jupiter. But the Gospel overcame the gods and brought the worship of the Greek Zeus, the Roman Jupiter, to an end. And as you know, it would lead to the abandonment and destruction of his Altar at Pergamon. And as you know, the Altar disappeared with the Christianization of the West—but then, ages later, reappeared at the time of the West's dechristianization.

"That was one side of the mystery and of the ancient war. But there was another.

"In the first centuries of the present age, two things disappeared from the world: the nation of Israel and the Altar of Pergamon. The first represented the kingdom of God, the second, the kingdom of Satan. So what would happen if the nation of Israel were to be resurrected and brought back into the world?"

"Then the Altar of Pergamon," I said, "would also be resurrected and brought back into the world."

"Yes," said the man, "The two kingdoms would again contend against each other, the kingdom of Satan against the nation of God. The Scriptures had long prophesied that in the last days, God would gather His ancient people, Israel, from the ends of the earth, bring them back to their ancient homeland, and resurrect His ancient nation."

"And it all happened," said Lara, "according to the prophecies."

"And the fulfillment of those prophecies, the resurrection of Israel, would represent a threat to the kingdom of Satan. So the Enemy would war against the resurrection of that nation with the resurrection of his Altar, the raising up of his Throne. And he would do so just as that prophesied resurrection was beginning."

"How?" I asked.

"In order for Israel to be resurrected, the Jewish people had to learn again how to farm the land, how to make the barren wasteland bloom. The first school to teach Jewish people how to do that was called *Mikveh Israel*, the Hope of Israel. It was the beginning of the land's resurrection. It was founded in 1870. It was right after that, at the start of Israel's resurrection—the very next year—that the Enemy moved to set in motion the resurrection of his Throne as Carl Humann stumbled on the Altar of Pergamon.

"But for Israel to be resurrected, there had to be a reason for the Jewish people to return to their ancient homeland. That would begin in what would be called the Odessa Pogrom. The name referred to a violent attack on the Jews of Odessa, a Russian city on the shores of the Black Sea. It is considered by many to be the first *modern* pogrom, or violent uprising, against the Jewish people and the harbinger of the large-scale Russian campaigns of anti-Jewish violence that would soon follow. It would prove to be a turning point, causing the Jews of Russia and beyond Russia to question their future in the nations. It would lead to the beginning of Zionism and the return of the Jewish people to their homeland."

"So when did the Odessa Pogrom take place?" I asked.

"In 1871, the same year that Carl Humann discovered the first pieces of the Altar of Pergamon. So the resurrection of Israel and the resurrection of Satan's Throne were both set in motion in the same year."

"And the same year that Germany was born," said Lara.

"Yes," said the man, "just as Israel's resurrection was beginning, the Enemy brought into being the nation that would seek to destroy the Jewish nation before it could be resurrected.

"It was that same decade, the 1870s, that saw the next milestone in Israel's resurrection. It was called *Petah Tikveh,* the Door of Hope. It was the first Jewish settlement founded in the hope of reviving the ancient Jewish homeland. It is considered the mother of all Israel's agricultural communities and the prototype of what would become the nation or State of Israel."

"And when did Petah Tikveh begin?" asked Lara.

"In 1878," the man replied.

"1878," I said, "the same year they began unearthing the Altar."

"And it was in the years of the Altar's unearthing," he said, "that massive persecutions against the Jewish people of Russia broke out, Zionism crystallized as a movement, and multitudes of Jewish people began returning to the land.

"The resurrection of Israel and the Altar of Pergamon happened at the same time. In the late 1890s, when architects, engineers, and builders gathered in Berlin to lay the foundation and begin building the Altar its first home, delegates from around the world gathered in Basel, Switzerland, for the first World Zionist Congress to begin laying the political foundation and structure for the future State of Israel, the resurrected Jewish national home.

"It was in the days of Israel's resurrection that the city of the Altar's resurrection gave birth to anti-Semitism and then the Third Reich, world war, and the Holocaust. Each was part of the Enemy's war to destroy the Jewish people and stop the resurrection from happening. And after that, it was the Soviet Union, in possession of the Altar, that sought Israel's destruction.

"The two that had disappeared from the world together had now together returned, as the ancient war now replayed itself in the modern world."

"It is time," said the man, "that we go to the center of that war and of the world to speak of things yet to come."

Chapter 88
THE END OF ALL THINGS

JUST THEN, WE came to the top of a large stone stairway. That's when I saw it. In the distance were the golden stones of the Western Wall, to which Jewish people have come to pray for ages. Above the wall was the Dome of the Rock, the shrine built by the Muslims on top of the Temple Mount.

The man led us down the stairs and then onto a walkway that brought us up to the Mount. We came to a security station with Israeli soldiers keeping watch. I had the impression that visiting hours were over, as it was now late in the day and no one else was there. And yet it seemed as if the man had favor with the soldiers, or as if they didn't care, or almost as if they didn't even see us. We just walked through.

The walkway ended with an open gateway that led into the Temple Mount. We walked through it. The Muslim authorities who guarded the Mount were known for their harsh dealings with visitors, but again we just passed by them as if they didn't care or notice, even though we appeared to be the only visitors there. The Temple Mount was a vast expanse, a gigantic square of Jerusalem stone with assorted buildings, domes, and trees, but it was mostly open. One could feel its gravity—a sense of awe, of conflict, and yet of peace, all at the same time.

"You are now standing," he said, "in the center of the world and the meeting place of heaven and earth, the most contested site on planet Earth and the focal point of the cosmic war.

"Over there," he said, pointing into the distance, "was where the Temple stood and on which they erected the Altar of Zeus. You were told of the coming world power. That power is linked to the beast, the Antichrist. It is prophesied that he will come here to the Temple Mount and desecrate it."

"The 'abomination of desolation,'" said Lara. "In biblical prophecy, that's what the desecration is called."[1]

"Yes," said the man. "It was the same name used to speak of the Altar that Antiochus erected on this ground. The abomination was the Altar of Zeus. And what King Eumenes erected in Pergamon was also the Altar of Zeus and was also an abomination. So there is a connection between the Altar of Pergamon and the desecration that is yet to come.

"There is, as well, a connection between the Altar and the Antichrist, as the Antichrist will embody in human form what the Altar embodies in stone. He will wage war against God and His people; against the Messiah, the Christ; against the Gospel and Christianity; against the Jews; against Israel; and against the kingdom of God.[2] He will be, as the Altar of Pergamon, a vessel of death and destruction and, as the Throne of Satan, that through which the Enemy will seek to rule the world. And as is the Altar, he will be an abomination.

"Come," said the man. "I want to show you something."

He led us over to the Dome of the Rock.

"This is what the Muslims erected on the ground on which the Temple of God once stood. Look over there," he said, pointing to a marble panel on the side of the Dome.

"What do you see?"

"A face," I said.

"It looks demonic," said Lara.

It was a menacing image, a dark face with two horns on top of its head, eyes that appeared to be glowing, a sharp downward-pointing nose, and a crooked mouth with sharp teeth or fangs. It was as satanic a face as one could imagine. At the bottom of the face was what could be taken as a reflection of the same face in the opposite direction.

"It looks," said Lara, "like a demonic painting of the face of Satan."

"How did it get there?" I asked.

"It was formed naturally in the marble, or unnaturally. In either case, this was the result."

"And why did they put it here," asked Lara, "of all places?"

"One would think they didn't realize it."

"It's hard to miss," said Lara.

"So here, in the middle of the holiest site on earth, in the place of God's dwelling, on the ground of His Throne, is an image of Satan...as a sign and embodiment of his ancient vow: 'I will exalt my throne above the stars of God, I will also sit on the mount of the congregation....I will be like the Most High.'[3] And so here he sits in an image of stone on the mount of the congregation, on the Temple Mount, the Throne of the Most High—the most unholy one in the most holy of places."

"The Throne of Satan," said Lara, "on the Throne of God."

"The sign of a cosmic war," he said, "of two kingdoms, two altars, two thrones."

"It doesn't end," said Lara. "The evil always returns, as if it's unstoppable..."

"No," said the man. "It is the nature of evil to appear that way...as if the darkness of night will overwhelm the light of a candle. But you must never believe it."

At that, he began leading us away from the Dome and toward the eastern side of the Mount.

"In the end, evil will not prevail," he said, "because it cannot. It exists only inasmuch as it opposes the Good. It cannot sustain its own existence but in the end brings about its own destruction. The darkness will never have the last word.

"Do you know which comes first in the Bible, day or night? The night comes first and then the day. The night, the darkness, is never the end...only the beginning. It must always lead to dawn. It is the day that remains and the Good that is forever.

"So the Good appears for now as a candle burning in the night, fragile and against all odds. But the darkness cannot overcome it, for the light overcomes all things. The first believers, the first followers of the Messiah, the early Christians, appeared as the weakest of peoples, defenseless in the hands of their persecutors. But the powers that towered over them, that persecuted and crushed them, are all gone. And yet they live.

"So too the Jewish people, the children of Israel—they've dwelt on earth as the weakest of nations, scattered across the earth with no king, no common language, no army, no defense, and with the world's strongest of powers seeking their destruction. But the powers that crushed them are gone. The mighty have all fallen, and yet, against all odds, the children of Israel live.

"And He who hung on the cross—naked, without defense, broken and crushed, the incarnation of love, the weakest of men...And yet no power on earth has so transformed the course of human history as has that one life...With no seat of power, no weapon, no army, He overcame the world and overcomes all things. For in the end, the weakness of God is stronger than the powers of hell, and the light of the Good greater than the darkest of evils.

"Do you see that mountain?" he said, pointing eastward, away from the Temple Mount. "It's the Mount of Olives. It is from there that Messiah will come and from here on this Mount that He will usher in the kingdom of God.[4] We know the end of the war. Your part is to stand on the right side of that war until the end. And, therefore, knowing the end, fear no evil, believe the Good, fight the good fight, shine the light, and overcome the darkness. For in the end, the night will usher in the dawn, and the kingdom of evil will give way to the kingdom of light. As it is written, 'The LORD is good…and His love endures forever.'"[5]

He let us dwell for a time on what was told to us, then led us down from the Mount and to the plaza in front of the Western Wall.

"So what are we to do with all this?" I said as he began walking away. He paused and turned around.

"I've heard that there is a place in these parts," he said, "where others have found revelation…and their calling. You might consider going there."

"Where?" I shouted back. But he had already resumed his departure and was heading to the Western Wall, where he disappeared among all the other bearded men in long dark coats. It wouldn't be long before we found the place of which he spoke and the revelation that awaited us.

PART XVII

JOURNEY'S END

Chapter 89

ANGELS

We caught a taxi back to our hotel in the new city. The next morning, Lara and I had breakfast at one of Jerusalem's outdoor cafés.

"I have good news and bad news," she said as she took out her notebook. "The good news is, I had a dream. The bad news is, I have absolutely no idea what it means."

"Tell me."

"It wasn't long. I was walking in the desert when I came to the base of a mountain. As I stared at it, lines began forming in the rock face, as if an invisible hand was carving them into the stone as easily as if into wax. At the end of the carving, the rock face had two columns of numbers. I took note of the numbers. And then I woke up."

"And?"

"As soon as I woke up, I jotted down the numbers in my notebook."

"And?"

"Here," she said, handing me her notebook, opened to the page with two columns of numbers. On the top of each column was a symbol. I couldn't make anything of it. I gave up and resumed eating my breakfast. We were almost done with our meal when it hit me.

"Lara, on your cell phone, look up the Hebrew word for *north*." So she looked it up and showed it to me.

"The symbol," I said, "at the top of the first column. It's the first letter of the Hebrew word for *north*."

"There must be a lot of Hebrew words," she said, "that begin with that letter."

"Now look up the Hebrew word for *east*." She did.

"It matches the symbol on the top of the second column."

"And what does it mean?" she asked.

"The numbers in your dream are coordinates, geographic coordinates. They're revealing the location of the place. The first column is its latitude; the second, its longitude. Try putting them into your cell phone, and see what happens."

So she did and then just stared at the results without saying anything.

"What?" I asked.

"It's here. It's in the desert—here."

"Try to find out where in the desert, if there's anything significant there."

So she spoke into her cell phone and then, after the results appeared on the screen, she just stared at it with a startled expression.

"What?"

"It's Mount Sinai!" she said. "We're going to Mount Sinai."

"That's why it was revealed to you as an inscription on the mountain. It's where God inscribed the two tablets of the Ten Commandments."[1]

"Two columns."

"The man told us it's the place where 'others have found revelation and their calling.' Moses found his mission there. Maybe we will as well."

And so we prepared to journey to the mountain that since ancient times had been identified as the site where Moses received the revelation and commandments of God. In order to get there, we had to drive to Eilat, Israel's desert city on the coast of the Red Sea. We spent the day there and then the following morning passed through the border, crossing into Egypt and the desert of Sinai.

The Sinai Desert was a different world, the blues and whites of Eilat giving way to the ocher, rust, and gold of the Sinai. As we drew closer to our destination, the road turned inland and began winding its way through dry riverbeds and towering, jagged mountains.

And then we arrived at the famed mountain. At its base was St. Catherine's Monastery, a fortress-like encampment in the middle of the desert. Nearby were dwellings and guest houses for the pilgrims, hikers, and other visitors who came to the site. It was one of these guest houses, run by local Bedouins, that would become our lodging place. The accommodations were simple, basic, and rustic, but at the same time warm and welcoming.

Later on the day of our arrival, as the sun was descending on the desert, our Bedouin hosts invited Lara and me to join them around a campfire in front of Mount Sinai. We accepted the offer. We sat on the desert sand, gazing into the fire, the surrounding mountains, and the desert sky.

"Did you ever wonder," said Lara, "about the ones who helped us through our journey, the guides?"

"What do you mean?"

"Who they were."

"They had to be members of an organization that worked against those who were against us."

"How did they all just happen to always be there at the exact places we happened to be and at the exact times we arrived there?"

"I guess the same way those who were against us knew...intelligence systems, surveillance. I don't know."

"And the boy in Nuremberg who didn't speak as a boy speaks? And the little girl at the Brandenburg Gate who didn't speak as a little girl? It was more than natural. And what would they be doing there—children on a mission, all alone? Why was there no one watching them if they had parents? And how did each one know what the others had told us?"

"What are you saying?"

She didn't answer. She seemed hesitant to say it.

"Who do you think they were?" I asked.

"I believe they were angels."

"Angels? Really? I know we've been shown things, and we've seen things that are way beyond anything we've known. I know it's more than natural...but angels? With wings and halos? The ones that appear on holiday greeting cards?"

"Angels are agents of God," she said, "spiritual beings who do His will, who fulfill His purposes, who protect His people, who lead His people, and who reveal His mysteries."

"Our guides were real people—real flesh-and-blood people with accents and quirks..."

"The Bible speaks of angels appearing as men. It's written that 'some have entertained angels unawares.'[2] That could only happen if they appeared as real flesh-and-blood people."

"I think this is..."

"Let me show you something," she said as she opened her notebook. "Do you know how angels are described in their natural form? As beings of light, as radiant, shining beings of light."

"And?"

"The man in the Turkish bazaar, Mr. Isik. Do you know what *Isik* means? It's Turkish for light. The woman on the bridge who showed us the Altar and then Hitler's birthplace, she told us her name was Yaira. Do you know what *Yaira* means? It's Hebrew for she will shine. The young Polish woman, the student with the knapsack and the long blond hair, *Alaina*—her name means bright. The old man in Sarajevo, the chess player, Zoran—*Zoran* is Bosnian for the light of dawn. The man in Red Square, *Yaroslav*, his name is Russian for bright. The little girl in the red coat, Ilka—*Ilka* means the shining one. And Meir, the Orthodox-looking man with the beard and the long dark coat who led us through Jerusalem, his name is Hebrew for he who shines and he who brings the light. All of their names describe angels."

"I don't know…It's too…"

"In the Psalms," she said, "it's written, 'He shall give His angels charge over you…to keep you in all your ways. In their hands they shall bear you up, lest you dash your foot against a stone.'[3] That's who they were, Ariel. That's why we made it. That's why we're still here…alive. He gave His angels charge over us, to guide us, to protect us, and to reveal to us the mystery."

I didn't know what to make of it or what to say. The journey had left me with only the smallest measure of residual skepticism. And even that was being brought to the breaking point.

The sun was now setting, and our desert surroundings were rapidly darkening. I couldn't help gazing up at Mount Sinai. What revelation was waiting for us there…?

Before that night was over, we would have the answer.

Chapter 90

THE MYSTERY ON THE MOUNTAIN

I BELIEVE WE NEED to go up tonight," I said.

"You want to climb Mount Sinai tonight?" said Lara. "I think I need to rest. Anyway, I believe it's for you. Whatever's there, it's for you to find."

"Are you sure you don't want to go?"

"Yes. But why do you have to do it now, in the dark?"

"I just feel it's the time."

We returned to the guesthouse, where I gathered up what I believed I should take with me on the ascent.

"Be careful," she said as I left the house and headed for the mountain. "Make sure you don't fall off."

There were two ways of ascending Mount Sinai. The first was called the Steps of Repentance, a steep and strenuous stone path of rocks built by desert monks. The second was called the Camel Path, a long, winding, and much more gradual ascent. I chose the latter.

So I began my ascent. The moon was nearly full that night, which helped illuminate my path. The higher I went, the quieter everything became, and with the increased elevation and the coming of the desert night, it grew noticeably colder. It took me about three hours. I finally made it to the peak. There I found a rock on which to sit and wait. I wasn't sure exactly what I was waiting for. But I was hoping that somehow, on top of that mountain, I would find some kind of an answer, anything that would give me direction.

I sat there on that rock for about half an hour until I almost fell asleep. And then I saw it. A tall, thin figure of a man in a long dark coat appeared under the light of the moon. Slowly, he made his way over to me. I got up from the rock, readying myself in the event that the approach was not of a friendly nature.

As he drew nearer, I was able to discern his features, illumined by the moonlight. His face was long, angled, marked by deep lines, distinguished, and crowned with a halo of white hair. I couldn't place it at first, and then it hit me.

"No," I whispered to myself. "It can't be…of all people."

It was the one who was more responsible for the journey than anyone else.

"Marinus," I said. "Professor Lorens Marinus."

"You were expecting perhaps a pillar of fire," he said, "or tablets of stone? Not everyone can have a Mount Sinai experience."

"I suppose it's not worth asking what you're doing here in the middle of the Sinai Desert on top of this mountain—*and right now*?"

"I'm here because of you," he said.

"You knew I would come here?"

"I did."

"Are you an angel?"

"No," he replied. "I'm a professor. The percentage of professors who are angels is still a relatively small number. I'm afraid I'm very much of flesh and blood."

"Then how did you know I would be here?"

"Those who knew you would be here told me as much. Shall we sit down?"

So I sat down again on the rock. The professor sat down on another rock to my left.

"Those who knew I'd be here," I said, "and told you to come, are they the ones who helped us on the journey, the guides?"

"Your guides are among their number."

"How do you know them?"

"Perhaps it was because I was open and willing enough to be used…and because of you."

"Because of me?"

"In the same way they knew you would be here tonight, they knew the day would come when you would be visited and given that page. And when that day came, you would have to be guided in a way you could receive it. You would have to be encouraged to begin the journey."

"So you knew it all from the beginning," I said, "when you arranged for Lara to come with me."

"That was my mission," he said. "That's why I came to New York. Do you think it was just to deliver a series of lectures on old manuscripts or to attend an honorary dinner? No, Mr. Herzog, I came because of you."

"So then you knew of those who would try to stop us."

"Yes, and those who would help you."

"And you believed I would survive?"

"I believed you would keep going no matter what. And yes, I believed you would make it to the end. And here you are. I was right."

"I'm glad you were."

"I would never have asked Lara to go with you if I wasn't sure of that."

"But why me?" I asked. "Why me of all people?"

"Because you were chosen," he said.

"Why?"

"For one, you were the least likely person, which made you the most likely person. What more powerful witness is there in testifying to a truth than one who starts out as an unbeliever, a skeptic?"

"So I'm the most likely because I'm the least likely."

"And more than that," he said. "Your family has a tradition concerning its origins, yes?"

"It's more of a family secret," I said. "I should be surprised that you know about it, but I'm not. The story is that we were descended from the royal house of Judea…but through the house of Herod. That's why we don't talk about it much."

"There's truth to it," he said. "But you don't have the story quite right."

"What do you mean?"

"The most famous person in history known by the name *Antipas* was of the house of Herod, Herod Antipas. Your ancestor was Antipas, but not Herod Antipas. Over time, it became confused."

"So which Antipas am I descended from?"

"Antipas of Pergamon."

"Antipas of Pergamon? I'm of Pergamon?"

"In that sense, yes."

"And who was Antipas of Pergamon?"

"He appears in the Book of Revelation. When it speaks of Pergamon, it says, 'Antipas was My faithful martyr, who was killed among you, where Satan dwells.'[1] Antipas was a man of God, a follower of the Messiah. He was the first person named in the Bible to be martyred for his faith outside the land of Israel. His martyrdom took place *where Satan dwelt*, at the Throne of Satan."

"At the Altar of Pergamon."

"That's why you were chosen to contend against the Altar and, by contending, to overcome it and the plans of the Enemy. It was for that mission you were born."

"But I went so much the other way."

"Yes, you hardened yourself…because of what the Enemy did to your ancestors, to your relatives. That's what he wanted…that you would believe the evil and lose faith in the Good. And yet you were always drawn to the supernatural, even if it was to disprove it—because you were called to it. If you could have disproved the supernatural, you wouldn't have answered your calling. But your calling was greater than your resistance to it."

"So what am I supposed to do now?"

"What are you supposed to do? You've come upon a mystery that involves nothing less than the future of this world. And yet those who dwell in this world have no idea. What must you do? You must reveal it to them. You must expose it. You must show them how real it is and how crucial are the stakes, the reality of evil…and the reality of good—of God. You must give them hope—their only hope…that they might come to Him, just as you did…that they might be saved."

"But how?"

"You're a writer, Mr. Herzog. That's not an accident. You became a writer because it was your calling to write. So write. Write a book. And in the book, reveal the mystery. Take what you were shown and make it known to the world."

And then he was silent. We both were. He wanted to give me time to take it all in. Finally, he broke the silence.

"So, Mr. Herzog, what do you think? Will you take up your mantle? Will you fulfill the calling for which you were placed in this world?"

I paused before saying anything. Then, in a whisper, I said, "*Yes.*"

"Then rise," he said. "We must pray for your protection and for your empowering."

So I got up from the rock and stood there with my eyes closed as he laid his hand on my shoulder and began to pray. In the middle of his prayer, I thought I was hearing other voices. I opened my eyes. And then I saw it. All around me, in a large, spread-out circle, they were there. They were all there, with their right hands lifted up toward me, each one praying along with the professor's prayer.

There was the custodian from the Altar; the man from the Turkish bazaar, Isik, in his red vest and fez; the woman from the bridge, Yaira, with her long, dark wavy hair; the old Bosnian man, Zoran, with his large white mustache, still wearing his fisherman's cap; the boy from Nuremberg; Alaina, the young Polish woman, with her knapsack still on her back; the man from the train who led us through Auschwitz; the man who appeared as a tourist at the Black Gate of Trier; the older Russian woman, Svetlana, from St. Petersburg; the mystical-looking man from Red Square; the little girl from Berlin with her long, wavy blond hair, still wearing her red coat; the Native American man who lit the fire in the New Mexican desert; the woman from Havana in her turquoise dress and large yellow hat; the light-blond-haired man from the Tiergarten who led us through the ruins of Rome; and Meir, in his long dark coat, who led us to the center of the mystery and the holiest place on earth.

They were all there—and each appearing as they did when we encountered them, each in the exact same clothes, and each now praying for me in different languages. And as they prayed, I thought I heard the rumbling of distant thunder even though there were no clouds in the sky. I was sure I was hallucinating.

I closed my eyes again and opened them one more time to see if they were still there. They were. And then suddenly, in a flash, each was transformed into a radiant figure of light. And then, just as the professor finished his prayer, they were gone.

Lara's words now echoed in my mind: "'He shall give His angels charge over you.'"[2]

"You saw them, didn't you?" said the professor.

"I saw them."

"Good. It's good to know who's on your side."

"I guess it is."

"Now you have much to do."

"The book."

"And this is a perfect place to begin writing it. You know where Moses started writing his book?"

"Where?"

"At Mount Sinai," he said. "And I've heard it became a bestseller."

"What about Lara?" I asked.

"Lara is a treasure. She's been invaluable to you. You couldn't have made it without her. But she can't help you now, not with this. This is for you to do. And you'll need to be alone to do it. But I think the two of you make a good team. Just something to think about.

"And now, Mr. Herzog, you need to go down the mountain. You have some things to take care of."

Chapter 91

TIME OF FAREWELLS

When I reached the bottom of the mountain, it was still dark. I entered the guesthouse, trying not to make a sound to avoid waking up Lara. That night I lay in my bed trying to absorb what had happened on top of Mount Sinai, overwhelmed, apprehensive, and in awe…and at the same time sad as I thought of Lara and what the next chapter would involve and what it wouldn't.

I woke up at midday. I knocked on Lara's door, but there was no answer. I decided to go for a walk in the desert. Shortly into the walk, I saw her. She was sitting on the desert sand, facing the mountain. I sat down beside her. She didn't see me at first, as her eyes were closed; she was in prayer. She looked up.

"Ariel! So tell me what happened! Did you find what you were looking for?"

"I found a person. I found Professor Marinus."

"Professor Marinus on Mount Sinai! What was he doing there?"

"The same thing our guides were doing: giving guidance."

"How could he have known you would be there? He's not…"

"An angel? No. But you were right."

"About?"

"Angels. I saw them…all the guides. They were there, for a moment, on the mountaintop, but they were there. You were right."

"And what happened?"

"I was told what I'm supposed to do."

"Which is?"

"Write a book."

"I knew you were supposed to write a book. So does that mean we can go home now?"

I paused. I didn't know how to answer her.

"What?" she asked.

"I was told I needed to write it here…in the Sinai."

"We'll be spending the next few months in the desert? I don't know that the museum would cover it."

"*I* need to stay, Lara. You don't."

"What do you mean?"

"It's something I have to do myself."

"I can help."

"Not with this."

I could see her eyes beginning to well up with tears.

"You've already given me more help than I ever could have expected or asked for. But I can't ask you to put your life on hold now because of me."

"It won't be on hold," she said.

"You'll have nothing to do."

"Is that what you want?"

"No," I said. "It's not what I want. But I know that you need to go, and I need to stay here to do this. It's not forever. It's just for now."

"Are you sure of that?"

"There's no one I would want to be with me on this journey more than you. But this is what I was told on the mountain. It's what I have to do."

It was only after that that she seemed to have some peace. We didn't say anything more. Tears were still streaming down her cheeks as we both sat there silent, staring at the mountain in the distance.

I spent the next few days with Lara, doing nothing in particular, but just being with her. We went on long walks in the desert, talking about everything we didn't have the chance to talk about during the time of our journeys.

And then the day came for us to part. I arranged for a driver to pick her up at the guesthouse and take her back through the desert to Israel, where she would fly home. After loading her luggage in the car, the driver signaled to us that he was ready to go. He didn't want to drive through the desert at night and wanted to leave as soon as possible. I signaled back that we needed a few more moments. Lara and I had to say goodbye. We walked away from the car.

"How are you doing?" I asked.

"Conflicted," she said. "You know, when I was first asked to go with you, I was horrified. You were the last person I would have picked to go on a journey with around the world—or, for that matter, anywhere."

"Was I that bad?"

"You were worse... You were the self-proclaimed nemesis of everything I stood for."

"And?"

"My impressions have changed a bit."

"A bit?"

"Just a little," she said with a smile. "It's ironic. You were the last person in the world I wanted to be with. And now..."

There was a long moment of silence. And then she broke it. "Take care of yourself, Ariel."

"You too," I replied. "Watch who you go into elevators with."

"And watch your step on that mountain."

"A wise person once told me, 'He shall give His angels charge over you.'[1] I believe that."

"Can I pray for you?" she asked. I nodded. She closed her eyes and began to pray that God would be with me to lead me, guide my steps, strengthen me, fulfill His will and calling for my life, and keep me safe. When she finished, she asked me to pray for her. I didn't really know how, but I placed my hands on her shoulders and spoke the blessing I had remembered from my youth: "The Lord bless you and keep you, Lara. The Lord cause His face to shine upon you and give you grace. The Lord lift up His countenance upon you, my friend, and the Lord give you peace."

We opened our eyes. It wasn't planned; it was just the moment, but what had never happened in all our journeying happened then. I leaned over and kissed her. Then we embraced for what had to be at least half a minute, an embrace that came to an end only because the driver couldn't take it anymore and began honking his car horn.

I walked Lara over to the car. Before getting in, she turned around.

"You stay alive, Herzog," she said, her voice breaking and her eyes welling up with tears. "You stay alive and come back."

"I will," I replied.

The driver started the car. It was then that the reality of our parting fully hit me.

"Lara," I said. "Do you know what Professor Marinus told me on the mountaintop?"

"No."

"He said we make a good team."

"I guess we do."

"I was thinking...maybe when I see you again, we could embark on a new journey. What do you think?"

"What kind of journey?"

"A different kind of journey," I replied.

"Not of mysteries?"

"A journey of mysteries but, I've heard, of a different kind."

"I think I might like that," she said, now with a smile, and tears rolling down her cheeks.

She got into the car.

"Goodbye, Lara," I said through the open car window.

"Goodbye, Ariel."

And the car drove away. I stood there, watching it go until it disappeared into the desert. The sun was now setting on the sands of the Sinai, on its rocks and mountains, and on the most unforgettable chapter of my life.

By the time of the next sunrise, the next chapter would begin.

Chapter 92

THE BEGINNING

I WENT TO BED early that night and got up while it was still dark. It would remain dark for several hours. I gathered what I needed for the day: a notepad, a pen, a small flashlight, my cell phone, food, water, and a pocket Bible. I put them all in a bag, left the guesthouse, and headed for the mountain.

I would begin the writing of the book, as had been suggested, on top of Mount Sinai. The desert sky was filled with stars that night and crowned with a moon still bright enough to illuminate my ascent. A gentle, cool breeze blew against the mountain rock, growing stronger as I ascended. When I reached the top, it was still dark. I sat down on a ledge; took out my notepad, my pen, my cell phone, and the Bible; and laid them down on the rock. All was still, calm, and quiet. I gazed out at the desert mountains silhouetted against the dark blue of the night sky, waiting for the sunrise.

And then it came. Slowly, the desert sky began to brighten, glazing the jagged mountain silhouettes with the golden orange light of dawn. Not long after that, the desert came alive with color: yellows, ambers, ochers, rusts, whites, and crimsons. It stretched out in every direction, a seemingly endless expanse of mountains and valleys, ridges, cliffs, winding paths, and dry riverbeds. It was my first sunrise on the sacred mountain.

I wanted to just sit there and take it all in. But the gravity of my task was weighing on me. I knew I had to begin. But my thoughts were racing in every direction. How could I put into writing the things we were shown? How could I convey the mysteries that were revealed to us?

Somehow, I was to speak to a modern audience of an ancient mystery that was altering the course of human history and on which the fate of the world and of their lives was hanging. Somehow, I was to share with them that this mystery was connected to an ancient object, an object linked to the greatest calamities and cataclysms of modern times. I was to bring to light the darkness and expose the ancient secret to the world.

On top of all that, I was to show them that the mystery and the object were linked to a being that many of them associated with pitchforks, red suits, and fairy tales, but that was, in fact, a profoundly real and dangerous ancient entity. If I hadn't come to know what I had come to know, that's what I would have associated it with, and did. I would never have fathomed that such things could actually lie behind everything from the forced labor camps of communism to the gas chambers of Auschwitz and nuclear destruction.

I decided to open the Bible to the Book of Exodus to see what Moses did on Mount Sinai. And then it hit me. What Moses did was simple; he wrote down the things he saw and heard, what God had shown him.[1] I couldn't begin to compare my calling to that of Moses. I didn't see myself as worthy to even sit on the same mountain. But it was what he did on Mount Sinai that revealed to me what I was now to do.

All I had to do was write down what I saw and heard: my coming upon the manuscript, my journeying with Lara, our encounters, the guides, the words they spoke to us, the dangers, and the mystery as it unfolded. I would write it as a story. I would change the names of the key people involved. I would write it as a novel, as if it were fiction, but what it would reveal—the mystery—would be real. I could title it after the object on which the mystery centers...The Altar of Pergamon.

I now had what I needed to begin. It was just then that the rays of the rising sun lit up the notepad that I had placed on the ledge. Moses had ascended Mount Sinai to come into the knowledge of God's ways and laws. The prophet Elijah had ascended the same mountain to come into the knowledge of God's power and plans.[2] And now I ascended the mountain, having come into a very different knowledge.

It was now time to begin. It was time to expose the secret of ages, to reveal the mystery that had shaken the world, altered its course, and nearly brought it to an end. It was time to make known the mystery on which the future of the world and everyone in the world was now hanging. It was time for the revelation to go forth. And whoever was meant to hear it would hear it.

I picked up the pen and, with a deep sense of awe and fear, set it down to my notepad. I didn't yet know what the first words would be. It was only at that moment that they came to me, and only then that I wrote them down on the sunlit paper on the ledge of that mountaintop...

I have come into a cataclysmic knowledge...

ABOUT JONATHAN CAHN

Jonathan Cahn caused a worldwide stir with the release of his first book, *The Harbinger*, a *New York Times* bestseller. Every book he's written since has likewise become a *New York Times* bestseller. He was named, along with Billy Graham, as one of the top forty spiritual leaders of the last forty years "who radically changed our world." He has addressed members of Congress and spoken at the United Nations. He is known as a prophetic voice for our times and for the opening up of the deep mysteries of God. His teachings and prophetic messages on his YouTube channel have had over one hundred million views.

Jonathan leads Hope of the World, a ministry of bringing the Word of God to the world and compassion to the world's most needy, and Beth Israel/the Jerusalem Center, his ministry base and worship center in Wayne, New Jersey, just outside New York City. He ministers and speaks throughout America and the world.

To get in touch, to receive prophetic updates, to receive free gifts from his ministry (special messages and much more), to find out about his over two thousand messages and mysteries, for more information, to contact, or to have a part in the Great Commission, use the following contacts. Go to: **HopeoftheWorld.org**; write to: Hope of the World, Box 1111, Lodi, NJ 07644 USA; or email: contact@hopeoftheworld.org.

To receive Jonathan's latest messages and prophetic updates, go to:

YouTube:	Jonathan Cahn Official
Facebook:	Jonathan Cahn (Official Site)
Instagram:	jonathan.cahn
X:	@Jonathan_Cahn

To find out how you can go with Jonathan on an adventure of a lifetime—on a Special Tour of the Holy Land, a Book of Revelation Tour, a Footsteps of Paul Mystery Tour, a Teaching and Prophecy Cruise to the Caribbean, or the Alaska Cruise—go to JonathanCahnSpecialTours.com or email contact@hopeoftheworld.org.

***To see Jonathan's other books**, go to: BooksByJonathanCahn.com, Amazon.com, or wherever books are sold.

If there are people in your life who should know about or read *The Altar of Pergamon*, let them know about it, or give it to them as a gift, available wherever books are sold.

NOTES

Chapter 5

1. Isaiah 14:13.
2. Isaiah 14:12.

Chapter 6

1. Revelation 2:13.
2. Revelation 2:12, author's translation.
3. 2 Corinthians 4:4, ESV.

Chapter 10

1. Alexander Conze et al., *Die Ergebnisse der Ausgrabungen zu Pergamon: Vorläufiger Bericht* (Weidmannsche Buchhandlung, 1880), 11, https://archive.org/details/dieergebnisseder00conz_0/page/n17/mode/2up.

Chapter 14

1. Revelation 12:1–5.
2. Revelation 12:13.

Chapter 18

1. Isaiah 14:16, NLT; Isaiah 14:17.

Chapter 21

1. "Rudolf von Sebottendorff," Timenote, accessed April 30, 2026, https://timenote.info/en/Rudolf-von-Sebottendorff.
2. Ian Kershaw, *Hitler 1889–1936: Hubris* (Penguin Books, 1999), 65.

Chapter 23

1. William A. Jenks, *Vienna and the Young Hitler* (Columbia University Press, 1960), inside flap.

Chapter 26

1. Isaiah 14:13–14.

Chapter 27

1. Albert Speer, *Inside the Third Reich*, trans. Richard and Clara Winston (Macmillan, 1969), chapter 5.

Chapter 28

1. Luke 10:18.

Chapter 35

1. Leviticus 9:1–24.
2. Leviticus 6:12.

CHAPTER 36

1. Alejandro Morales, "Panel Report: The Holocaust and Beyond," *International Journal of Psychoanalysis* 77 (1996): 147–48. https://pep-web.org/search/document/IJP.077.0147A.
2. Leviticus 6:9, author's translation.
3. Leviticus 16:1–24, DRA.

CHAPTER 37

1. Stefano G. Caneva, "Shaping the Elite of Attalid Pergamon," *Electrum* 30 (2023): 75–101, https://share.google/38LLBXxv18b9Petmi.
2. Exodus 19:6.

CHAPTER 38

1. Leviticus 14:13, KJV.
2. 2 Chronicles 29:7, KJV.

CHAPTER 39

1. Leviticus 24:19.
2. "Leviticus 24," Sefaria Library, accessed May 29, 2026, https://www.sefaria.org/Leviticus.24.1?lang=bi&with=all&lang2=en.

CHAPTER 41

1. "The Union of Believers with Christ According to John 15:1–14, Showing Its Basis and Essence, Its Absolute Necessity, and Its Effects," Marx/Engels Archive, accessed April 17, 2026, https://marxists.architexturez.net/archive/marx/works/1837-pre/marx/1835chris.htm.
2. Karl Marx, "Invocation of One in Despair," Marxists.org, accessed June 12, 2026, https://www.marxists.org/archive/marx/works/1837-pre/verse/verse11.htm.
3. Isaiah 14:13.
4. Marx, "Invocation of One in Despair."
5. Marx, "Invocation of One in Despair."
6. Richard Wurmbrand, *Marx: Prophet of Darkness* (Marshall Pickering, 1986), 15, https://dn790007.ca.archive.org/0/items/ProphetOfDarkness/Prophet%20of%20Darkness.pdf.
7. Karl Marx, "Human Pride," Marxists.org, accessed June 12, 2026, https://www.marxists.org/archive/marx/works/1837-pre/verse/verse20.htm.
8. Isaiah 14:14.
9. Wurmbrand, *Marx*, 13.
10. Robert Payne, *Marx: A Biography* (Simon and Schuster, 1968), 317, https://archive.org/details/marxrobertpayne/page/313/mode/2up.
11. Wurmbrand, *Marx*, 30.
12. Jerry Newcombe, "Karl Marx's Favorite Quote," *The Stand*, August 26, 2021, https://afa.net/the-stand/culture/2021/08/karl-marx-s-favorite-quote/.

CHAPTER 42

1. Karl Marx, "Marx to Dr Kugelmann Concerning Paris Commune," Marx Engels Internet Archive, accessed May 6, 2026, https://www.marxists.org/archive/marx/works/1871/letters/71_04_12.htm.

2. "Marx to Dr Kugelmann Concerning Paris Commune," Marx Engels Internet Archive, accessed May 6, 2026, https://www.yorku.ca/comninel/courses/4090pdf/Civil_War_in_France/71_04_17.htm.

Chapter 45

1. "Karl Marx to Ludwig Kugelmann, 11 February 1869," Marxists.org, accessed May 3, 2026, https://www.marxists.org/archive/marx/works/1869/letters/69_02_11.htm.

Chapter 48

1. "April 10–16: Lenin Arrives at Finland Station," World Socialist Web Site, April 10, 2017, https://www.wsws.org/en/articles/2017/04/10/twrr-a10.html; Joshua Hammer, "Vladimir Lenin's Return Journey to Russia Changed the World Forever," *Smithsonian Magazine*, March 2017, https://www.smithsonianmag.com/travel/vladimir-lenin-return-journey-russia-changed-world-forever-180962127/.
2. Catherine Merridale, *Lenin on the Train* (Metropolitan Books, 2017), 8.
3. Isaiah 14:13–14; Isaiah 14:16, KJV; Isaiah 14:16.

Chapter 58

1. America's National Churchill Museum, "Churchill's 'Sinews of Peace' Speech at Westminster College," YouTube, March 5, 2019, youtube.com/watch?v=ZA5ISi9yhhs&source_ve_path=OTY3MTQ&embeds_referring_euri=https%3A%2F%2Fwww.nationalchurchillmuseum.org%2Fsinews-of-peace-iron-curtain-speech.html.
2. Mao Tse-tung, "On the People's Democratic Dictatorship," Marx Engels Internet Archive, accessed May 29, 2026, https://www.marxists.org/reference/archive/mao/selected-works/volume-4/mswv4_65.htm.
3. Wurmbrand, *Marx*, 13.
4. Newcombe, "Karl Marx's Favorite Quote."

Chapter 64

1. Exodus 19:6.

Chapter 65

1. Isaiah 1:1–27.
2. Isaiah 1:7.

Chapter 66

1. Isaiah 14:13.

Chapter 68

1. John F. Kennedy, "Address During the Cuban Missile Crisis," October 22, 1962, John F. Kennedy Presidential Library and Museum, transcript and audio, 17 min., 46 sec., https://www.jfklibrary.org/learn/about-jfk/historic-speeches/address-during-the-cuban-missile-crisis.
2. Newcombe, "Karl Marx's Favorite Quote."
3. Wurmbrand, *Marx*, 15–16.
4. Isaiah 14:16–17.

CHAPTER 69

1. Chris Matthews, "How John F. Kennedy's Appeasement Strategy Averted a Nuclear Holocaust," *The New Republic*, October 14, 2012, https://newrepublic.com/article/108575/how-john-f-kennedys-appeasement-strategy-averted-nuclear-holocaust.
2. Revelation 2:13, ESV.

CHAPTER 75

1. Barack Obama, "Address in Berlin at the Victory Column in Tiergarten Park," The American Presidency Project, July 24, 2008, posted by The American Presidency Project, https://www.presidency.ucsb.edu/documents/address-berlin-the-victory-column-tiergarten-park.
2. Obama, "Address in Berlin."

CHAPTER 76

1. The Debate Chronicles, "Barack Obama (2006)—Faith and Politics," YouTube, July 4, 2023, https://www.youtube.com/watch?v=q_pCumWYMLo.

CHAPTER 78

1. Revelation 2:13, ESV.

CHAPTER 83

1. Job 36:32; Psalm 18:13–14.

CHAPTER 86

1. Isaiah 14:13.

CHAPTER 88

1. Mark 13:1–2, 14.
2. Daniel 7:21–25; 11:31–33; Revelation 19:11–21.
3. Isaiah 14:13–14.
4. Zechariah 14:4–9.
5. Psalm 100:5, author's translation.

CHAPTER 89

1. Exodus 31:18.
2. Hebrews 13:2, ESV.
3. Psalm 91:11–12.

CHAPTER 90

1. Revelation 2:13.
2. Psalm 91:11–12.

CHAPTER 91

1. Psalm 91:11.

CHAPTER 92

1. Exodus 34:27.
2. 1 Kings 19:8.

Loved this book?

Leave a review and help others discover it.

★★★★★

Your next read starts here

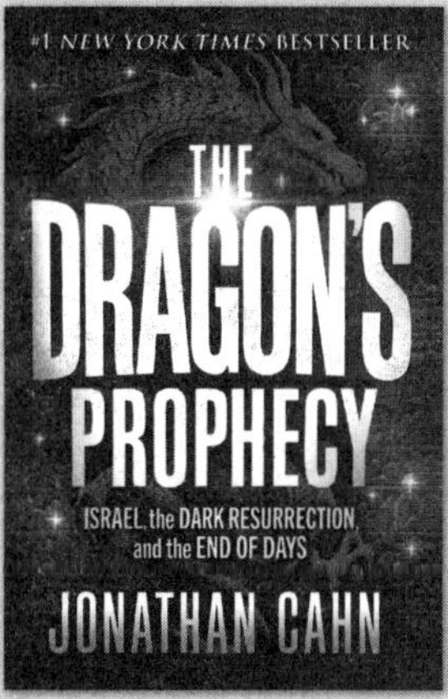

CHARISMA HOUSE — Equipping readers with Spirit-empowered books that ignite faith.

FRONT LINE — Thought-provoking titles where journalism, faith, and truth meet.

SILOAM — Guiding readers to wholeness in body, mind, and spirit.

MEV MODERN ENGLISH VERSION — Bibles and devotionals with clear, modern translation.

REALMS — Inspiring stories that uplift and reflect Christian values.